Fredrick Huebner

Shades
of
Justice

A Novel

Simon & Schuster
New York   London
Toronto   Sydney   Singapore

SIMON & SCHUSTER
Rockefeller Center
1230 Avenue of the Americas
New York, NY 10020

DESIGNED BY DEIRDRE C. AMTHOR

Manufactured in the United States of America

10 9 8 7 6 5 4 3 2 1

Library of Congress Cataloging-in-Publication Data
Huebner, Fredrick D.
    Shades of justice : a novel / Fredrick Huebner.
        p. cm.
    I. Title.

PS3558.U3127 C+
813'.54—dc21   00-066075

ISBN 0-684-81847-7

Canst thou not minister to a mind diseased,
Pluck from the memory a rooted sorrow?

William Shakespeare

Part I

Mark's Murder

September 9–10, 1997

Chapter One

The medevac chopper fell like a stone from the hazy night sky in the bleak chill hour before dawn. Its turbines screamed as the pilot killed his speed and hovered for an instant over the Harborview Hospital helipad. The rear doors slammed open as the skids touched the ground. Two paramedics jumped from the rear of the chopper, pulling a metal gurney with the body of an unconscious woman strapped to its frame. The gurney stuck in its rack, then came free with a sudden jolt and bounced hard on the concrete landing pad. A paramedic cursed loud enough to be heard through the white noise of the prop wash and checked the electronic monitor cuff on the woman's arm. "Blood pressure seventy over— shit! Go! Go!" he shouted, shoving the gurney forward, his face green in the halogen glare of the pad lights.

Not too bad for Labor Day weekend, Roy Black thought to himself as he sipped at his seventh cup of coffee. It was 4:45 Tuesday morning. Black had been an ER surgeon for six years, two at L.A. General and four at Harborview, in Seattle. The night rhythms of an ER, he mused, seldom changed. The first part of the shift brought the part-time jocks with torn Achilles tendons and green-sticked collarbones from Seattle's softball and touch football fields. Between midnight and three they caught the heavy work: fistfights and domestic brawls, gunshot wounds, overdoses, and the bleeding old men scraped off Pioneer Square cobblestones, their guts ravaged by alcohol. The final hours usually produced battered women, able to call the cops and get the hell out of the house when their old man passed out at last.

Black stretched upward, then bent over and touched his palms to the floor to ease the mounting strain in his lower back. "The chopper down yet?" he called to the new trauma nurse, a blonde woman of maybe thirty with solid curves and a handsome face with high cheekbones. Her name was Paula something or other, Black thought, wishing he'd listened more closely for her name in last week's staff meeting. She'd handled herself well during the shift, and they'd had a bad one, a Samoan gangbanger with an assault rifle wound the size of a baseball carved into his chest, caught on the wrong side of a drive-by shooting.

"The chopper's down," Paula said. "None too soon. Blood pressure's bad, pulse is thready. They've got a unit of plasma going."

"We have a blood type?" Black demanded.

Paula checked the computer screen to her right. "Yes. They called it in. O-positive, so it should be easy to match."

"Good, get a unit ready. Suicide attempt?"

Paula nodded. "They've got a deputy on the chopper. He says she shot her husband, then cut her wrists up. She was outside for at least an hour, maybe more. She was lying on the beach half in the water when they found her. They've been trying to warm her up in the chopper, but she's still going to be pretty cold."

Black sighed. Blood loss, shock, hypothermia. This one would be close. He could feel his adrenaline falling as it always did near the end of the shift. He had seventy-two off-duty hours coming up. Maybe Paula something would like a Bloody Mary with breakfast. Worth a try, anyway, Black decided.

Black took a deep breath and blew it out through pursed lips. "One more," he said as he turned to scrub up. "You did good tonight, Paula. Breakfast's on me, if you're interested."

Paula thought it over, then smiled tentatively and nodded.

"Good." Black paused to adjust the splatter shield over his face, then regloved. "We know who she is?" he asked idly.

"Yes. The painter. Laura Arcand."

Black frowned, thinking sourly of the wall of press that would be waiting outside for them when they left their shift. "Let's go for it," he said tiredly. "Notify the psych floor. If she lives, we've probably got a customer for them."

The paramedics slammed the gurney through the doors into the ER. A short, dark, heavy man in a blue police uniform puffed up behind it, winded by the sprint up the hill from the helipad. Black waited with one eye on the approaching gurney, the other on the computer screen with the last vital-sign information from the helicopter's monitors. The fat cop, whose nameplate read MARTINEZ, stayed beside the gurney as the paramedics slid Laura Arcand onto an examination table. Black took a shears and began to cut away the thick blood-soaked bandages around Laura Arcand's wrists. He looked up, irritated by the cop's wheezing.

"Mask!" he barked, pointing at Martinez. "Get the fuck out of here." Black turned away, checked the blood pressure monitor, and cursed. "Whole blood! I want it now!" he commanded.

"I got to stay with her," Martinez said, still breathing hard. "She's in custody."

Black ignored the deputy's words and pointed again with a gloved finger. "Mask. Or I'll have your ass for breakfast." Black returned to the task of removing the bandages. When the wounds were exposed, he swore. "No marks for neatness," he said under his breath. This woman hadn't slit her wrists, she'd gouged them, ripping at the arteries and tendons with some kind of sharp-pointed object, maybe a fork or something, Black thought. "What the hell could have done this?" he asked aloud.

"Her ring," Martinez said numbly. "She had a big diamond wedding ring. The stone was long and sharp. We found it in her hand."

Black shook his head and reached for a suture on a sterile tray. As a second nurse started to pull a blue privacy curtain around the surgical bay, Laura Arcand suddenly jerked upright, flailing at the air. Black caught her and tried to push her down on the table. Laura Arcand fought him, her body rigid, her skin ghostly gray-white from shock and blood loss, her eyes wide and sightless and dark.

"I killed them!" she screamed, surging against Black's embrace. "Oh God, *both* of them."

Chapter Two

Will Hatton suppressed a yawn, then gave in to the urge, shrugging his shoulders in the witness chair to ease the knot of tension between his shoulder blades. The air-conditioning in the Dallas County Courthouse had broken down over the weekend and the courtroom air was thick with the draining September heat of central Texas.

Jennifer Dale McKinnon looked up sharply from the defense table across the bland modern courtroom of beige wool carpet and blonde oak. If the heat bothered her, she gave no sign of it, cool and precise in a simple starched white linen dress. In idle moments during the trial Hatton had appraised Jennifer McKinnon with carnal interest. In her late thirties she retained a tightly muscled, sculpted body that bespoke Perrier and devoted exercise. Her breasts were small but high and rounded. Serious breasts, he concluded, not that he was ever likely to touch them. Her dark eyes were both fierce and guarded. A tight smile played across her sharp, rather feral features. "Are we boring you this morning, Dr. Hatton?" she asked sarcastically.

Hatton smiled back. "No, Counsel. I apologize. The jet lag must finally be catching up with me."

"Yes, from the London conference you took half an hour to tell us about last week."

The judge, Walter Forrester, a stout, balding black man in his mid-fifties, sighed heavily. He mopped his face and neck with a white handkerchief that was already soaked with sweat from the hot morning. The trial was now in its fifth week. Forrester had given up trying to control the lawyers' catfights a week into the trial, comforted by the knowledge that the damned case would be appealed nine times anyway. He scratched idly on the desk calendar in front of him, circling the date of his scheduled departure for two weeks of golf and bourbon on Padre Island for the sixth or seventh time. "Get on with it, Counsel," he said tiredly.

"Of course, Your Honor," McKinnon said smoothly. "Dr. Hatton, let's go back to the report of Dr. Kincaid. Page three, please."

Will picked up the report. His mind was still wandering from lack of sleep. You cut it too close this time, Hatton, he thought, coming straight from the London Psychiatric Conference to the trial. It had been five long days since he had first settled into the witness chair, smiled at the jury, sworn to tell the truth, and begun the ritual testimony of his qualifications as an expert witness: William Girard Hatton, born at the naval air station hospital at Pensacola, Florida, March 9, 1954. Grew up on Bainbridge Island, Washington, with my mother, a legal secretary. Joined the marine corps out of high school, trained as a rifleman. Stationed in California; Guantanamo Bay, Cuba; and Washington, D.C. Graduated from Colorado College, Colorado Springs, B.S. in biology, what they gave you in the premed program there. Medical training at the University of Minnesota, residency at St. Paul Ramsey Hospital, returned for a Ph.D. in forensic psychology. I'm a consulting forensic psychiatrist, certified by the American Board of Psychiatry and Neurology. Life fellow of the American Psychiatric Association. I evaluate mental states for legal purposes. I've taught at Columbia, Johns Hopkins, and the University of Washington. Worked with more medical examiners than I can name; you've got my vita. Fifteen pages of publications. Ever married? Quiet chuckle and wince for the benefit of the jury. Not for lack of trying. Move to qualify Dr. Hatton as an expert, Your Honor. Any voir dire? We'll reserve, Your Honor. So, qualified. You may examine, Counsel.

Hatton had given one day of direct testimony, rebutting the insanity defense, then spent the weekend in evidence reviews and conferences with Ben Culver, the tall, athletic, and driven Dallas County prosecutor, and his fatigue was beginning to show. McKinnon was a relentless cross-examiner, patiently inflicting a thousand careful, cutting questions, probing endlessly for weak answers that she could use in summation to cast a doubt into the jurors' minds. Hatton finished rereading the defense psychiatric report and glanced across the courtroom at the defendant, John Henry Soames, the pale younger son of a Midland oil family, who retained, even at fifty, the lanky blond hair and weak-chinned good looks of the perpetual boy. Soames had managed the peculiar 1980s trick of riding a $30 million inheritance into the bankruptcy court, courtesy of dry oil wells, failed real estate investments, three ex-wives, and a misbegotten run for Congress on a right-wing platform so extreme, even for Texas, that $7 million worth of advertising netted him less than eighteen thousand votes. When his family finally cut off the money, Soames had brooded with his extensive collection of guns and combat knives in a rented Turtle Creek condo for six weeks before breaking into his ex-wife Sheila's home and shooting her and her lover, a Dallas Stars hockey player, nine times with a silenced Colt automatic. Soames had bundled his two sleeping sons, ages seven and nine, in their blankets and taken them to the swimming pool, then cut their throats with a razor-sharp k-bar combat knife before turning the blade on himself. He had been dragged half dead from the water with more than twenty self-inflicted stab wounds, and charged with four counts of aggravated capital murder. Texas was a death state, and John Henry Soames's more prudent brothers had ponied up the million dollars needed to buy Jennifer McKinnon's growing and formidable reputation as a criminal defense lawyer in order to save John Henry from the last possible indignity—from being the only rich white man in the history of Texas to sit on death row.

McKinnon paced slowly, circling the defense table.

"You've reread section two of Dr. Kincaid's report."

"Yes. Several times now, Counsel," Hatton replied, voice on the edge of exasperation. Patience, Hatton told himself. Listen, answer. Don't fight her.

"You concur with Dr. Kincaid's finding, based on your own personal examination, that John Henry Soames was severely depressed?"

"Yes."

"You're aware that no less than three treating psychiatrists over the past two years diagnosed Mr. Soames as suffering from clinical depression?"

"Yes."

"You're also aware that one of those treating psychiatrists, Dr. Brecht, diagnosed Mr. Soames as suffering from depressive psychosis less than two months before the events of this case?"

"Yes."

"Do you challenge that diagnosis?"

"I was not there. I've read Dr. Brecht's report. I see no reason to challenge that diagnosis."

"You considered John Henry Soames's voluntary service in Vietnam?"

"Yes."

"You are aware that in the course of his infantry service he was required to assault Vietcong camps with sudden, silent, deadly violence?"

"Yes." Killing was the only thing Soames was ever good at, Hatton added to himself.

"That John Henry Soames was trained to commit these assaults with silenced weapons, and with knives?"

"Yes."

"And for which Mr. Soames was awarded the Bronze Star."

"Yes, I know that."

"You are aware that alcohol and cocaine use can trigger episodes of traumatic memory flashback, particularly when coupled with clinical depression or depressive psychosis?"

"I agree that the literature suggests a link."

"So the answer is yes."

"Yes."

McKinnon dropped Kincaid's report on the defense table and began a slow stalk toward the witness stand. We're near the end now, Hatton thought. She's recited her case, and now she's going to try to come straight at me. Stay sharp.

"You're aware that on the day before the assaults, Mr. Soames told three witnesses that he was still in the 'boonies,' a reference to combat areas in Vietnam, and couldn't find his way back?"

"Yes, I read that testimony."

Ben Culver began to slump in his seat, wondering how he was going to rehabilitate these concessions on redirect. McKinnon pressed on.

"And you yourself concluded—referring to your own report— 'that it is quite likely that Mr. Soames has experienced one or more episodes of spontaneous flashbacks as a consequence of posttraumatic stress disorder during his life'?"

"Yes."

McKinnon paused ten feet in front of the witness stand, as though wondering how far to push. The graying Vietnam veterans in the courthouse pews, bellies spilling over ancient fatigues, were nodding their approval to one another. When Soames had run for Congress he'd advocated reinvading Vietnam to find the hundreds of MIAs he said were still rotting in prison camps. The small band of veterans had attended every day of the trial, a silent Greek chorus for one of their own.

"Dr. Hatton," she said sarcastically, "do you know what *Newsweek* called you two months ago?"

"Yes."

"Why don't you tell the jury?"

"Objection," Culver called out.

"Overruled."

"The *Newsweek* writer," Hatton said calmly, "referred to me as 'Dr. Lock 'Em Up.'"

"Why did he do that?"

Hatton shrugged, then smiled. "I have no idea. Why don't you subpoena the reporter? Or are you concerned what *Newsweek* will call *you,* Counsel?"

"Why don't you answer my question?" McKinnon shot back.

"Knock it off," Judge Forrester said sharply. "Move on."

"Certainly, Your Honor. Let's talk about that article, Dr. Hatton. It refers to you as 'the favored psychiatric expert of prosecutors across the country,' does it not?"

"It does."

"It also calls you a 'leading skeptic of posttraumatic stress disorder and repressed-memory claims,' correct?"

"Correct."

"And all for a mere $4,000 a day," McKinnon said caustically. "Now, Dr. Hatton, it's a fact that you've testified in sixty-one trials, correct?"

"That's true."

"Fifty-four times for the prosecution, correct?"

"I believe so."

"Doesn't that indicate just the slightest bias, Dr. Hatton? As a 'leading skeptic' of repressed-memory and PTSD claims?"

"It indicates," Hatton replied calmly, "a scientific view that murder is usually a volitional act, Counsel."

McKinnon shrugged the answer away. She smiled slightly, taking two measured steps toward the witness stand. "Usually. But not in all cases, correct?"

"That's right, Counsel. In a very small number of cases, the act of killing is not volitional and is the result of insanity."

"And if someone is in the full grip of a delusion, caused by posttraumatic stress disorder, then the act of killing is not volitional, is it, Dr. Hatton?"

"That's also correct, Counsel."

McKinnon paused, as though uncertain. You should stop right there, Hatton thought, but there's one question more and you're itching to ask it. Just do it, and watch me hit it out of here.

McKinnon resumed her march forward. She placed both hands flat on the bar of the witness stand. "Dr. Hatton," she said, dropping her voice to an intent husky whisper that carried throughout the courtroom, "you really cannot exclude, on the basis of the evidence you have heard and seen, the possibility that John Henry Soames committed these acts in the grip of depressive psychosis that triggered a posttraumatic stress flashback, believing he was a soldier back in Vietnam and carrying out acts of violence he was trained to commit, can you?"

"Yes, I can," Hatton said succinctly. "May I have state's exhibit number 27?"

McKinnon froze. "No."

Culver leaped to his feet. "Your Honor, I object. The witness has a right to complete his answer."

"Your Honor, I'm through with the witness," McKinnon said quickly.

"Let him finish," the judge commanded. "Hand him the exhibit."

McKinnon picked up the exhibit from the evidence clerk and dropped it on the bar of the witness stand, then stood with her arms folded skeptically in the well below the bench.

Will took the exhibit. "This is a photograph of the neck wounds suffered by Garrett Anson Soames, Mr. Soames's nine-year-old son," he began. "You'll notice that there are two small marks, knife cuts, on the skin above and to the left of the slashing wound that the medical examiner testified caused Gary Soames's death. They are called hesitation marks. You see them most often in cases of suicide. Gary's brother, John Henry junior, had three similar cuts or marks on his neck." Hatton paused, let his voice take on weight for the jury. "You see, Counsel, your client hesitated before he cut the throats of his children. That tells me that he knew right from wrong. And that, ultimately, is why I do not believe that he was legally insane when he killed these people."

The courtroom filled with a dense silence, suddenly broken by the sighs of the jurors. They had something solid now, something they could understand. Jennifer McKinnon saw the danger she was in and tried to extricate herself.

"You've never been trained as a pathologist, have you?" she snapped.

"No. I *am* a medical doctor trained in evaluating and using the findings of physical pathologists as part of my evaluation of mental states."

"You've never conducted an autopsy."

"Not since medical school. I don't need to."

"Then how can you draw a conclusion from looking at autopsy photos you aren't qualified to understand?"

God, that's a bad question. Hatton refused to gloat. He turned to the jury, spoke calmly. "By consulting with John Grier, the medical examiner of Hennepin County, Minnesota, over the weekend. He is perhaps the nation's most respected pathologist. When I saw the marks on the photographs I asked John to review them with me. He confirmed that they were hesitation marks."

Jennifer McKinnon sat down abruptly, biting her lip. "As I said, Your Honor, I've concluded my examination. May we have a brief recess?"

"It's only ten-twenty," the judge replied. "Let's start the redirect first."

Ben Culver had enough sense to read the jury's approval before opening his mouth. "No redirect," he said with quiet triumph.

"Let's take fifteen minutes, then," the judge replied.

Will Hatton struggled to get his feet under him as the judge went off the bench and the courtroom stood. His exhaustion was nearly complete. When the jurors had left the courtroom he slumped back down in the witness chair.

Ben Culver grabbed his elbow. "By God, Will, I don't know whether to thank you or get really pissed," he said, exultant. "When were you going to tell me this stuff about the hesitation marks?"

"I just figured it out last night," Hatton replied, oblivious to the excited buzz from the press row as the reporters rewrote their mid-day lead. His fatigue had started to evolve into a dull headache. "I faxed the photos to Grier at three o'clock this morning, used up a lifetime's worth of favors to get him to look at them."

"Well, it paid off." Culver's triumphant grin was cut short. He turned away as a deputy prosecutor, a younger man with a mop of orange curly hair and thick rimless glasses, tugged at Culver's arm and whispered in his ear. "No fucking way," Culver exploded, shaking his head. The young deputy looked like he wanted to hide inside his ill-cut blue suit.

"What is it?" Hatton asked.

Culver lowered his voice. "Jenny Mac wants to talk in chambers," he said. "She says her client's willing to plead if we offer him life without parole."

"Why don't you take it?" Will asked.

"Why give up when we're winning?" Culver demanded.

"Because John Henry Soames is a very disturbed man, Ben. He's not legally insane. He's been a shit all his life, and he murdered these four people. But he's got a long history of mental problems—severe depression, episodic flashbacks. Let him go, Ben. He'll have no peace in prison. Without good psychiatric treatment, John Soames will kill himself within two years. If the other inmates don't get him first." Will shook his head. "I think the most courageous thing you could do now would be to show some mercy."

Culver snorted. "My voters want John Henry Soames and killers like him dead. They don't want displays of courageous mercy."

"Ben, you won't like my testimony at the penalty phase," Hatton said. A tone of polite warning entered his voice.

"Then we won't call you," Culver said stubbornly.

"Take the deal, Ben," Hatton said coldly. "Either side can call me as a witness, you know. I think my credibility with the jury is pretty high right now."

Ben Culver stared. "You are one arrogant son of a bitch," he said at last.

Hatton nodded without sympathy. "All doctors are, Ben. What's the best way to get to the airport?"

The red-haired kid standing at Culver's side slapped himself on the forehead. "I'm sorry, Dr. Hatton. They took this fax message for you at our office before court this morning. You're supposed to call right away."

Hatton opened the fax and read it quickly. "God," he said quietly. "It's Laura."

Chapter Three

Will Hatton sagged into the first-class seat of American's midday flight to Seattle and put down his vodka and ice, the second of the flight. He reached for the in-flight telephone without enthusiasm and punched the numbers that he knew from memory again.

"Hauser and Todd. How may we help you?" The receptionist's voice was professional, female, and spoke with a clipped British accent.

"It's Will Hatton again. I'm trying to reach Ed Hauser."

"I know, Dr. Hatton. I'm sorry, but he's still at Harborview. Mary Slattery has her cellular, though, and needs to speak to you urgently."

"Who's she?"

"Mr. Hauser's associate. She is working on the Laura Arcand matter. Please hold while I put you through."

A pause, a click, followed by a rumble of static. "This is Mary Slattery, Dr. Hatton." The voice was low and competent. A good jury voice, Will thought absently. Then his mind snapped back to reality. "What the hell is going on?" he demanded. "I got handed a fax two hours ago to call Ed, that he was representing Laura and it was urgent. Nothing more."

"I'm sorry. We couldn't take the risk of putting details in the fax. It could come into evidence."

"Of what? What's going on?"

"Ms. Arcand is at Harborview Hospital. She has attempted suicide. Her condition is serious but stable."

Will shut his eyes. "Oh shit," he sighed.

"Yes. It gets worse, I'm afraid. Laura's husband, Mark, was shot outside the beach house at Laura's mother's estate on Bainbridge Island last night. He is dead. I'm at the crime scene now. The Kitsap authorities believe Ms. Arcand murdered him."

Hatton was silent. He gripped the phone tightly to steady himself. "Did she?" he asked, his voice rasping.

"I don't know, Dr. Hatton. And it's not something I can discuss on a cellular phone."

"How's Ellen holding up?" Will asked. Ellen was Laura's mother and Ed Hauser's longtime lover.

"As best she can, I suppose. She is still with Laura at the hospital." Slattery's voice sounded cooler, more distant. "There's nothing more that can be done at present. Ed said that he wants you to examine Laura as soon as she is medically able."

"I can't do that. I've known the family too long."

"You'll have to take that up with Ed. I'm sorry, but I must go. You'll be met by a Kitsap Industries car at the airport. Please hurry."

Mary Slattery folded the cellular phone and dropped it in her shoulder bag. She stood on a path at the edge of a wide ryegrass meadow, facing the green water of Port Orchard Passage. Behind her stood the oversized two-story shingled Craftsman house still known on Bainbridge Island as the Stenslund place, named for Henrik Stenslund, the eccentric fishing boat owner who had built it as a summer home for his young second wife and their five children in 1910. The house faced west, to the water. Slattery paused to order her thoughts, then started down the narrow path that led from the house through the meadow. The path ran parallel to a small unnamed salmon stream, to the edge of the bluff. The stream trickled over an exposed rock shelf, then cut a V-shaped hollow into the side of the bluff. It spread lazily across the bright sand of a small cove as it flowed into the salt water of Puget Sound.

Slattery paused again at the top of the new redwood stairs that had been anchored to pilings driven into the bluff, and looked down. The beach cabin on the far side of the stream below her originally had been built as a playhouse for the Stenslund children and their friends. It was newly rebuilt, sided with cedar shingles stained cinnamon brown, with bright white trim. A new deck, framed on pilings, faced the water.

A large tide pool had formed in the coarse, gravelly sand below the cabin. Mark Talbot's nude pale body was lodged beside a large basalt rock at the far side of the pool. Slattery gave silent thanks that the shooting had occurred outside. The breeze was fresh and blowing in from the west, bearing the smell of sea salt and the kelp bed that drifted a hundred yards offshore. At least I won't need cigarette smoke to get me through this one, she thought grimly as she descended the stairs.

When she reached the beach, Slattery stopped, slipped off her Ferragamo heels, and placed her shoes carefully on a wide sun-bleached cedar log that had washed ashore and settled at the high tide line. She gritted her teeth against the chill of the water as she stepped into the tide pool.

The pool was thigh deep in the center and the footing was soft. Slattery braced herself on the lean, bony shoulder of Jon Sorenson, the Kitsap County coroner, as he crouched over Talbot's body. Sorenson was shirtless, his pants legs rolled up over his knees. Sorenson had been a deputy medical examiner in King County when Slattery was a King County prosecutor. He was a tall, angular Norwegian, normally reserved to the point of shyness, utterly lacking in the pomposity Slattery associated with anyone who had an M.D. after their name. Sorenson was a very rare man in another sense, an elected rural county coroner who was also a meticulous pathologist rather than a politician. Slattery did not relish the idea of having to cross-examine him.

"Hey, Slats," Sorenson said, greeting her with her prosecutor's office nickname, one that made her sound like a bookie but that she'd liked nonetheless. "We always meet in the best places, don't we?"

"That we do, Jon. And with the best company." Talbot lay on his back, head toward the shore, feet toward the water. Slattery pointed over Sorenson's shoulder at Talbot's exposed chest, the two entrance wounds within four inches of each other, bloodless and puckered by the exposure to salt water. "Two shots, Jon?"

"Back off, Mary, I'm not done yet," Sorenson said genially as he probed under Talbot's back, his arm up to his shoulder in the cold Puget Sound water.

"Relax, Jon, you can tell me that much. You're sure it was two shots?"

"Yeah, Mary, I am. Now back off, please." Slattery stepped back as Sorenson gently lifted Talbot's body with his left hand braced under the neck, and probed again with his right hand in the tide pool beneath the body. His wiry back and arm muscles were visibly strained by Talbot's weight, but Sorenson continued to probe. "Nothing underneath him that I could find," he finally said, as he eased the body back into the pool. "Nothing like his own gun, or knife, or a stick. Nothing that might make me think it was self-defense. Talbot was kind of a bulky guy, though; carried a lot of weight in his chest and shoulders," he mused. Sorenson stood up and appraised Talbot again. "Getting a little soft around the waist, but still not anybody you'd want to take on by yourself. I guess that's why she used a gun. Laura Arcand, I mean."

"Made up your mind awfully quick, haven't you, Jon?" Slattery asked.

"I think it's pretty obvious, Mary. Look at the witness statements. She had a fight with him last night, he gets stripped for bed, they fight some more, take it out on the beach, and she nails him. Look," he added, pointing to two long scrapes on the side of Talbot's face. "When they look under her nails I bet they find his skin."

Slattery shook her head. "Still kind of early for me, Jon. For all of this."

Sorenson's assistant, a pale, thin young woman with coppery hair pulled flush against her scalp, appeared on the path at the top of the bluff. "You ready?" she asked.

"Did the photographer want anything else?" Sorenson called up in reply.

"He's done," she answered.

"I think we can take him out of here, then," Sorenson replied. He waded out of the tide pool, the pale flesh of his arms and legs mottled from the cold water. He sat on the bleached driftwood log next to Slattery, wiping his arms with a ragged towel as Slattery hiked up her skirt so her legs could dry in the sun.

"We're six, maybe seven feet below the high tide line," Mary Slattery mused. "Why didn't he drift out of here, Jon?"

"What do you mean?"

"The tide should have floated Talbot's body away, shouldn't it? He was under the water; you can see that by the salt drying in his hair. Why did the body stay on the beach?"

"The killer might have had that in mind," Sorenson said slowly. "But Talbot wouldn't have gotten far. If he'd drifted out into the pass, he probably would have been pulled south because of the flushing action of the currents between the islands and the peninsula, down to Point White, then west toward Bremerton. But there're a couple of reasons it didn't work. His body wouldn't have much buoyancy until decomposition set in, and the cold water retards that. There's not that much wave action in the pass unless there's a storm, and the tidal movement is slow. It looks like his hand got stuck under the edge of that rock in the tide pool. It wouldn't take that much friction to hold him in place. Why do you ask?"

"No reason," Slattery said quickly. "Just thinking out loud." She paused, then added, "Did you find the gun?"

"Not yet. And that's the last thing you get from me, Mary. Everything else is going to have to come from the Kitsap prosecuting attorney's office."

"Okay, okay. Can I have a look inside the beach house? I guess they were staying there."

Sorenson shook his head, no. "Not yet. I've got a crew from the state lab coming down. Maybe tomorrow."

Slattery took a frustrated look up at the beach cabin. Below the cabin's deck, at the edge of the tide pool, she noticed three piles of round washed beach rock, balanced on top of one another, as though to form three stone cairns.

"What're those, Jon?" she asked, puzzled. She pointed to the stone cairns.

Sorenson dropped the towel on the log and started to shake the sand out of his socks. "Beats me. Looks like something a kid would do. Why?"

"Same answer, I don't know. Just looking around."

Sorenson's assistant returned and called out as she skipped down the redwood stairs. "Better get off the beach, Jon, and away from the enemy," she paused. "*She's* headed down here," she added nastily.

Mary Slattery looked up. A thickset woman of fifty with frosted blonde hair stepped carefully down the narrow winding path, then stopped at the top of the stairs, peering down at them below. Her bright white leather walking shoes shone in odd contrast to the dull gray-and-green plaid of her two-piece suit, worn with a ruffled blue blouse and black string tie. The woman stepped quickly down the stairs, then strode angrily across the beach to confront Mary Slattery.

"What are *you* doing here?" she asked sharply.

"My job," Slattery said calmly, extending her hand. "I'm Mary Slattery, one of Laura Arcand's attorneys. And you are . . . ?"

The woman grew angrier, refused Slattery's offered hand. "I'm Judith Watkins, the Kitsap County prosecuting attorney," she snapped.

Slattery withdrew her hand and stood for a moment, perplexed. This pop-eyed, angry woman could not be recognized from her press photos, the ever smiling, ever righteous defender of children who had risen from a shopping center divorce-and-car-crash practice to the prosecutor's chair on a wave of Christian rectitude. "I'm glad you're here," Slattery said cautiously. "I'd like to talk to you about the arraignment. Our client's still in shock. Her competency is going to be in doubt until we can get her examined. We'll need an extension on the arraignment date."

Watkins stared at her coldly. "I know all about Laura Arcand. A godless woman who paints sex pictures. And now has murdered."

"I suspect *Art in America* has a slightly different view," Slattery said dryly, "of a woman named one of the best American painters of this decade."

"They would," Watkins said, her voice heavy as stone. "I repeat, what are you doing here? This is a crime scene."

"Our client's mother owns this property," Slattery said evenly. "Surely you uphold private property rights. She has asked me to observe the work of the coroner."

"Get out. Or I'll have you removed."

Slattery smiled. "You don't want to risk *that,* do you? Concealing evidence from the defense, unreasonably restricting access to the alleged crime scene?"

Watkins hesitated. "You've got no business here," she said stubbornly.

"Care to find out? I've got my car, we can be in Port Orchard at the courthouse in half an hour."

Watkins grimaced. She has got, Slattery thought to herself, not the slightest clue about criminal procedure. But somebody in her office will set her straight soon enough. Far too soon to do us any good.

"We're charging Laura Arcand," Watkins said grimly, "with first degree murder. She'll be arraigned tomorrow on the nine-thirty calendar."

"Laura Arcand," Mary Slattery said evenly, "isn't even conscious yet. You can bring on the arraignment, but all you're going to get is a motion to extend time until we can talk to our client. You know," she added sarcastically, "fair trial, due process, all that constitutional stuff judges worry about."

"God," Judith Watkins said firmly, "will judge Laura Arcand."

"I don't doubt that," Mary Slattery replied.

Chapter Four

Will Hatton climbed into the wide leather backseat of the Kitsap Industries car, a dark green Range Rover, and tossed his flight bag into the cargo space behind the seat. His dull headache returned as the effect of the airline vodka and two hours of troubled, sweaty sleep wore off. His mouth felt dry and full of cotton. The driver was young, no more than twenty-two, a stocky, well-muscled kid with short, bristling black hair that was still growing out from a military buzz cut. Ed must have picked him, Will thought. He'd want Ellen to have a driver who could protect her in a tight spot. "Is there any water in the car?" he rasped.

"There's mineral water and ice in the cooler, sir." The Rover rounded the last curve in the highway loop that surrounded the airport and edged into traffic. "We should make the three o'clock ferry, if the line isn't too long. Mr. Hauser would like to see you on the island, at Ms. Arcand's home."

Will found the small cooler, twisted the cap off a bottle of Perrier water, and swallowed three aspirins with the first swig. "What's your name?" he asked the driver, taking another pull from the bottled water.

"Owen Dietrich, sir."

"What the hell happened out there, Owen?"

"I don't know, sir," Dietrich replied. "Ms. Arcand had a house party this weekend, maybe a dozen guests. Some brought their own cars. I wasn't at the house. I come in on call when Ms. Arcand wants to be driven into the office or into town for meetings. I didn't hear anything about it until I was called to take some of the guests home this morning." He paused, then repeated, "I was awfully sorry to hear about Mr. Talbot. I liked him, and Laura too—she always told me to call her that, and to knock off the 'Ms.' and 'ma'am' bullshit. Sir. I just don't know how she . . . I mean, what happened."

"I never understood her either," Will replied. "Take me to Harborview."

"Sir?"

"Take me to Harborview Hospital. Get off the freeway at James and head up the hill."

"But sir, Mr. Hauser said that I—"

"You're not listening, Dietrich," Will snapped with the low, cheerful growl he'd acquired as a marine squad leader twenty-five years before. He had not been much of a marine but he'd learned the command voice at Twenty-nine Palms and bulled his way through it. "Take me to Harborview or I will have your balls roasted and served with drinks this evening. Understand?"

Dietrich permitted himself a small smile of recognition, visible in the rearview mirror. "Perfectly, sir," he said cheerfully, cutting across three lanes of traffic to make the exit. "*Semper Fi,* sir."

Will Hatton talked his way past the psych duty nurse and the locked ward matron before running into a squat, stolid psychiatric resident. "Avrim Becker," he said, offering his hand. "Look, Dr. Hatton, I can't authorize access. Ms. Arcand is still unconscious, and will be for another thirty-six hours, at least." Becker spoke with a harsh Israeli accent, overlaid with a veneer of Oxbridge English.

"Can you fill me in, Doctor?" Will replied. "I'm an old friend of the family. They've called me back from Dallas to consult. I'd like to be able to explain Laura's condition, let them know what she's facing."

Becker thought, standing with his feet squared in military fashion on the dull brown linoleum floor outside the heavy locking door that led to the psych wing. "Let's get a coffee," he said finally. Becker led Will to the basement, picked up two coffees from the stand in the cafeteria, and strode to an outdoor smoking area behind the main hospital building, overlooking the parking lot, the helipad, and the rooftops of Pioneer Square across the droning lanes of traffic on I-5. Becker lit a Dunhill and offered the red box to Hatton with a rueful smile of silent apology. Hatton shook his head.

"I'm trying to quit again," Becker said. "A bad example for a doctor, I know."

Hatton nodded impatiently. "Tell me about Laura, Doctor."

Becker took a deep drag and blew the smoke out in a narrow plume, squinting into the afternoon sun. "A nasty suicide attempt. Deep gouges aligned to the veins, no hesitation at all. She was brought in with deep shock, blood loss, and hypothermia. The medevac crew said she was wearing only a T-shirt and panties when they found her, and she'd been partially submerged in the water for at least an hour."

"Has she been conscious at all?"

"Briefly. She regained consciousness three times. Screaming each time."

"What did she say?"

"Nothing intelligible. She said something about a killing in the ER, but nothing at all in the other two episodes. We've given her a light Valium drip, but I don't want to medicate her very much. After each semiconscious episode her life signs drop. We've almost lost her twice."

"The police are saying she killed her husband."

"Yes, I know. She may have, of course. But I'm troubled. Do you know if she'd experienced any kind of life-threatening trauma before this happened?"

"No. Why?"

Becker tossed his cigarette into the sand-filled urn beside the door and looked into the distance. "I knew a girl from the army, six years younger than I," he began. "She was nineteen, a truck driver, doing her national service. Her unit was called into south Lebanon during the *intifada,* some years ago. The road was supposed to be secure. It wasn't. Her truck was cut off from the convoy near a Hezbollah village. The mujahideen captured her. Dovuh was a very sheltered girl. Very innocent. They raped her. Repeatedly. To make a political point, I suppose. My squad went into the village the next day and found her. We captured the men who had raped her. Before we could get them out, she snatched up an Uzi and shot them, all of them, again and again. While they were bound and gagged. They screamed from the backs of their throats."

Becker lit another cigarette, his hands trembling with the memory. "We hushed it up, of course. Six weeks later Dovuh was still in an army hospital. I stayed with her. She had nightmares about her captivity every night and relived it in flashbacks nearly every day. When she screamed I would go to her, hold her, try to bring her back to reality. The episodes diminished after a couple of months. I hoped Dovuh was all right. She was not. The day after they released her she threw herself off the balcony of her parents' apartment in Tel Aviv. She fled from her memories the only way she could."

"I'm very sorry," Hatton replied.

Becker shook his head, still troubled by his own memory.

"Your friend reminds me of Dovuh," he said sadly, "in an unscientific way that I cannot explain. Perhaps it is her eyes, when she breaks out of unconsciousness. Full of rage and fear. But seeing nothing."

Becker dropped his second cigarette and stepped on it. "I've got to go back to the ward," he said. "Come back in a day, maybe two. And take good care of Laura Arcand. She'll need it."

Chapter Five

Jesus Christ, Mary Slattery said to herself, what a god-awful mess. She sat on the porch of Ellen Arcand's home and leaned against one of the rough fieldstone pillars that supported the roof above, while she scraped the wet sand from her legs. Drying salt stained the hem of her pale gray wool skirt. In her haste to get to the crime scene she hadn't had time to stop at her Belltown apartment and change her clothes or even grab a pair of rubber boots.

Slattery sighed, said a quiet "What the fuck," squirmed out of her sodden panty hose, and tossed them behind the rhododendron bushes at the end of the porch. She lit a Camel Light and pulled a legal pad from her briefcase, to add to her case notes. *NEW QUES-TIONS,* she wrote quickly in the small, slanted block capital letters she favored. *TIME OF DEATH???* headed the list of questions. She added *TIDE, MARK NAKED?* and *WHERE'S THE GUN??* then put the pad down on the deck. She took a deep drag and stubbed the cigarette butt on the flagstone step between her legs before dropping it into the base of the hedge beside her.

Ed Hauser emerged from the double front doors of the house carrying two highball glasses filled with gin, crushed ice, and lime. "I thought you might be ready for this," he said, settling his bulk on the porch step beside her.

Mary Slattery nodded gratefully, took a full swallow of Tanqueray, and sighed. "What a mess," she repeated.

"Whatever can't be cleaned, we'll buy," Hauser said quickly.

Slattery turned a warm smile on her boss. "Thanks. But I'm talking about the crime scene," she said, reaching into her purse and extracting a second Camel Light. "The physical evidence is going to be pretty inconclusive. The county coroner, Jon Sorenson, is a good pathologist but isn't going to get much," she reported. "The water in the tide pool lowered Talbot's body temperature so quickly they can't get an accurate time of death; they'll be within an hour at best, either side. But somebody in Illahee must have heard the shots across the water. We should get an investigator over there, see if we can nail down the time. The water's effect on the edges of the entry wounds could mess up the ballistics analysis for the angle of the shots. Both slugs lodged against his spine, so there're no exit wounds, and they may not have enough of an internal bullet track to be precise about the angle. They haven't found the gun, but the state crime lab crew hasn't been through the beach house yet. We can't get access until they do. If any of this matters," she added, with a sideways glance at Hauser.

Ed Hauser nodded as if to acknowledge her unspoken question. He reached for her cigarette, took a quick forbidden drag, then handed it back to her. "Tell me the story of the case," he said. "Start at the beginning. I want to hear how it sounds. I'll fill in what I know as you go."

"You know how it's going to sound, Ed. Like shit." But Slattery took a quick look at her notes of the witness interviews she'd conducted that morning and began to recite, in the clipped professional cadence she'd learned from her father, once chief of detectives for Silver Bow County, Montana. "Laura Arcand, thirty-nine years old. One of the country's best-known modern painters. Tall, striking looks. Native of the Northwest, grew up in Bremerton and on Bainbridge Island. Five years ago she left New York, where she'd lived since 1979, and moved back to Seattle. A history of drug and alcohol abuse. Three years ago she married Mark Talbot, president and chief operating officer for Kitsap Industries, a conglomerate mostly owned by her mother, Ellen Arcand, who has been your lover for over twenty years. Ellen Arcand has shown good sense by refusing to marry you, despite your repeated heartfelt pleas."

"That much I remember," Hauser said dryly. "Limit the editorial comment where possible, Slattery."

"Not always possible, Ed," she replied. "Laura's marriage to Mark was thought to be shaky from the beginning. It's also rumored that Laura's manic-depressive, been hospitalized for mental illness before."

"She has, but let's hold that subject for a minute. Take us to the party."

"Ellen was having a house party for ten guests this weekend, twelve people in all. You and Ellen; Laura and Mark; Jack Stephens, the crime writer from Port Townsend, and his wife; Tony Alpert from SeaFirst Bank and his wife, Joan; Bob Tierney, a real estate investor, and his third wife, who looks like she's about fifteen; and Marcia Wiegand from Kitsap Industries and her boyfriend, the guy who stomped out at the dinner, Tom Guenther. Kind of an odd mix, if you ask me."

"Not so odd," Hauser responded. "Except for Guenther and the spouses, they were all investors in the Elk Run office project that KI has been developing in north Kitsap County and just moved into. It was half business, at least. We had meetings about the project for most of the day on Monday."

"Mark was roasted on the spit, I take it, given that it was his deal, the project was behind schedule and, aside from Kitsap Industries, less than fifteen percent occupied?"

"Pretty much. Mark was directly in charge of all Kitsap Industries real estate projects. Marcia Wiegand was his number two, and neither of them had a very good time answering all the questions. Keep going."

"Mark and Laura were staying at the beach cabin. It was Mark's pet project this summer, rebuilding the old cabin from the pilings up. He did most of the work himself, at first. Laura worked on it with him, but quit. Mark then hired a contractor; they finished it about two weeks ago. I haven't been able to look at the cabin, by the way—

the crime lab's still going through it. You can't see the cabin from up here at the house—it's below the bluff, maybe thirty feet down, beside the stream. Laura stayed down there by herself except for meals. According to the witnesses, Laura was quiet, polite, not very sociable. Until last night. Laura got drunk and blew up at dinner."

"Did she ever." Ed Hauser sipped at his glass of gin, troubled. He looked out from the front porch over the bluff-top meadow, still deep green in September thanks to the rainy spring, and out over the pass to the forested Illahee shore on the Kitsap Peninsula. "Laura was in a mood all weekend, dark and distracted. She was quiet during most of the dinner, drinking pretty steadily. When dinner was over Mark tended bar, pouring brandy for whoever wanted it. He was sharing some kind of joke with Marcia Wiegand when Laura came up to the bar. 'So how is she?' she asked Mark, looking straight at Marcia. 'At giving head, I mean.' She said it very distinctly, in that theatrical way of hers, just loud enough for everyone to hear. Then she threw her drink at Mark and stormed out of the house. Mark followed her, I guess down to the beach cabin."

"Great," Mary Slattery answered sarcastically. "The defense lawyer's a witness to the motive. The prosecutor's going to love that." She paused, then added, "How much truth was there in Laura's little outburst?"

Hauser hesitated, trying to frame the answer in a way that would put Laura in the best available light. "Laura's had a bad summer. She hasn't really been able to paint since she married Mark. I could never figure the marriage, to tell you the truth. Mark was so stiff and unemotional, on the surface anyway. A perfectionist, pretty tightly wound up with his work, a classic workaholic. Ellen rode him hard, demanded a lot. Laura, on the other hand, is very self-absorbed with her painting and her problems. She's not submissive, not the doting-helpmate type. Whatever fire there was in the marriage seemed to be dying out. They had their good times, of course, right up to this summer. She loved him, maybe more than he did her, but I think she sensed she'd been a prize, Mark's way of cementing his position with KI."

"Meaning?"

"Meaning that I wouldn't be surprised if Mark found sex in the office. And the way Tom Guenther, Wiegand's boyfriend, took off—

he had some words with her, and I guess she told him it was true."

"So the jury's going to hear that Mark's getting laid on the side," Slattery said, making another note on her legal pad, thinking aloud. "Laura storms out, cursing. Mark follows her. Everybody else turns in pretty quickly, the party atmosphere a little soured, to say the least. At four A.M. Jack Stephens is up, wrestling with a new book idea, and decides to walk down to the beach. He finds Mark shot to death in the tide pool. And Laura lying on the beach half dead just above him, her wrists gouged. With her wedding ring. You don't need Freud to see the symbolism here, do you?"

"No." A breeze kicked up from the water and Hauser shook slightly from fatigue and the sudden chill. "Mark didn't stay with Laura all night. He got her calmed down and came back up to the house. Ellen had gone to bed, but we talked. Mark said Laura was okay, that she was sleeping. He stayed a couple of hours at least, till maybe one o'clock or so, when I finally had to drive back to my farm in Island Center. I slept there because Tor and I were supposed to go down to my boat in Westport early this morning for some fishing." Hauser paused and rubbed his arms against the slight chill entering the late-afternoon air. "I'd better get a sweater. Anyway, there's no physical evidence linking Laura to the shooting, and no witnesses. Nobody up in the main house heard or saw the shots. At low tide you can walk the beach all the way around to Fort Ward. It could have been anyone."

Mary Slattery shook her head. "That's not going to fly, Ed. Not with the fight they had at dinner. You know how they'll put it together. Mark comes back late, strips down for bed. Laura wakes up, still drunk, still mad, even angrier that he left her alone in the beach house for hours. They fight. She gets the gun, chases him out on the beach, shoots him. Her suicide attempt is an admission of guilt."

"There's still no witnesses," Hauser said stubbornly.

Slattery snorted impatiently. "They won't need one. What about the gun?"

"What?"

"The gun. Did Laura know how to shoot? Did she own or have access to one?"

Hauser nodded. "Possibly. Years ago, when Ellen and I began to see each other, I tried to teach Laura and Ellen a few basic things about handling a gun because I had them in the house. Ellen took to it, but Laura fought me on it, said she hated guns. But she might have learned enough. It's not all that difficult." He paused, his voice tentative. "Do they know what kind of gun killed Mark?"

"Not yet. You have a Colt automatic in the main house, and Ellen has a .38 Smith & Wesson. They're being checked, but neither looked like it had been fired to me. What about Mark? Did he own guns?"

"Several. Mark was quite a shooter—it was his hobby. Mark might have carried a handgun with him, maybe in their truck. I think he had a concealed-carry permit."

"If he did, it's not there now, Ed. So far, no one's found it."

Edwin Hauser looked out to the west and stared at the sun dropping over the Kitsap mainland. He seemed suddenly ancient, the vitality draining from his red-faced bulk, artfully clothed in ancient corduroys and a pressed denim shirt.

"Oh my God," he cried, his voice suddenly choked with sorrow, all his lawyer's dispassion gone. "She must have been insane. Laura was diagnosed as a manic-depressive when she was in her mid-twenties. This summer . . . she came out here with all kinds of ideas, really up, ready to rebuild the beach house with Mark. They tore it down to the studs and slept out there, under the open sky, happy as a couple of teenagers. Her mother and I were so pleased for them . . . we thought her therapy had finally kicked in and she was ready to get on with her life. But when they started rebuilding it, her mood changed. She started drinking again, more heavily than I'd ever seen her. Some days she couldn't work until noon, other days she just disappeared, took the ferry back into Seattle, didn't reappear for two or three days. Mark was patient, for him. He tried to jolly her out of it, tried to get her back to her therapist in the city. She refused to go. But something about this whole summer set her off. I never figured out what it was." He stopped and buried his face in his hands. When he finally looked up his expression was firm. "Call the office. Get Reuben Todd and the two summer clerks going on the research. I want a complete memo on the status of the insanity and diminished-capacity defenses by tomorrow."

"They've already started. I called Reuben two hours ago. The county prosecutor out here, Judith Watkins, is pushing the case. We're facing an arraignment tomorrow. Reuben's also working on discovery requests and a custody motion, to get Laura out of Harborview."

"Good," Ed Hauser replied. "I'd better check on Ellen."

"Ed," Mary Slattery said softly, "what in hell are we doing in this case?"

"Because Laura needs me and I'm going to defend her."

"That's crazy, not to put too fine a point on it. Even though you and Ellen never married, you're pretty damned close to being her stepfather. You're a witness to some of the events last night that the prosecutor is going to use to prove jealousy, and motive. You're sixty-three. You've got a bad heart, and haven't tried a major criminal case in ten years. You're not going to be able to help her."

Ed Hauser looked at her with sudden anger. "I'm sterile," he said abruptly. "I had rheumatic fever when I was thirteen. Laura is as close to a child as I'm ever going to have."

"Except for Will," Mary Slattery reminded him.

"Except for Will," he agreed. "But I'm damned if I'm going to sit around and watch them hang Laura."

"Ed, you can't do this."

"Yes, damn it, I can." Hauser stopped, still red faced with anger. "Look," he added plaintively, the anger slowly beginning to drain out of him. "This is the only thing I can do. Hell, it's all I really know how to do." He shook his bulk to chase the chill out of his bones and walked heavily into the house.

Chapter Six

Two television news vans stood at the head of the private road, parked inside the stone gateposts off Crystal Springs Drive, their dish antennas pointed skyward to dump the satellite feed to the six o'clock news. The Rover bounced past them without slowing. Will grinned as Dietrich dropped a gear and slewed around the turn in the loose gravel, throwing a spray of dust in the faces of the camera crews and the blue-blazered reporters who leaned against the side of the vans, smoking and gossiping. They dropped down the steep hill through a thick stand of Douglas firs and pulled into the graveled parking area, screened by a row of Lombardy poplars from the house. Will grabbed his bags from the back of the Rover and set off down the sloping path through the trees into the meadow.

He paused on the porch to drop his bags, then opened the double screen doors. "Ed? Ellen?" he called out, entering the house.

Ed Hauser opened the glass-paned pocket doors and stepped out of the living room into the wide, cool central hallway. He wrapped Will in a bear hug. "It's good to see you, kid," he said huskily. "I just wish the times were better."

"How're you and Ellen holding up?" Will asked, pounding the old man's back, then letting go, but keeping an arm around his shoulders.

"Not great. I had to practically drag Ellen back here from Harborview. You went to the hospital? Should have figured you would. Has Laura's condition changed?"

Will stepped back to look at Ed. Hauser was still wide as a fullback in his fishing sweater and shapeless corduroys. His broad face was red and sunburned under his short white brush-cut hair. But his skin had a grayish tone under his sunburn, and his eyes were red with fatigue and worry.

He looks old, Will thought suddenly, old and tired for the first time I can remember. "Ed, Laura's still unconscious, in deep shock, likely to remain that way for a day or two. She's had several . . ." Will fell silent as Ellen Arcand entered the hall and put her arms around Ed Hauser's bulky middle.

"Hello, Will," she said softly. Ellen was casually elegant even in grief, her straight gray-blonde hair pulled up in a twist, dressed in a simple white tunic and denim jeans, a blue cotton sweater knotted loosely around her waist. At fifty-five she looked a decade younger, a small, slender woman with lightly tanned skin, scarcely creased by time. Only the bloodless pallor beneath the tan and the bloodshot eyes revealed her feelings of shock and loss.

"Ellen, I am so sorry," Will said, abandoning a search for better words. "Are you all right? I've got my prescription book, I can get you something in town if you need it."

Ellen smiled ruefully. "I've learned to take my troubles straight, Will. But thank you. Tell me," she added with quiet bitterness, "are those television vultures still out at the gate?"

Will nodded. "I'm afraid you've got to expect that, given Laura's fame."

"I know," Ellen replied. "But that doesn't make it any easier." She stiffened for a moment, seemingly lost in her own thoughts, gazing past Will through the double front doors to the brighter, more peaceful world outside. After a long minute she shook away whatever thought was pressing on her and turned back to him. "I'm sorry, Will. You've had a long flight, and I'm being a terrible hostess. Let me get you a drink. This young lady from Ed's office wants to take down my life story, and we might as well be comfortable on the porch while she does it. Ed," she added, taking Will's arm, "please send out your young shark. And tell Grace to bring the drinks tray. I think I'm finally ready for one."

They stayed on the front porch in deep, ancient wicker chairs for the better part of two hours in the dry, slanted, end-of-summer light. Mary Slattery sat with a legal pad poised on her knee, pausing between questions to scribble notes or sometimes just to sit with her chin cupped in her hand, pondering her next question. Will sat back, appraising her. There's a solid quality there, he thought to himself. The classic Irish face is too wide for beauty, but her auburn hair and green eyes are handsome, and she knows it. I just hope she's as smart as Ed seems to think she is. "Tell me about yourself and Laura," Mary Slattery had said, and Ellen, for all her dislike of talking about herself, had spoken at length.

Ellen Arcand had been raised by strict Catholic foster parents in a working-class Bremerton neighborhood. In 1957, sixteen years old and pregnant with Laura, she married Laura's father, Russell Lund, a twenty-year-old fisherman, who quickly tired of married life and abandoned wife and child eight months after Laura's birth.

"Russ was just a boy, with a wild streak as wide as Laura's," Ellen Arcand said dispassionately, at ease with a past she could not change and would not try to color by editing memory. "He had the same dark hair and gray-blue eyes. We were still legally married when his boat went down in the Bering Sea, six months after he left. I didn't know he'd bought insurance. The settlement was $20,000, which seemed like all the money in the world to me. I was able to take my high school equivalency exam and start business courses at the junior college. I'd never had a childhood or an adolescence, and part of me wanted to take the money out of the bank and just spend it. But I never did. I wanted Laura to have a better life than I had. So I went to work. We lived in a tiny rented house on D Street, near the Bremerton Shipyard, and a neighbor woman looked after Laura for $10 a week while I was at work." Ellen Arcand paused to pour herself a small glass of scotch. She lit one of the four Benson & Hedges cigarettes she allowed herself each day and looked at Mary Slattery severely through the smoke. "I still don't understand the relevance of all this ancient history," she said abruptly, a tone of frustrated anger suddenly rising to the surface.

Slattery put down her pad and leaned forward, her gaze intent. "Ms. Arcand, your daughter is going to be charged with murdering her husband tomorrow," she said bluntly. "There are no other reasonable, or even plausible, suspects. We're probably going to have to plead that Laura was insane when she shot Mark. The only chance we have of helping her is to know as much truth about her life, her upbringing, as you can give us. It hurts now, I know. But it will hurt more later if you're not willing to talk about this."

Ellen looked at Ed Hauser. "She's right, Ellen," he said softly.

"I understand," Ellen Arcand said at last. She began again. "I worked in a factory at first, one that made plastic radio housings for the navy. My job was to sand off the rough edges when they came from the molds. The plastic shavings made the skin of my hands swell, then dry and crack. When I came home at night Laura would wait for me, rub lotion on my hands, and tell me very somberly that she loved me. She was four." Ellen's eyes teared up but her gaze was steady, holding Mary Slattery's eyes. "Other children got to run home and tell the stories of their play, their friends. Mine had to rub my hands before I could make her dinner. After we ate, before she got her bedtime stories, she would sit at the kitchen table, draw with her crayons, and listen to me while I read my high school correspondence lessons aloud to her. It was the only way I could study and we could be together."

Ellen Arcand drifted through factory work and office jobs while finishing her high school and accounting courses, searching for some way out of a single mother's working-class poverty. In 1963 she took a bookkeeping job with Renner Tool & Die, a twelve-man metal shop that machined specialty parts for the navy. The company grew quickly in the Vietnam military buildup, and Ellen Arcand was promoted to office manager. In 1967, Curt Renner, the owner of the company, had a chance to bid on a steel fabrication contract that would triple the company's revenues. Ellen had gone with him from bank to bank, but no one would lend.

"We'd tried everywhere," she said, sipping her scotch in the first evening chill. She pulled her sweater tighter and folded her arms under her breasts. "We didn't have the cash flow to service the loan unless the contract came through, and there was no assurance that it would. Curt stood on the shop floor in tears when I told him that our last bank had refused us. He knew I had the money I'd saved for Laura, nearly $35,000 by then. He begged me to loan it to him. I refused. He asked me what I wanted; I took a deep breath and told him that the book value of the company was a hundred thousand dollars, and I'd take thirty-five percent of the stock. Curt didn't want to make me his partner. But he had no choice. It worked. We got the contract, and the business grew. Within five years, sales had gone up thirty times, and I was getting almost $40,000 a year in dividends on top of my salary. In 1971 I was able to buy this house. It was run-down, and cheap because of the Boeing depression. Laura and I began to fix it up. It was hard, but it got Laura out of Bremerton, into good schools here on the island. She was so gifted artistically, even as a child, that she needed schools where she could stretch and grow."

"When did Laura's mental problems begin?" Mary Slattery asked softly.

"I don't know," Ellen Arcand replied, her face darkening. "Laura was terribly quiet, even through puberty. I suppose we were too close, having been alone together for so long. She had a hard time making friends. We moved to the island when she was thirteen. She'd skipped two grades in Bremerton, and they put her in the high school here. It was hard on her. She grew up too fast; she looked like a grown woman at fourteen. I lost control of her for a while. I took her to therapists; they said to ride it out, it was just normal adolescent rebellion. It didn't help. She had one episode . . . the second summer we were here she ran away, disappeared for four days. It might have been drugs, I don't know. After that summer she boarded at Seaside School, over in Seattle, and seemed to straighten out. You might ask Will, he knew her a little bit in those days, even though he was a couple of years ahead of her." Ellen smiled briefly, reached for Will's hand, and held it for a moment. "And to be truthful, I had my own problems at that time. With Curt Renner."

"What kind of trouble?"

"Curt was a brilliant engineer, self-taught, really the soul of the company. But he'd long since divorced his wife, Mark's mother—"

"Curt Renner was Mark Talbot's father?" Mary Slattery asked, surprised.

"Yes, of course. That's how Mark came to look for a job with me—he'd inherited the part of his father's stock that wasn't covered by our buy-sell agreement. Is that surprising?"

"No," Mary Slattery replied. "I just didn't know, that's all."

"Curt was a heavy drinker," Ellen Arcand continued, "not to mention chasing every woman in Kitsap County. In 1972 he drowned in a boating accident, the same summer Laura ran away. I had to hold the company together, keep the customers from pulling their business away. It was too much—I was only thirty-one. I worked so hard those next few years . . . we were on the edge all the time. We made it, but I'm not sure Laura ever forgave me—or got over—the time I had to spend working."

"Why would you think that, Ellen?" Will asked, surprised.

"Isn't it obvious, Will? Laura's addictions, her depressions, her craziness—what part of that did I cause? What part do I claim as mine, or not mine?"

"Perhaps some of it, perhaps none of it. Addictions are chemical, with a genetic predisposition, Ellen. And we don't know what mix of genetics and environment results in depression, or most other types of mental illness. What part do you want? If you take some of the pain, you should take some credit for Laura's skill, her genius . . . ."

"Her killing Mark Talbot," Ellen Arcand said bitterly. She stopped abruptly, eyes clenched shut. She stood up, whispered, "I'm sorry," and walked off the porch into the meadow, alone.

"Let me check on Ellen," Will said, standing.

Ed Hauser waved him down. "Ellen will be all right," he said. "I'll talk to her. She's the strongest woman I've ever known."

Mary Slattery closed her eyes and rubbed the bridge of her nose. "I think," she said carefully, "that I need to know the rest. Can you fill it in, Dr. Hatton?"

"Will," he responded. He squinted into the last of the sunlight, watching Ed catch up to Ellen and wrap his arm around her as they walked slowly to the edge of the bluff. A thin fog had drifted up from the water and clung to the meadow floor at their feet, shot through with the first orange-and-gold light of sunset. "If you're asking about Laura's running away when she was a teenager, I don't know much more than you've just heard. I left the island earlier that summer—1972—and went to New Orleans to see my father, about two weeks before Laura disappeared. I got a wild hair when I was down there and joined the marine corps, didn't come back for a long time. As for Laura, all I could do is guess. It might have been a bad drug trip of some kind—1972 was sure the right year for it. Or maybe Laura just plain ran away. She's never remembered anything about it."

"What about Laura's relationship with her mother now, Will? I'm going to want to have Ellen tell that story in the trial, if it comes to that."

Hatton sipped at the iced tea he'd been nursing. "You'd have to ask Ed. I don't think they're day-to-day close—so far as I know they don't call each other every morning, that sort of thing. I don't know if you've represented Ellen on any of her business deals—if you have, you know she's one tough, demanding businesswoman. I'd guess that Laura's lifestyle has caused her a lot of pain. But Ellen genuinely loves and values Laura and her work as a painter. I know it hurt her when Laura came back here, unable to paint with the brilliance she had before. Not because of status or anything like that. Ellen understands the trauma of not being able to work at what you're good at, knows how much pain that caused Laura. And there's the history they share. Ellen has always been fiercely protective of her strange and wonderful child, and Laura knows it. My guess is, if you scratch one, the other would bleed."

Ed Hauser returned, his bulk looming over them before he settled onto a wicker chair with a fresh glass of gin and ice. He drained the glass and set it down sharply on the glass-topped wicker table beside him. "Talk to Laura, Will, when she's conscious again. If Laura shot Mark she did it in some kind of insane mental state. She'd never do it out of jealousy. I know that."

"I can't, Ed. I've known Laura since we were kids, and I'm too close to the family. If you put me up as the defense forensic and I say she was insane, they'll rip me to shreds with that."

"Please, Will. Just talk to her, assess her condition. Even if we never put you on the stand, there's nobody better than you are at building a case. Maybe the families, at least, will know that Laura didn't intend to kill Mark." Ed Hauser stood up unsteadily, badly flushed from the alcohol hitting his weakened heart. "I've got to go now," he said tiredly. "I've got to talk to Mark's family, try to help them see that."

Chapter Seven

When the docking announcement came over the ferry *Tacoma*'s loudspeaker, Will Hatton stood to go. "Thanks for the lift to the ferry," he said. "I'll get a cab from here."

Mary Slattery looked up, troubled. She had been silent for most of the return sailing, leafing through a stack of faxes her office had sent to her over Ellen Arcand's home computer system. "Hang on just a second, please," she said, thinking. "Can you give me some more time on this tonight? I've still got about a thousand questions. I'll buy dinner, anywhere you like."

"Thanks," Will said, "but I've been up for most of forty-eight hours. Could it wait?"

"I don't think so. We've got to be in court in the morning. And frankly, I'm worried about Ed."

"Okay," Will said. "How about this—you drive me home, we'll talk as long as you need or I can stay awake. I'll send out for Chinese or something. At least I can take a shower and have some coffee to keep me awake."

"Done."

They returned to Mary Slattery's gunmetal BMW convertible on the car deck. Will got in the passenger side.

"Pretty slick," he said, running his hands over the leather seats.

"Ed's been generous about money. I decided to splurge."

"You like Ed a lot, don't you?"

"Yeah," Slattery said, breaking into a grin for the first time. "I do. He's a great lawyer, a fair boss. And a good friend." She paused. "What's your relationship to Ed, exactly? He talks about you like you're a son."

Will hesitated before delivering the answer. He normally found personal questions distasteful, but there was something in this woman that he found interesting. "My mother worked as Ed's legal secretary, back in the late 1960s, when he was still practicing criminal law out of his old office in Bremerton. They were close. Lovers, but very proper around me. She died when I was sixteen, just before they were to have gotten married. I didn't want to live with my father, or with my mother's parents. So Ed took me in. He lived on Bainbridge Island then, in the old farmhouse he still has in Island Center. He fixed up the bunkhouse for me, so I could stay in high school on the island."

"How long did you stay with him?"

"Two years, until I finished Bainbridge High School. We got along pretty well. No, it was more than that. I was pretty lost after my mom died—I'd never really had anyone else. Ed saw that, got me hooked on a reading program—Dickens, Chaucer, Shakespeare, Melville, Hemingway. He wouldn't take a dime from me—invested my mother's insurance money instead. I clerked in his law office to pay my room and board. He taught me the rudiments of evidence, trial work, how to put a case together. I got fascinated by law and medicine." Will smiled, bemused by ancient memory. "Ed even taught me how to box. Badly, of course. When he'd taught me everything he knew, he found an old washed-up welterweight who had a gym down by the waterfront in Bremerton, and we took lessons together every Saturday morning. He liked my company. I needed that, a lot."

"What about your real father? Biological father, I mean."

"He was," Will said precisely, "not very interested. My parents divorced when I was two years old. He stayed in New Orleans. Sometimes I think my father viewed procreation as a sort of aesthetic experiment, one he decided he wasn't crazy about."

Mary Slattery heard the strain in Hatton's voice and changed the subject. "Sorry. I cross-examine everybody. Which way?" she asked as the ferry car deck emptied out onto the dock.

"Turn left on Alaskan Way, cut up to Western, take Elliott over the Ballard bridge. I'll talk you in from there."

"Ballard?" Slattery asked, amusement in her voice. "I figured you for a slick downtown condo, Dr. Hatton."

"It's Will. And you'll see when we get there."

Slattery followed his instructions and found herself on Ballard Avenue, a brick-paved street of boat brokers, fishermen's taverns, used furniture stores, machine shops, and restaurants. "There," Will said, pointing to his left. "Just do a U-turn and pull up in front."

Mary Slattery got out of the car and looked up at the narrow four-story brick building. The name CHRISTIANSEN was chiseled into a stone lintel piece just below the roofline. "My great-grandfather built it," Will explained, "around 1904."

"I thought your family was from New Orleans."

"Just on my father's side," Will explained. "My mother's folks came from Norway—all fishermen. Come on." He led her past the offices of a boat brokerage to a freight elevator at the rear of the small stone-floored lobby. They rode in silence to the top-floor loft. Will opened the sliding elevator gates and switched on the lights in an oak-floored vestibule. A pair of bright red Tabriz rugs hung on the wall over a Stickley library table stacked with mail. "There's wine and liquor and coffee in the kitchen," Will said, pointing to the left. "The living room's on the right, facing the street. You'll find restaurant menus in the kitchen drawer next to the stove—I've got accounts at all of them, and they'll deliver. I'm not much of a cook. Pick out whatever you like. I'm going to shower off this airplane smell."

Will returned twenty minutes later, in time to tip the waiter from Julia's, a restaurant two blocks north toward Market Street. He quickly made coffee, set plates and silver and napkins on a polished oak trestle table in the open living room, opened the oversized, steel-framed loft windows to let the stale air of absence escape from the room, then put the food back in the oven to reheat. When he finished he found Mary Slattery standing in front of a pair of Laura Arcand's paintings hanging on the exposed-brick far wall, a glass of Ravenswood zinfandel held loosely in her hand.

"Tell me about Laura's paintings," she said.

"These are two early ones," Will replied. "Around 1982 or so, just when she was beginning to build a reputation. Part of her flower series. I bought them from her studio through Ed. God knows I couldn't afford them now."

"They're not realistic. There's just swirls of color, of paint."

"Right. They are abstract. But they're suggestive of flowers."

"And other things," Slattery said, coloring slightly beneath her light summer tan. "When you look at it long enough, it looks like . . . a woman's . . ."

"Vulva. Laura always did have an ironic sense of humor. You know anything about her career?"

Slattery shook her head. "Not much. An occasional newspaper story, some remark Ed or Ellen would make around the office."

"Laura got her B.F.A. in painting from Yale in 1979. She was only twenty. By then she'd already shown in New York. She moved down there after graduation. Her ascent in the art world wasn't seamless, but it was pretty quick. Mark Loudin, a very good dealer, picked her up right out of college and promoted the hell out of her. She was a color-field painter, a kind of abstract expressionist, but her work was almost unique in the way she could merge fields of color into comprehensible images. Some critics called her—I guess they still do—the heir to Helen Frankenthaler. It was the beginning of the 1980s art boom in New York, and Laura's work was big and bright, with strong sexual overtones. It appealed to a lot of the new-money types, investment bankers and arbitrageurs and other financial riffraff. It was great art that also looked good hung over a white silk sofa. By 1988 a single Laura Arcand painting cost $600,000. The prices have fallen some, I guess, but if Laura held on to what she made then, she's probably got nearly as much money as Ellen does." He paused, then added, "I don't think sudden fame does anybody much good. I don't think it was good for Laura. Those were wild years. Lots of alcohol, lots of cocaine, lots of late nights, none of it good for a woman whose bipolar disorder was pretty well established. In the end it hurt her work, hurt her. Eventually she realized that, came home."

"Did you see her back then?"

"Not when she was getting started. I spent three years in the marine corps, didn't finish medical school until 1981. I did see her later, briefly, when I was teaching at Columbia." Will stopped abruptly. "Dinner should be warm, now."

They settled at the table. Slattery had ordered smoked salmon ravioli and salads. Will realized that, for the first time in days, he was hungry.

"How much do you know about Laura's medical history?" Mary Slattery asked, piling warm spinach salad on her plate.

"Can we wait just a few minutes longer?" Will pleaded. "Every meal I've had in the last eleven days has been business, including breakfast. I'd like to just eat. Tell me about yourself. I thought you did well with Ellen, pulling all that personal information out of her under tough circumstances."

Mary Slattery thought it over. Will sat across the table from her in a shapeless straw-colored cotton sweater and faded jeans that hung loosely on his lean frame, his dark blond hair still wet from the shower and slicked straight back, bags the size of boxcars under his strained blue eyes. He's too tired to make a pass at me, she decided, but if he did I'd give it some thought. God knows I've had worse offers lately. "I'm a cop's kid," Mary finally said, "the oldest of six. I grew up in Butte, Montana, which is not exactly the garden spot of the universe."

"I know, I've been there. And as the joke goes, it really does look best in the rearview mirror."

"That's Butte. I was a scholarship student at the University of Washington, undergrad and law school. You lectured in my law-and-psychiatry class."

"That properly ages me. You must be about thirty." Will cocked his head and studied her more closely. It's the eyes that draw you, he thought, that dark green . . . no. I am *way* too fucking tired to be thinking like this.

Hatton busied himself with his salad. "Did you always want to be a lawyer?" he asked, a bland question to hide his sudden embarrassment.

"No," she said, smiling. "I wanted to be a cop. But my father told me that lawyers had better jobs, made more money, and seldom got shot at. And that he'd break my arm if I came home to Butte. So I went to the King County prosecutor's office. I made senior deputy before the office politics got to me. I joined Ed as his firm's in-house criminal specialist a year ago."

Will looked up as he finished his salad. "You must be good, if Ed took you in. You married?"

"No," she said perfunctorily.

"Me neither. I think I've missed something, but I'm not sure what, looking at most of my married friends. Children, I guess." Will put down his fork, surprised at how quickly he'd eaten. "Thanks," he said. "You've been patient, and I appreciate it. I know that with a major homicide case you've got more to do than you can handle. So let's get on to business. You and I both know that I shouldn't be involved in this case, that I'm too close to Laura and the family. Ed shouldn't either. What are you going to do about it?"

"Hope that we get disqualified," Mary Slattery replied, forking a last bit of ravioli and following it with a sip of wine. "I'm never going to be able to talk Ed out of it. You and Laura are like his own children. He loves you both, and the best I'm going to be able to do is get him to sit back in the front row and let me do the talking."

"I think Laura'd be in good hands that way," Will said. "I didn't like Ed's color when I saw him at the house. Is his heart all right?"

"No. He's been scheduled for bypass surgery twice. He keeps putting it off."

"Damn it. You're right, you know. You'll never keep him out of this. What about me? Can you keep me from being subpoenaed if all I do is evaluate Laura, steer you to another shrink?"

"No. If we file an insanity plea, the privilege is waived as to any treating or evaluating psychiatrist. We'd have to turn you over to the prosecution, even if you were just consulting. I don't think Ed knows that. The law changed four or five years ago. You file an insanity or diminished-capacity plea, and any evidence of medical condition comes in, privileged or not."

Will frowned. "That's worse than I thought. But let's burn that bridge when we get to it, if we do. What else do you want to know?"

"More about Laura. And Mark, of course. You don't like Laura very much, do you?"

Will stared, surprised by Slattery's sudden challenge. "Why on earth would you say that?"

"There's something clinical in the way you talk about her. In the way you approach this whole mess."

Will's jaw set with what Slattery decided was probably anger. "I think you're out of line, Mary. I've just not been that close to Laura or Mark in recent years."

Slattery shrugged and tried again. "What was Laura like in high school? When she ran away. Give me a picture of her if you can."

"I remember her as pretty young," Will mused. "She came into Bainbridge High School as a sophomore transfer, I think, in the fall of 1971. I suppose I considered myself a lot older, didn't take a lot of notice of her until the next summer. Laura hung around with a group of us, all island kids, mostly older than she was. In the summers we ran pretty wild, camped in the fields of the old army post at Fort Ward. If it rained we slept in the abandoned barracks, built bonfires on the beach below. We had everything kids that age and in that time could want, beer and cheap, weak dope and temporary freedom. It's a happy time, you know? You've discovered sex but not death." Will looked away, then added, "Laura was quiet then. Not shy. She simply didn't talk if there was nothing she wanted to say. At fourteen . . . tall, slender. Looked much older. Long dark hair, very straight, the way girls wore it in the early seventies. She worked hard at her painting, even then. She set up a studio in the old beach house, slept there most nights." He smiled. "I mostly remember smells, somehow. The musty funk of that old beach house, turpentine, paint, smoke from incense or stolen cigarettes."

Slattery paused while Hatton's distant look of remembrance faded. He may be cold now, but he sure remembers her as a teen angel, Slattery thought silently. He must have had a pretty good crush on her.

"And what about Mark?" Slattery asked aloud.

"I've known Mark since high school, but not as well. He was two years ahead of me. His stepfather was a navy rear admiral, commanding the Bremerton Navy Yard. Mark, as you've no doubt heard, was pretty high-strung. Driven. Not always ethical. He got caught up in a cheating scandal at the naval academy in the early seventies and washed out, got law and business degrees at Wharton, had a couple of different jobs back east, then came home. He owned some piece of Kitsap Industries—maybe ten percent—that he'd inherited from his biological father, Curt Renner, and approached Ellen for a job. They hit it off. He's been Ellen's number two for over ten years now. God, I don't know what she'll do without him."

Will paused, then added, "You were halfway right. I did not like Mark very much. Nothing I could ever put my finger on—just uncomfortable with him. Three years ago I was stuck at a Christmas party at Ellen's house on the island. Mark was working the room like a politician and I was trying to get the hell out of there. I ended up having a drink with Laura. She was newly married, seemed happy, despite the problems she was having trying to paint. I asked her why she'd married Mark. 'I got bored fucking strange men,' she said."

"Great," Mary Slattery replied. "Be sure to leave that part out if you get called as a witness, okay?"

"I will. But that's part of Laura you need to understand. She's enormously sensitive, and the talent—her gifts come from places that no one begins to understand. God, DNA, social environment—pick an explanation that fits your beliefs. Laura likes to live behind that public persona she created in the eighties: hard-drinking, sexually aggressive. When she came home from New York she hid, our own local version of J. D. Salinger. No interviews, no receptions. The bitch goddess persona's a shtick, but there's a real core of bitterness that comes out in the downside of her bipolar phases. In New York she'd been on lithium, then on Prozac, and I'd guess she's also been treated after moving back home. According to Ed her condition's been pretty stable the past few years. But she always stops taking her medication. She says she can't paint when she's medicated, and I suspect she may be right. She thought so, anyway. I tried—"

"You *treated* her?"

"No. I suggested. She didn't take my advice. That was some years ago." Will paused with his coffee cup in midair, then asked, "Has Laura been painting lately?"

"No. Ed said she hasn't been able to paint for years, ever since she came back here."

"I don't buy that. I don't think Laura's ever stopped trying. When you get her psychiatric records, look for that issue. The way Ed says she fell apart this summer . . . I wonder if she went off her lithium to try to paint."

"Why would she do that?"

"Lithium has a lot of side effects. When I was a psych resident in the early eighties, lithium was the best available drug for people suffering from manic-depression. It's still the only drug that works for many of them. The biggest problem in treating with it is that people stop taking it. Headaches, nausea, irritability, lassitude—I had one patient who compared it to trying to fight with a giant pillow. I think a lot of Laura's early, and best, painting was done in her manic phases. If she was trying to paint again she might have tried to recapture that state of mind."

"Okay," Mary replied, jotting a note on her pad. "That's good. What else would you look for if we retained you to evaluate her?"

Will leaned forward, intent and professional, his exhaustion temporarily forgotten. "If I were doing this, I'd want to look at her surroundings, where she's been living. Her home. Her studio. The beach house. What she's been doing in those places. If she's been painting, I'd want to look at her work."

"Why?"

"I'm not sure. I don't know what I'd find."

"Good idea, though." Slattery made another note, then poured herself another glass of the zinfandel. "So let's try this. Say you were in my shoes, trying to set up the best *legal* insanity defense for Laura. What would you do?"

Will considered the question carefully. "I'd try for a posttraumatic stress disorder defense," he said at last. "Check out Laura's disappearance, her loss of memory when she ran away as a teenager. I didn't know she'd been gone a full four days. That kind of long-term amnesia and memory loss is damned unusual, no matter what the repressed-memory crackpots say. It usually indicates some kind of physical trauma, as well as emotional distress." Will paused, then added, "I stopped at Harborview on my way out here today. I talked to the psych doc there when I couldn't get in to see her. His name's Avrim Becker. He's been in the Israeli army and he's seen combat PTSD cases. He seemed to think Laura's case was similar."

"Why a PTSD defense?" Slattery asked.

"Legally, it *is* an insanity defense. If the accused is truly reliving a traumatic episode, there's a psychotic break with reality. It meets M'Naghton's rule, because the patient can be in the grip of a delusion so powerful that they don't know they are committing legal or moral wrong. Juries buy into it because it seems logical to them that a person could be so traumatized that they'd relive a horrifying experience. Everyone has some kind of intrusive memory, relived, if you will, some stupid or terrible thing they did or experienced. Jurors remember that when they're deciding on a verdict. The only problem is, in real life true PTSD that is severe enough to cause a complete psychotic break with reality is about as rare as an orchid growing in the snow."

"Like that painting behind you," Mary Slattery said. Will turned to look again at the painting. It had hung on his walls so long that he'd momentarily forgotten what it depicted.

An orchid on a field of white. Or the sex of a woman on a bank of frozen snow.

Chapter Eight

SUPERIOR COURT OF WASHINGTON FOR KITSAP COUNTY

STATE OF WASHINGTON,
      Plaintiff,   No. 97-1-01664-3

v.   INFORMATION

LAURA MARIE ARCAND,
      Defendant.

I, Judith E. Watkins, Prosecuting Attorney for Kitsap County, in the name and by the authority of the State of Washington, do accuse Laura Marie Arcand of the crime of murder in the first degree, committed as follows:

That the defendant Laura Marie Arcand in the City of Bainbridge Island, Kitsap County, Washington, on or about September 9, 1997, did intentionally assault and murder Mark J. Talbot, a human being.

Contrary to RCW 9A.32.030, and against the peace and dignity of the State of Washington.

/s/Judith E. Watkins, by Thomas M. Tiernan, Chief Deputy

CERTIFICATION FOR DETERMINATION OF PROBABLE CAUSE

That Thomas M. Tiernan is Chief Deputy Prosecuting Attorney for Kitsap County and is familiar with the police report and investigation conducted in Kitsap County Sheriff's Department Case No. 97-04178;

That this case contains the following upon which this motion for the determination of probable cause is made:

On September 8, 1997, Laura Marie Arcand argued with her husband, Mark J. Talbot, at the residence at 1194 Crystal Springs Drive, Bainbridge Island, Kitsap County, Washington, about his alleged affair with another woman. Thereafter, at approximately 2:30 o'clock a.m. on September 9, 1997, Laura Marie Arcand did shoot Mark J. Talbot, a human being, twice in the chest with intent to cause his death. The shots fired caused the death of Mark J. Talbot in Kitsap County, Washington. Laura Marie Arcand then attempted suicide by cutting and gouging the veins in her wrists with a long-pointed diamond engagement ring. Said Laura Marie Arcand then lapsed into unconsciousness. Upon being removed to Harborview Hospital in Seattle, Washington, for treatment at approximately 5:03 o'clock a.m. on September 9, 1997, Laura Arcand regained consciousness in the presence of Guillermo M. Martinez, a Sergeant of the Bainbridge Island police. Laura Marie Arcand, upon regaining consciousness, called out, "I killed them. Both of them." Laura Marie Arcand thereafter relapsed into unconsciousness.

Under penalty of perjury under the laws of the State of Washington, I certify that the foregoing is true and correct. Signed and dated by me this 10th day of September, 1997, at Port Orchard, Kitsap County, Washington.

/s/Thomas M. Tiernan

• • •

"Shit," Mary Slattery said.

"What is it?" Ed Hauser asked. He put his hand over the mouthpiece of his cellular phone. Concern widened his reddened, sleepless eyes.

"They have an admission. In the emergency room. Laura regained consciousness for a few seconds and admitted killing Mark."

"Any chance it's doctor-patient privileged?"

"No. The ER doc's notes indicated that a Bainbridge Island cop was in the surgical bay with them the whole time. He didn't record what Laura said, but the cop apparently heard it and it's in the certification of probable cause. It's weird, though. Laura said something about killing 'both of them.' What does that mean?"

Hauser slumped against the grayish yellow wall of the Kitsap County Courthouse hallway, breathing heavily. He took the information and read it quickly. "Well," he said, closing his eyes, "that makes it tougher. I don't know about the 'both of them' aspect, maybe we can use that. Let's get into the courtroom; they're going to call the calendar in ten minutes." He grunted as he stood up, squared his shoulders, and strode off down the hallway.

They pushed past the knot of courthouse reporters and camera crews clustered outside the door with a string of blank-faced "No comment's" and into courtroom 3. They found a clear space in the third row of benches. Mary Slattery turned away from Ed to riffle through her briefcase and looked up to see a portly man in his forties approaching them. His features were close and foxlike in a broad fleshy face, with squinting, colorless eyes beneath a helmet of carefully styled flowing gray hair that seemed his only indulgence.

"Good morning," the man said briskly. "I'm Thomas Meeker Tiernan, chief criminal deputy for the county. You're Mr. Hauser and Ms. Slattery?"

They nodded. "Sorry we couldn't get the information to you sooner," Tiernan continued. "But we had to review the facts against the statute and make a charging decision."

"Funny how the decision always seems to be to charge the maximum offense," Hauser said dryly.

"That's what the prosecutor and her constituents want," Tiernan replied evenly. "Any special issues for the arraignment?"

"Just that our client is not conscious, and therefore not presently able to comprehend the charges and intelligently plead," Hauser replied, with broad sarcasm.

"I figured that," Tiernan said, unruffled. "Suppose we go forward on a rolling ten-day basis, see how your client's condition changes, set the plea and the omnibus hearing date after you've had a chance to talk and assess the case?"

"Fine," Ed replied. "But let's get our discovery requests and motions out on the table right away. Mary's got a set for you to take with you." Slattery passed an inch-thick stack of discovery requests and motions to Tiernan, who raised an eyebrow, hefting them in his hand.

"Great. You'll have ours by fax later today." Tiernan smiled acidly. "They'll be lots shorter, of course, because the county doesn't pay us three hundred bucks an hour."

"One more thing, Tom," Hauser added, ignoring the insult. "I'm going to want to move Laura to Northlake Hospital for psychiatric treatment. Her treating physicians are on staff there, and treatment will be more effective."

Tiernan considered the request, then shook his head. "Better take that one up with the judge. Northlake doesn't have a hard lockdown, and Mrs. Watkins doesn't much like having murder defendants staying at the country club of their choice. The fact that her sort-of daddy used to be a big-time lawyer over here doesn't change that. Well," he added, checking his watch, "talk to you after the calendar."

Tiernan moved away with his peculiar rolling gait, the walk of a fat man new to his girth. Mary Slattery paused until Tiernan was out of earshot and her voice would be muffled by the clatter of the county prisoners being brought in on the chain. "I know him," she said through clenched teeth as they rose for the judge. "Tiernan was brought in from L.A. to head the drug prosecution unit in King County during my last year there. He's a lifer and a world-class asshole, but he's a pro. If Watkins wants to be in court for the publicity, he'll give her a written opening statement to deliver and some witnesses she can't screw up. But he'll be running the case."

Hauser nodded, seemingly distracted. "Be ready to argue the motion on custody and the hospital transfer. I don't think we should wait."

The clerk droned on with the call of the arraignment calendar. When the clerk called out, "State versus Laura Marie Arcand," Hauser strode forward out of the pews. "Edwin Hauser and Mary Slattery for the defense, Your Honor," he said briskly.

The arraignment judge, Henry Thorvaldson, nodded. He was nearly seventy, with a thatch of thick white hair above deep-set blue eyes in an angular, hawklike face. "Appearance noted. Welcome back to Kitsap County, Mr. Hauser. Do you waive reading of the information?"

"We do, Your Honor."

"Is the defense prepared to plead?"

"No, Your Honor. Our client remains unconscious due to shock, blood loss, and hypothermia. She is presently in custody at Harborview Hospital. We have not been able to communicate with her. We would therefore enter a plea of not guilty at this time, without prejudice to future plea of any type when we are able to talk to our client."

"I see. Any comment from the state?"

Tiernan stood at the state's table. "We've agreed with the defense to roll forward on a ten-day schedule until Ms. Arcand is competent to communicate with her counsel," he said. "The state has no objection to a tentative plea of not guilty, entered at this time."

"Noted," Thorvaldson said crisply. "We'll have a formal arraignment and plea, and set the omnibus hearing date by motion after the defense has an opportunity to speak with their client. Any problem with the speedy trial date being waived? No? Any other matters?"

"Just the issue of custody, Your Honor," Hauser replied. "May my associate, Ms. Slattery, address the court?"

"Of course. Let's hear it, Ms. Slattery."

"Thank you, Your Honor. The defense requests an order permitting the transfer of Ms. Arcand from the Harborview Hospital psychiatric wing to the Northlake Hospital in Snohomish County, Washington. Ms. Arcand's treating physicians are on staff there, and the hospital is recognized as having the best psychiatric program in the state. We have declarations from the treating physicians to the effect that their services can be provided in a more effective and efficient manner there. We will not seek release from Northlake without further motion to the court."

"Pass them up and I'll consider them. Your proposed order, also." Thorvaldson glanced at the declarations, then raised an eyebrow at Thomas Tiernan. "Why's the state refusing to stipulate to this?" he asked.

"Your Honor," Tiernan said, rising to his feet and hitching his pants over the mound of his belly, "the state questions the adequacy of the security. Northlake Psychiatric does not have a hard lockdown wing. I'm personally familiar with their security systems, and a child could walk out of there. Ms. Arcand has substantial financial resources, as does her mother, and the flight risk is great."

"Even if she's unconscious? What do you say, Ms. Slattery?"

"The defense is prepared to tender Ms. Arcand's passport to the state to hold for the duration of the trial. The defense is prepared to pay the county for stationing guards at Northlake, if they choose. And the defense is prepared to post bond, which should be reasonable. Ms. Arcand has no prior criminal history."

"We haven't had a chance to evaluate her, Your Honor," Tiernan protested. "We don't know what her mental state is."

"I wouldn't be too eager to inject mental state in this case if I were you, Counsel," Thorvaldson said with a dry, sarcastic tone. "But the charge is serious. Ms. Slattery, I'm going to order bond at $300,000. That should hold Ms. Arcand, even when she wakes up. If the county wants you to surrender her passport and pay for additional guards, I'll hold you to your offer. I'll sign your order authorizing transfer to Northlake Hospital. Let's get the lady well enough to try her."

"Your Honor?" Tiernan asked.

Thorvaldson's gray, bushy eyebrows shot up. "Have I missed something, Counsel?"

"My argument on bail."

"This is preliminary, Counselor. Demonstrate some serious risk of flight and I'll consider increased bail, or pretrial detention in a harder facility. You've shown me nothing so far."

"But Your Honor, our prefiling investigation is not complete. This is a murderer. Court services can't talk—"

A crease of anger passed along Thorvaldson's lined face. "This is a citizen," he shot back, "who stands before *this* court completely innocent, in the law. If you weren't ready, you shouldn't have arraigned her. That was your choice, Mr. Tiernan. Or that of your boss. Next case."

At the end of the calendar, Tiernan caught them as they were packing up to go.

"You've won the easy one," he said. "The rest'll be tougher."

"I'm assuming," Ed Hauser replied shortly, "that there's some point to this conversation."

"Oh, there is. I know about you, Hauser, and your reputation over here, from the old days. But you don't know this county anymore, Hauser. This jury won't be a bunch of hookers and navy yard men, ready to acquit a husband killer. They're God-fearing family people now. And the other judges—"

Hauser put up a hand, silencing the smaller man. "You really are a nasty little shit," he snarled. "I'm just old enough to prefer the days when officers of the court served this county under the law, not with their personal views on religion." Hauser banged his briefcase down on the courtroom rail and strode from the courtroom without another word. Mary Slattery followed him, her expression grave.

Mary Slattery was silent until they reached the parking area outside the courthouse. The September sunlight cast diamonds on the distant water of Port Orchard Bay.

"Goddamnit, Ed, did you need to go out of your way to make an enemy?" she exploded.

"I think so," Ed Hauser replied thoughtfully. "He's overcharged the case, trying to put pressure on us to plead out fast. He's the kind of born-again right-wing creep that makes old-fashioned Republicans like me want to cringe." Hauser's jaw set, his expression grim. "Damn it, I want the little bastard to know he's in a fight."

"That's personal," she said harshly.

"It is," Edwin Hauser agreed. "We're not going to win this case on points, Mary," he added. "These pricks are out for blood, and publicity, which these days amounts to the same thing. What's the earliest we can all meet?"

"Probably about three-thirty. I've got to go look at the beach house, see what's been taken as evidence."

Hauser nodded and took out his cell phone. "I'll call Reuben and set it up. We need a defense we can sell, even to the God-fearing."

Chapter Nine

"Good morning," Will Hatton called out.

Mary Slattery turned in surprise at the edge of the bluff above the beach cabin. She watched Hatton trot down the path from the main house. He wore jeans, running shoes, and a turtleneck sweater against the chill morning fog that had not yet burned off the west side of the island.

"What are you doing here?" she asked when he had caught up with her.

"I just brought Ellen back from Harborview. She went back into town late last night to sit up with Laura at Harborview. The ward doc wouldn't let her stay—he thought Laura might be coming out of her coma. Ed said they argued it all the way to Harborview's chief of psychiatry—getting him out of bed at five-thirty in the morning. It's one of the few arguments anyone can remember that Ellen didn't win."

"How'd you get involved?"

"Ed asked me to go to Harborview to talk with Ellen, calm her down. He had to leave for court on the early ferry. Ellen's all right, just exhausted—I gave her a light sedative, and she's sleeping now."

Slattery looked worried. "Do you think Ellen will be able to stand up to the stress of testifying at trial?"

Hatton nodded. "Hell, yes. Ellen's tough in a fight. Laura's mental illness is something she can't control, and it eats away at her, that's all. How did it go in court?"

"Okay, as far as it went. They're letting us transfer Laura to Northlake so she can start treating with her regular psychiatrist, Dr. Treadwell."

Hatton frowned. "If that's what she wants."

"What do you mean?"

"Nothing. I know Treadwell a little bit, that's all. I'm not sure whether he's right for her now. We'll see. Anyway, what brings you back?"

"The beach house. The crime lab's done, so I can take a look at it."

"Can I come along?"

"Sure, I guess so. I don't have an extra pair of gloves with me, so don't touch anything, okay?"

Hatton nodded and followed her down the path. It switchbacked once, then stopped at the new redwood stairs that led the rest of the way down to the beach. The stairs ended between a drift of sea grass and the stream that emptied into the tide pool near the cabin's new deck. The view as he descended the steps was serene, gray sky merging with green water, meeting the stone-and-sand beach. It's as if, Hatton thought, the nightmare had been swallowed by the morning.

Hatton paused on the beach to breathe the clean moist air scented by salt and the kelp bed offshore. He turned to look up at the bluff, gestured for Slattery to look at the height of the bluff above them. "I'd forgotten how private this little cove is," he said. "No wonder Mark wanted to build right on the same spot."

"Right now I'd rather have a witness," Mary Slattery replied dryly.

The rebuilt beach cabin was shingled in reddish stained cedar, the trim bright white. They stepped up onto the deck that surrounded the cabin on three sides. The only entrance was through a pair of French doors on the west side of the house, facing the water, near a large hot tub that had been set down into the decking. Strips of yellow crime scene tape remained stuck to the glass doors.

The interior of the cabin was filled with cool gray light from the wall of west-facing windows and a pair of skylights above. It consisted of one large room with a boat-style galley kitchen, and a small shower bath on the north side. The walls were rough whitewashed cedar planks that extended to the open roofline, the floor dark-stained, polished fir. The beach rock fireplace from the old cabin remained where Hatton remembered it, filling the southwest corner, but the stone had been sandblasted clean. A large convertible futon bed was pulled out from the far wall. Four wicker chairs surrounded a glass-topped table near the kitchen wall. Mark and Laura's suitcases rested on a low chest in the corner opposite the fireplace, beside an open French pine wardrobe partly filled with clothes and towels.

The futon was down and the bed was an unmade mess of twisted sheets. Clothes were strewn on the bed, the chairs, and the floor. A thick hardcover Tom Clancy thriller lay open and facedown on the floor at the foot of the bed, as if thrown there.

"Would the cops disturb anything when they searched this place?" Will asked.

"The cops would, but the state crime lab personnel wouldn't," Mary Slattery replied, not pausing in her survey of the room. "They would take what they needed for testing and disturb everything else as little as possible. They've probably photographed the interior pretty thoroughly."

"It sure looks like they had a fight." Will stepped closer to the bed and sensed something sticky under his foot. He moistened a finger, bent down, touched the floor, and brought the finger to his mouth. "Spilled wine," he said, wincing at the sour taste.

"Shit," Mary Slattery said, shaking her head. She quickly searched the kitchen and the bath and returned with a troubled expression on her face.

"What is it?" Will asked.

"Take a look in the bath." Will went in, Slattery behind him. There was a long tiled shower with glass doors sandblasted to look like Japanese shoji screens, a stainless steel sink in a wood vanity, and a row of open shelves on the inside wall next to the sink. A pair of canvas-and-leather toiletry bags with the L. L. Bean logo stood on the bottom shelf; a scatter of combs and brushes and razors was on the counter beside the sink.

"I'm not seeing it," Will said.

"I can't believe they missed it," Mary Slattery replied. "If they did." She pointed to the toiletry bag that bore Laura's initials, LMA. "See the oil stain on the canvas? I spotted it because I've got one just like it."

Will leaned forward and sniffed the dark stain. "Mineral oil?" he asked.

Slattery shook her head. "Gun oil. Talbot didn't bring the gun here. Laura did."

"Let me begin with the obvious bad news," Reuben Todd said, rising at precisely 3:30 P.M. from the head of the conference table in the thirty-sixth-floor war room in Hauser and Todd's offices. "We have a very difficult case." Todd, Edwin Hauser's partner for nearly fifteen years, was a former United States Supreme Court clerk and Justice Department prosecutor. He now spent most of his time out of court, advising on everything from criminal defense strategy to corporate acquisition financing at $400 per hour. Unfolded to his full six and a half feet, he loomed like an angular stork over the assembled trial team of Edwin Hauser, Mary Slattery, Michael Spellman—a summer clerk from Harvard Law School who would take a leave of absence to stay through the trial—and Anthony Guzzo, a former King County police detective who worked on call as Hauser and Todd's firm investigator.

Todd's legendary stamina for legal work had been tested by trying to develop a legal strategy for Laura Arcand's defense in little more than twenty-four hours. He pushed his round, black-rimmed reading glasses up on his balding head, rubbed his dry, reddened eyes, and began again. "Washington is a M'Naghton rule state. Insanity is an affirmative defense. Ms. Arcand must prove by a preponderance of the evidence that because of mental disease or defect she was unable to perceive the moral quality of, and was thus unable to determine, right from wrong when—I still hope *if*—she shot her husband.

"There has been just one successful insanity defense in a capital murder case in this state in the past fourteen years," he continued. "Public opinion polling has firmly established that most prospective jurors dislike the insanity defense and would cheerfully discard it.

They find most expert psychiatric testimony incomprehensible and believe that the defense is an escape for a wealthy or well-connected defendant. Which, of course, is the case here."

"Got any *good* news, Rube?" Mary Slattery asked sarcastically around a mouthful of tuna fish sandwich.

"None to speak of," Todd replied. "My first suggestion is to find another suspect."

"Tony Guzzo's going to work on that as soon as he nails down the timeline," Hauser said. "I sort of like the idea of Tom Guenther, myself. He left right after Laura threw the drink at Mark. The man was just seething with anger."

Guzzo shook his head. "Won't work, Ed. After I heard the story out at Ms. Arcand's house about Guenther, I headed for the nearest bar," he said. "Captain K's in Winslow. Sure enough, Guenther'd been there. From nine o'clock on the night of the murder. He closed the joint down and got DUI'd on the last ferry by the state patrol. He spent the rest of the night in the King County jail. I think we have to forget him."

"Then," Hauser said heavily, "I suppose we have to assume the worst."

"If we assume that Ms. Arcand shot her husband," Todd continued, "there are three questions. First, did she do so with the requisite intent to cause his death? If not—if what we have is a heat-of-passion killing prompted by jealousy—it may be wise to try the case to obtain a manslaughter verdict. Second, what was her capacity? Did she have a mental condition that precluded her from forming any intent whatsoever? Diminished capacity usually involves some form of involuntary intoxication, such as an unintentional drug reaction or a diabetic coma. This is the rule in Markham's case: an English sailor who murdered while in a state of delusion brought on by diabetic shock. Third, if medically insane, is the insanity of a type which causes an inability to determine right from wrong? Full-blown schizophrenia is the normal diagnosis that can prove the defense, if it is sufficiently severe to cause well-defined delusions. For example—"

Slattery cut him off. "What about posttraumatic stress disorder?"

Todd smiled thinly. "In theory, it works, Mary. After PTSD was accepted in the third *Diagnostic and Statistical Manual* of the American Psychiatric Association in 1980, there were several well-publicized acquittals of Vietnam veterans suffering from combat flashbacks. But the psychiatrists, and our friends the tort lawyers, have debased that particular coin. A PTSD claim for mental trauma damages gets raised in nearly every car crash case, and there are enough hungry shrinks in the world willing to testify to it. The result is a mass of bad case law rejecting the claim."

"What if it's all we've got?" Hauser asked.

"Then it's what we've got. We have to prove the existence of a severe and well-defined stressor—a trauma-producing event—in Ms. Arcand's past, a coincidence of circumstances between the prior events and the events charged, and an actual mental flashback to those prior events that would make the present use of deadly force against her husband legally or morally justified in her mind—self-defense, defense of others, or combat. Fail to prove any one of those elements and you won't get the insanity instruction. Fail to tell a compelling story and the jury will laugh it out of the courtroom."

"Which means Laura has to take the stand," Hauser said.

"Perhaps. There are ways around that. We could tape her psychiatric evaluation, at the risk of handing the state testimony it otherwise could not have compelled."

"What about procedural requirements?" Hauser asked.

"We have to provide notice of the insanity or diminished-capacity plea to the prosecution within ten days following arraignment, unless extended. Once the notice is given, the privilege is waived as to any of the accused's treating physicians or mental health providers, and as to any expert, whether consulting or testifying. As a result, you get one shot at picking an expert. If your first expert concludes that Ms. Arcand was sane, the state can subpoena that expert and require them to give that opinion in court."

"No," Hauser exclaimed, shocked.

"That's the law, Ed."

"Okay," Hauser said wearily. "Run through some comparable cases and tell me what went wrong."

"I had to pick cases quickly, given the time pressure, but read the trial transcripts in two leading cases last night. The first, *State v.*

Porter, involved a suburban-love-triangle double homicide where the defendant, Mr. Porter, attempted suicide by knife after killing his lover and the man he believed was going to take his place. The defense was insanity as a result of depressive psychosis. The jury rejected the insanity defense in large part, I would guess, because of extensive evidence of premeditation—Mr. Porter prepared himself by buying the murder weapon more than twenty-four hours before the actual killings, drove from Yakima to Issaquah, where the killings occurred, and ate a large breakfast along the way."

"That's not so bad," Hauser mused. "We don't have that kind of premeditation evidence here."

Todd shook his head. "But we do have the fight, the drink throwing, and the missing gun," he said skeptically. "Remember, premeditation takes only a moment. In the second case, a twenty-two-year-old man named Dan Schenck shot and killed his former high school teacher, who had sexually abused him for years. The defense was delusional schizophrenia, the expert testimony was convincing, but the jury convicted quickly, despite the sexual abuse." A sharp look of distaste crossed Todd's hawkish features. He volunteered his time as a Juvenile Court guardian *ad litem,* representing the interests of abused and injured children. "I would have voted the other way on that one."

"So even if we put Mark's character on trial, proved that he was actually having the affair Laura accused him of, it wouldn't do us any good," Slattery said, thinking aloud.

"Correct. We'd catch the sharper side of that blade. All we would accomplish is proving motive."

Hauser sipped at his coffee, made a face, and went to the coffee bar for a fresh cup. "How good were the experts in those cases?" he asked, his back still to the room.

"Quite good, Ed. National reputations. Perhaps not as good as Dr. Hatton's, but close."

Hauser returned to his chair and sat heavily, his face ashen with worry. "So we've got ten days to decide on a plea," he said grimly, "and insanity is a long shot where we have the burden."

"I've got an idea about that, Ed," Todd suggested, thinking aloud. "There's nothing in the statute that requires us to plead *only* the insanity defense. We could plead not guilty and give notice of *both* diminished capacity and insanity, without waiving our right to insist that the state prove the fact of the murder and that Ms. Arcand committed it."

"Wouldn't we have to elect our theory at trial?"

"Nothing in the statute requires it. It's usually not a good strategy to float multiple theories before a jury, but we wouldn't have to. We *could* keep the state guessing for a good long time." Todd grinned maliciously, a born tactician.

"I think I like it, Reuben. Let's give it some more thought. Thank you. Immaculate reasoning, as usual." Hauser rose to start going over a draft pretrial investigation checklist, but Todd refused to yield the floor.

"Ed? I'm not quite through."

"Oh?"

"There's an ethical issue to consider here. As a member of the firm, I have to raise it. Perhaps I should wait for a partnership meeting?"

"No. Let's hash it now."

"The rules of professional conduct prohibit a lawyer from participating in a matter in which he has a personal interest. Your family interest in Laura's welfare would probably be sufficient to invoke the rule."

"Bullshit. Cite me the case."

"I've found none in Washington where a family member was actually disqualified from representing another family member under these circumstances."

"Which I'm not. Ellen and I aren't married, and Laura isn't my daughter."

"But the prosecution can exploit the appearance of your bias, Ed. Particularly if Dr. Hatton is involved. The argument would be powerful. If we went outside, we could get any number of qualified lawyers. Lewis Brock, say, or Sam Kemper. There's also Matthew Riordan. I know he can be damned hard to get along with, but he has good insights and is good before a jury."

Hauser shook his head, no. "They're sole practitioners. They don't have the horses this firm does."

"Which we could still provide as cocounsel. You could also let Mary take the lead chair, or me. We have about ninety criminal trials between us. The problem, Ed, is your direct day-to-day appearance before the jury."

"You've never tried a murder case, Reuben, and they're nothing like those massive racketeering cases you did at Justice. Mary's damn good, but . . . I think my thirty-five years brings something to the table that outweighs any risk."

"We could still be exposed under the RPCs, Ed."

Hauser's reply was flat but emphatic. "No. The reason behind the rule is that the lawyer's personal interests get in the way of the client's. My only interest here is to win Laura's acquittal because I do not believe that she could have killed Mark unless she was insane. To avoid even the appearance of a conflict of interest, I will refuse any part of the fees for my time; they will go to the other partners in the firm, and to Mary, Michael, and Tony as bonuses. I think this concludes the subject of possible conflicts. I want everyone except Reuben collating the witness interviews, gathering documents and Laura's medical records, and creating a timeline for the case. Michael, you're on the trial brief. Reuben will supervise you. Let's have a draft assuming an insanity defense in ten days, and keep updating it right through trial. In addition, you back up Mary and Tony on witness interviews, discovery motions, and the timeline. Let's review—"

The telephone at the conference table rang. Hauser snatched at it impatiently. "Yes? Ellen? She's awake? Good, darling, good. Don't overstay, just let her go back to sleep when she's ready. I'll see you downtown tonight."

Hauser broke the connection and redialed. "Will? She's awake, kid. She's being moved to Northlake tomorrow. Go see her. As soon as you can."

Part II

The Crossing
Staircase

September 11–17, 1997

Chapter Ten

On Wednesday morning Will Hatton drove up the cheerless road that led to Northlake Hospital, offended, as he always was, by the fortress sensibility of the modern hospital, with its concrete, airless buildings, gated entrances, and guarded checkpoints. The oak-paneled Laura Ashley–print lobby struck him as cheerless and false. The air was thick with a pine-scented disinfectant that amplified rather than masked the corrupt odors of illness and death.

Hatton showed his medical credentials to a grim-faced, overweight security guard at the psychiatric floor's nursing station and filled out a visitor information form. He followed the xeroxed hospital floor plan, unsure of his directions despite a half dozen previous visits. He pulled open a heavy door and entered the artificial cheer of the south psychiatric ward. The concrete walls were painted with bright, childlike colors, yellows and sky blues. Crude cheerful pictures painted by patients were framed in Plexiglas and hung on the corridor walls. Hatton knew that the bright colors were helpful to patients suffering from clinical depression, but the skylighted and sunlit hallways somehow made him yearn for the dark, mythic, tobacco-stained consultation rooms of Freud's Vienna.

Hatton paused to show his paperwork to the Kitsap County

deputy guarding the door to Laura Arcand's private hospital room. The deputy, a thin, taciturn black man in his mid-twenties, with the name ELLIS etched on the plate pinned to his uniform, put down the dark brown criminal law casebook he was studying and read the form with interest. "You're a new addition to the lady's team of physicians, Dr. Hatton," he said politely. "You're working the case for the defense, I take it?"

Hatton shook his head, no. "I'm just an old friend of the family, Mr. Ellis," he replied edgily. "Trying to help."

"Yeah, right," Ellis exclaimed, his expressionless face breaking into a sudden grin. "The West Coast's leading forensic psychiatrist, and you're just here to say hi. I'll see you at the trial. I'm a first-year law student. Should be interesting." He returned the permission form to Hatton and picked up his textbook, still smiling.

Hatton slid quietly through the doorway and stopped, saying nothing. Laura was propped up in the bed, staring blankly at the television, tuned to one of the morning news shows. Her beauty seemed to have coarsened since Will last saw her. Her eyes were still the same startling, intense gray-blue, but the lines of her face had grown more angular, overwhelming the softness that gentled her features in the happier moments of years past. Her long dark hair had been washed and pulled into a braid, courtesy of a conscientious nurse. The gray in her clean hair stood out now, more clearly than he had ever noticed before. Her skin, however, looked surprisingly soft, given the ravages of alcohol and tobacco, although it had taken on the hospital pallor Hatton knew too well. She tugged and pulled at the thick bandages surrounding her wrists.

Hatton knocked loudly on the door frame, twice.

"Oh, shit," Laura Arcand whispered when she saw him.

"Funny. I was thinking the same thing," he replied, sarcastically.

She sighed. "Female vanity should send me diving under the sheets. Fortunately, I was never afflicted by it."

"You were. You just never admitted it."

Will crossed the sunlit room in three steps, pausing at the foot of the bed to read her medical chart. "You want to see this?" he said, offering the clipboard to her.

"Not particularly." Her voice was still limited to a broken whisper.

Hatton started to say something but stopped himself to look hard at Laura Arcand. There's no sense of either movement or energy, he thought. Even in the worst times she always had that. "How do you feel, Laura?" he finally asked, the lame question shielding his feelings.

"Broken," she said, coughing. "Foreign. Like my body belongs to someone else and is trying to crawl out of my skin, looking for a place to hide. I'd *like* to find a place to hide. Yesterday they told me my husband was dead."

"And?"

"And the deputy outside my door has me convinced I'm responsible. I killed Mark, didn't I?"

"I don't know that. I'm not sure what happened. What can you remember?"

"Very little." Laura Arcand closed her eyes and grimaced, as though steeling herself for the ordeal to come. "I don't suppose you brought me any cigarettes."

"Every hospital in this state has a strict no-smoking policy." Will produced a box of Marlboros and a pack of matches. He took a plastic coffee cup from the remains of the breakfast tray and filled it with an inch of water from the faucet in the bathroom. Laura lit a cigarette as though her redemption depended on it. "God," she said as she exhaled, a thin plume of smoke drifting toward the opened window, "it *is* possible that you loved me once."

"Can you tell me what you remember?" Hatton repeated blandly, ignoring what she'd said.

"Why *are* you here, Will?" Laura asked, her voice suddenly edgy, fearful.

"Ed asked me to come down here. I've filled out the paperwork as a visitor. If I get subpoenaed I will say that I came here as your old friend, bearing flowers and solace."

"I don't want that." Laura leaned her head back and sighed, her eyes pressed tightly closed. Her voice was thick. "Especially from you. I should just plead guilty."

"Just shut up and tell me what happened, Laura," Will snapped, his patience wearing thin. "At this point there's very little you can do to me that you haven't already accomplished."

She looked up at him, surprised; then she broke into a sudden, rueful smile. "Poor Will," she said softly. "You got the full course, didn't you?"

"Not quite, Laura," Hatton replied sharply. "I'm still breathing. Mark isn't."

His words seemed to strike like a blow, and she winced. Then she was silent, inhaling from her cigarette, filling the air around her with smoke. "You know, Will," she said at last, "you've always been a cold-blooded bastard." She finished the cigarette, dropped it into the water-filled coffee cup, and immediately lit another.

Hatton smiled for the first time and sat down on the edge of her bed. "You're probably right," he replied. He felt as though the tension of their meeting again had finally broken. "Look, at this point I'm the best friend you've got. So you'd do well to tell me what really happened."

Laura remained tense and guarded. "Damn it, I told you, Will. I don't know."

She is holding back, Will Hatton thought to himself. "Tell me what you do remember," he said. "Anything at all."

"A party." Laura sighed, then reached for the squeeze bottle of water on the table beside her hospital bed and gulped desperately. "One of those awful business-houseguest weekends that Ellen does twenty times a year. She ought to open a fucking bed-and-breakfast. I got drunk. Mark and I were fighting, I left, went to the beach cabin, fell asleep. And that's it."

"The witnesses were a little more specific," Will replied. "It seems you asked Mark about his assistant's fellatio skills. At theatrical volume."

Laura grimaced. "I didn't really blame him, you know. I was just pissed that she was *there*—in my *mother's* house, for God's sake. With all I'd put him through the past year, if Mark found someone kind to him he deserved it."

"Tell me about the last year, Laura. What went wrong?"

She closed her eyes again. "Everything. I couldn't work. The paintings were dreck, Will, absolute dreck. Mark was stressed, my mother pushing him for cash profits on long-term projects that were going to take a couple of years to work out. Mark would stay up until two or three in the morning, working on his computer. He was preoccupied, buried, scared. Sometimes he couldn't get hard. When he could, I couldn't get pregnant."

"You wanted a child?"

"Mark did. But the scrape I had obviously took a little more than anybody anticipated. Just as well. God would give me an aardvark for a child."

Will forced her forward. "What else?"

"The beach house. Mark thought it would fix things for us, be our special place. I really wanted that. But then the dreams started again. Bad ones."

"About what?"

"Being . . . afraid. Attacked. Frightened. Alone. I woke up soaked with sweat. Sometimes I peed in the sheets, I was so scared."

"What else can you tell me about the dreams?"

"Nothing . . . Just afraid."

Will watched Laura carefully as her affect turned flat and her answers got shorter. She's not lying, he thought, but there is something there that she doesn't want to deal with. And she's going to lose it pretty soon now.

"How did you feel about Mark after the dreams started?"

"Okay. Good. I mean, he tried to help me."

"How?"

"With my dreams. He'd sit up with me, change the sheets, ask me about the dreams, try to help me understand them." Her eyes brightened with sudden animation; her voice warmed. "Mark *tried*, Will, he really did. And I made his life hell."

"Why do you say that?"

"Oh God. My life. My shrinks. That I couldn't get pregnant. Everything." Laura's hands shook as she put the cigarette to her lips and dragged.

Will leaned forward and gently brushed Laura's hair away from her forehead. She flinched at his touch, then accepted it. "What did you tell Mark about the dreams, Laura? You said you talked about them."

Laura shut her eyes, squeezing them tight, as against real pain. "I don't remember. Just . . . flashes. Fragments. The door, the lights, the crossing staircase . . ."

"What door, Laura? What staircase?"

"I don't remember. They're just things I saw. Things I still see."

"Were these dreams about Mark?"

"No, I had them before Mark. For years. Every once in a while. And they didn't seem that threatening. Until this summer, when we were on the island most of the time."

"You woke up once at Harborview, Laura. When they took you into surgery. You said something about killing them. 'Both of them,' you said. Did that have something to do with these dreams?"

She shook her head violently. "How could it?" she asked. Sweat suddenly darkened the hair at her temples.

Will moved closer, touched her chin to raise her eyes to his own. "I have to ask some hard questions, Laura," he began. She nodded.

"Did you bring the gun to the beach house, Laura?"

"I don't know."

"Did you fire a gun when Mark was killed, Laura?"

"I don't know. I must have."

"Where is the gun, Laura? What did you do with it?"

"I don't know."

"Did you hide it after you shot Mark?"

"No!" she shrieked, shoving him away. "He's dead! And I should be dead with him," she sobbed. Her body pulsed in the bed as though she were having a seizure. When she finally recovered, she whispered, "Stop, Will. Please stop. I can't stand any more. Not today. Get out of here."

Will nodded. He took the lit cigarette that had fallen from her fingers to the floor, dropped it in the cup, and flushed the sodden mess of filters and ashes down the toilet. When he returned she was still sobbing, her face buried in her hands. He took the cigarettes and matches with him when he left.

· · ·

"**She knows what** she's up against, I think," Will Hatton said, leaning back in the cast iron chair in the narrow, walled outdoor garden of the Vine Street Grill on Second Avenue in the Belltown district. It was, he thought, both a shrewd and a pleasant choice for lunch. The walled garden's old brick held the morning sun's warmth, yet was screened from the street and too far north of the financial district to fill up with the courthouse crowd, who might see and remark on their meeting.

"Did you get a look at her charts?" Mary Slattery asked. Her luncheon wineglass was empty. She took a sip of her double espresso, found it still too hot, and set it carefully on the glass-topped table.

"Yes, and they're consistent with what her treating shrink, Robert Treadwell, told you. She's massively depressed, not a big surprise; you *should* be depressed after you find out that you killed someone you loved. They've got her on enough desipramine to blast a crack addict in withdrawal to the moon. But it won't reach effective therapeutic levels for another week, at least. All she has now are the side effects, dry mouth, sweating, hot flashes, anxiety. She's crawling out of her skin with it."

"But she understands the nature of the charges against her?"

He nodded. "She does. But in her present state of mind it's a close question whether she can help you, or *wants* to help you, and that limits her ability to withstand a trial. She says she doesn't remember anything, but she's convinced she killed Mark."

"So she's probably going to be found competent to stand trial, at least by Kitsap County standards," Slattery replied. "Is she faking the lack of memory?"

"Hard to tell. She claims no memory of anything after the party. My gut feeling is that she remembers more about the night Mark was killed than she's willing to admit to now." Will hesitated, then added, "I don't think she's intentionally lying to me. It's more like . . . she's desperately afraid of something that she associated with Mark, or the night he was killed. Whatever it is, it frightens her more than the idea of Mark's death . . . or her own, I'm afraid."

"What were her feelings about Mark?"

"Grief, of course. Genuine affection for Mark. She's wracked with guilt for what she sees as her failings as a wife. She knew that she was cracking this summer, and sought Mark's help. You don't usually ask for help from someone you're deeply angry at. And you don't kill someone who is helping you—"

"Until you find out they're fucking the office staff," Slattery cut in dryly. She read Will's stony expression and apologized. "Sorry. Did you read the medical records I sent you?"

"Of course. They only go back for the last few years, since she moved back to Seattle. I'd need to see everything for an evaluation, back to early childhood if possible." Hatton frowned, thinking. "I don't think there's anything wrong with Treadwell's basic diagnosis of bipolar disorder, but . . . he never goes deep enough. He's a checklist shrink—one symptom, one pill, out the door. If I were doing this I'd want to find out what happened to her this summer, what caused the downward spiral that Ed described. She complained about her painting. I think she went off her medication to paint. The time she was spending on the island probably didn't do her any good, either."

"Why?"

"I'm not sure. She kept talking about being on the island in her dreams, of being afraid, attacked. There's some images that she recalled—a door, some kind of light or lights, and a staircase. I have no idea what they mean. But she associates them with being on the island, being home. She said that she'd had the dreams before but they didn't frighten her until this summer, when she was staying on the island again."

"Do you think you could give a sanity or diminished-capacity opinion that would hold up in court? If you were to do this case?"

"Not based on what she's said so far, and maybe not ever. Laura's got to cooperate, open up about the night of the murder. I don't know if she will do that or not. It's going to be a kind of race. Someone's got to give Laura a good explanation of what happened to her and Mark, one that gives her a reason to believe that she's not beyond redemption, that she needs to keep on living. Her depression is very real and very painful. She can't see any daylight. If it persists she will kill herself. It won't matter much whether it's a gun, a knife, or the courts. She'll use whatever is handy."

Their mutual silence was broken by the persistent buzz of Slattery's cellular phone. She took it from her purse and listened. "Oh, shit," she said. "They've gotten a search warrant for Laura and Mark's house on the peninsula. We haven't gone through it yet. They're going to execute it at three o'clock today."

"If I were you," Will said, "I'd get there. Now."

He need not have spoken. Slattery was already moving from her chair, bolting for her car, parked on Second Avenue. Will Hatton sighed and paid the bill, blinking in the late-summer light.

Chapter Eleven

"I said I wanted to see the warrant," Mary Slattery said distinctly, raising the tone of her voice two notches louder than necessary.

Kitsap County sheriff's detective Joseph Schweiger shook his head. "We served your office, Ms. Slattery."

"Exactly one hour and forty-four minutes ago," she replied, stepping up to confront Schweiger's 240 pounds of polyester-clad bulk. "While I was at lunch. I barely made the ferry. Don't try to fuck with me, Schweiger, it won't do you any good. I prove defective service and anything you pull out of here is going to get suppressed. Which will cause Tommy Tiernan to turn you into dog food. Just hand it over and you'll get what you want."

Joseph Schweiger ran a hand through his graying brush-cut hair, sighed, remembered that he had another three years before he could retire at full pension, and turned the warrant over. Slattery read it quickly: it called for books, records, diaries, notes, weapons, and telephone records of Laura Marie Arcand and/or Mark Jerome Talbot, and was signed by Kitsap County Superior Court judge Rachel Browning. She handed it back with a wave and a sweeping arm gesture, ushering the detectives into the house.

This must have been Mark's idea of heaven, she had thought to herself as she had waited on the front lawn for the detectives to arrive. The house stood on three acres, at the end of a concrete drive in a new golf course and riding development called Equestrian Ridge. Two lines of struggling young poplars, browning from lack of water, straddled the curving drive. The house was massive, nearly cubical in an effort to capture the maximum nine thousand square feet of floor space from the allowable footprint under the zoning laws. The bulk was not redeemed by the broken pediment in the roofline, the arched Palladian windows, or the beige and off-white tones of the stucco walls, already stained by a season of winter rains.

Slattery followed the detectives through the two-story entrance hall into the forty-foot-long white-on-white living room, the monochromatic decorating scheme broken only by the bright bursts of color Laura's paintings cast on the walls. She watched as the detectives methodically searched the drawers and bookshelves flanking the marble fireplace. Each shelf was carefully segregated to Mark and Laura's tastes, her side given to art history books and oversize painting folios, his to investment guidebooks and Tom Clancy technothrillers. The police came up with nothing of any interest to them, even in Mark's pseudobaronial cherry-paneled study, with its Carver sound system and perfectly reproduced rolltop desk.

"Christ, it's like nobody lived here," Schweiger complained, searching the drawers of Talbot's desk and matching credenza. Slattery kept a mental inventory of Mark's study, to be recorded later on the handheld Dictaphone she kept in her purse: telephone books, Standard & Poor's stock and bond guides, real estate market reports, a Rolodex file, about two feet of what looked like work files, some old Christmas and birthday cards, and a personal computer. The detectives ignored the navigation and tide charts of Kitsap County and Bainbridge Island waters that were thumbtacked to the paneling beside framed photographs of Mark, Laura, and their parents. When they finished they bundled the computer's central processing unit and computer disks out of the room and into the front hallway, where they would make up the service return on the warrant. The detectives spent the next hour in the bedrooms, pawing through the clothes drawers, remarking occasionally on the better designs in Laura's collection of lingerie, which seemed extensive, and sexual items not unusual in any married couple's bedroom: a couple of soft-core blue videotapes, a diaphragm and a canister of spermicidal foam, vials of scented massage oil. "Come on, you guys, snap it up," Slattery said, unable to resist a grin. "If you're looking for better stuff there's a porno shop on Aurora Avenue in Seattle that I busted when I was a prosecutor. They liked me. I think I can get you a discount."

They ignored her as much as they could and hurried through the rest of the search, examining the kitchen, the three furnished guest rooms, and the home gym in the basement. They finished with a quick check of the garage and Laura's studio, set a hundred feet behind the house in the backyard. Schweiger stood in the kitchen and laboriously wrote out the service return and grudgingly handed it to Slattery. "Thank you, boys," she said grandly. "Take good care of the computer stuff, because you're going to get another discovery request by fax this afternoon. Try not to fuck it up."

Schweiger took the crack with a sly smile. "Don't get too cocky, Counselor," he said. "Remember, it ain't always what's in the search. Sometimes it's what isn't."

Slattery felt a cold finger trace itself down her spine. "What's that mean, Joe?"

"Just what I said. Mark Talbot had six guns registered to him: two shotguns, a rifle, and three handguns—a .22 Colt target pistol, a .44 Browning, and a .38 Smith & Wesson Ladysmith he must have bought for the wife. And the Ladysmith, Counselor, is missing from this house. You have a good one now." Schweiger winked at her once on his way out the door.

When they were gone Mary Slattery helped herself to a can of Diet Coke from the restaurant-sized stainless steel Sub-Zero refrigerator and walked into the backyard. She sat in a green cast iron lawn chair on the sand-set brick patio at the edge of the lap pool, quickly dictated her notes of the search, then stopped to think. Laura and Mark's house was seven miles from the Agate Pass bridge that linked the Kitsap Peninsula to Bainbridge Island. It was another six miles, at least, to the beach cottage from the bridge. With the narrow roads, Slattery guessed it was at least forty minutes round trip. Could Laura have gone home to hide the gun after the shooting? It was unlikely but possible. Women are better at hiding stuff than men, she said to herself, so if I were Laura, where would I hide something? When the Coke can was empty and the sun had grown uncomfortably warm, Slattery returned to the kitchen, methodically checking the food tins in the pantry, the oversized glass jars of flour and sugar, bags of coffee, and canisters of dry pasta. She found nothing. She ran her hands under each of the shelves; nothing was taped there. The freezer yielded frozen orange juice and ice cream; nothing had been tampered with. She went back to the yard, thought more, and headed for Laura's studio.

The studio was above the four-car garage behind the house. The garage itself held three vehicles: Mark's silver Jaguar sedan; his thirty-year-old, fully restored, dark green Austin Healey roadster; and Laura's black Jeep Wrangler. Their Ford pickup, she knew, was still on Bainbridge Island. The door to the studio was set in a corner of the garage. It opened to a flight of stairs leading to the loft above.

The studio loft was airy and bright from six large skylights set into the sloping roof, three on each side of the ridge line. Dust motes shimmered in the bright afternoon sun. A painting table dominated the center of the long room, with two blank, stretched canvases lying on its surface. Slattery ran a finger across the surface of the canvas. No ground of white lead paint or gesso had been applied to the canvas. The room had been closed up for at least a week, yet there was no smell of paint or solvent or Laura's cigarette smoke in the air. The hardwood floor was clean, no paint splatters or spills. A wooden rack had been built in a corner to hold finished canvases or work in progress; it was empty.

She doesn't really work here, Mary Slattery said to herself. Or she can't. But maybe she spends some time here, anyway. Slattery opened the doors of the white Formica-faced cupboards that lined one of the walls, tucked under the sloping eaves. Rows of paint and solvent, in tubes and cans, faced her. "Shit," she said with a sigh. She took a Swiss army knife from her handbag, opened the screwdriver blade, and began to search.

It took the better part of an hour. At the back of the last cabinet shelf Slattery found a round gallon can of linseed oil that felt lighter than it should have. She pried it open eagerly. The can was empty, carefully wiped dry. It held five five-by-eight-inch cardboard-faced notebooks with sewn bindings, held together with a rubber band. Each notebook cover bore a white gummed-paper label, with the year written in India ink, from 1993 to 1997.

"Damn," she said.

Mary Slattery fished a Camel Light out of her purse, grabbed an ashtray from the painting table, and sat down on the floor to read.

Chapter Twelve

The journals began in 1993, the year before Laura Arcand had married. At first they read more like account books than a diary: Laura had methodically recorded canvas and paint ordered, paintings completed and named or destroyed or painted over, paintings consigned and sold. Cursory observations of colors, shapes, weather, moods, and occasional lovers were scattered in between. Laura's October 1994 marriage to Mark Talbot had been noted with a single arch comment: "Married Mark today, during lunch hour at the courthouse. Mother is very happy at last."

As Laura's productivity as a painter waned, there were long stretches of days and sometimes weeks with no entries. In 1995 she was hospitalized for depression and the entries stopped for almost three months. By mid-1996 a dense self-loathing had crept into Laura's words.

September 14. Up all night. Feel like my skin doesn't fit me. Dawn pale gray, no color. Worked for a few hours in morning, wasted canvas. Mark wants a baby, or thinks he does. Me as a mother? I can't keep myself fed and straight and sober. I would laugh but I want to give him what he wants . . . when did I start needing his approval, or anyone else's?

November 17. Clouds. Cold dim light. Worked until four, painting is shit, trite, sentimental. Had drinks with Sandy. Mark got home at ten. Wanted him to fuck me, hit me, anything so I'd feel him being alive, being with me. He went into study and played with computer until midnight. He hasn't touched me since I failed him at the fertility clinic. Damn him to hell . . . he should be with me.

Slattery read on, steeling herself in grim expectation. To her surprise Laura's mood lightened and her relationship with Mark seemed to improve in the early part of the new year.

February 7. Break in the rains, sun, very low on horizon, but very clean light. Worked well for three hours. Maybe I'm outgrowing this blackness or maybe I'm just tired of wandering around the house in my bathrobe all day. Mark is terribly stressed but he seems better, too. Maybe he's over the baby thing. We're having dinner tonight at La Casa, the Spanish stuff he likes so well. I hope he doesn't bring his business friends, it would be fun to get him so hot at the table that he drives like a bat out of hell to get me home.

March 9. Returned from a week in Baja California with Mark. I'd like to spend a year down there, maybe someplace like Loreto, away from the tourists and closer to the Sea of Cortés. Wonderful light, hot pure whites and sere yellows. Mark could never take the time but I found myself thinking as we danced in the zócalo that I wouldn't want to be there without a lover and I'd want that lover to be him. Surprised me. I married him because he was a convenience and I was . . . what? It suddenly does matter to me.

In April Laura began to write about the beach house.

April 25. No paint but not a bad day. Mark and I went to the island with final plans & permits for the beach shack. I like the idea of tearing it to the ground. I'd burn it if I could, but we need the pilings and foundation to keep the permit and build right on the beach. Ellen staying with Ed in New York, so the house is ours for a week. No cigarettes in two weeks now, no alcohol for three. Ran and stretched on the road and worked out at Ellen's gym in Winslow. Mark taking a long weekend off, so tomorrow we start tearing it down. Odd, I had old dreams again . . . I don't usually have them after a good day.

The next day she wrote:

Huzzah. Clear, hot, first warm day of the year. Today we started the teardown. I ripped shingles from the roof and tossed them into the Dumpster, sweating like a coolie and working the crowbar until my hands were raw. We stopped at three and had bread and cheese and wine on a blanket in the meadow, and each other for dessert. I just kept coming, loving the feel of Mark inside me. God! Like kids.

Laura's mood stayed upbeat and determined as the old cottage was torn down and the new walls went up.

May 17. Three weeks of rain! I've been painting, though. The only bad thing is that the dreams have started coming nearly every night. I'm trying to work through them. Mark had to work at his office this morning, but the sky cleared in the afternoon and we finished the teardown. Mark wanted to just hire it done when he got busy, but I loved every pulled nail and every swing of the breaker bar. I felt like cheering and crying all at once when we were down to the pilings. The sunset was so grand I took a mat down there and sat on the sand, inside the pilings, watching the sky and stars coming out. I wanted Mark so badly but he went in to work after supper and stayed until almost one. Ellen is riding him so hard. That damned office project is going to kill him if she doesn't stop it. I just wish she'd stay in town with Ed and leave us alone out here forever.

June 12. The new frame is up! I feel like a journeyman car-penter. I can spit, chew, pound nails, pee in the bushes, and swear with the best of them.

As the construction continued, Laura's moods darkened.

June 14. Roof on. The frame is beautiful in its simplicity and I want to leave it that way. I begged Mark, please just screen it in, give ourselves a pavilion where we can feel the wind and the rain and not be closed in. There's over 12 acres here, we could put a house up at the other end of the meadow, but Ellen doesn't want it. They both sit there with those damn smiles and tell me I'm crazy, it will wreck the place or something. They're both such bitches, the two of them! I've got to get off this rock and get to work.

June 21. The walls are on, damn them. I wouldn't do it and Mark hired a carpentry crew to finish. It feels so closed in and dark, even with the skylights. The dream's still coming every night. It's not my fault, I swear, I haven't had anything but a lit-tle wine in three months, I've taken my damned pills, and they're back anyway. It's so unfair! I can't breathe here any-more. I've got to work.

June 28. 2:30 A.M. The electricians and plumbers have fin-ished and the walls were Sheetrocked today. Yesterday Mark worked and it rained and I said fuck it, went to Captain K's in Winslow and got myself good and loaded. Fuck him. He's been working late and I think I know what he's working on, that as-sistant of his with the tits. More dreams tonight until I woke up dripping sweat and Mark snoring like a cow. I can't stand to have him touch me, I don't know why but I can't. I'm going to the city in the morning to paint and if Carlo is still around I'm going to see him. He's usually worthless but he'll talk for hours if he thinks I'll fuck him.

Laura stopped writing in her journal for nearly six weeks. When she wrote again her pen nearly ripped through the page.

> *August 15. The dreams won't stop and I'm trying to see them in the daylight it's so hot and I drink beer and cold coffee and smoke and work until my hands bleed the noise of the cars and trucks don't bother me I just work and work and work. The black dreams are closing in but if I can paint them maybe they will stay on the canvas. The pills don't work and I threw them away. THAT FUCKING TREADWELL DOESN'T KNOW SHIT! I can find the man and if I paint him I can kill him.*

Laura's journals held only one more entry. Slattery turned the page reluctantly, wanting to stop the pain of what she was reading.

> *August 31. Mark went to San Francisco with his "assistant" to see the "money boys" about the office park. They've got meetings all weekend so they'll have to stay. THE LYING SON OF A BITCH! His damned shack is done and I can't set foot in the thing. Christ, when he gets back I am going to kill him. Just fucking kill him.*

Mary Slattery carefully closed the journal and gathered the small bound memo books, bundled them together, and dropped them in her bag. "And you did, didn't you, Laura?" she said to the air.

"Jesus," Edwin Hauser said as he put down his photocopy of Laura's journals. It was seven o'clock Wednesday night. He sat at the head of the small conference table in the litigation war room, rubbing his face with both hands. Coffee in a blue mug with a stylized Hauser and Todd logo embossed in silver sat untouched on the table beside him. The police reports and documents that the Kitsap prosecutor's office had produced in discovery lay in a pair of open boxes at the center of the table. Thick folders with Laura Arcand's recent medical records filled a third box beside them. A surveyor's map of Ellen Arcand's property had been blown up, mounted on foam core boards, and hung on one wall; architect's drawings of the floor plans of the beach house and the main house filled another.

"This is just awful stuff," Hauser finally said. "Have the cops got it?"

"No," Mary Slattery replied. "They didn't search the studio carefully."

"Incredibly stupid. We shouldn't produce this diary, then."

"That won't work, Ed," Mary Slattery replied. "It's covered in their discovery request. Section three. 'Journals, diaries, notes, or other documents referring to Mark J. Talbot.'"

"Damn it. What about Laura's Fifth Amendment rights?"

"We could try, I suppose. But we'd have to show it to the judge in camera anyway."

Hauser pressed his lips together in a grim line. "Got any more news for me, Mary?" he asked, his voice heavy with concern.

"None that you'll like. The Kitsap sheriff's office interviewed six people living or staying in waterfront houses in Illahee, across the pass from Ellen's place. Three of them heard the shots. One of them, Frederick Barstow, put a precise time on it, two-oh-five A.M."

"Can he be shaken?"

"I doubt it. Barstow's a retired electrical engineer from Boeing. His statement says he's prone to insomnia. He was up reading in his living room with his deck doors open, facing the water, and glanced at his watch when he heard the shots."

"Maybe he heard something else. A boat engine backfire, or something."

"Unlikely. They asked Barstow about that. He's a Korean War vet, says he knows what a pistol shot sounds like. But what does it matter, Ed? We're going to have to concede that Laura fired the shots."

"It's the timing, damn it," Hauser said. He picked up his coffee cup and sipped, then grimaced at the taste of cold coffee. "Remember, Mark and I stayed up talking until around one A.M. That leaves too much time for Mark and Laura to have had a second fight, down at the beach house, before the shooting." He sighed heavily and reached across the table for a bottle of aspirin. "Anything else?"

Hauser said wearily, shaking two tablets loose from the bottle.

"It gets worse. The McKenzies"—Mary Slattery checked her notes—"live four houses south of Ellen's cove, down the beach. They went out on their deck at one-thirty A.M. that night to use the hot tub and stayed for over an hour. They weren't sure about hearing shots—they just said they heard something—but they didn't see anyone crossing their beach."

"They got married only two months ago, didn't they? They might have been looking somewhere else," Hauser replied dryly.

"Maybe," Mary Slattery said, flashing a sour grin, "but I leave all cross-examinations south of the navel to you, old man."

Hauser nodded, refusing to smile. "Okay. Get the paralegals back to work under Tony Guzzo's direction. I want all evidence and witness statements excerpted and a revised chronology built from every document and witness statement. Have them break the events down to the minute. Is there anything on Mark's gun yet?"

"No. The Kitsap sheriff's people haven't found it, but the bullets they recovered came from a .38 Smith & Wesson, like the one Mark apparently bought for Laura. I don't know whether that's bad or good. If I were them I'd argue that Laura took it from the house—that would show premeditation—then hid it after shooting Mark, which is not exactly the act of an insane person."

"Do they know about the gun oil stain on Laura's toiletries bag?"

"I don't think so. The bag wasn't taken in for testing."

"That's a small blessing." Hauser turned. "Will?" he asked. "Anything?"

Will Hatton looked up from where he sat at the far end of the room, interrupted in his rereading of Laura's journals. "Were there any recent paintings in Laura's studio, the one at her house?" he asked.

"No," Slattery replied. "Nothing. It looked like it hadn't been used in a while. Weeks, maybe."

"Did she have another studio, a work space in Seattle, or maybe someplace in Bremerton?"

"Not that I know of," Hauser answered. "Why?"

"Look at what she writes on August fifteen. 'Work until my hands bleed the noise of the cars and trucks don't bother me I just work and work and work.' Where was she working that had traffic noise? Not at her house. It's on a couple of acres, next to a golf course."

"Who would know?" Ed Hauser asked.

"There're references to somebody named Carlo, and to going into town to see him. That sounds like he was in Seattle. Do we know who he is, where he lives?"

"No. And I hope that prick Tiernan doesn't find him. I do remember Mark calling me about a month before he died. He said Laura hadn't been home in two days. God help us if she was screwing around with somebody herself. The jury will hate her."

"We've got to expect that," Mary Slattery replied. "I'll get him found and interview him before we turn the journal over. Maybe her art dealer knows about him. Weren't she and Laura pretty good friends?"

"I think so," Hauser replied, distracted. "What're you looking for, Will?"

"I'd like to see what Laura was trying to paint. It sounds like she was using her painting to pry some meaning out of the nightmares she'd been having."

"Then let's find out where she was working," Hauser replied, heaving himself out of his chair. "I just talked to Dr. Treadwell again, Will. Laura won't talk to him, won't work in therapy sessions with him. She says she won't talk to anyone but you. How soon can you be ready to interview her for the tape?"

Will shook his head. "Ed, we've talked about this. I can't testify. They'll kill me on cross because I've known Laura for years. And there's something you don't know, Ed. I had an affair with Laura. When we were both living in New York in 1987."

Hauser frowned. "How long did it go on?" he demanded.

"Six weeks. Then she dumped me."

"Christ." Hauser drummed his fingers on the table.

"What do your psychiatric ethics say about this?" Slattery demanded.

"They're different for forensic psychiatrists and treating psychiatrists," Hatton replied. "You shouldn't be treating a patient with whom you've had a sexual relationship. And current sexual relationships are completely forbidden. In forensic work the test is looser—

it's whether you have a personal or professional relationship with the person you are evaluating that could impair your professional perspective."

Hauser thought. "How many times have you seen Laura since your relationship with her ended?"

"No more than five or six times briefly, except for the hospital the other day."

"Do you think your professional opinion would be impaired?"

Will thought hard. "I don't think so," he said slowly. "Laura seems willing to work with me. And my knowledge of Laura as a teenager could help."

"Then it's settled. I want you to—"

"Like hell it's settled," Mary Slattery said hotly. "I don't want to go into court like this, Ed. You, Hatton—Christ, I'll be the only person at this table who doesn't have a preexisting relationship with Laura. I want somebody else."

Hauser glared. "Goddamnit, Mary, I—"

"No, you don't. You do this case *with* me, and Reuben. For chrissakes, Reuben, help me out on this."

Reuben Todd finally broke his silence. "I can see advantages and problems both ways, Mary. Let me ask this. Dr. Hatton, who would you choose to replace you if you couldn't testify? Someone with similar skills in PTSD-type cases."

"Fred Leermentov, at UC-Berkeley," Hatton said promptly.

"Could Dr. Leermentov check your work, advise you—and us—if he felt your personal feelings were interfering?"

"He could. He could also step in and take my place, if necessary."

"Then we will retain him." Todd turned to Hauser. "With that precaution, I'd be satisfied, Ed."

"So would I," Hauser rumbled. "How soon can you be ready to interview Laura on tape, Will?" he repeated.

Hatton pursed his lips and sighed, realizing what he had just gotten himself into. "Two or three days," he said. He tried to ignore the sound of Mary Slattery slamming the door as she stormed out of the room.

Chapter Thirteen

Mark Talbot's funeral service was abrupt and cold and suffused with anger. Talbot's mother, Jean, and stepfather, Luther Talbot, a retired navy admiral, stood stiffly next to Talbot's coffin during the reading of the austere burial service. When it was over they listened without expression as Ed Hauser and Ellen Arcand offered words of condolence. Their pain and fury were plain below the surface of the skin.

Will Hatton turned away and walked to the grove of fifty-year-old cedars at the far edge of the small country cemetery near Rolling Bay, where his mother had been buried more than twenty-five years before. He paused at the edge of her grave and knelt to sweep away the leaves and twigs that had accumulated near the headstone, then placed the bouquet of yellow summer roses he had brought with him at the base of the stone. As he rose to go he felt a tentative hand on his shoulder.

"Will?" a woman's voice asked.

He turned to face a petite woman in her mid-forties with artfully lightened, short blonde hair, dressed in a black skirted suit. Her face was oval, its normal prettiness marred by tear-swollen grief. "I'm sorry if I startled you," she said. "I'm Sandy Demerest—my name was Sandy Hollings. Do you remember me?"

"Of course," he said, smiling. He bent forward to kiss her cheek, then put his arms around her as she broke down again.

They sat in her sun-bright kitchen in the carefully restored blue farmhouse on a grassy hill above Agate Pass, which Sandy Demerest had kept when her marriage had ended. The room was warmed by butcher-block maple counters and racks of copper pots. Will studied the pictures of Sandy's two daughters, both now grown. The younger girl, Sarah, looked much as he remembered her mother from high school. It seemed impossible to him that so much time could have passed.

"I wasn't sure if you would remember me," she said, pouring coffee into stoneware mugs.

"Surely you didn't think I'd forget," he replied. Sandy smiled and colored slightly, then took a fifth of cognac from a cabinet and held it out to him. Will nodded. She added a carefully measured shot to each cup and put the bottle away.

"I'm glad you haven't forgotten. I was quite proud of myself, you know."

Will laughed. "And I was quite amazed."

And in truth he remembered her with amazement. Sandy Hollings was a bright, pretty girl in Will's high school class, with good grades and a hulking football player boyfriend. The boyfriend—Wade Demerest, a ferocious defensive tackle that Will's teammates had nicknamed Thug—had coldly dropped her in the week before the school's winter formal dance. Her friends had caucused and selected Will as the best available replacement. Dateless himself, he'd gone along with the plan, renting a tuxedo and stealing two bottles of Korbel champagne from Ed's modest wine cellar. To his surprise they both enjoyed the dance; with no real expectations, he'd invited her back to the small bunkhouse he lived in on Ed Hauser's old Island Center farm. He'd made a fire and offered her the first champagne of his life. After an hour of talk she'd suddenly kissed him, then slipped out of her long, formal dress with sweet efficiency, already naked beneath. They made love twice in the three hours before her 2 A.M. curfew. A week later she had reconciled with her boyfriend, whom she married within the year. Will never saw her again.

"I didn't know you were such close friends with Laura," Will said, pulling himself back to the present.

"We were actually pretty close in high school, even though she was a lot younger. We were in the honors art course together, and I was in awe of her ability, even then." Sandy Demerest broke into a sudden laugh. "In fact, Will, she's the one who suggested you as my replacement date. I don't think you ever knew that."

"I didn't," he admitted, joining her laughter.

"After I got married I lost touch with Laura, until she moved back to Seattle. I was living in the city then, running my antique importing business out of a warehouse south of the market, watching my kids go away to school, my marriage to Wade fall apart. I was drinking too much. Laura came in one day, looking for some old teak furniture for her new apartment. She was a mess, too, and we became our own little mutual therapy group, with our famous all-vodka dinners." Sandy shook her head ruefully. "It took me a year to come out of it, but when I did, I had a good friend again."

"What was Laura like?"

"She was pretty manic for a while. Highs and lows. As I came out of my spiral I pretty much forced her back into psychotherapy. It helped quite a bit, I think. She steadied down and started seeing Mark and decided that if he wasn't quite perfect, he was better than a lot of the competition."

"Was she still trying to paint?"

"Oh, yes. She experimented with a lot of things—representational landscapes, folk art, Northwest coast scenes, Southeast Asian stuff. But she burned most of it. She didn't think she had anything left to say as a painter, and said she couldn't come up with anything new even when she was real high."

"What kind of high?"

"Coffee, cigarettes, vodka, speed."

"Speed? Methamphetamine?"

"Not meth, not street drugs. Diet pills she'd score from friends. Women can bullshit male doctors into prescribing nearly anything.

They give us drugs hoping we'll go away and stop reminding them of their wives."

Sad but probably fairly accurate, Will thought. "What did Mark think?"

"He didn't care if she still painted. He said she'd already proven herself and could just quit. She tried, too. She decorated their new house and doted on him and tried to turn herself into a sexier version of Suzie Homemaker. But it didn't work. The longer she stayed away from her work, the more she got depressed, had to be hospitalized for it."

Will finished his coffee and Sandy poured him another cup, this time without the brandy. Her hands and voice shook as she returned his cup with a question. "Will? Could Laura have really killed Mark?"

"It's possible, Sandy. Even probable. At this point the police aren't looking for anyone else, and there was enough evidence to arrest and arraign her."

"God. It's just so awful. Yet it doesn't seem like it can be real."

"I know. Did you spend any time with Laura this summer?" Hatton asked, to keep Sandy Demerest talking.

"Some. She and Mark—actually, Mark—came up with the idea of rebuilding the beach house, so they were on the island a lot. Laura had fun for a while, but then her dreams started up again. And she just fell apart."

"Tell me about the dreams, Sandy. Laura couldn't remember much of them when I talked to her the other day, but she said she was having them."

"Well, they were—are—awful. She'd wake up screaming . . . but she never could remember them, not the whole thing. Just pieces. Mark was really concerned about them, too. He came to see me alone, to talk about them. They started years ago, when Laura disappeared. The summer we graduated."

Will shook his head. "I wasn't here. I went to New Orleans to see my father, then went into the marine corps down there."

"I'd forgotten that. It was quite a big deal. Laura disappeared, and the whole island was in an uproar. The sheriff's office set up search teams to look in the parks and along the roadsides for her, or actually for her body, because a lot of people thought she was dead. Then they found her in Seattle, and she was so beaten up, she couldn't remember anything about what had happened. Anyway, Mark was really interested in that. He wasn't here then, either—he was in his second year at Annapolis. He only came home later that summer, after his birth father died—and so it was pretty new to him. But he seemed to think that Laura's disappearance, and whatever happened to her when she was lost, was the reason for her dreams."

Hatton kept his face neutral. "Did Mark ask anything specific about Laura's disappearance?"

Sandy Demerest frowned and sipped at her now cold coffee. "He did. Let's see . . . he wanted to know if she'd had a boyfriend that summer, who she was hanging out with, where she was right before she disappeared."

"What did you tell him?"

"That I didn't know, really. Sometimes she went out with Danny Donnelly, you remember him, a jock like my ex-husband. The one who later played for the Rams. Laura and Danny both hung out with the group at Fort Ward that summer. I told Mark I didn't know why she disappeared, only that she was kind of on the outs with her mother, doing a lot of drawing and painting and sleeping at the beach house most nights so she could come and go when she wanted to." Sandy Demerest shook her head. "I thought it was kind of weird that Mark was so interested, to tell you the truth."

"Maybe not. It's pretty clear Laura had some kind of traumatic experience while she was missing."

"Just like now," Sandy replied. "The papers said Laura tried to kill herself, Will. Is that true?"

He nodded. "She tried. And very nearly succeeded."

"Is she going to get well?"

"I don't know."

"Do you think I can see her?"

"You'd better check with her doctors, Sandy. I'm not treating her—I'm just trying to figure out what happened." Hatton looked at his watch and realized that he needed to get back to Seattle. "I do have to go. If you think of anything else about Mark or Laura that might bear on her breakdown this summer, be sure to call me, or Ed Hauser. Okay?"

"I will," she said. She suddenly leaned across the table and kissed him on the lips, the gesture so like the impulsive kiss she had given him years before that his mouth was suddenly dry. "Thanks for talking with me, Will. I'm so afraid that I've lost both of them. I just don't understand how Laura could ever . . . We never really know one another, do we?"

"Not enough," Hatton admitted.

Chapter Fourteen

At six-thirty on Friday morning Will Hatton was in the Hauser and Todd offices, reading Laura Arcand's recently located childhood medical records. Her general practitioner on Bainbridge Island, one Dr. Ted Wilson, had treated her after her return from Juvenile Hall in Seattle. The key entry read:

8/28/72. PT Laura Arcand, age 14 years 3 months. PT presents as well-developed young woman returned this morning from a runaway episode. Bruising in areas of head, face, chest, arms, and abdomen. No fractures observed or reported by hospital examination but my X ray of skull shows possible hairline fracture in lower occipital area. PT is visibly agitated, upset. No recall of recent runaway episode although recall for events prior to runaway now appears normal or nearly so; unclear whether PT in fact remembers or does not want to remember recent events. Just as well. This young woman has clearly been through some kind of trauma, probably on streets as a runaway. Fear reaction to touch or to requests for information. Recommended bed rest, fluids, rich foods. Referral to psychiatrist Steven Terry for explanation of episode.

Will looked up from his reading to see Ed Hauser stride into the room. "Good morning, Will," he said. "You had breakfast?"

"Just coffee. What about you?"

"The same. Did my thirty minutes on the exercise bike at home, just as the doctor ordered." Hauser grinned like a child proud of a new toy. "I still feel ridiculous pedaling away on a thirtieth-floor balcony, but it's kind of pretty to look out over the city and the harbor at dawn."

Hatton did not smile. "That's not all I've heard the doctor ordered. Ed, what are you doing? You were scheduled for a bypass six months ago."

"It's a very minor blockage, Will. Just slows me down a little. As soon as Laura's case is over, I'll go in for it."

Will shook his head. "You're taking risks you don't have to."

"No, I'm taking risks I have to. Let's get breakfast at the Athenian and kick this thing around."

"It's going to be hard to get Laura to open up," Will said, digging into a smoked salmon omelet.

Ed Hauser sipped coffee and stared out the steel-framed windows beside their second-story booth. The dawn rain had ended and a crease of blue had opened to the west, the sun catching the first snow lacing the peaks of the Olympic Range. "Why's that, Will?" he asked, his voice low. There was a rising clatter from the bar below their perch on the balcony as a Russian cargo boat crew arrived in the downstairs bar for a fish and vodka breakfast.

"There's something about these dreams that she's afraid of, more afraid than she is of being found guilty," Will continued.

"And you're sure that these dreams are linked to the four days that she disappeared?"

"I'm not sure of anything. But there's nothing else in Laura's life to suggest any kind of serious physical or emotional trauma. She keeps talking about the same things in her dreams—doors, lights, a staircase. I can't tell at this point if they're symbolic or real things she remembers, although very badly. When she ran away—is it possible she was hurt, concussed before she ever got to Seattle? Dr. Wilson found plenty of signs of head trauma that would interfere with memory formation, but if it happened later, I'd expect her to be able to remember *something* about running away, and she never has."

Hauser shoved away his half-eaten bowl of cereal and picked up a banana, the victim of a low-fat diet. "Imagine," he growled. "Me eating this crap. I'd kill for a four-egg bacon cheddar omelet." He paused, sighed. "So what do we call this, repressed memory?"

"Not the way the repressed-memory hysterics would. Memory isn't a perfect recorder. We don't just record and repress a traumatic memory until Dr. Freud puts us under hypnosis and pulls it out, wriggling and screaming. Memories form imperfectly. They grow and shrink and change as we create ourselves, our personal myth or legend about who we are and our place in the world. There's recent neurological research that suggests that the very process of memory formation and remembering can actually 'rewire' the brain, change it physically. The one thing we *do* know is that when someone is as emotionally vulnerable as Laura is, they can be very suggestible—a psychotherapist can plant a memory more easily than they can find a real one. I'm being very careful not to suggest anything to her because that might contaminate an expert opinion, whether from me or Leermentov. But there's something . . . there's a core of something that she's holding back. Consciously or unconsciously, I don't know. But she associates it with Mark's death, somehow. And with these dreams."

Hauser drummed his fingers uneasily on the table. "That's not good . . . you're telling a complicated story, Will. And you know what juries like."

Will grinned. "Hauser's rule number one. Juries like simple, understandable stories."

"It's good to know you recall some of the training from your youth."

"Yeah," Will replied, still smiling. "But I wanted to ask you— what do you remember about this? You're the one who picked Laura up from the juvenile facility when she ran away."

Hauser munched on a mouthful of banana and dry toast. "Not

that much, to tell you the truth," he said, reflecting. "I got a panic-stricken call from Ellen that morning after Laura had disappeared . . . I think it was a Friday, might have been a Saturday. I called the Kitsap sheriff's department, told them that Laura was missing. No, it must have been Friday, because Ellen and I spent Saturday and Sunday combing the island together, didn't even consider that Laura might have gone into town on the ferry. Dumb, in retrospect. The Seattle police called us on Monday. We picked Laura up at Twelfth and Alder in the city—that's where the old Juvenile Hall was—and took her to Dr. Wilson. He's dead nearly fifteen years now. Ellen took over from there." Hauser paused, old memory growing into fresh anger. "God, I was pissed at the Seattle cops! An obviously injured kid and they tossed her into Juvenile Hall with a bunch of tough cases. Poor Laura. The hell of those four days, I'm not surprised that she doesn't want to remember it."

"Were any drug tests done on Laura?"

"I don't think so. You've seen both her medical records and the Kitsap and Seattle police reports. She just took off like all you kids did, headed for the city and got in over her head. What about you? Did you ever see her take anything?"

"Nothing but a puff of marijuana. The stuff we got on the island was so weak, I think half the high was imagined. Damn, I wish I'd been there when she ran away."

Hauser smiled. "You got that wild hair to see your father. You had your fishing money, from your granddad's boat, and I figured it was about time for you to light out for the territory. Why'd you go on the bus? I could have sent you down on a plane."

"I thought it was time I started doing things for myself." Will pushed away his plate and reached for his coffee. "Anyway, I always wanted to tell you that I appreciated your not interfering when I joined the marines down in New Orleans."

"I would've preferred you started college, but how could I object? The navy was my ticket out of North Dakota, got me out here, where I made a life." Hauser grinned, then broke into a laugh, gesturing out the open window toward the island. "Every time I see the water and those green hills I thank God I'm not still breathing dirt on the farm we had south of Bismarck." He reached for his wallet and laid a $20 bill on top of the check. "You ready to interview Laura?"

"I'm getting close. I've got to go back through all the medical records and tackle Treadwell next. Maybe Saturday morning, if they'll let us tape out at Northlake."

"They will. Anything you need in the meantime?"

"Just Dr. Steven Terry. Or his records. He's the missing link, the person who might have gotten the truth out of Laura back in 1972."

"We're looking. It's going to be a tough hunt. It seems Terry started screwing his female patients a couple of years after he treated Laura. Some of them sued, and he took off. He let his Washington license lapse, and left the state with a string of default judgments pending against him. Tony Guzzo's got a national skip-tracing firm looking for him, but I'm not too hopeful."

"Get him," Will replied. "We're going to need whatever he's got in his records. We've got to know what happened to Laura in those four days."

Chapter Fifteen

Marcia Wiegand sat behind her mahogany desk at Kitsap Industries' Elk Run offices and stared out the window. The carefully manicured fringe of the second-growth Douglas fir forest that had once covered most of the office campus was visible in the distance, beyond the cedar-and-glass three- and four-story office buildings connected by winding concrete walks. "I suppose I get to play the scarlet woman in all this, don't I?" she asked bitterly.

"That depends," Mary Slattery said evenly, "on what the truth is."

"Truth." Marcia Wiegand laughed, a short bitter bark. "Like that's important in a courtroom."

"It's vital, Ms. Wiegand. If you prefer, we can do this under oath, in a deposition, and you can get your own counsel. However you would like to proceed." Mary Slattery looked at her watch, fighting impatience and the fatigue that weighed on her like a heavy blanket.

Marcia Wiegand turned back to face Slattery. Her severely cut suit did not hide her heavy-breasted, wide-hipped body. She suddenly smiled. "The truth, Ms. Slattery, woman to woman, is that I did sleep with Mark Talbot. I enjoyed it. I would do it again, if I could."

"And why is that, Ms. Wiegand?"

"Because he was a good lover and a good man dealing with a wife who was the nearest thing to crazy, and a mother-in-law who runs this company with an iron grip and does not suffer failure. Period. Ellen Arcand has never failed at anything. Ask her. She'll tell you herself."

"Look," Mary Slattery said wearily, "you don't have to be so defensive. I'm here to find out what you will say if called as a witness, find out what Mark was working on before he was killed, and take a look at his office before the search warrant gets served this afternoon. That's it. I'm not some kind of avenging angel for Laura Arcand. Or her mother. You slept with a married guy, fine. It happens. I'm sure it was a good idea at the time. And frankly, aside from the fact that the prosecutor is going to try and twist that into a motive for my client to kill her husband, I don't give a shit. Period."

"You sound like you're speaking from experience."

As a matter of fact I am, and it cost me a job I liked a hell of a lot, Mary Slattery thought, but I'll be damned if I'll give you the satisfaction. Slattery kept her voice neutral. "Let's just stay with the facts, please, Ms. Wiegand. When did you first meet Mark Talbot?"

"Two years ago, when I interviewed with him for this job. Kitsap Industries had just started planning the Elk Run development. I was hired to coordinate marketing, design, leasing, and tenant satisfaction functions."

"What was Mr. Talbot's job? This real estate development?"

"No. Much more. Mark was KI's president, chief operating officer, and corporate secretary—he had a joint M.B.A. and law degree, though he never practiced law. He took care of administration, finance, records—pretty much everything except the engineering and contracting divisions. He really made this company, you know. When he came here, KI was still a small custom engineering and manufacturing company that did military and aircraft work. We're ten times as big now, we sell products all over the world, and the real estate projects he planned will be worth over $300 million someday."

Mary Slattery scribbled notes to give herself time to think. Mark Talbot got himself one pretty committed cheerleader in you, lady, she thought. "How is this office project working?" she asked.

Marcia Wiegand colored slightly and tapped her manicured red nails on her desk. "We're a little slow leasing up," she admitted.

"Which explains the empty parking lots out there," Slattery said, gesturing out the window.

"Well, yes. The investors haven't yet received the returns they wanted."

"Is that why Ellen had that meeting at her home the weekend Mark was killed?"

"Yes. KI holds seventy-five percent of the project. The people at the meetings were the minority investors. Mark and I went to San Francisco two weeks before the meeting to talk with potential investors who might take a piece of the project and cut some of the initial investors' risks."

"Did they buy in?"

"Not yet, but they were still considering it."

"Are your bankers getting nervous?"

"We don't have any bankers. The investors have put up all the money, roughly $20 million."

Which means Ellen must have been hell on wheels about this, Slattery thought. She's got over $12 million tied up in this place. "Were the meetings tense?"

"Not really, but Ellen . . . she'd been driving Mark pretty hard."

"How was Mark handling it?"

"Fairly well, I thought. Determined, but upbeat. At least until his wife . . ."

"What about Laura?"

"Mark said they were having problems this past summer. She'd fall into these black moods, then disappear for days at a time, and Mark would brood about it . . . I don't think he ever got a decent night's sleep. Some mornings he took caffeine pills to get going, and he'd check out of the office suddenly, saying he had to meet with Laura's doctors about her problems. Whatever time he lost to that he'd make up at night."

"How often did that happen?"

"Quite a bit, toward the end of summer. Once or twice a week, in August."

"Was Mark working on anything besides this office project?"

"Oh, yes. He was reorganizing the company, preparing to restructure it into a more modern kind of holding company with separate subsidiaries and defined profit centers so that we could see which businesses were profitable and which weren't. Moving the office from Bremerton this summer took a lot out of him. There were thirty-five years of old records to review and streamline, decide which could be discarded and which ones we had to keep because of environmental liabilities or whatever. And on top of everything else we had the Bremerton environmental lawsuits that your law firm is handling. Some days Mark would have to spend ten hours with the records and the lawyers. Then he'd go to the beach house he was building and pound nails just to get rid of the frustration."

"Did Mark keep any kind of diary?"

"Just his Filofax, as far as I know. He was pretty computer oriented. He'd jot notes in his Filofax, then every night before he went home he'd organize everything into a list for the next day on his PC or his laptop. If he absolutely couldn't get to it here, he'd do it at home and e-mail it to his desk."

"Are his company computers both here?"

"Yes, and we haven't touched them, just as you instructed. Your paralegal has been here for two days, copying and downloading everything."

"I'll look at everything shortly, but let's finish here first. When did your affair with Mark begin?"

"I don't know if you could call it an affair. It was just . . . we were in San Francisco. We had our initial meetings with the potential investors on Friday, the twenty-ninth, and it was pretty clear we were going to have to stay the weekend to go over everything with them. We checked into the St. Francis that night, had dinner, then drinks in the Compass Rose. Mark was worried. The meetings hadn't gone that well, and he was pretty sure he wasn't going to get any sleep. I think I drank more than he did . . . Anyway, we went upstairs, and an hour later I stopped by his room. He was working on his laptop, looking miserable . . . and I said I thought I knew how to help him sleep. And that was that. We slept together both nights."

"Any declarations of undying love, promises to divorce, anything like that?"

"No. If he had said anything like that I would have stopped him. I think Mark loved his wife . . . but he couldn't figure her out, and her craziness was going to kill him." Bitter anger flashed in Marcia Wiegand's dark eyes. "And she did."

Tony Guzzo sat at Mark Talbot's computer as Slattery entered Talbot's spacious office. Guzzo overflowed Talbot's desk chair. A former Garfield High School and University of Washington football tackle, Guzzo's devotion to northern Italian cuisine was barely held in check by his three weekly visits to the Gateway Health Club's weight room. After seven years as a Seattle cop, Guzzo became Hauser and Todd's sole in-house investigator, working on call when needed. He spent the rest of his time studying literature and making desultory starts on a first novel. He'd befriended Slattery when she'd joined Hauser and Todd; the friendship lasted and deepened despite a brief weekend affair that left them both convinced they were not suited to be together.

Slattery looked around the office. A wall of glass overlooked the artificial lake at the center of the office park. Talbot's various awards and civic citations were hung on the left wall; bookshelves filled the right, stacked with notebooks and bound financial summaries. The office was furnished in standard upper-executive ware, a modern cherry-wood desk and matching conference table, its oxblood leather chairs stacked with boxes of documents and original files that had been returned from copying.

"We got it all, I think," Guzzo said, looking up from the computer. "They're going to be able to tell that I retrieved Talbot's erased files from his hard disk if they get someone who knows what they're doing to bleed his computer."

"Anything interesting?"

"Not unless you're a defense contractor or a real estate speculator. And the grammar in business letters . . ." Guzzo shuddered. He had six credits to finish before completing his master's in Renaissance English literature at the University of Washington.

"What about his Filofax?"

"It was here, along with a desk calendar his secretary kept. But I didn't see anything matching the list of names you gave me. This guy was all business, Slats."

"What about doctors? Laura's, I mean."

"Nada. Did you expect them to be there?"

"I'm not sure," Slattery said. "I thought he was spending a lot of time talking to her doctors."

"If he did, he didn't write the appointments down." Guzzo paused, tapped a key, then waited for the last download from Talbot's hard drive to be complete. He looked up from the computer screen to make sure the door was closed. "How was the mistress?"

Slattery started to laugh, then thought better of it. "Loved him. Hated our client. She'll be about number three on the prosecutor's witness list."

"Sounds like I better invade her privacy."

"Correct. I want to know everything about Marcia Wiegand. Something doesn't register right." Slattery yawned with fatigue. "Are we out of here?"

Guzzo nodded. "Reuben called. He's sending Mike Spellman over to baby-sit when the search warrant gets served, so we can take off. The copies of Talbot's files are in your car. Eight boxes. Looks like you've got some reading to do tonight."

"Yeah," Slattery replied, grinning sourly, "and it ain't going to be Milton."

Guzzo grinned. "Better to rule in hell, Mary, than serve in heaven."

"The devil got that one right," Slattery agreed.

Chapter Sixteen

The name ROBERT DARRINGTON TREADWELL, M.D. was spelled in raised gold capital letters on the lobby wall of a converted brick-and-timber First Hill mansion on a tree-lined block of Spring Street, three blocks from the ever expanding campus of Swedish Hospital. The names of five junior psychiatrists and six non-M.D. therapists graced the wall in smaller gold letters. Will Hatton stepped back and took it all in with a smile.

"*This* is a fucking money machine," he said under his breath.

The receptionist sitting in a walnut-paneled alcove on the far side of the grand entry hall looked up and eyed him sharply. "I beg your pardon?"

"Nothing. Dr. Hatton to see Dr. Treadwell. Let me know when he's free."

"I will, Dr. Hatton. Would you care to sit down?"

"Thank you." Hatton settled on a low leather sofa, a bemused smile still on his face. Treadwell owned one of the last silk-stocking psychiatric practices in Seattle, one not dependent upon the increasingly tightfisted insurance companies, with their preapproved twenty-minute therapy "hours" and heavy use of psychiatric drugs. Treadwell's steady flow of wealthy clients came from his careful but relentless marketing at corporate seminars and retreats, and his willingness to be showcased on television news and in his monthly "Mental Wellness" column in *Seattle Lifestyles* magazine.

Hatton had just finished rereading the last of Treadwell's chart notes on Laura Arcand when Treadwell himself appeared in the lobby, a well-fed but fit man in his early fifties, with a great head of flowing white hair above his tanned, seamless face. "Dr. Hatton," he said, offering a large, soft hand. "This is a pleasure. It's been far too long since we've talked, but I have read your papers with great attention."

"Thank you," Will said, shuffling the copied chart notes back into his canvas briefcase. "I'm here to ask you about Laura Arcand."

"Of course. Won't you join me for coffee in my office?" Will followed him through the lobby and down a gently lit hallway into what was once the home's grand library. Walnut bookcases lined the walls, flanking a carved marble fireplace. A rich cream-and-blue Isfahan rug graced the brightly polished hardwood floor. Treadwell ignored his desk in favor of a fat brown leather chair, across a glass-and-iron coffee table from the slipcovered sofa he offered to Hatton. He sat down and started a tape recorder on the coffee table. "Do you mind?" Treadwell asked. "I'm such a poor note taker. I don't keep these tapes; I just use them for chart notes and erase them at the end of each day." Hatton dug into his briefcase for a moment, then laid it on the table. He shook his head, no. "Please go ahead and tape this if you like," Hatton said distinctly.

Treadwell poured coffee for both of them, then settled back into his chair with a fixed look of compassionate sorrow spreading across his features. "This is tragic, just tragic," he began. "Poor Laura. Like so many artistic people, her gift comes coupled with the curse of mental instability. I've worked so hard with her since she returned to Seattle five years ago, and now this. I truly liked and respected her husband, you know. A fine businessman." He sighed heavily. "I just came back an hour ago from Northlake. Laura's handling her medication all right, but she can't or won't talk to me about her husband's death. I really wish that she would let me help." Treadwell paused, clearly frustrated. "So, what can I do for you? I understand you've been retained by Laura's attorneys."

"I've not yet been retained to testify," Hatton replied cautiously. "I'm merely evaluating Ms. Arcand. I've reviewed your chart notes and have a few questions."

"Really? I should have thought Ms. Arcand's situation was obvious. Bipolar disorder, mixed, intermittently arrested, mostly because the patient would not cooperate in maintaining her medications." Treadwell put his cup down on the table and shrugged dispassionately. "Did her condition make her legally insane, under M'Naghton's rule? I doubt it."

Hatton decided to skirt that issue.

"Have you given Laura a thorough physical examination to determine if there have been any changes to organic brain condition?"

"Of course," Treadwell replied. "I oversaw a detailed physical and neurological examination as soon as Laura's condition stabilized. CAT scan, PET scan, brain chemistry—the works. I saw no new physical abnormality. Not that I expected any. I'll have the results copied for you."

"Thank you. What was it like to treat Laura?" Hatton asked, changing the subject.

Treadwell's eyebrows shot up in surprise. "I'm not sure I should answer that. Well—doctor to doctor—Ms. Arcand was one of the more difficult patients I had. She began well enough, after her move here from New York five years ago, but she simply would not stay with lithium."

"Why not?"

"Her claim, of course, was that she could not paint under its influence. I've heard such claims before—I have quite a number of patients who are active in the arts and letters. Most of them have worked through the medication quite successfully—in many cases, their work has improved without the distractions of the manic and depressive phases."

"What was your conclusion about Ms. Arcand?"

"Like others, she grew addicted to the manic phases—prolonging them with coffee and cigarettes and alcohol, staying up all night to produce her work. Work as nonstop party. She did try, at first, to work while under medication. I thought some of the painting she did while in balance was very good, particularly the series she based on Northwest coast Indian artifacts and mythology about four years ago. But she hated them."

"Why?"

"She said she found them lifeless, unemotional. 'Like painting dead things,' if I remember her statement correctly."

"Did you review her paintings regularly?"

"Only through her shows, not as part of her therapy. I'm a fairly devoted art collector myself, as you can see." Treadwell gestured toward the paintings on his walls. "That picture on the left, for example—"

Hatton cut him off, unwilling to change the subject. "Did you notice any significant changes in Laura's paintings or in her work patterns?"

"Only deterioration. As she got older she could not handle the physical consequences of her manic phases—to put it bluntly, she couldn't paint with her hands trembling from hangovers. She also had developed rather rapid cycling between the manic and depressive phases, which resulted in her hospitalization. About eighteen months ago I counseled her to take a sabbatical from painting and focus on her health and her relationship with her husband, who seemed like a patient man, all in all." Treadwell shook his head sadly, and picked up the case file resting on the table. "Yes, January of '96. She took my advice at first—maintained her lithium, stayed away from alcohol, seemed to enjoy life more." Treadwell chuckled as he reviewed his notes. "She seems to have had much more sex with her husband, and fewer visits here. A good indicator, I think."

"Did you consider or treat her potential alcoholism?"

"Of course. Laura did not seem to me to be a true alcoholic in the sense of addiction—her heaviest alcohol use was as self-medication during the depressive episodes, to blunt the pain. I urged her to keep away from it and to substitute therapy and possibly antidepressants during those periods. I did not think that aversion therapy or an AA-type twelve-step program would be effective with Laura."

Will stayed with his prepared list of questions. "Did you notice any disturbance of her condition this summer, Doctor?"

"Yes, I did," Treadwell said defensively. "Really, Dr. Hatton, it's all in the chart notes. Ms. Arcand's condition did deteriorate, again because she stopped taking her lithium. On her last visit with me, at the end of June, she claimed that it was interfering with her painting. She also claimed it gave her headaches and other flulike symptoms, which as you know are perfectly common side effects."

"Did she say anything about her dreams, say in the last six months?"

"She did mention her dreams from time to time, relating them to unpleasant colors and professing that they were painful. I was interested in them because they appeared to be a recurrence of some dreams she'd had years ago, while living in New York. Her therapist there, Dr. Milstein, referenced them in his chart notes. Have you seen Milstein's notes?"

"No. The attorneys are still trying to track down all her medical records from the years she lived in New York."

"I have Milstein's stuff, which I maintained separately from her current file. Dr. Milstein's notes referred to several episodes of these dreams during the winter of 1985, but then they ceased, and Ms. Arcand had no further pain from them."

"Did you have an interpretation of Laura's dreams?"

Treadwell threw back his head and laughed. "Heavens, no! I'm not some bedraggled old Freudian hack mumbling away about symbolism and such. Like you, I'm a medical doctor. I look for medical symptoms and medical solutions, not the old talking cure." Treadwell paused, reconsidering his answer. "Don't misunderstand me. I listened to Laura's descriptions of these dreams—mostly fragmentary—and evaluated them carefully. They seemed to be an indicator of stress in her life."

"How so?"

"The frequency increased with other stressors. Most recently, Laura's inability to bear children. I understand that was a great disappointment to her husband."

"I thought that was sometime past."

"No, I believe it was a recurring issue, at least for her husband, even though medically there was very little hope for conception."

"Did Laura report any other stressors?"

"She missed her work—she isn't built or inclined to enjoy leisure. She resented her husband's long hours, wanted his attentions. As you probably know, Laura has a tremendous need to be the center of attention, and her work has always made her that."

Will kept his voice neutral. "So far, I haven't heard anything that points to a condition that could lead her to murder."

Treadwell shook his head sadly. "No. I'm afraid your evaluation will be precisely the same as mine."

"What about the last three months?"

"I'm sorry, I don't understand."

"There's only one meeting and one phone call logged between you and Laura between mid-June and her husband's death. If she was starting to spiral down, why didn't you increase the frequency of her therapy sessions or alter her medication?"

Treadwell frowned. "I was on vacation in France for most of July and August. What are you getting at?" he asked gruffly.

Will kept his voice businesslike. "That Laura Arcand shot her husband after spiraling down into a severe depressive condition, that you were aware of her declining condition, aware she was experiencing painfully intrusive dreams and memories that coincided with a prior traumatic episode, and that you did nothing effective to attempt to arrest it. If you were absent, you failed to provide for Laura to be able to continue therapy with another doctor. In short, Doctor, I'm suggesting neglect."

"You accuse me of malpractice, Dr. Hatton? Say it again and I will sue you for libel."

"It is plausible, Dr. Treadwell." Hatton's voice was cold.

"You're not a clinician, Dr. Hatton. You're not qualified to render that opinion."

"There are others who are."

Robert Treadwell leaned forward intently, a thin, cold smile on his face. He snapped off the tape recorder. "Before you go reaching for those experts, Doctor, you'd do well to consider my differential diagnosis."

"I saw none in your charts."

"I maintain a separate file for situations that can be embarrassing to a patient, particularly one with a husband who wanted to read her medical records."

Hatton's voice took on a steel edge. *"You let Mark Talbot read . . ."*

"I did not. When he asked about Ms. Arcand's condition this spring and early summer and demanded to read her records, I put him off. I then separated her file, pulled out documents that would hurt her in the event that she requested her file, which she has the statutory right to do."

"Why?"

Treadwell's thin smile grew still colder. "Laura Arcand's personal conduct reflects problems with impulse control, and histrionic and narcissistic tendencies, whether or not they merited a formal differential diagnosis. It's not the current scientific fashion to use these terms, but were I to be pressed for a differential diagnosis my gut would tell me that we are dealing with a basic character disorder. I administered an MCMI Two—the Millon Clinical Multiaxial Inventory—to Ms. Arcand when she was first referred to me. I'll send you a copy, along with Milstein's files. Ms. Arcand tests strongly for anger, self-absorption, and a willingness to engage in antisocial behavior. To use the lay terms, Dr. Hatton, I can persuasively describe Ms. Arcand as a self-absorbed, lying, hostile bitch, entirely capable of killing her husband. And if I am hauled into a courtroom, or my reputation is sullied in one, you can be sure that I will explain it to the jury just that way."

Hatton was on his feet, struggling for self-control. "Resign," he demanded. Hatton wanted to say more but anger thickened his tongue. "Immediately."

"Oh, I shall," Treadwell replied, still seated. "But mark this, my friend. You and I both know this is going to end with a trial in which Laura's sanity is put in issue. And if you and her lawyers think I am going to sit still and allow my professional conduct to be attacked, you will be very wrong. I *will* make the jury understand that Laura is a lying, jealous, violent woman who could easily kill her husband— and is legally sane. I've sweet-talked a hundred juries, and they will believe me. Do you understand?"

"I've heard you," Hatton said thickly, the words forced out through his fury. He picked up his briefcase and turned to go.

Treadwell's caustic voice followed him to the door. "Do remember what you've learned here today, Doctor, about the *defensive* practice of medicine," he said.

Hatton looked back at the older man. "I think we all will," he said quietly, then walked silently out of Treadwell's offices. He waited until he was out of the building before switching off the tape recorder in his briefcase.

Chapter Seventeen

The loft was over a hardware store owned by an elderly Japanese man named Kimura in the 3400 block of Rainier Avenue South. It was nearly six o'clock on Friday night, but the bright Indian summer sun still slanted in the west-facing storefront windows. Dust shimmered in the air over the rows of tools and above the steel bins of screws and nails and bolts. Kimura brewed Will Hatton and Mary Slattery strong green tea on a hot plate tucked in an alcove near the back of the store as they waited for Laura Arcand's art dealer to arrive and let them into the loft.

"The lady changed the locks, and I didn't get a key," he said by way of apology, handing Mary Slattery a steaming cup. "I let it pass because she had paid six months' rent in advance. Foolish of me, I know."

"We don't mind waiting, Mr. Kimura," Slattery replied, accepting the cup. "Thank you." Will accepted a second cup of tea and nodded his thanks as Kimura returned to the front of the store.

"How'd you find the place?" Will asked Mary Slattery, his voice low.

"Basically, I just bludgeoned Laura's dealer, Lisa Thayer, into telling me the truth. I told her we knew Laura had some hiding place in the city, and that we had better get there before the cops did. She thought it over, decided I was right, and called me back this afternoon." Slattery blew on her tea to cool it. "How did it go with Treadwell?"

"Swell. He's withdrawing as Laura's treating physician."

"What?" Slattery's surprise raised her voice enough to be heard in the front of the store. Kimura looked up, concerned. Will waved him off with a smile.

"He malpracticed Laura, Mary. Pretty badly. He knew that she was in a declining phase of her bipolar disorder this summer. He only saw her once in the three months before Mark was killed. His chart notes say he just handed her another lithium prescription and lectured her about staying on her meds before leaving on a seven-week vacation. He never considered hospitalizing her, and his chart notes don't show any assignment to another therapist. I'm no clinician, but even I know that isn't the required standard of care."

Slattery thought quickly. "That's not bad, Will. It always helps a jury to have someone other than the defendant to blame for what happened."

"It could be very bad. Treadwell's kept some things out of Laura's file, because Mark wanted to see it. He did a full MCMI II on her when she came to treat with him. That's a kind of personality inventory. Laura's scores aren't very flattering. If Treadwell gets accused of malpractice, he'll fight back by using the MCMI to tell the jury that Laura is latently deceptive and violent."

"Can you deal with that?"

"Possibly not. It could very well be a plausible interpretation of her test scores—and there're enough bad incidents in Laura's history to make that kind of smear believable. But Treadwell's so obviously used the test to protect himself from a malpractice suit that I think you could hurt him in front of a jury, attack his bias, maybe even show that he manipulated the scoring of the test."

"I see." Slattery was still deep in thought when Kimura returned.

"Do you own the building, Mr. Kimura?" Will asked.

"Since 1956." Kimura nodded. "We lived upstairs at first, but business was good and we bought our house in Beacon Hill shortly after that, in 1960. Since then we've rented the loft when we could. It has been vacant the last few years, but I kept the *For Rent* sign in the window." Kimura paused, then added, "Are you sure you wish to wait?"

"Yes, please. I know it's close to your closing time." Will glanced at his watch.

"Has anyone come around recently, asking about the upstairs loft?" Mary Slattery asked, coming back into the conversation.

"No, not since Miss Johns rented it," Kimura replied.

"Johns?" Will asked, foolishly.

"Yes, the lady who paints." Kimura's genial expression was replaced by momentary confused suspicion. He nervously brushed his hands through his thick white hair. "Is there something wrong?" he added.

"No," Mary Slattery replied quickly. "Ms. Johns instructed her sales agent to meet with us here to show us her paintings. Will got the names mixed up, that's all."

Kimura nodded, then went to the front counter to close out his cash register. "Why would she use a false name?" Hatton asked when he had gone. "To keep Mark from finding out?"

"Probably," Mary Slattery replied grimly. "But all we can do now is wait."

Lisa Thayer, Laura Arcand's art dealer, arrived ten minutes later. "I'm so sorry," she said, exasperated. She was tall, nearly five-ten in flat-heeled shoes, and at least seven months pregnant, her bulging belly covered by a light cotton summer dress. Sweat dampened the blonde hair at her temples. "I haven't been on time since I was three months into this pregnancy. I get so spacey." She smiled briefly and touched her abdomen, before her expression darkened. "This whole thing with Laura and Mark is just so tragic. I hope I'm doing the right thing here," she added, looking at Will, puzzled by his presence.

"You are," Mary Slattery replied. "This is Will Hatton. He's a doctor, and a childhood friend of Laura's, here to help me out."

Will stepped forward and shook Thayer's hand. "How long have you known Laura?" he asked.

"Years. Until 1989 I worked at Mark Loudin's, the gallery that represented her in New York. Then I came home and started my own gallery, and we kept in touch, talked on the phone every few months or so. And of course, I saw her when I went to New York, on buying trips. When Laura moved back to Seattle, she wanted a local dealer. We were already friends, so she picked me." Thayer looked again at Will, face tilted in puzzled appraisal. "You look familiar somehow," she said. "Did you meet Laura in New York?"

Will laughed and shook his head. "Nope. Bainbridge Island High School. Anyway," he added, "did you bring the loft key?"

"What? Oh, of course. Here, let me show you the way."

Lisa Thayer led them up the narrow twisting stairs that rose from the back of the store to the loft above, pausing every third step to hold her belly. "He's kicking up a storm," she explained, smiling again. When she reached the landing at the top of the stairs she worked the key in the lock of the door to the loft, then stepped through the doorway. "It's not much," she said, leading them into an oversized, high-ceilinged room nearly the size of the hardware store below. The skylights had been recently cleaned and a thick coat of white paint had been slathered on the cracked, flaking plaster walls, but that was the extent of the renovation. The air was hot and still, even though the double-hung windows overlooking the street had been left open. Traffic noise drifted up from Rainier Avenue. An old camping cot lay in the near corner with a tangled bundle of sheets and blankets piled on it. A washstand and toilet stood on the opposite wall, cracked and stained by age and the constant drip of water. A narrow table on the far wall held a coffeemaker and an open cooler with water in the bottom. A large flat worktable stood in the center of the room with a clutter of paints and bottles and cans of thinner, and a two-pound coffee can cut down to serve as an ashtray. An easel stood with its back to them, its face oriented to the west, facing light from the windows fronting on the street. Stretched canvases leaned against the worktable and the walls.

"What was Laura doing in this dump?" Slattery asked. "She has a beautiful studio at her house on the peninsula."

"I don't know," Lisa Thayer replied. "Laura rented this place in early June, gave me a key in case she lost hers or wanted me to look at some of her work when she wasn't here. All she said was that she felt suffocated trying to work at home, and she didn't think she could work on the island."

"Because of Mark, or her relationship with him?"

"I'm not sure. Mark wasn't spending much time at home. He was a workaholic, often worked nights and weekends. I thought whatever spare time he had was spent rebuilding the beach house on Bainbridge. Laura liked the idea of rebuilding the beach place at first, but by midsummer she was having one of her black periods again, one that didn't seem to lift."

"Can you describe the moods?" Hatton asked.

"Just from what I know, or saw. Laura'd go weeks without calling me, then she'd call at three o'clock in the morning, happy because she'd had a good day with Mark, or they'd just made love and she was still jazzed. The next day, crash. Black thoughts, angry that she couldn't have a child to please Mark, jealous of me for having a baby, worried that Mark was seeing someone else. Sometimes she'd spend a whole day in bed with the covers pulled up over her head, other times she'd be drinking, hanging out in town, acting like the old, wild Laura. I asked if she was still taking her medication. She'd fudge, say she was, but I knew damn well she wasn't. Her mood swings were just too extreme."

"Did you call anybody? Her mother, her shrink, anybody?"

"I tried. Her shrink—Dr. Treadwell?—has got to be the coldest man alive. I called him two or three times, left him long voice mails, but he never returned my calls."

"Why did you call him?" Hatton asked.

"Because Laura was becoming so manic. In late June, after she got this place painted and cleaned up, she moved in and started working. She worked for two days straight, no sleep, and then got really drunk. I told Treadwell I was worried that Laura might crash again."

"And Treadwell never responded?" Will was incredulous.

"Not to me. He must have said something to Laura, though. When she found out, she came into the gallery raving that I had no business messing in her life. After that, since Treadwell didn't seem to be worried, I thought it was better to leave it alone."

The dense hot silence in the room was broken by the sound of Will's voice. "Has Laura shown any new work with you lately?" he asked gently.

"No." Lisa Thayer hesitated, then added, "Laura stopped painting almost two years ago, saying she wanted to put her energy in her marriage for a couple of months. A couple of months stretched into six, then a full year, then more. I was glad when she said she was going to start again. Her work still sells very well. It's the mainstay of my gallery, and it's been tough not having new work of hers to sell. Laura consigned a few paintings from her own collection just so I could have some sales to tide me over. It was a kind of a gift—God knows she and Mark didn't need the money. I've seen a few things she's worked on here, but it's nothing like what she's done before. I don't even know if it could be sold. It's so dark. Let me show you."

Thayer stepped awkwardly to the stacked canvases and began spreading them out around the room. The paintings were indeed dark, fully abstract, with stormy masses of angry reds and dull browns, dark biting grays, and flat blacks.

"When were these painted?" Hatton asked.

Lisa Thayer turned the canvases and checked. "Late July. Early August. These are the ones I've seen before."

"Did you talk to Laura about them?"

"Of course. But there wasn't that much for me to say. They're unsalable, really, even with her name attached. There's no theme, no presentation. Just these ugly masses of paint."

"I wouldn't say that," Hatton said slowly, pausing in front of each canvas, dropping to his knees to examine them. "There's a theme. Anger. Frustration. Bitterness. I've seen this kind of painting before. In therapy work, by hospitalized patients. These pictures have more structure, more skill, than the therapy stuff I've seen—what I'd expect from an artist. But there's no mistaking the emotion."

"No," Lisa Thayer said, "I suppose not. But no one in their right mind would want to hang one of these in their homes. It'd be like living with a manic-depressive."

"Just so," Hatton said mildly. "Is there any later work?"

"There might be. There's a storeroom by the stairs." Lisa turned and stepped into the stairwell, opening a storeroom door Hatton hadn't seen before. "About six more pictures," she said, pulling the first one out. "Could you give me a hand, please?"

Will helped her drag the paintings out of the storeroom and propped the paintings against the long side of the worktable. "They're not dated," he said, checking the back of the canvases.

Thayer brushed her hand across the surface of the paintings. "No varnish," she said. "Still very new. Not more than three or four weeks old, I'd say."

Hatton stood in front of the row of paintings, staring. "Step back and look at them," he said slowly, touching Mary Slattery's arm. His voice dropped with sudden intensity. "What do you see?"

Mary Slattery looked down the line of paintings. If anything, these pictures were angrier than the others. The color theme of red, brown, black, and gray was carried forward, but with a new savagery. Brush strokes had been replaced by angry smears from a palette knife. Clots of black paint were sometimes smeared, sometimes hurled at the canvases, as though in a new and higher level of fury. The last three paintings had been slashed, long angry gashes that tore through the center of each painting.

"Rage," Mary Slattery said softly.

"Perhaps," Will replied. "Focus on the masses of black paint. What do you see?"

"Rorschach blots," Slattery said, frustrated.

"Exactly. Look again, just at the black paint at the center of each painting. Look at how it changes over time. What do you see?"

"A man," she said slowly. "The silhouette of a man. From the shoulders or chest up. Sometimes in three-quarter relief, sometimes full front."

"That's what I see," Hatton said quietly. "A man. Rage. And also, fear."

Chapter Eighteen

T he videotape began with silence. Laura Arcand sat dumbly at a table in the Northlake Hospital library wearing a washed-out blue hospital gown. Her dark hair had been tied back so that the camera focused on her pale, haggard face. Black circles rimmed her eyes. Her hands twitched on the tabletop, fumbling for the cigarettes that weren't there. Rows of medical texts filled the wall behind her, lending an odd formality to the scene.

"Laura," Will spoke softly, out of the camera range. The camera would be trained on Laura alone, so that if the videotape was shown in court, Laura would appear to be speaking directly to the jury. "It's Saturday, September 13, 1997, at ten A.M. Do you understand why you are here?"

"Yes," Laura Arcand said, her voice shaking. "I'm going to try and answer your questions, Dr. Hatton."

"Have you taken any medications today, Laura?"

"Just my prescriptions, this morning."

"Laura, I want you to try to relax, and take yourself back in your mind to the day that Mark died. Can you remember the first thing you did that morning?"

She nodded, her expression blank. When she spoke, her voice was flat. "I woke up alone, in the beach house."

"The beach house is at your mother's home, on Bainbridge Island?"

"Yes. Mark, my mother, and their guests were having some business meetings in the main house. It was late morning. I . . . I didn't feel well. I'd had a lot to drink the night before. I took a long bath and drank some coffee that Mark had left for me in the little kitchen. When I felt better I went for a walk."

"Where did you go?"

"Down the beach. The tide was falling, and I walked. For a couple of hours, I guess. When I came back everyone was eating lunch. I didn't want to join them, so I stayed at the beach house."

"What did you do in the afternoon?"

"I read some magazines, tried to start reading a novel. Then I laid in the sun, out on the deck. I might have slept a little more, but I don't really remember. I was very tired. I hadn't slept much the night before."

"Why didn't you sleep well?"

"I had dreams. The bad ones I told you about before."

"Do you remember your dreams from that night, Laura?"

"Just pieces. Like shards of colored glass. I always remember them as broken, colored glass."

"How do the dreams make you feel, Laura?"

Fear began building in Laura Arcand's eyes. "I'm afraid. I remember that I was afraid, and angry. I remember breathing hard, feeling winded, like I'd been running. I remember the door. I wanted to go out the door and up the path. It took me a long time to get through the door."

"Was something stopping you?"

"The black thing. A black blur." Her voice rose and she spoke rapidly now, her breath coming in ragged, short puffs. "There was noise, like a storm, lightning and thunder, and I finally got away, got out through the door. I ran again, over the hills, for a long time."

"Was it night, or day, Laura? In your dream."

"Sometimes both." She relaxed slightly, breathing deeply. "But the staircase was always in the daylight."

"What staircase, Laura?"

"The crossing staircase. I run up and down the hills, rest, and then I see the crossing staircase, where it's always daylight."

"How did you feel when you found the staircase?"

"Good. Sometimes, anyway. But the staircase is very high. Sometimes I make it to the top, sometimes I don't. And if I don't make it to the top, it's always night again." The fear returned, filling her like cold, rising water, remorseless and inevitable.

Will pressed on, his voice still soft. "Does that make you afraid? That it is night again if you don't get to the top of the staircase?"

"Yes." Nearly the same level of fear as before, but not quite, Will thought, looking at the tape. Why?

"Do you remember anything else about the dreams you had the night before Mark died?" he had asked.

"The good part. I had a little piece of the good part."

"What is 'the good part'?"

"There's a warm wind. It makes me feel good. I feel clean. But then it stops."

"Is it night, or day, when you feel the warm wind?"

"Day, I think. In between. Colored daylight. Maybe it's morning, I don't know. But the daylight has color in it, and I like that."

"What colors?"

"Good ones, like the ones I used to paint in. Cadmium orange and ocher and strontium yellow. Crimson. Cerulean blue."

"Do you paint in those colors now?"

"No."

"Why don't you paint in those colors anymore?"

"I can't. They feel wrong. They don't feel like me." Laura's recorded voice grew tense again. She pressed her hands together on the table to stop their constant shaking.

"You said before that you remember this dream like shards of broken glass. What color is the glass that's broken?"

"Different colors. Dark reds. Black. Burnt sienna. Sometimes there's a piece or two in the daylight colors, but not often."

"Is there anything else you remember about the dream you had the night before Mark died?"

Laura bit her lip and thought hard, the effort plain on her face. "No," she said at last.

"Laura," Will said quietly, "can you talk about your paintings? The new ones that you've been doing."

Laura Arcand stared blankly at the camera, as though unaware of its presence. She wrapped her arms tightly around herself and said nothing.

"Laura," Will repeated. "Can you talk about your new paintings?"

"I didn't want anyone to see them," she mumbled, eyes cast down.

"Why, Laura?"

Her words came in a sudden rush. "They're about the dreams, the bad parts of the dreams, the broken glass, the blackness at the center. I tried to paint them . . . I thought if I could paint them and stick them to the canvas that I'd stop having them."

Will, off camera, had listened to the rush of the words, noted their childlike cadence. "Have you had the black part of the dreams for a long time, Laura?"

"Years. They started when I was a teenager. But then they went away for a long time."

"When did they start coming back?"

"This spring. Early summer. When Mark and I slept in the old beach house the night before we started to tear it down. That's when they started coming back."

"Did you talk to Mark about them?"

"Yes. A lot. I knew they were bad for us. I wanted to talk them out with him."

"Did he listen?"

"Yes." The adult Laura returned, more assured, more measured in her speech, her voice softened by affection. "Mark really listened. We talked about them, almost the way we've done today. He . . . he really wanted to help me with them. I'd wake up frightened and sweating, sometimes throwing up, and Mark would hold me and help me clean myself." Tears swelled in her eyes and ran down her cheeks but she did not sob. "I loved him so much for doing that," she said softly.

Laura Arcand froze. Her hands clenched into fists. Her head fell back and her eyes rolled back into their sockets. She drew her arms up to her body and began to convulse as she slipped out of the chair to the floor.

Will Hatton leaped out of his chair and punched the emergency alarm on the wall intercom. "Get an emergency team to the library!" he shouted. "She's having a seizure." Hatton shoved the furniture out of the way of Laura's rolling convulsions and dropped to the floor. He rolled Laura's head to the side and shoved his wadded handkerchief between her teeth. When the convulsions eased he pulled the handkerchief out of Laura's mouth and listened to her broken sobs. Hatton stayed on the floor with her and held her in his arms until the emergency team arrived, five long minutes later.

Chapter Nineteen

Laura Arcand lay back on her hospital bed. "I really do feel stronger, Will. I'd like to finish this today if we can."

"I'm not sure you should," Will replied. "The seizure ran its course in about six minutes, but—have you ever had a seizure before? You don't have any history of epilepsy."

"I think I must have. Twice, anyway. It happened when I was working on the new paintings. I was working very hard, really slashing away, both times late at night, and I found myself on the floor." She laughed hollowly. "I thought it was just fatigue. And vodka." She sighed. "Let's finish this, Will."

"It's only going to get harder. I'm going to have to ask you about the night Mark died."

"I know. But if we don't do this now I may never be able to do it."

"It's one-seventeen P.M. on Saturday, September thirteenth," Will Hatton said on the tape, when they had returned to the hospital library. "At eleven-oh-four this morning Ms. Arcand suffered a seizure of unknown origin that lasted six minutes. In the past two hours, her life signs have returned to essentially normal and we are continuing this interview at her request."

Will paused. "Laura, I want you to go back to the day Mark died. You're on the deck, lying in the sun, reading. What did you do after that?"

Her eyes closed in thought. "I dozed for a while, I think. I felt warm, and good. But when I woke up I felt very anxious." Her word choice was adult, her voice was strong and sounded nearly normal. But her hands continued to twitch until she hid them under the table.

"What were you anxious about?"

"Mark." Her voice and expression softened. "He'd been working so hard, and these meetings were important to him. I felt that by sitting there I was letting him down with his problems, even though he was trying to help me with mine."

"What happened next?"

"Mark came back to the beach cottage. It was late in the afternoon. He looked exhausted, like he'd had a really hard day. I wanted him to stay for a little while and make love with me. But he said we couldn't, we had to go up to the house for dinner, and some of the people there wanted to meet me. It was important to him, so I got dressed for dinner and we went up to my mother's house."

"Why did you want Mark to make love with you?"

She looked down at the table. "So Mark would feel happier. So I wouldn't feel so alone. I always felt alone in the beach house."

"Did you and Mark make love often?"

"No. It was difficult for him when he was feeling stressed."

"You and Mark rebuilt the beach house just this past summer, right?"

"Yes." Laura brightened; her voice took on a new intensity. "I *loved* tearing the old house down. I wish we'd left it that way."

"Why?"

"Because I hated the old house."

"Why?"

"I don't know. I loved it when my mother and I first moved there. It was like having a grown-up-sized fort all my own. I spent a lot of time painting there, even slept there in the summer. But it changed. It felt cold and dark and musty, like a haunted house. I stayed away from it for years. But when we tore it down . . . the wood frame was *beautiful,* like old weathered bones, purified by fire and opened up to the wind and sky."

Where the hell did that come from? Hatton asked himself. For most of the interview Laura had been tense and reticent, her affect almost flat until she had spun into the seizure. Yet somehow the re-membered sight of the nearly demolished beach house filled her with something very close to joy. Hatton glanced at the tape counter and jotted the counter number into his notes.

"How did you feel after it was rebuilt?" Hatton said on the tape.

"I thought it was ugly." Laura's voice was harsh and her eyes glinted with anger. "I stayed on the deck whenever I could."

"Okay," Will said. "It's nearly two o'clock, Laura, do you want to take a break?"

"No, I'm all right."

"Fine. Laura, I want to talk to you now about the night that Mark died. Are you prepared to do that?"

Laura Arcand stared straight at the camera. Her eyes flooded with new tears. She made no move to brush them away as she nodded her agreement.

"Laura, you're at the dinner, seated at the table. What are you feel-ing?"

"Nervous. Mark has gotten upset at something. He's very quiet. I'm drinking a lot of wine, and not eating very much. After a while I can feel the wine hit me and then I'm not so nervous anymore."

"As the dinner goes on, what are you thinking? Are you angry, happy, sad, what?"

"I'm not really feeling much of anything. I tried to smile and be polite. When dinner was nearly over I went outside to smoke." She shook her head ruefully. "I was fairly drunk by then, Doctor. Things start to blur about that time."

"Do you remember throwing a drink at Mark?"

Laura blushed faintly, but nodded. "It was so childish."

"Were you angry with Mark when you left?"

"Yes." Her voice was slowing, in embarrassment, or fear of what was coming. "I thought Mark might be having an affair with a woman who worked for him. I really wasn't angry about that. You have to understand . . . I hadn't been a good wife for him, I knew that, and if he—well, I wouldn't complain. But I didn't like having her *there*, in my *mother's* house, smiling at him, fawning on him."

"How did throwing the drink at Mark make you feel?"

"Embarrassed," she responded. "Silly. Poor Mark, his crazy wife at it again."

"What do you remember after throwing the drink at Mark?"

"I left. I was crying because I was ashamed. I went out of the house and ran down the trail toward the beach house. Or actually, I know I *must* have done that, but I don't remember it."

"Did Mark come with you?"

"No . . . I went back by myself. I drank some more wine that we had in the beach house. And then I passed out."

"What happened after that?"

"It got very late, I think. It felt like I had been asleep for a while, because I felt stiff and my mouth was dry. Then Mark came in."

"What was he like?"

Laura looked bewildered at her memory. "It was so strange, Mark was drunk. Really, really angry drunk. That wasn't like him. Mark usually didn't drink at all. Beer on a hot day, a glass of wine at dinner. But he stumbled into the beach house calling my name."

"Calling your name? How?"

"Kind of singsongy. 'Little Laura.' He kept calling me 'little Laura,' 'sweet little Laura,' things like that." Laura looked confused again, then uneasy, her eyes darting around the room, breathing hard as the fear built up inside her. "Then his voice turned angry, and mean."

"Did Mark talk to you that way in bed, or during sex?"

"*No!* He never did. He seemed . . . different, not himself. He peeled off his shirt and walked around the room, drinking out of a bottle, still talking that way."

"What did you do?"

"I was afraid. I was in the bed and I kind of shrank into a corner."

"What did Mark do?"

"He got angry. He wanted me to suck him, and I wouldn't, and he got angry. He hit me, a couple of times."

"Where did he hit you?"

"In the face. In the belly. On my breasts."

"Did Mark ever hit you before?"

"No. Never."

"How did he hit you?"

"He slapped me, hard. Then he hit me with his fist, in the face."

"What did you do?"

"I just tried to get away from him."

"Did he come after you?"

"Not right away. He slid down his pants. I wouldn't play with him, so he played with himself."

"With his penis?"

"Yes. He stroked it until it got really big and hard. And then he came after me again."

"Did he say anything else?"

Laura's eyes widened. Her voice grew soft, her cadence almost childlike. "Yes. He said, 'Take me in your mouth, get me wet, and I'll teach you. Just touch it, touch it.'"

"Did you want to do that?"

"No. I was really frightened. I . . . I didn't know what to do."

"Did Mark do anything else?"

"He grabbed my hair and pulled me to him and put his penis in my mouth. I didn't want to do that, so I tried to get away again."

"Could you get away?"

"No. Not right away." Anger flashed in her eyes. "I was really scared. And then I remembered."

"What did you remember?"

"The nightstand. There was an old wooden nightstand beside the bed, with a drawer. I remembered there was a gun in the drawer. I got away from him and found the gun. I pointed it at him and told him to go away."

Hatton felt the room shrink to claustrophobic proportions. His mouth was suddenly dry.

"What happened then?" he asked softly.

"He laughed and got the bottle and took another drink. Then he got angry again. He balled up his fists and started to walk toward me."

"What did you do?"

"I pulled the trigger. There was a big blue flash."

"What happened to Mark?"

Laura's voice rose in fear and dismay, the childish cadence back in her words. "He was shot—there was blood on his arm. He screamed. He fell down. When he got up he went out the door, up the hill, the bluff path."

"What did you do?"

"Nothing, at first. I was too scared to move. Then I ran. I ran for a long time. It felt like I'd run for hours. But then I was back on the beach again."

"How did you get to the beach again, Laura?"

"I don't know. It's like I went all the way to the top of the crossing staircase, and then fell all the way back down again."

"Where was Mark?"

Laura looked confused again. "He was gone. I'd thought he'd run away, and I was glad. But then I looked down at the water. He was there, lying down, in the sand. His legs were in the tide pool." Her voice grew breathy, panicky. "I called his name, over and over. He didn't answer. I tried to pull him up. I couldn't. He was too big, too heavy. I turned him over but he wasn't . . . wasn't breathing."

"What happened then?"

"I laid down beside him." Laura's voice grew soft. Dark, weary pain filled her eyes. "I knew he was dead. I knew what I wanted. I wanted to die with him."

"Do you remember cutting your wrists with your ring?" Hatton asked.

"No." Laura shook her head wearily.

"Do you remember anything else about that night?"

"No." Laura was looking down at the table in front of her, her head bowed as if in prayer, or in shame. "No."

"Laura."

No response.

"Laura, did you want to kill your husband?"

She reared up from her chair, screaming. "No! Oh God, no!"

Laura Arcand threw herself on the table in front of her, sobbing.

Will Hatton's flat voice came on the tape again. "Ms. Arcand is not able to continue this interview. It's three-forty-six P.M."

The replay of the tape ended. It was nearly eight o'clock on Saturday night.

Edwin Hauser sat back in his chair. There were tears in his eyes. "Jesus Christ," he whispered.

"What?" Mary Slattery said impatiently, her voice strident. "That was great fucking TV! This gives us a *chance,* Ed. Self-defense. Spousal rape is still rape."

"No, it doesn't," Ed Hauser said, his voice bitter with anger and frustration. "She made it up. Goddamnit, she must have made it up."

"Why?"

"Her story is just all wrong. Mark and I talked in the library in the main house until quarter to one in the morning about the problems in the Elk Run project. Mark wasn't drunk, he wasn't even drinking. Mark didn't drink at business dinners, period. And look at the hospital records." Hauser picked up a half-inch stack of paper, then threw it on the conference table.

"Look at them!" he shouted, venting his frustration and anger. "There's no bruises on Laura's face, chest, or arms. Mark was six-two and weighed about two twenty-five. If Laura'd been in the fight with him she describes, she'd be black-and-blue from the waist up, have a couple of broken ribs, maybe a broken arm." Hauser turned to Will Hatton, furious. "Damn it, you said she could handle this interview. Didn't you tell her that she couldn't lie? That if she lied they would convict her with this tape?"

"Of course I did," Will said mildly. "But you're partly right, Ed. It didn't happen the way Laura said. It couldn't have."

"Why not?" Slattery demanded.

"Three impossibilities. No, four of them. First, Mark wasn't shot in the beach house. There was no blood spatter inside the house, and the autopsy report says the first bullet clipped an artery. If Mark'd been shot inside the beach house, there would have been blood all over the floor and the walls.

"Second, Laura says she shot Mark in the arm. She didn't. Both bullets hit him in the chest, at least six inches away from his shoulders, much less his arms."

Will got up and picked up a diagram mounted on a large foam core board that was leaning against the far wall. "Third, Laura's got the layout of the beach house wrong. Look at the architects' drawings." Hatton pointed to the floor plan. "Laura said that after she shot Mark he got up, went through the door, and stumbled *up* the path, but there's no door there. The only entrance or exit is through the French doors facing the deck, on the water side. Fourth, Laura couldn't have gotten the gun from a nightstand. There isn't a nightstand in the beach house—not now, anyway."

"So she's lying, and we're fucked," Slattery said flatly. "We can't hide that tape from the prosecution if we're going to plead insanity. It's part of Will's examination record. We'll have to plead her out."

"Hold on," Will said. "I didn't say Laura was lying. I remember the old beach house pretty well, the way it used to be. There *was* a door on the land side, right at the foot of the old path down the bluff." He pointed to the drawing. "Here. Just as Laura said. That path up the bluff isn't there anymore; the slope north of the stream has been reinforced with rock, and the stairs were built to go down the bluff." Hatton hesitated, then went on. "I don't think Laura's lying. I don't think she made this up. I don't think she was acting when she had that seizure. She's got no history of epilepsy, but the seizure she had was almost certainly psychogenic, stress induced."

"What are you suggesting?" Ed asked.

"That what happened to Laura in 1972 and what happened to her last weekend are connected," Will replied.

"How?" Ed Hauser demanded.

Will shook his head and frowned. "I need another day, maybe two."

Hauser's face fell in defeat. "Don't take too long, Will. If we're going to have to plead her out, the price is only going to get higher," he said wearily. He stood up. "I need a drink," he said abruptly, then stalked out of the room before anyone could follow.

Chapter Twenty

Mary Slattery gritted her teeth and sipped at her hot black coffee with great care. The harsh fluorescent lights in the MV *Walla Walla*'s galley seemed to hurt her eyes.

"Tough Saturday night?" Will Hatton inquired gently.

Slattery glared at him, drank more coffee, and spooned rubbery scrambled eggs onto her toast. "Not at all," she said archly. "A late dinner meeting of the Prosecutorial Women's Association, retired division."

"Any particular points of discussion?"

"The worthlessness of men in general, and you in particular."

Hatton grinned. "I'm flattered. I think. Did we make any more progress on locating Steven Terry?"

"Tony's still working on it. He's following up on a couple of unsatisfied malpractice judgments against Terry. One of the lawyers who has a client holding a judgment—Ted Brack, do you know him?—thinks Terry left the state at least ten years ago. It looks like he dropped pretty far down the food chain, wherever he went. Why do you want him so bad?"

"Because he just might be able to confirm what we're about to try to do."

"And what's that? Ride the six-twenty A.M. ferry to Bainbridge Island on a Sunday morning?"

"No. Ride it back to Seattle and see if we can figure out where Laura went during the four days that she disappeared."

"I still don't get it," Mary Slattery said stubbornly as they trudged up Western Avenue from the Madison Street ferry terminal, up the hill toward the Pike Place Market. "Laura's disappearance was over twenty-five years ago. And you think these dreams are going to tell you where she went? That's crazy. No pun intended."

"There's lots of ways to interpret Laura's dreams," Will responded patiently. "A Freudian analyst would view them as symbols, pushing Oedipal or Electra notions. I don't believe that. Laura's dreams may be the result of badly stored, fragmented memories. The repressed-memory folks believe that traumatic memories are perfectly stored, then repressed because they are too awful for the conscious mind to deal with. To put it mildly, there isn't much scientific evidence to support that, even though it was the prevailing wisdom for more than sixty years. Today we think that memory is a complex bioelectrical process that stores both true and false information. The hippocampus portion of the brain is involved in ways we don't fully understand yet. But we know memories can be suggested, distorted, or scrambled on formation if the person is under stress or on drugs, or whatever. Distorted, fragmented memories can show up in recurrent dreams. Give old Freud at least that much credit. So what I'm trying to figure out is if any of Laura's dreams can give us a clue to what happened to her, to identify the stressor that caused her PTSD."

"How are you going to prove what happened?"

"'Prove' is too strong a word. But a good working hypothesis, with some facts, would help me sell a PTSD diagnosis in court."

"But we can't get Laura's story in evidence without at least some proof."

Will grinned. "That's what you pay expert witnesses for, Slattery."

Will paused and looked uphill, past the University Street stairs to the bulk of the market's buildings, set like building blocks on the steep slope up to First Avenue. "Look, we know Laura showed up in Seattle after she ran away. I'm just going to try to follow the key points in the dream: the door, the path, the running, the wind, the crossing staircase. Assume the door and the path were real, and represent the beach house. Laura's been badly abused, possibly raped. She's frightened and runs. She was too young to drive, but Laura and her friends often hitchhiked or walked to the ferry terminal in Winslow and went into town, usually to come here to the market. I did the same thing. I was always haunting the used-book stalls in the lower market, or buying grass from some hippie in Post Alley. My guess, if I've got the sequence right, is that Laura was attacked, fled across the island, got on the ferry, and headed up toward the market. She'd have found other kids hanging out there, maybe somebody to take her in."

"That's a lot of long guesses."

"Maybe." Will paused below a blank-faced yellowed stucco warehouse and pointed ahead. "Tell me what you see."

Mary Slattery looked, paused, looked again. "A staircase."

"A crossing staircase, one that switchbacks up the hill."

"Okay," Slattery said reluctantly. "That's the way it looks now. What about 1972?"

"The vote to save the market from redevelopment was in 1969. By 1972 they'd started to renovate it, and rebuilt the staircase connecting the market to Western Avenue and the waterfront. The elevator and the kids' play area and landscaping came later, but the staircase was here."

"So where would she go from here?"

"Up. The lower stalls sold all kinds of junk back then—books, used clothes, beadwork—plus there were old record stores, head shops. The produce stalls and fish markets were on the upper level, where they are now. If Laura was hungry, there were day-old bread stores, a soup kitchen, the produce stalls, cheap cafés. If she had to, she could panhandle the tourists. I bet she was hungry."

Slattery followed him up the steps. They ended at the center of the market, where Pike Place turns to the north, under the market clock. When they reached the top of the stairs, Will pushed his way through the late-season tourist crowd onto the cobblestones of Pike Place. He turned to look back into the market and idly patted Harriet, a life-size bronze piggy bank that had been mounted on the sidewalk under the clock, thinking. "I'm trying to remember what was here," he said, suddenly unsure of himself. "City Fish was here then. Loback Meats. They're gone now, but the sign is still there. The produce stalls look about right. There used to be a kind of a garage sale thing, used clothes for fifty cents a bag, down that way. But nothing strikes me as a landmark she might have picked up on."

Will led her down the row of produce and craft stalls, occasionally stopping to buy sausage, cheese, tomatoes, and fruit, and stowing them in his canvas rucksack. "I thought I might as well do my shopping," he said apologetically, picking up six ears of late-season white sweet corn. "But this isn't getting us anywhere."

They walked on the grassy knoll in Steinbrueck Park, Slattery watching the clouds begin to roll in across the sound.

"What now?" she asked.

"I'm not sure," Hatton replied. "If Laura ran from the market, she could have caught a bus anywhere in the city. Most likely to Broadway, on Capitol Hill, or the University district. But those neighborhoods have changed so much we'd probably never track her. Let me take another look at the police reports." Slattery passed over the thin file, the cardboard dusty from years in storage. Will quickly scanned the yellowing sheets of old thermofax paper. "Yup, the U district. The cops picked her up from the alley between University Way and Brooklyn, down near where the law school is now, around midnight on Saturday, the twenty-sixth. I suppose I should call Joel Richter again. He's an assistant secretary of the Department of Social and Health Services now, but he ran the juvenile facility at Twelfth and Alder between 1970 and 1982. I called him last Friday to see if he could find any old files on Laura. Let's see if he's come up with anything." Will strode off to find a phone booth in the Cutter's Restaurant building at the north end of the park. He returned a few minutes later, a bemused smile on his face.

"Joel says he found a couple of things," Will said. "He's home if we want to come get them. He said to bring two pounds of salmon fillets, four ears of corn, a pound of asparagus, four Yellow Finn potatoes, and two bottles of chardonnay."

. . .

Joel Richter roasted the potatoes and corn in a gas grill on the back deck of his modest Shoreline district split-level. "They'll take half an hour or so," he announced, his slight, wiry figure leaning against the deck rail. A carefully nurtured perennial garden filled most of the small backyard behind him, alive with late-season flowers. An unaccustomed smile split his dark, normally mournful features. A rabbi's face, Will had always thought, radiating intelligence and compassion, but always at a distance. "The kids are away at camp, so we can indulge in a modest vice or two. Will, Mary, you guys want a martini or something?"

"Vodka, not gin," Will replied. "Please."

"Coward. Typical M.D. Afraid of gin, the vice of the people. Okay. Wait, here comes Susan, bearing gifts."

Susan Richter placed a drink tray on the garden table at the center of the deck. She was a slightly stocky, honey-haired woman in her late forties, a child psychologist with a thriving if not lucrative practice, an Alabama drawl, a husband and children she loved, and an air of impenetrable calm that came from knowing that the world could be both wonderful and bestial at the same time. Will had worked with her on court-ordered child abuse evaluations, a part of his practice that he detested and had given up five years before.

"I read the records on Laura Arcand, Will," she said. "And I remember her. I was working at Juvenile as a psychology intern that summer she was brought in." Susan busied her hands with building a pitcher of martinis as she spoke. "Joel and I had just started dating back in '72, that might be why I remember that summer so well. We caused a *substantial* scandal." She smiled at her husband, busy brushing a peach glaze on the salmon fillets beside the grill.

"Take a look at a picture of Laura," Will said, "just to double-check."

Susan Richter accepted the picture and sat down as her husband began to pour drinks. "Yeah, I remember. Such a beautiful girl. She came in pretty beat-up. She had a shiner a couple of days old and some traces of dried blood on her face, and a lot of old and new bruises, face and body, some not more than twelve hours old. I had our duty doctor take a look at her. I wanted her sent to Harborview for evaluation, but he said she'd be all right. I was so new I didn't fight him. I thought the girl had been hit pretty hard, maybe concussed."

"How did she present?" Will asked.

"Hungry, disoriented. No sense of place or time. And scared. Very, very scared."

"Could she identify herself? Speak coherently?"

"No. I checked on her a couple of hours after she was brought in, and she couldn't even remember her own name. That's when I got really scared myself. So I called Joel and demanded that he override Dr. Sarkanian, that drunken old fool. He did, and we sent her to Harborview. They did a series of X rays, didn't pick up any fracture or internal bleeding, and sent her back a couple of hours later."

"Jesus," Will said. "Even though she was displaying traumatic amnesia?"

"Even so. We were off duty when she came back in. I'd marked her file for special treatment, to hold her in the infirmary. Some idiot didn't look at the file and sent her into the pit."

"The pit?" Mary Slattery asked.

"Yeah," Joel Richter replied, clearly embarrassed. He ignored a warning look from his wife and lit a small dark cigar. "Before Twelfth and Alder was rebuilt in the late eighties, there was a general area for the kids, segregated by gender but still pretty open."

"What happened?"

"The Arcand girl got beat up again. She got crosswise with a couple of other girls and they took her."

Mary Slattery reached for a cigarette from her purse. "How bad was it?"

"Not that severe, physically. But God knows what it did to a kid who'd already been traumatized for two or three days."

"What did you do?" Slattery asked.

"We both came back on duty on Monday morning," Richter replied. "We found what happened and pulled her out of there, back into the infirmary. By that time the SPD had picked up the missing persons report from Kitsap County and identified her. Her mother's lawyer showed up with an order, and we released her."

"What did you think happened to Laura?" Slattery asked, finishing her martini. "Sexual abuse, street violence, what?"

"I was pretty sure it was sexual abuse," Susan Richter replied, rising to place the salmon on the grill. "I called the Kitsap County sheriff's department and they said the girl lived alone with her mother, there wasn't a man in the house, and the mother was a successful businesswoman who clearly loved her daughter and was very distressed by her daughter's disappearance. So I decided I was wrong."

"Maybe not," Will Hatton replied. "I'm pretty sure somebody tried to rape Laura, maybe succeeded, and that's what caused her to run. The question I can't answer is, who did it?"

Later that Sunday night Hatton and Slattery returned to the war room at the Hauser and Todd offices. Ed Hauser and Reuben Todd joined them shortly after eight o'clock. Todd looked thoughtful but rested after a half day's sail on the sound. Hauser was drained and pale after spending Sunday with Ellen and Laura at Northlake Hospital.

"Let me try to lay this out," Will said. He rummaged nervously for a marking pen on the conference table, then opened the white drawing board set in a cabinet on the wall.

"Here's what we know," he said, printing rapidly in block letters on the board.

"First, Laura disappeared for four days, Thursday night, August 24, to Monday afternoon, August 28, 1972. She returned emotionally traumatized, physically beaten, with a head injury that left her no apparent memory of what happened to her during those four days.

"Second. We can assume that she was traumatized, perhaps by an attempted rape, in the beach house, and that's where she ran from."

"We can't be sure of that," Ed Hauser said. "If I remember right, Ellen said Laura had gone out with a crowd of island kids to a party that night."

"Maybe," Will said. "But Laura was sleeping in the beach house nearly every night that summer, and it's probable she went back there after the party. It's also consistent with the fear and distaste she displayed for the beach house, even after the house was rebuilt.

"Third. In the past five months Laura has been heading for a major depressive episode, all the way to psychosis. She has had repeated intrusive dreams and memories of a traumatizing event that she associates with a man. She can't suppress the memories during the descending phase of her bipolar mood swings. The dreams and memories are fragmentary but—again, my assumption—are of real events: a sexual attack in the beach house, her flight across the island, and her subsequent beatings in Seattle.

"Fourth. Laura's mental condition deteriorated even further in late summer of this year. She cycled rapidly between manic and depressive phases, heading for a major crack-up. In her manic phases she tried to remember what had happened to her, by talking her dreams out with Mark and by trying to identify her attacker by painting him. The intrusive memories of her trauma, which she experiences mostly as dreams, are now driving the cycling of Laura's manic and depressive phases. It's like a feedback loop: the depression gets worse, which makes the memories more intrusive and painful, which makes the depression worse. On and on.

"Fifth. Laura's shrink, Robert Treadwell, failed to treat her adequately. By Labor Day weekend she was in the grip of a major depressive episode, near suicidal. She was self-medicating with alcohol, which only makes her depression worse. She was approaching a psychotic state, beginning to lose contact with reality.

"Sixth. Conclusion. When Mark came back to the beach house on the night he was killed, he somehow re-created the conditions that Laura remembered from the attack she suffered in 1972. Maybe it was nothing more than Mark coming into the beach house late, in the dark, stripping off his clothes, possibly trying to engage Laura in sex. Laura then suffered a psychotic break with reality. She had a flashback—in essence, her mind lost the ability to sort and distinguish the memory of her prior attack from reality. And believing herself in terrible danger, Laura reached for a gun that either she or Mark had brought to the beach house. Mark retreated onto the beach, where Laura shot him. She then attempted suicide."

Will put down the pen and stared at the list of points he had written. When he turned, he saw Ed standing next to Reuben Todd at the back of the room. Todd was shaking his head, his lips pursed skeptically.

"Better find Laura's 1972 psychiatrist, Will," Todd said. "You need him to corroborate the nature of the trauma, explain that Laura has never been able to consciously remember it. Next, you'd better find the rapist who attacked Laura in 1972. At least find somebody—a drifter, a convicted sex offender who was in the area—anyone who could look plausible. But above all else, we've *got* to find out what happened to the gun. If Laura really wanted to kill herself, why didn't she use the gun on herself as well as Mark? Why did she gouge her wrists instead? If Laura really did hide the gun, no jury will believe she was insane."

"I agree it's got holes," Will said. "Mary?"

"It sounds like a great story, Will," she said sardonically. "Too bad you could pack all the evidence that supports it into a raindrop, with room left over."

"Ed?"

Hauser looked pensive. He tapped a tape cassette he was holding against the tabletop. "Mary, call Tiernan tonight, at home. Tell him we're ready to plead. Don't say what we'll plead. Call the court tomorrow morning and set the continued arraignment for Tuesday morning. Draft notices of the insanity and diminished-capacity defenses." He tossed the cassette on the table. "I've got an idea."

Part III

1972

September 16–October 18, 1997

Chapter Twenty-one

"Please stop the car," Laura Arcand said quietly. "I'm afraid I'm going to be sick again."

Mary Slattery nodded sympathetically and pulled off Highway 3 onto a side street in Gorst, a nasty slash of used car dealerships, RV repair shops, and dark taverns just south of the Bremerton Navy Yard. It was not quite seven-thirty in the morning and the skies were leaden with promised rain.

"Take your time," Mary said. She got out of her BMW as Laura paced restlessly in front of the car, walking off her nausea. When the spasms had passed, Laura remained on the street and lit one of the Marlboros that Will had insisted Slattery bring for her. Laura wore a gray skirted suit, the sort of bland off-the-rack outfit she normally detested, but one selected by Ed after much thought and care. The arraignment would be Laura's first public appearance since Mark's death. The odds were that at least one of the jurors would have his or her first look at Laura Arcand on the local six o'clock news that night, and Ed wanted Laura to look as saddened and conservative as possible.

"Thank you," Laura said politely after she had finished her cigarette and gotten back into the car. "Could you please tell me again what is going to happen? I wasn't able to focus very well yesterday."

"Of course," Mary replied. "We're going to the courthouse early so that the Kitsap County sheriff's office can fingerprint you and take your picture to enter into their information system. We've been promised that they won't perp-walk you into the courtroom—"

"Perp-walk?"

"Walking you down a corridor lined with press and photographers so that you get jostled and butted, and have bad pictures taken that make you look guilty. They've promised not to do that, but I don't trust them. If it happens, I'll guide you through the mob. Just relax and follow me. Once we're inside the courtroom, the judge will control the crowd. The judge will ask you a few questions, to confirm that you're represented by counsel and able to understand everything that's going on. Then you'll plead not guilty. Whatever you do, don't lose your temper, don't smile, don't acknowledge anyone other than Ed, me, and the judge. Do you understand?"

"Of course," Laura replied, her face ashen. "It's just not something I ever expected I'd have to do."

"No one does," Mary Slattery replied.

They faced a gauntlet of press, strobe lights exploding in their faces.

Thomas Tiernan, the Kitsap County chief criminal deputy, looked blankly at Mary Slattery. "Someone must have leaked," he said unctuously.

"Fuck you, Tiernan," Slattery hissed between clenched teeth. She pulled Laura's arm and urged her forward into the corridor, using her and Laura's height to deny Tiernan, a full three inches shorter than either of them, the press photos he had so clearly tried to set up. By the time they reached the door to courtroom 2, Laura's composure and belly had nearly given way to another bout of nausea, but she gulped at the slightly fresher air of the courtroom and put her arms around Ed Hauser's stocky chest. He gathered Laura under one arm and swept her past the remaining reporters into the courtroom, a confident, somber frown stitched across his blunt, reddened face. Slattery followed, suppressing a grin. You've got to love Ed for it, she thought. He lets his ego off the leash with more style than any three lawyers I ever knew.

They had barely found seats in the second row of benches when the clerk announced the judge's arrival. Henry Thorvaldson took the bench briskly, waving the packed courtroom back down. "Please hold the chain for a moment," he said to his bailiff, who quickly telephoned the jail captain to have him keep the prisoners waiting for arraignment out of the courtroom until Laura's arraignment had been completed. They would wait in the jail, shackled hand and foot to a steel chain, kept on hold until the media feeding of Laura's arraignment was over.

Thorvaldson called the calendar. "This is the Superior Court of the State of Washington for Kitsap County," he said. "This is the criminal calendar. Before the clerk calls the first matter, I do understand that there is extensive press interest today. The rules of this courtroom when I'm in it are pretty simple. No talking, joking, outbursts, smoking, or photography. I enforce these rules harshly on everyone. Clerk, please call the first matter."

"State versus Laura Marie Arcand," clerk Sylvia Morita called out, more loudly than usual. Judith Watkins, the county prosecutor, moved to the bar with Thomas Tiernan at her side.

"Defendant is ready, Your Honor," Ed Hauser said, shepherding Laura past the bar and into the well of the court.

"The state is also ready, Your Honor," Judith Watkins replied.

Thorvaldson nodded. "Ms. Arcand," he began, "are you well enough to understand and participate in this court session today?"

"Yes sir," Laura replied, her voice barely above a whisper.

"Are you taking any medication that could interfere with your understanding?"

"Only my prescribed medicines, sir. I think I can understand."

"Mr. Hauser and Ms. Slattery are your attorneys, correct?"

"Yes sir."

Thorvaldson looked at Hauser. "Since this is a continuation of arraignment, your client doesn't have the right to have the information read again, but I'll allow it if she wants it."

"Not necessary, Your Honor," Hauser replied. "But thank you. Ms. Arcand is ready to plead."

"Ms. Arcand, do you understand the charge against you?"

"I do, Your Honor."

"And how do you plead?"

"Not guilty, Your Honor." Laura's ragged whisper carried across the silent courtroom, the expectant buzz from the press section following in its wake.

"Very well. Today is September sixteenth. Omnibus hearing is set for"—Thorvaldson tapped a few keys on the computer hidden below the railing of the bench—"Friday, October third. Anyone on either trial team going to be out of the office for Rosh Hashanah?"

"Reuben Todd will be, Judge, but sometimes he lets me come to court by myself," Hauser replied.

Thorvaldson refused to smile. "I'll take that as a no," he said gruffly. "What about trial dates?"

"As soon as possible, Your Honor," Hauser said, scowling for the benefit of the press. "Ms. Arcand wants to resolve this case and resume her life as best she can after her tragic loss."

Thomas Tiernan hesitated, suspicion plain on his wide-boned, fleshy face. Judith Watkins broke the silence for him. "I agree, Your Honor. The sooner the better. This is a simple case. I'd say three days for jury selection, five trial days for the state."

"Mr. Hauser?"

"Five days jury selection, five trial days for the defense case," Hauser replied, looking at Tiernan, who still appeared worried.

Thorvaldson looked at them both with close appraisal, then suppressed a smile. "You're all in luck, Counsel. Judge Cairns just had two very lengthy matters settle. She has a four-week block open . . . starting October twenty-seventh."

Hauser's voice boomed. "Thank you, Your Honor. We accept. October twenty-seventh."

Slattery closed her eyes and repressed a curse. October 27? They couldn't possibly be ready.

Tiernan's face was glazed with a look of slow calculation. "Your Honor," he began.

Thorvaldson looked down, his eyes narrowed in irritation. "Excuse me, Mr. Tiernan, but it's customary, at least in this court, for the elected county prosecutor to speak for the state on the days when he or she is present." Thorvaldson looked hard at Judith Watkins. "Madam Prosecutor? Can the state be ready?"

Watkins hesitated, an angry scarlet blush spreading across her face, acutely conscious of the three-deep wall of reporters packing the courtroom. "Of course we can be," she snapped, ignoring Thomas Tiernan's barely perceptible shaking head.

"So ordered," Thorvaldson barked. "Trial is set for October 27, 1997. Anything else?"

"I'd like to get a formality concluded in open court, Your Honor, so there's no dispute about this later," Hauser said.

"Go on."

"Your Honor, the defense tenders its notices of insanity and diminished-capacity defenses to the prosecution, as required by statute." Hauser handed the notices to Judith Watkins with a flourish and a small nod, his head turned away from the bench to hide his grin.

"What?" Judith Watkins's voice rose an octave in outrage.

"Is that a request, Madam Prosecutor?" Thorvaldson asked acidly.

"He can't do that," Watkins stammered. "He can't plead her not guilty and then plead her insane at the same time. It's got to be one or the other."

"Nothing in the statute requires it," Ed replied smoothly. "The law clearly allows alternative not guilty or insanity pleas, or both pleas to be made simultaneously. If you have any doubt, please review—"

"I'm familiar with the statute."

"Thank you, Your Honor."

"Wait," Judith Watkins called out again. "I mean, Your Honor, we can't be ready for an insanity trial in just six weeks."

"But that is what you agreed to, ma'am."

"But he didn't tell me . . ."

Thorvaldson smiled for the first time all morning. "That's correct, Mrs. Watkins, he didn't. You have to know what you're doing. At least in my court. Take it up with Judge Cairns. Ms. Arcand, you're subject to the same conditions of release and hospitalization as I set before. Next case."

. . .

"On behalf of my client, I would like to thank the court and the prosecution for setting such a prompt trial date. It is, I hope, the first step in bringing this tragedy to a just end. Thank you." Edwin Hauser shook off the reporters' questions and moved through the crowd to his "court car," a plain blue ten-year-old Ford sedan, Laura on his arm. Slattery followed him in her BMW to the Port Orchard ferry terminal, where Laura was picked up by the Kitsap Industries Land Rover, staffed with a psychiatric nurse from Northlake Hospital. Slattery waited silently while Ed said good-bye to Laura, praising her strength and courtroom performance. As soon as they were alone, Mary attacked.

"So, tell me just how we get this case ready to try in six weeks, Ed," she said bitterly. "The timeline's a mess. We still don't really know what happened to Laura, the murder weapon is still missing, and we haven't even found and talked to all of the witnesses yet. Are you insane?"

Hauser ignored her, his mouth twitching with pleasure.

"Did you see the look on that awful woman's face when Thorvaldson lit into her?" Hauser said, breaking into a grin. "I've never seen a worse courtroom performance. Never. Hah!"

"That doesn't answer my question, Ed. We don't have time!"

"Okay, I know it's a risk," he replied. "But our problems are fixable, with enough work, and the prosecution's problems may not be. We've assumed all along that Laura shot Mark, and focused on the insanity defense. Watkins and Tiernan may have thought that's where the case was going, but they didn't know for sure—and now they still don't know. That means they have to put on a complete liability case—prove, beyond a reasonable doubt, that Laura shot Mark. It's going to take a lot of work. They don't have an eyewitness, they don't have the gun he was shot with, and they can't place her with Mark at the time he was killed. An hour later, yes. But not for that critical moment."

"What about Laura's suicide attempt as an admission?"

Ed shook his head. "Won't fly," he said shortly. "Admission by conduct has to be unambiguous, and a wife seeing her dead husband could kill herself out of grief."

"There's still her statement in the trauma center at Harborview. 'I killed them' is pretty unambiguous."

"Reuben's working on that one. He thinks if he can show that she made that statement in extreme shock or unconsciousness, he can keep it out. If the judge goes our way at the omnibus hearing and excludes it, they could be in real trouble on their prima facie case."

Mary shook her head. "I doubt it."

"It still means they have to put more work into it," Ed said stubbornly. "They won't have as much time to get a shrink, so they'll probably go for Laura's treating psych, Treadwell, who's already told them he doesn't think she was insane."

"And how does that help us?"

Ed looked up and saw that the ferry line was beginning to move. "Better get back to your car. You coming on this boat?"

Mary shook her head. "I'm heading up to Laura's house."

"Then listen to this tape. Thank God Will had the balls to make it. When we play this for the jury, there won't be enough left of Treadwell to clog a drain."

Chapter Twenty-two

Will Hatton stared at the faces in the faded black-and-white photographs: the 245 members of his high school class, frozen in time on the yellowed newsprint of a twenty-five-year-old *Bainbridge News-Review*. The faces stared back, some friendly and confident, some shy, others clowning, all unlined, unworn. He searched for a word to describe how he and his classmates had looked; "unfinished," he decided. "Unfinished" was the best word.

He paged through the fifty-two weekly papers for the entire year of 1972, his mind open to absorb stray bits of information about a past that seemed impossibly ancient, even to him. I was there, he thought, and I can't remember much of this. The Boeing bust, with its mass unemployment, had entered its third year after the billboards had gone up in Seattle advising the last person to leave the city to please turn off the lights. Bainbridge Island had weathered the local depression better than most parts of the region, bolstered by solid union paychecks from the Bremerton Navy Yard and the veneer of wealthy doctors, lawyers, and trust fund heirs who owned the big old houses along the shorelines. Island Center acreage could be had for a tenth of its current value; the Japanese and Filipino berry farmers still had their co-op strawberry cannery; working boats still fished out of Eagle Harbor. Hair and clothing styles had been as clownish as he remembered them. He laughed out loud at a picture of Ed Hauser leaving the Kitsap County Courthouse after winning the acquittal of a local politician on bribery charges. Ed was resplendent in a garishly striped three-piece suit, his then-dark hair hanging in long waves to his shoulders, muttonchop sideburns spreading down his beefy face.

Laura's disappearance had brought a twelve-point agate headline: ISLAND GIRL MISSING, FEARED DEAD, it declared. The story, below the byline of a reporter named Ira Klein, read:

> *Bainbridge Island, August 26. An island-wide search will be mounted today for Laura Arcand, 14, of Crystal Springs. Arcand, the daughter of Ellen Arcand, office manager of Renner Tool & Die in Bremerton, was reported missing Friday morning. Arcand was last seen at a beer bash thrown by graduating island seniors on the north side of Stenslund Lake in Island Center late Thursday night. Kitsap County sheriff sources say that the party had been moved to the remote wooded area after they had closed the Fort Ward Park beach to the teens. Kitsap County Sheriff John Stansbury said that volunteers for the search should report to the high school parking lot at noon today. The sheriff's search-and-rescue squad and the Bainbridge Explorers Troop No. 2 will form the core of the search party. Stansbury refused to comment on rumors that the Arcand girl had met with foul play.*

Hatton paged forward to the next week's issue, looking for the story on Laura's return. He found a page three story, again written by Klein, under the headline ISLAND GIRL FOUND.

> *Bainbridge Island High School sophomore Laura Arcand was found in Seattle late Monday afternoon. Arcand, 14, was picked up by Seattle police near the University of Washington on Saturday night and taken to King County Juvenile Hall. The teenager*

carried no identification and was apparently the victim of an assault. Seattle police said that no charges were planned. Family attorney Edwin Hauser said that the family would have no comment on Miss Arcand's disappearance, other than to express their gratitude to all who participated in last Saturday's island-wide search, the largest and most intense in recent memory.

Kitsap County Sheriff John Stansbury also refused comment, saying that he wanted to respect the family's privacy. "We're just glad this story has a happy ending," Stansbury said. "But every family in this county should know that teenage runaways and teenage crime are a growing problem. We urge any family feeling the stress of these hard economic times to get help, and counseling, before tragedy strikes."

Will spent another hour looking for crime stories, pursuing Reuben Todd's notion that Laura might have been attacked by a random rapist. He found nothing—no rapists, no escaped convicts, almost no violent crime. The island, Will mused, was as he remembered it from childhood: a haven of green rolling hills and sunny meadows, somehow blessed and remote from the cares of the city just eight miles away.

Sandy Demerest looked at the photocopied pages of the "1972 Senior Salute" and laughed ruefully, the laugh lines in her tanned face etched sharply by the slanted afternoon sunlight. "It's hard to imagine being that young again," she said, sitting at a sidewalk table outside Café Nola, on the edge of Winslow Way. Warm September sun had burned through the morning clouds and evaporated the last of the morning rain from the concrete terrace. She forked a mouthful of arugula salad and made a face. "The next time I come here I'm ordering lasagna. Or a hamburger, if they have it." She sipped a glass of chardonnay and pointed to the date on the cover of the *News-Review* that headlined Laura's disappearance. "I know I didn't go to that party when Laura disappeared. That was the week I found out I was pregnant with Mara. Wade—my boyfriend, now ex-husband—

had already gone off to Washington State, over in Pullman, to start football practice. When I called him he said he was still in two-a-day practices and couldn't come home to talk to my parents. I told them by myself. I cried all week."

"Who would have been at that party?" Will asked. "I've looked at the names and faces and they all kind of blur together. I guess I've been away too long."

"You might have had people in mind if you'd gone to the reunion last summer," Sandy replied. "Come to think of it, Laura and Mark came to that reunion with us. Wade called and asked me to be his date. I guess he was feeling nostalgic or something. I invited Laura and Mark along, since they both knew a lot of the people in our class. Anyway, Mark did ask a couple of people about that party."

"Who did he ask?"

"Danny Donnelly, of course. It was his party, if I remember right." Sandy Demerest frowned in thought, pulling at her chardonnay.

"The only others I know for sure are Julianna Morgan and Tom Greenlee. Who else, Will? You hung out with these guys."

Will picked up the paper and looked again at the pictures and names. "Sam Goltz would have been there. Susan Brickell, too."

"She died last year. Breast cancer."

"I didn't know."

"Do you remember Joni Berman?" Sandy Demerest asked.

"Yeah, she would have been there." Will took out a pad and began jotting down a list. "Anyone else?"

"It wouldn't have been huge. Maybe thirty, forty people." Sandy thought. "What about Henry Ryan?"

"Possibly. The people I want to talk to are the people who would have been close to Laura then, probably more women than men. Anyone who might have seen her, talked to her before—or at the time—she took off."

Sandy frowned. "She was there with Danny Donnelly, Will. You knew that he started taking her out that summer, right?"

"Of course." And it's one of the reasons I left the island that summer, Will thought, but kept the thought to himself. "But if Danny didn't take her home, where did she go? I keep thinking she must have left the party without him."

"Maybe." Sandy Demerest gave up on her salad and gestured to a waitress for another glass of wine. "How well did you know Danny, Will?"

"Not that well, I suppose. He was our mighty football hero—he was a good quarterback, and I liked him. I remember the year before when I told Ed I wanted to try out for the team, as a tight end. Ed said that I'd have a better chance of making the team if I worked out with the starting quarterback. I didn't know Danny then, but I called him up and asked, and he worked with me most of the summer before my junior year, teaching me pass patterns, football smarts. I wouldn't have made the team without his help."

"Didn't you hear him doing his locker room boasting? About women, I mean."

"Some. Getting laid seemed to be the national obsession in 1972. It certainly was for teenage boys. I didn't think much about Danny's boasting. It just seemed like Danny had a way with the girls."

"Oh yeah, he did," Sandy Demerest said sarcastically. "These days, they'd call it date rape. There were a couple of girls in the school that he'd forced himself on. He came pretty close to the edge of being prosecuted. That's why I tried to steer Laura away from him. But you know how she was . . . is. It probably made him more attractive to her."

"Did the police question Donnelly after Laura disappeared?"

"I think so. But you'd have to ask Danny."

Chapter Twenty-three

Mary Slattery blasted her way up Highway 3 at nearly eighty, straight north up the backside of the Kitsap Peninsula, still seething. Six *weeks* until the trial? Ed must have taken leave of his senses. If Tiernan hadn't cleared his calendar and prepared to go to war already, he surely would after Ed's trick dual pleading of innocence and insanity. It was too much of a gamble, she thought grimly. Ed must hope to embarrass Treadwell and rely on Will's reputation to carry the jury. Mary didn't buy it. It wouldn't be enough.

Her mood remained dark as she pulled into the winding drive that led to Laura and Mark's home. The two-story marble entry felt cold and damp despite the warmth of the emerging sun. The house had taken on the slight musty edge of absence in the ten days since Laura and Mark had left it. Mary climbed the carpeted stairs to their bedroom, intent on gathering the makeup and toiletries Laura had asked for and still making the next ferry back to Seattle. She shoveled the contents of Laura's bathroom vanity drawers into a small overnight bag and descended the stairs quickly. At the bottom of the steps she slowed, sensing something out of order. She turned away from the living room to the windowless back hallway leading to the kitchen.

As she turned she saw that the door to Mark Talbot's study was closed, but light leaked from the gap under the door.

Slattery hesitated in front of the door. She was sure that no lights had been left on when she had left the house; the habits of a hard-scrabble Butte upbringing, where wasted light was wasted money, had been too much to break. "Oh, this is just stupid," she said aloud, then pushed the door open.

A halogen desk lamp burned on Talbot's rolltop desk, casting a bright pool over the dropped writing surface below. Slattery turned on the overhead lights, then opened the heavy curtains to let in the sunlight. Nothing seemed changed; the same scatter of papers and files lay on the floor beside Talbot's chair. The computer table still had a dark gap where the CPU box had rested before being removed by the police. The same tide and navigation charts covered the walls, thumbtacked into the expensive cherry-wood paneling as though they were a corkboard.

Talbot sure wasn't much of a housekeeper, Slattery thought. My mother would have killed him for what he's done to that paneling. She stepped toward the wall and idly pulled one of the tacks out, staring at the chart. It was a tidal and navigation chart for Agate Pass and waters north from Bainbridge Island to the far tip of Whidbey Island and the entrance to Deception Pass. Talbot had marked tidal flows with red ink arrows; various sites were checked with Xs. Slattery stopped, puzzled. Talbot wasn't a sailor, she thought, or at least I never heard anyone around the office talking about it with him. And he and Ellen are our largest client. She looked at her watch, saw she'd missed the next ferry, and decided to make another pass through Talbot's credenza files to see if the search had missed anything. A half hour later she opened the last file drawer. It contained nothing but Kitsap corporate documents—sales reports, accounting records, a file of legal correspondence—the same files she'd seen before. She leafed through them quickly. A sheet of yellow printer paper had been stuck in the middle of the correspondence file as a place marker. She stopped, puzzled. I know that paper wasn't here before, she said to herself slowly. I went through that file myself with Joe Schweiger in order to make sure that anything privileged got tagged for the protective order. She closed the file and placed it back in the cabinet, the yellow marker still in place.

Somebody else has been in this house, she thought, suddenly cold again. I wonder who the hell it was.

John Stansbury's cottage stood in an island of sunlight, surrounded by a carefully tended garden, three blocks north of the general store in Indianola, an old village of summer cottages and woodcutters' shacks set in heavy second-growth forest on the edge of the Duwamish Indian reservation. The acrid smell of wood smoke still hung in the air from morning fires.

Hatton mounted the steps to the cottage and found the door open to a small living room filled with books. A large oak desk was pushed against the front wall, to take advantage of the southern light that streamed in the old double-hung windows. A pair of ancient leather chairs faced the small brick fireplace on the far wall.

"Hello?" Hatton called out.

"Be right with you," a voice called out from a back room. "I'm just airing the place out. Got to take advantage of the sun when we have it, you know." A man emerged from the kitchen door of his house, smiling, hand extended. "You must be Dr. Hatton. I'm John Stansbury. Care for some tea? Iced or hot, as you please."

Hatton shook hands and appraised Stansbury. He was a fit, compact man with close-trimmed white hair and beard. He must be well over seventy, Will thought, but looks barely sixty. "Iced tea, thanks," Will began. "Please call me Will, or anything except 'Doctor.' We've met before, a long time ago."

"Really?" Stansbury said. "I know who you are, of course, but I don't recall we'd met."

"In 1971," Hatton replied, smiling, "and it had to do with a six-pack of beer in the back of my jeep while I was parked at Battle Point."

"Grew up on the island, did you? Ah. I remember now, you're the boy that lived with my friend Ed Hauser after your mom died. Well,

I assume you survived the lecture I gave you on the evils of underage drinking and driving?"

"I did," Hatton said, breaking into a small laugh. "It was pouring out all the beer in front of my date that hurt."

"I probably should have busted you," Stansbury said briskly. "Come round back with me. The sun should be hitting the garden about now, and it's pleasant."

Hatton followed the older man through the neat kitchen and out the back door to a square, low cedar deck, surrounded by beds of raked gravel and carefully planned grass and flower beds. Japanese-style stone garden lanterns marked the corners of the garden. A freshly painted black iron table stood in the center of the deck, surrounded by four iron chairs. The table held a pitcher of iced tea, glasses, and a yellowed manila file weighted down by a smooth, round granite stone to keep the contents from blowing away in the light breeze.

When they had settled into their chairs and the tea had been poured, Stansbury leaned back into his chair and studied Will with shrewd hazel eyes. "You're asking about Laura Arcand's disappearance, you said over the phone," he began.

"That's right. You were Kitsap County sheriff in 1972, when she ran away. The island was still policed by the sheriff's office back then."

"Correct," Stansbury said. "I was sheriff until 1980. My wife died shortly after I lost the election that year, and after losing Betty, too . . . well, I had no interest in police work as such. I decided to retire rather than go back in rank and work for a man I didn't much care for."

"What have you done since?"

"This and that. Worked as an investigator for some of the local attorneys up until last year or so. Now I pretty much split my time, up here in the summer and fall, then down to Mexico for the winter and spring." He leaned forward intently. "I have a sporting interest in this case of yours," he said. "Laura Arcand and her late husband, probably Kitsap County's leading businessman. I still have some friends in the sheriff's office, and they gossip, particularly about this case. Ms. Arcand's lawyers have drawn quite a bit of fury from the local prosecutor, you know."

"It seems that way."

"Judith Watkins is an ass, pardon my having opinions. But she's shrewd, got a real steady base with the voters. Kitsap's a funny county, you know. You have Bremerton, with its navy yard and sailors, the old downtown deserted and boarded up, like a miniature Cleveland. Then there's the rest of the county, suburbs down Gig Harbor way, small farmers and loggers up here in the north. Finally there's Bainbridge, with its lawyers and doctors and trust fund heirs. Watkins pulls together the conservatives and the Christians, and in this county those folks vote and are pretty powerful, even if the islanders look down their collective noses at them. If she gets a jury full of her true believers, you're going to have a hard time selling any kind of insanity defense for Ms. Arcand." Stansbury watched Hatton's surprised expression, then put a hand up to reassure him. "Relax, Will. One of my old friends told me what happened in court this morning. Don't worry, I'm not going to give your ideas away to the prosecutor."

Hatton offered a guarded smile. "Thanks. But what can you tell me about Laura's disappearance in 1972?"

"Some. That was a major case for me. At the time I feared greatly that the girl had been killed. When I got voted out as sheriff, I kept a copy of my personal files on every case I considered unsolved, and that was one of them."

"Why would you think of it as unsolved? The case was closed when Laura was found."

"Closed isn't the same as solved, Will. Not for me. Anyway, I never could understand Laura Arcand's reason—or reasons—for running away. By all accounts she was a decent student, worked hard at her art classes, had a pretty good relationship with her mother. So she didn't really figure as a runaway. At first I thought she had been kidnapped, raped, and killed right away. That's why I ordered that all-island search—I thought surely that we were looking for her body. I was as surprised as anyone else when Laura Arcand turned up alive in Seattle." Stansbury paused to sip tea, then opened the top file. "We got the call around seven A.M. on Friday morning, the twenty-fifth of August," he said, reading from his reports. "Ellen said her daughter had been at a party with some of her high school friends on Thursday night, then hadn't come home. She hadn't worried until morning, because Laura sometimes slept in the beach cabin on her place; and when she'd checked on her for breakfast she wasn't there."

"That doesn't sound like Ellen," Will said. "She's always been very protective of Laura."

"That's what I thought too. But Ellen Arcand was following the advice some idiotic counselor gave her about giving Laura space to find herself, or some similar kind of 1970s touchy-feely therapeutic shit." Stansbury cocked his head and looked sideways at Hatton to see if he'd drawn blood. Hatton was unruffled, long since used to being lumped in with the idiots of his profession.

"There was a keg party that night, Thursday, for the seniors going off to college that weekend," Stansbury continued. "It was supposed to have been down at Fort Ward, but I got wind of it and closed down the park. The kids outfoxed us, of course, and moved the party to Stenslund Lake. It wasn't a park then, just a two-hundred-acre patch of second-growth woodlot that old man Stenslund's youngest kids still owned and cut timber from." Stansbury read ahead in his notes, then continued. "By noon the next day we had a pretty good list of who was there. We started with the boy she was supposed to be dating—Danny Donnelly, the football player. He swore up and down that she wasn't his date, but when he saw her that night she looked drunk, or drugged up, so he'd asked Seth Gwynn to make sure she got home all right."

"Gwynn? Wasn't he an English teacher at the high school?"

"Theater teacher. A young one—twenty-four or -five. Claimed he was there at the party as a sort of unofficial chaperon. I guess the school board believed him, but I didn't. He was just a little too slick and a little too interested in the high school girls."

Hatton leaned forward, intent. "Did Gwynn take Laura back to the beach cabin?"

Stansbury shook his head. "He swore he hadn't. Said he didn't remember Donnelly telling him anything about Laura, didn't recall seeing her drunk, or seeing her much at all."

"What about the others at the party?"

Stansbury returned to his notes, leafed through several Accobound pages. "At least forty kids went. We questioned every one of them that I could identify. No one saw Laura Arcand with Gwynn, although several remember her standing with Donnelly near the keg, her arm around him. No one could remember seeing her leave."

"Was anyone able to give you the approximate time Laura left, or went missing?"

"Not really. I pegged it about eleven P.M., because a couple of people remembered Donnelly being by himself after that, and hitting on some of the other girls after midnight."

"What about Donnelly and Gwynn? How late did they stay?"

"Donnelly said he stayed until two or so. We picked him up for questioning about ten the next morning, and he was still in bed with a hangover. Gwynn said he'd left earlier, maybe twelve, and had gone home to read. He was living in a little rented mill shack in Winslow, down at the foot of Madison Street, where the marina and all those condos are now." Stansbury looked thoughtful. "Never could shake their stories. But both of them were plenty scared, for some reason. I held them for twenty-four hours to see if either'd change his story, but both stuck to what they told me."

"What happened then?"

"I had to assume that someone else had gotten the girl. She'd have been pretty vulnerable, walking by herself late at night along Baker Hill Road, especially if she'd been drinking. Like I said, my guess was that she'd tried to hitch a ride with someone and gotten killed. That's why I called for the search. Which found nothing, of course, and had the whole island in an uproar."

"Did you talk to Laura after she was found?"

"Some. Ed was helping Ellen with her, and they didn't like it, but I finally got through to see her. She couldn't remember anything. Complete amnesia for the four days she was missing. The last thing she remembered was catching a ride to the party with Donnelly and a couple of other kids."

"Whatever happened to Donnelly and Gwynn?" Hatton asked.

"Now, you mean? Donnelly's back in the area, trading on his pro football days, selling himself as a dinner speaker. Has an office over in Silverdale. Gwynn got himself fired as a teacher two years later, in 1974, when he got one of his students pregnant. She was over sixteen, so there was no criminal case. But the school board had his number by then." Stansbury flipped through his file, then extracted a news clipping. "Gwynn went to L.A., but he's up in Port Townsend now. He seems pretty well fixed. Has a bookstore and café, owns a hotel and some rental property, works on the Centrum Arts Festival. Cuts a pretty substantial figure in the community now."

"When you went to the beach cabin the morning after Laura disappeared, what did it look like?"

"Not bad. Messy, as you'd expect a teenager's room to be—sheets on the cot all twisted up, a cluttered table where the girl painted, bottles of thinner, tubes of paint, brushes. No real signs of any violence, no blood. That was my first thought, you know. And when I didn't see any blood, I figured it was more likely that Laura got kidnapped on the road, not from the cabin. That's why I ordered the all-island search."

"Anything else?" Hatton asked.

Stansbury frowned in concentration. "No. The windows were open—that figures, it was a hot night. The place was kind of damp, but being that close to the water, that didn't seem unusual."

"What happened after Laura was found? I mean, aside from questioning her, did you try to find out where she had gone?"

"No," John Stansbury said, scratching his beard. "I wanted to, of course. The gaps in the story nagged at me. But I had a county to police with half the officers I needed, and we just couldn't spare the time."

Will glanced down at his list of questions, found all of them checked off. "Thank you, John. I'm amazed that you remember as much as you do about this."

"Well, it was quite a sensation at the time. And of course, I've been asked about this before."

Will cocked his head to one side, puzzled. "By who?"

"By Mr. Talbot. Just this past summer."

"*What?*"

"Oh, yes. Talbot came around in . . . let's see. Early August. The fourth."

"What did Talbot ask you about?"

"Pretty much the same things you did. He said his wife was having some nightmares that he thought might be tied to her disappearance, and that her regular psychotherapy wasn't helping much. I told him what I'd told you."

"Did Talbot ask about anything else?"

"He wanted to know about his dad's drowning. But that was a city of Bremerton case, so I didn't have much for him."

"How did Talbot's father die?" Hatton asked. "I wasn't around here when it happened."

"Curt Renner died from combining two dangerous things—a boat and a bottle. He lived summers on his boat at the Bremerton Yacht Club, and had a little open skiff that he used to run around the sound in, slip over to his lady friends' houses by boat when their husbands weren't around. Anyway, he drowned off Whidbey Island, same summer as Laura Arcand went missing. Maybe a week or two after." Stansbury paused. "Oh, and Talbot asked one other question."

"What?"

"He said he was trying to find out about a lawyer who used to practice in Bremerton, by the name of Elder. Lawrence Elder."

"Did he say why?"

"Talbot said he was trying to track down some old records he thought Elder might have, about Kitsap Industries' ownership and insurance coverage. Elder was Curt Renner's lawyer, a long time ago."

"What did you tell him?"

"That I'd known Elder, of course. He was county prosecutor until 1975 or so."

"What happened to him?"

"Elder? Died in 1977. Car crash."

"Did Mark Talbot ever find the records he was looking for from Lawrence Elder?"

"Not that I heard. Of course, Talbot was dead just over a month later."

Chapter Twenty-four

Mary Slattery knocked hesitantly, then opened the door. It was just past eight o'clock on Tuesday, the end of the long day that for her had begun at 5 A.M.

"Laura?" she said, stepping quietly into the darkened room.

"It's all right, Mary. I'm awake. Here." Laura Arcand switched on the bedside light. The soft yellow glow filled a corner of the darkened room and illuminated Laura's puffy, tear-stained face. "Give me a minute," she said, and took a hospital washcloth to wipe the tears from her eyes.

Mary held out the bag of cosmetics and toiletries as an offering. "I'm sorry I'm so late," she said. "Long day at the office."

"No doubt trying to save me," Laura said, a sardonic edge to her voice.

"That seems to be what we do right now," Mary replied evenly, suppressing her irritation. Why does this woman want to bite every hand that tries to help her? she thought.

"Difficult work, saving me. I wouldn't bother, if I were you," Laura continued, the edge still in her voice.

"But you're not me, and it *is* my job." Mary suddenly tired of what she took as self-pity. "Then again," she added, "I'm charging you $250 an hour. That does take the sting out of it."

Laura was silent for a moment, then smiled. "Touché, Mary. Can I have a cigarette, please?"

Mary thought about it, shrugged, then opened one of the room's small, high windows, cranking the glass pane out until it touched the heavy white plastic-coated screen that covered the window. She lit a Camel Light for herself, then passed the pack and matches to Laura, who climbed out of bed, slipped into a print silk robe, and sat down with Mary at a white Formica table beneath the small window.

Laura lit a cigarette, then exhaled smoke gratefully. "Thanks. And for bringing my stuff."

Mary nodded. "So, tell me how you're doing," she said politely.

"Ever been crazy?" Laura asked, her tone rising, a crooked smile on her face.

Mary laughed, "Sporadically, due to occupation. Clients like you."

Laura chuckled. "Fair enough," she replied, her voice low and scratchy. "Well, if it gets bad enough, I can recommend this hospital. Three squares, nutritionally balanced if tasteless, no alcohol, reasonably plentiful drugs, plenty of time to be alone. This is my fourth trip through one of these joints, and I think I know the secret to their success—you can be alone."

Mary laughed again. "I'm surprised they don't have more lawyers in here."

Laura smiled. "Might not be a bad vacation, doing what you do. Spending every day with someone else's problems and trying to fix them. Painting pictures is easier, believe me."

Only if you can, Mary thought, and that is such a gift . . . Never mind. If she's talking, I've got to take advantage of that.

"Listen," Mary said urgently, "can I ask some questions? If you're feeling okay. There's just so much—"

"I know. Do you mind if we just talk first, maybe have you answer a few questions for me? I'm stuffed in a cocoon here, and the drugs . . . I've got another Cloznepfemine at ten o'clock, and that will whack me out for another eight hours."

"What's that like?" Mary asked, suddenly curious.

"It's an antipsychotic. Like you're still on the cross, only you can't feel the nails."

"Doesn't sound like it would be one of my favorites. Okay, Laura, ask, or talk, whatever."

"What are they—you—doing? I don't understand. Ed comes in here with my mother, strokes my hair, tells me everything will be all right. It's wonderful to watch them together—have you ever seen how much he is in love with her? Really seen it, I mean."

"I think so."

"Then you know that everything Ed tells me is for Ellen's bene-fit—he looks at her the whole time. It doesn't tell me what I'm up against."

"I understand," Mary said. "Tell me what you want to know."

"I guess I want to know what's being said. Not to me, to the world. What your thinking is. How you're going to defend me, if there's anything to defend."

"Will's been driving it so far," Mary replied. "The theory for your defense, I mean."

"That sounds like Will. But he won't tell me much either."

Mary hesitated. How much should she say? How much would be too much, possibly affect Will's work? She thought carefully, then said, "Will believes that when you shot Mark, you were acting out an old traumatic memory. Of something that happened to you in the beach house a long time ago. It's called posttraumatic stress disor-der."

"So even Will thinks I killed Mark," Laura said slowly. Tears welled in her eyes and she began to cry again, silently. Mary waited patiently, regretting that she had no comfort to give. Finally Laura wiped her face again and sat straighter in her chair, lighting another cigarette. "Go on, please," Laura whispered.

"Did you kill him, Laura? If you didn't, if there's anything else you can give us, we can go to work on that, change the case we're build-ing."

Laura looked at her plaintively, the tears welling out of her eyes, yet without sobbing. "I wish I could tell you that. I wish. Was it my gun that killed him?"

"They think so. They can't find it."

"What do you mean?" Laura asked, puzzled. "I brought it; it was in my travel kit."

"I know. I saw the gun oil stain on the canvas. Why did you bring a gun with you to the island?"

"To kill myself, of course," Laura replied, her voice even again. "Didn't you know that?"

"No," Mary replied. "Why?"

"Because I'd reached that point, Mary. I was once a good painter, and lost that, drank and drugged until it was gone, or until even with alcohol and drugs I couldn't reach it anymore . . . I was never sure which way it was. I tried to be a good wife. I tried to be a mother. I failed . . . and I found I couldn't escape my life. I couldn't change." Laura felt Mary's hand touch her shoulder, and roughly pushed it away. "I don't need sympathy yet. I've had a better run than most people, you know. I was famous . . . more importantly, I was good. My failures are my own." She stopped, hit on her cigarette, and blew smoke toward the window. "What else does Will say?"

"He thinks you were raped in the beach house in 1972. And when Mark came to you on the night he died, you relived that earlier experience, and tried to defend yourself."

"But that doesn't . . . I've tried so hard to reach back . . . I've been trying hard tonight, and . . ." Laura's speech began to slur and she appeared to drift away, her eyes closing. She slumped back against the back of her chair, shaking. Mary, alarmed, ran to the bathroom and wet a washcloth, then placed it on Laura's forehead as she slumped in her chair, head back. A long minute passed before Laura opened her eyes.

"It happened again, didn't it?" she whispered.

"Yes," Mary replied.

"Shit." Laura straightened up and dropped the damp cloth on the table. "Thanks," she said, still shaking a little. She picked up her cigarette, inspected it, saw it had burned almost to the filter, then drew a new one from Mary's pack and lit it from the old one. "There are two comforts when you're crazy, Mary," she said, drawing on the new cigarette. "One is this: Inside your crazy self is a sane self trying to get out. It's small and scared, but it's there. You can reach that self from time to time. The other is that sometimes you just blank out. And that is a mercy." Laura's voice was tense, but got firmer as she spoke. "I wish I knew what happened. I hope—hell, I pray, can you

imagine that? I pray that I didn't kill Mark. But even if I did, I want
to *know*, damn it. I want to regain some control over my life. And
until I know what really happened, I won't have that."

"I think I'd better go," Mary said. "You're stressing."

"No, please stay . . . This is really, well, not pleasant, but almost
normal, like having drinks or dinner with one of my friends. Just
talk. I know you've got lots to do. I appreciate the time, Mary, I do."

"Not at all." Mary thought for a minute. I might never get another chance to ask questions, she thought. So I might as well.

"Your journals," Mary began.

"You found them? I thought I was pretty clever in hiding them."

"There's a mention of a man named Carlo. Lisa Thayer told me
that might be Carlo Aguilar."

"And I wrote?" Laura paused, her cigarette poised near her
mouth.

"Something about fucking him, actually," Mary said dryly.

Laura laughed. "Oh, that was long ago. In New York, although I
saw him a few times after Carlo got some jobs out here."

"Were you sleeping with him recently?"

"No, but I thought about it. Carlo—well, let me put it this way:
Carlo never hides the fact that he wants to get you horizontal. Sometimes I like that. He's been out in Seattle a couple of times, doing big
ugly metal sculptures for computer company lawns, or some damn
thing. I tried to help him establish himself, but the fact is Carlo's not
a very good sculptor. What did I write about him?"

"Just that you were angry at Mark and wanted to see him. You
wrote that in June."

"God, I must have been hard up. But I never called him. The
funny thing is, I was actually faithful to Mark. Isn't that a hoot?"
Laura's eyes lit up with humor, the first time Mary Slattery had ever
seen her that way. "Got any other deep dark secrets you want to ask
me about? I have at least a hundred lovers for you to choose from."

"Tell me about Will," Slattery asked, surprising herself with the
question.

"Will? What do you mean?" Laura said, puzzled.

"He told me you went to school together. What was he like?"

Laura sat back with her cigarette poised at her lips, her eyes suddenly cool and appraising. "Really? What's the interest, Mary? Personal, or professional?"

Mary shrugged defensively. "I asked him the same question about you. I'm trying to get a feeling for what you were both like when . . . in 1972."

Laura nodded. "Sorry. You're supposed to be too good a lawyer to get sidetracked by personal feelings. Ed says so, anyway. Are you asking whether Will had a crush on me when we were children, wondering whether that affects his judgment now that he's become Dr. God? He did. But it wouldn't affect his medical judgment now. How was he when we were kids? Hmm. He was older, he wanted to be indifferent to me . . . but he spent time with me, watching me paint, trying to understand why I could do it and he couldn't. He was cool and scientific, even then. Would he have fucked me if I had given him the chance? Of course. He was seventeen. Skinny. Bookish. All knees and elbows . . . and dick, though I was just fourteen and didn't have a really advanced appreciation of that fact then."

"I thought he played football, and boxed."

"Oh, he did, part of his compensation. He wasn't any good, but he kept at it until he was black-and-blue."

"Compensation for what?"

"His father."

"Ed?"

"Oh no, his biological father. Didn't you know? After Will's mother died—she was Ed's lover, before my mother—Will went to live in New Orleans for a few months. His father had explained to him that he was gay, and raising a teenaged boy wasn't something he could handle. Will came back here to live because of that. And then after I ran away . . . well, I'd heard that he'd gone down to New Orleans again that summer, to have things out with his father, and nothing had changed. His father had his life, he was happy, and Will wasn't part of it. That's why Will enlisted in the marine corps. To prove he was different. Heterosexual. Tough."

Mary frowned. "How do you know this? I don't think Ed even knows it all."

Laura shrugged. "Will told me. A long time ago. Does it matter? You see, he *is* tough, Mary—he's made himself that way. Don't underestimate that cold bearish scientist inside him. It's as real as any other part of the man. He didn't make himself one of the best forensic psychiatrists in the country by being soft."

Mary decided she had to ask one more question. "Do you love him?"

Laura looked away, then back to Mary, startled. "Will? Good God, no." She laughed, briefly. "I know this will surprise you, but I actually loved my husband." Laura looked at Mary steadily, then went on. "It does, doesn't it? I had a hundred different lovers . . . but I only really loved my husband, the rough and nasty uncultured businessman. Most people never saw the heart in him. The caring. I did. Isn't it funny . . . the man I never expected to love. But it's the truth, Mary. It is, by God, the truth."

Laura's head suddenly dropped forward, as though in exhaustion. When she was able to raise it again the exhaustion showed in her bloodshot eyes and the lines on her face. "You'd better go," she said. "It's nearly ten, and I'm due for my drugs . . . a little death in lieu of the big one. You're more than I expected, Mary Slattery. I'm glad you're on my side. Thank you."

"We haven't won *yet*."

"That doesn't matter. I'm grateful for what you're trying to do. Even though I'd have rather died with my husband, as God intended."

"As God?" Mary Slattery asked.

"Sorry. That was presumptuous of me. As I intended."

Chapter Twenty-five

Daniel Donnelly's office was on the top floor of the Silverdale Professional Center, a six-story mirrored cube overlooking Silverdale Bay. The glass double doors to his suite were lettered, in bold italic script, *Donnelly Personal Dynamics: Performance Enhancement.* Will Hatton gave his name to the receptionist, was told to wait, and passed the time peering into a huge glass trophy case that, divided into three sections, told the story of Donnelly's football career. The first held the awards for passing won at Bainbridge Island High School and Portland State University; the second, pro jerseys from the Chicago Bears, Atlanta Falcons, and the then Los Angeles Rams. The third section of the case contained a signed game ball and photographs from Donnelly's last professional game, when he had come off the bench in the third quarter of the 1986 Super Bowl, with the Rams trailing the Bengals by fourteen points, and passed them back into the game. With the score tied in the final seconds of overtime, Donnelly had driven the overmatched Rams seventy-eight yards, then faked a screen pass and dove the last six yards himself. The tackle at the goal line had blown apart Donnelly's right knee and ended his career, but the Rams won the game, 27–21. Will, who usually detested spectator sports and had watched the game only because of his past friendship with Donnelly, had cheered himself hoarse in the bar of the Washington Athletic Club.

"Everybody gets at least one day where everything goes right, and that was sure mine," Danny Donnelly said, following Will's gaze as he came out of his private office. Will turned to shake Donnelly's outstretched, oversized hand.

"Even if it cost you your knees, Hoss?" Will asked, using Donnelly's old high school nickname.

"Yeah, even that," Donnelly replied, grinning. "How are you, Will? It's been a long time. I was hoping I'd see you this summer, at the reunion."

"I was out of town on business," Will replied. "You look good." Donnelly grinned again and shook his head. But Will had spoken the truth: Donnelly had lost some of the beef from his playing days, and now stood thin but still broad shouldered, in a hand-tailored two-button gray tropical wool suit. His face was tan from a summer on the golf courses, where he gave inspirational lectures to real estate agents and corporate sales conventions. Donnelly's thinning sandy hair was now streaked with white. His eyes were pale blue, and he looked, Will thought, like a slightly older version of Mickey Mantle in his final days with the Yankees.

"Come on into my office." Donnelly led him past a pair of conference rooms to a large office furnished with an oak bookcase with glass doors, a glass-topped desk on a marble base, and a pair of leather-and-steel sling chairs. More photographs lined the office walls: Donnelly shaking hands with Ronald Reagan and George Bush after his Super Bowl win; Donnelly with Billy Graham; Donnelly with Stephen Covey—discussing the habits of highly effective people over lunch, Will guessed. He was more troubled by the recent additions to Donnelly's vanity wall: Donnelly speaking from a podium with an Operation Rescue antiabortion banner; Donnelly introducing Pat Buchanan at a political dinner; Donnelly raising the hand of Kitsap County prosecutor Judith Watkins in victory at the last election.

Donnelly settled into his chair and reached behind him into a small refrigerator. "Want something to drink? I've got mineral water, orange juice, diet Fresca—that's my weakness now."

"No beer?"

"Nope. I can send Tracy down to the corner, though."

"I'm kidding, Dan. Mineral water, thanks. My high school memory of both of us is with a beer bottle in hand."

Donnelly nodded. "I know. But I haven't had a drink since 1985. I was in Detroit, the Lions had just kicked the shit out of us, me especially, and I had about ten beers after the game. I was sitting in the lounge at the hotel in Renaissance Center and I somehow knew that I just wasn't going to drink after that night." He paused, smiled, then added, "So I had another Heineken with a shot of Gentleman Jack, and that was that. I didn't go through any twelve-step deal or anything like that. I just knew I was getting older, my legs were starting to go, and if I ever wanted to achieve anything in the game, I'd have to stop drinking."

"Well, you sure as hell did. Achieve, I mean. What's performance analysis about, anyway?"

"That's what I've been wanting to talk to you about. I've been doing counseling—performance coaching, helping people figure out why they fail, and how they can avoid it in the future as they work toward getting in the zone of success. I've been taking more psych courses—hell, I'm six credits and a thesis from a master's degree—but I need someone with top-flight credentials in psychiatry to review the book I'm working on, and make sure I've got the science right. I thought that you—hell, with that great piece about you in *Newsweek*—that you'd be perfect."

Will stared for just a moment in astonishment, then caught himself and decided the offer was genuine, if misguided. "Thanks, Dan. But I'm not the right guy—I don't treat people anymore, and I've never studied performance psychology. I'm a forensic psychiatrist—I come in after something awful's happened and try to figure out why."

Donnelly nodded, his face beginning to flush. "I was afraid of that. This is about Laura Arcand, isn't it, Will?"

"It is. I'm trying to figure out what happened to her."

"Damn, I knew it."

"Why does that trouble you, Dan?"

Donnelly's face darkened. He grabbed at the glass of Fresca on the desk in front of him and downed half of it. "Look, how would you like it if the husband of some woman that you hadn't even seen in over twenty years walked into your office and accused you of raping her?"

"I don't get it. What are you talking about?"

"Laura's husband, Mark Talbot. He knows who I am; I've done some motivational work out at Kitsap Industries, trying to get their sales force to improve their performance. I see him and Laura at the class reunion, we say hello, Laura smiles, and the next week the guy is threatening me with lawyers for raping his wife. I tell him I don't know what he's talking about. Then the next thing I hear, it turns out he's been fucking around, and she got mad and shot him."

"Slow down," Will said. "Tell me what Talbot said to you."

"He said Laura'd been having some kind of traumatic memories coming to the surface. I understand what that's about; I've talked to Judith Watkins—who's a good friend of mine, by the way—about repressed memory and child abuse. Terrible things come out, I know. But this is about Laura—somebody I dated for about a month in the summer of 1972. Then Talbot says Laura's all screwed up now because I raped her when she was fourteen. It was crazy, to put it mildly. I almost threw Talbot out the window, I was so mad." When he was finished talking Donnelly paused, deflated, the anger temporarily spent. "What are you going to do, Will? Accuse me of the same thing, try to get Laura off the hook for murder because she was such a poor abused little rich girl?"

Will ignored the outburst. "Did Talbot ask you about any specific time or place?"

"Sure. You know. The party at Stenslund Lake, the night before we all took off for college. You were there, weren't you?"

"No, I wasn't, Dan. I went down to New Orleans a couple of weeks before to see my father, then joined the marines when I was down there. I didn't come back to the island again for two years."

Donnelly looked puzzled. "Huh. I could have sworn you were there."

"Nope. Tell me what happened."

Donnelly looked away, into the distance across Silverdale Bay. "It was our usual kind of Fort Ward kegger, maybe a little bigger, more people, because we were all graduating and heading off into the world and everybody knew that life was going to be different, never the same again. Laura called me that afternoon and asked me if I could pick her up for the party. I said sure." Donnelly swung his chair back from the window and stared at Will. "I never had sex with her, Will. Never. I knew she was only fourteen. Christ, I could have if I'd wanted to. She even asked me once why I hadn't tried to fuck her."

"What did you say?"

"I laughed it off. Told her that if she was interested when she was sixteen, we had a deal, she could name the time and place."

"Why did you go out with her, then? You were the biggest swinging dick in that school, and you weren't shy about exercising it. Or so you said."

"I wasn't shy, Will. And there were some times when some girl saying no was just a challenge, another way of hearing yes. I admit that, but it was a long time ago. I'm a Christian now." Donnelly paused, seemed to struggle for words. "Why did I go out with her? She lived in the Stenslund house, man. Her mother was getting rich. Maybe that didn't mean anything to you. But to me . . . there were eight Donnelly kids who grew up in a mobile home up in Battle Point. My old man practically broke himself in two trying to feed us after they laid him off from Boeing in 1969. He ran the last shingle mill on the island, did you know that? We cut cedar all winter, stealing it from the county land when the money to buy it ran out. Dad fished up in Alaska as a deckhand in the summers to keep us going, and he was nearly sixty years old by then. So when this rich, beautiful kid wanted to ride in my old truck, I didn't tell her no. I was from hungry, and I liked it. I liked having her out late at night and having her rich-bitch mother wondering what her little girl was doing."

Hatton was silent, stunned. This man had been cheered by thousands of people and made millions of dollars, yet the scar of growing up poor on a wealthy island lay just beneath the surface of his skin.

"Danny, I need to know what happened at that party. It could be critical to Laura's defense. What do you remember?"

Donnelly stared back at him, calculation on his face. "Or what, Will? I get subpoenaed, dragged into court?"

"I can't control that. It depends on what you know. And did."

"I told you, I didn't do a damn thing. I brought Laura to the party, but she drifted away pretty quickly. And I thought, Well, if that's how she's going to be, there's still plenty of quiff in the neighborhood, no problem. Laura started out pretty mellow, had a couple of beers, maybe a joint, and then went off with a couple of other kids who had a pot of vodka punch going. She got pretty drunk. I was kind of pissed, to tell you the truth, because I thought I was going to have to leave early and get her home. But when I saw her again, she was hanging with Seth Gwynn, and he said he'd get her home. That's the last I saw of her, I swear."

"Do you know how she got home?"

"No. I got interested in Terry Slaney and we wandered off down to the lake. That was maybe one, one-thirty in the morning."

"Was Laura gone by then?"

"I don't know. I kind of think she was but I don't know for sure."

"Did you find out anything later? I understand that John Stansbury held you for a couple of hours on Friday morning, after Laura's disappearance was reported."

"It wasn't a couple of hours. The son of a bitch held me in the county jail in Bremerton for the entire weekend, until Laura was found. I had a hell of a time explaining that when I finally got down to Portland State. We were supposed to report for practice that Saturday night, and I damn near lost my scholarship over it."

"Stansbury said you told him you hadn't seen her."

"What in hell was I supposed to say? My scholarship, everything I'd worked for was on the line."

"Even though Laura was missing?"

"I told you. I didn't have anything to do with it."

Hatton nodded. "Did you ever hear anything again from Mark Talbot over this?"

"Just once. The bastard called me up like nothing had happened. He said he had a couple more questions, but I told him to fuck off." Donnelly sighed. "Sorry. I'm trying to give up that kind of language."

"It's all right. You should hear doctors."

"Yeah." Donnelly peered at him, his voice cautious. "So what happens from here? Am I going to be some kind of witness?"

"I don't know," Will said carefully, fairly certain that whatever he said now would end up in the ear of the Kitsap County prosecutor. "I'm just trying to figure out what happened to Laura, whether it's related to her problems now."

"Lots of luck on that. From what I hear, she's going to spend the next twenty years painting pictures inside a prison. And deserves it."

Will stood to go. He turned to the door of Donnelly's office, then turned back, seized with a sudden anger. "Laura Arcand is in wretched pain, Danny. Something terrible happened to her that night, when you watched her get drunk and left her alone. It's something she's lived with for twenty-five years. She was just fourteen, for Christ's sake. Doesn't that mean anything to you?"

Donnelly stared at him, his eyes narrowed. "You know, there's only three real sins left in this country, Will. Not being rich, not being famous, and being a loser. Laura had the first two easy. Now she's a loser. Don't expect me to break up over something that happened over twenty years ago."

"I won't," Hatton replied, rising to go. "But hell, finish your book, Danny. The way you think, it'll probably sell a million copies."

Chapter Twenty-six

Will Hatton paused before the carved plaque that proclaimed PROSPERO'S BOOKS/MIRANDA'S CAFÉ, hung in a cast iron frame on the red acid-washed brick of a Water Street storefront in downtown Port Townsend. It was, Hatton thought, far too arch for his taste, but every town needed a place for its self-appointed intellectual and artistic crowd to meet, Port Townsend more than most others. A once thriving seaport later abandoned by the railroads, Port Townsend was reborn in the 1970s as an arts and tourist town, its quaint Victorian streets choked with galleries and guest houses, selling hundred-year-old knickknacks to elderly tourists who arrived by the busload every day.

Hatton entered the building through handsome fir-and-glass doors. The bookstore itself was on the main floor of an old shipping warehouse, the rough pine bookshelves and dark oak reading tables well lit by a large square of skylights in the ceiling. Hatton browsed the shelves for a moment, looked at the psychology section, grimaced at the titles he saw, and went off to track down Seth Gwynn.

He found Gwynn at a table in the basement café, halfway through a plate of vegetarian ratatouille. Gwynn was over fifty now, but still slender; his long, dark hair was either untouched by gray or carefully retouched to hide it, the skin around his face tight and unlined. His lunch date was a slender girl of sixteen or seventeen with a bright, intelligent face and lovely thick, cascading auburn hair. She had already polished off a spinach salad and was listening, rapt, as Gwynn held court.

"Then, when we finally had the scene wrapped, we all drove back to Polanski's apartment in Paris for the party. It was—" Gwynn broke off the story and looked up sharply at Hatton, hovering just inside earshot. "Sir? Something I can help you with?" he asked coldly.

"Sorry," Hatton apologized. "Don't let me interrupt your lunch. But I'd like to speak with you as soon as it's convenient."

"And you are?"

"A former student of yours. My name's Will Hatton."

Gwynn's eyes narrowed, but he smiled brightly. "Of course. Fee," he said, turning to the girl, "this is an old student of mine, now a rather well-known psychiatrist. Dr. Hatton."

"I'm very pleased to meet you," the girl said, affecting poise beyond her years.

Hatton took her offered hand and shook it briefly. "And I to meet you," he said, offering a cautious smile. "I didn't quite catch your name. It's Fee?"

The girl sighed. "Short for Phoenix Starburst. My parents were into that sort of thing when I was born. Now they sell real estate."

"I understand," Will said, suppressing a grin. "I'm sorry to interrupt. Let me come back—"

"Oh no," the girl said. "I've got to sneak back into school before fourth period or they'll kill me." She stood to go. "Thanks, Seth. When should I have the monologue ready?"

"By Thursday next. Call me if you have questions, okay?"

"I will. Ciao!" She gathered up a loose pile of papers and books and dashed up the stairs.

Gwynn gestured rather sourly at the girl's empty chair. "Sit down, Doctor. Something you find amusing?"

"Just that no one's said 'Ciao' to me in about twenty years. The girl is a student? You're still teaching?"

"That's what you get for living in hospitals and courtrooms, I'm afraid. Yes, I teach an acting seminar every fall and winter for five or six brighter students. Part of the Fort Worden Center arts education program. I charge them just enough to cover books and materials, nothing for myself." Gwynn self-consciously smoothed back the waves in his hair, as if he were onstage.

"That's good of you, Seth. I'm sure the kids appreciate it. And you must be busy, owning and running this place."

"Thank you. I actually own quite a bit more here in Port Townsend than just this bookstore," Gwynn replied, another piece of his natural arrogance coming to the surface. "One of the benefits of inheriting money—you end up succeeding even if you fail at everything else. Now suppose you tell me why you're here, Dr. Hatton."

"John Stansbury says you're one of the last people who may have seen Laura Arcand on the night she disappeared, in August 1972. I'm trying to find out what happened to her."

Gwynn sighed, exasperated. "Surely that couldn't matter after all these years, could it? Or does this supposedly have something to do with her husband's death? The television news said that an insanity defense was going to be offered."

"It may. I'm trying to find out."

"It seems absurd. But yes, I was at that party—a stupid thing for a young teacher, as I was to find out."

"It didn't seem to take. I understand you were fired for having an affair with another student a couple of years later. One that produced a child."

Gwynn stared angrily at Hatton. "For the last time," he said theatrically, "what in hell is this all about?"

Hatton leaned forward intently. "Several highly paid investigators and lawyers have been looking into your past for quite a while now, Seth," he said, his voice low. "They know about the Bainbridge Island High School student. Your son, by the way, is majoring in geology at the University of New Mexico. Good grades, I understand—you should be proud. They know that you moved to L.A. to work as an actor in 1975, landed a TV series, something called *The Apartment House*—I never saw it, but I understand you were one of the leads— then broke your contract six months later and moved rather abruptly to Paris. Just ahead of an indictment for statutory rape. It took you several years to get that one settled, before you could come back to the States. The investigators are looking for the person who raped and traumatized Laura Arcand on the night she disappeared in 1972. You were the last person to see her before she disappeared. And with your record of sexual deviancy with very young women, you fit the facts of the case quite well. Is the charming young actress I met your current conquest? Or your next?"

Gwynn looked at Hatton with bitter anger, his face pale. "Follow me," he commanded. He led Hatton up the stairs, through the bookstore, and into a loft office at the back of the old warehouse, tucked under the ceiling beams. Review copies of books and publishers' catalogues were piled on an old oak library table that Gwynn used as a desk.

Gwynn sat down in a leather swivel chair behind the desk, started to move the pile of books out of his way, then abruptly swept them to the floor. "It was her husband, wasn't it?" he said angrily. "He's the one who was behind this. Let me tell you what I told him: I had nothing to do with what happened to Laura Arcand. Nothing. And if I'm accused—"

"You'll call your lawyer," Hatton said placidly. "And if he or she is even marginally competent, they will tell you that anything that is said about you in the defense of a criminal case, in court, no matter how libelous, is privileged—which means that you will have all of the legal rights and remedies of a pre–Civil War Alabama sharecropper."

Gwynn drummed his fingers on the tabletop. "What is it you want?"

"Just the truth, Seth. Tell me what happened the night Laura disappeared. If you tell me the truth, and if you didn't have anything to do with it, I promise you that the investigation will stop." Hatton stopped, then added with sudden intuition: "You won't have to run away anymore, Seth. You can stay right here, with your money and property and your small piece of fame, that once modestly known actor who guides the art festival and volunteers to teach the high school students, and you can keep on seducing the town daughters until they catch you with one who's under sixteen and they lose their sense of humor about you. If you don't tell me the truth, I promise you it will continue."

Gwynn stared at him. "I'd never known doctors could be such sons of bitches."

Will glanced at his watch, impatiently. "You obviously don't know many doctors. Your choice, Seth."

"All right," Gwynn said abruptly. "All right. I was there. And I saw Laura Arcand."

"Tell me all of it, Seth. From the beginning."

"It was August—a terrific night, very warm, clear skies, light until ten o'clock. Magic. The kind of night when you itch to do something, when you're young—I was only twenty-four. I'd seen a couple of my students in Winslow that day, and they invited me to the party. I drove up to Stenslund Lake around ten, maybe a little earlier, on the old logging road that ran to the lake from Vincent. It was just getting dark. I could see the bonfire on the west side of the lake, so I hiked in the rest of the way. When I got there I saw Laura talking to Danny Donnelly, that year's resident football hero. I guess she came with him, but they were arguing. I . . . I'd always admired Laura, thought she would make a wonderful actress—those dark emotions she seemed to have, even though she was just a kid. But she never took any of my classes, was interested only in her painting. So I sought her out."

Gwynn paused, licked his lips. His words were taking on the rhythm of a reverie, an old memory that, Hatton guessed, Gwynn found desirable, even exciting. "Go on. What condition was Laura in? Drunk, stoned, what?"

"Laura was a little drunk, not too badly," Gwynn said. "She was mildly upset—pouting would be the best way to describe it. I asked her what was wrong. She said she'd wanted Danny to trip with her, but that he refused—he said he wanted to stay at the party. And then she'd asked me if I'd trip with her."

"Did she have the LSD already? Or did you give it to her?"

"She had it. She'd bought it several weeks before, but was hesitant about trying it. She asked me what it was like. I told her that I'd tried it, but that it didn't do that much for me—that some of the colors and images were wonderful, but that I couldn't use them in my work. She said that was what she was after—new colors, new images, to see beyond what she could already imagine. I told her that it

wasn't best to take it at a big party—she needed to be someplace rel-
atively quiet, with her own music and space. She said she had the
place. We were already pretty far away from the main part of the
party. I said okay, I'll get my car. But she said no, she knew a better
way, a secret way. She took my hand and started leading me down a
path around the south side of the lake, one that I didn't know was
there. It was dark by then, with only about a quarter moon. I kept
stumbling after her, trying to keep up. After a while it became a game
with her. She would dash ahead of me, just out of reach, then let herself be caught, laughing, then slip away again. It was pretty sexual.
At least it felt that way to me. And I kept on following her, watching
her dance ahead of me. Lithe, like a sprite. The trail was narrow,
overgrown—I could hardly see ten feet in front of me. It went up
over a ridge, then down to a spring that flowed out of the hillside—a
big one, with a pool of water beneath it that was full even in summer.
The spring emptied into a stream that flowed down the hill, forming
a little canyon. Laura got ahead of me and I couldn't see her, so I just
kept stumbling down the hill, following the streambed. And then it
opened out onto the beach, and I saw Laura there, standing beside a
small beach cabin.

"'It's my place,' she said. 'Isn't it cool?'

"I followed her inside. She lit a candle, and I reached for her, but
she slid away. 'I want to trip, not fuck,' she said, and then she swallowed the tab of acid.

"I was winded—I smoked then—and so we waited for the acid to
hit her, smoking cigarettes and drinking the warm beer she had hidden in the cabin. I still remember how it looked—she had a painting
table and an easel, a narrow bed, a fireplace in the corner. It didn't
take too long—it must have been a fairly good batch—and she began
to get quiet, then tuned in to the drug. At first her trip was fine. Then
we heard the boat."

"What boat?" Hatton asked, puzzled by the sudden shift in
Gwynn's retelling of his story.

"I don't know. Like a fishing skiff—an open boat, low to the water. The moon had gone down, and it was hard to see. We heard the
growl of the engine, then the boat scraping on the beach, just north
of the cabin. I went to the window and saw a man jump out and

stumble, then curse as he landed the boat. I was terrified—I knew I'd
be shitcanned if I was caught with a student who was loaded on
drugs."

"I thought you were rich," Hatton said skeptically.

Gwynn smiled ruefully. "Not then. My father'd cut me off . . . we
Gwynns don't get our money until we're forty, when we're old
enough to know how to use it to make more."

"What happened then?"

"The man headed up the bluff, on a winding path that headed up
behind the cabin. When he had gone over the edge of the bluff I followed him, just close enough to look over the top of the bluff. I saw
him cross the meadow to the big house. The lights came on, and I
knew I had to get the hell out of there."

"Where was Laura?"

"Still in the cabin. The whole thing had started to weird her
out . . . she might have been reacting to my fear, I guess. I told her the
man was gone, she had nothing to be afraid of, and I had to go."

"Did she react?"

"She seemed afraid, but it was hard to tell. The LSD still had her.
She just curled up in a corner of the bed."

"And you ran?"

Gwynn nodded. "Down the beach about a quarter mile, to the
next house. I could see a driveway. I followed it up to . . . maybe
Baker Hill Road? It came out near the old movie house in Lynnwood
Center. I can't remember the names of roads on the island anymore.
It took me nearly two hours to walk back to my car."

"What time was it by then?"

"Three, maybe four in the morning. I wasn't wearing a watch."

"And when the sheriff popped you in the morning you lied your
head off, right?"

"Absolutely," Gwynn replied. He drummed his fingers on his
desk. "So, where does this go from here?" he added anxiously.

"I think," Hatton said, "against my better judgment, that you've
told me the truth. At least some of it. How much of this did you tell
Talbot?"

"An edited version. Not the LSD, and not my wanting to fuck his
wife, thank you. I said Laura had gotten drunk at the party, I was

worried about her, and that I'd helped her back to the beach cabin, heard a boat, realized my predicament, and left." Gwynn paused and licked his lower lip nervously. "I'll be left alone if I testify to this?" he asked again.

"If you've told the truth," Hatton replied. "What about the man in the boat? Can you describe him?"

"No. I never even got a look at his face, and the moon was down. He was just—what's the word? A silhouette, against the starlight reflecting from the beach."

Like the black image Laura painted, Hatton thought. But who else could it have been? Ellen never said someone had gone to her house on the night Laura disappeared.

Hatton said his good-byes and left Gwynn's office. When he reached his car he pulled out his cell phone and called the Hauser and Todd offices.

"Tony? Will Hatton. I've finished with Gwynn. Do you still have that process server here in Port Townsend?"

"Absolutely," Guzzo replied.

"Have him serve Gwynn. Both the deposition and the trial subpoenas. Now, Tony, as soon as you can. Gwynn might just be the guy we have been looking for."

Chapter Twenty-seven

At two-thirty on Friday afternoon Mary Slattery ignored the persistent buzz of her telephone long enough to open a plastic container of pasta salad, now nearly four hours old. When she saw that the delicatessen on the first floor of the building had forgotten to put a fork in the bag with the salad, she swore, gave up, and punched the intercom button on her telephone.

"Can't I for chrissakes eat lunch?" she asked plaintively.

"Not today, darling," Angela Sayers, the firm's British-accented receptionist, replied firmly. "A woman named Wiegand says she has to talk to you about Mark Talbot. She says it's urgent, because Laura's mother is trying to destroy evidence, or something."

"Oh, Christ," Slattery said wearily. "Just what I need. Put her through." Slattery rubbed a hand over her face, composed herself, then said, "Ms. Wiegand. What can I do for you?"

Marcia Wiegand's words tumbled out in a rush. "Look, I know we didn't get along very well before, but I decided you were just doing your job and were a pretty honest person. Anyway, I thought it might be important. Ellen wants me to destroy evidence. Well, I think she does, anyway. You see, there's some more files of Mark's that we found at the old offices—"

"Slow down, Ms. Wiegand. What are you talking about?"

"Ellen. She was here, and she told me to throw away Mark's files."

"She has the right to do that. Those are company files, and she owns the company."

"But they might be about Mark! Or Laura. Or the environmental lawsuit that Mark was working on. They could be important."

Mary Slattery frowned. Environmental lawsuit? Oh, the toxic dumping case, now over two years old. "All right. Ms. Wiegand, I'm going to check with someone here who's working on that lawsuit. I'll ask about the documents. Then I'll come out, and we can talk to Ellen. You're at the corporate offices in Elk Run?"

"No. These were down at the old office, on Burwell Street in Bremerton. Where Mark was working this summer."

"All right. There's a Bremerton ferry at four, and I'll meet you there at five o'clock."

Slattery picked out a piece of pasta from the plastic box in front of her, tasted it, and dropped the box into the garbage. Well, maybe I can eat on the boat, she thought as she sighed. She punched her intercom again. "Angie, I need to talk to Dave Dworshak. I've only got ten minutes. He around?"

"Down in his dungeon. Want me to ring?"

"No, I'll go dig him out."

Slattery slipped through the mail room and took the freight elevator to the sixth-floor document storerooms that Hauser and Todd had created for the never-ending Bremerton environmental lawsuits involving Kitsap Industries. Kitsap, along with a hundred other companies and landowners, had been sued for the cost of the federal government's toxic waste cleanup in Port Washington Narrows and Dye Inlet. Kitsap, in turn, had sued every insurance company it had ever held a policy with to cover the costs. Like most complex environmental lawsuits, it had generated a mountain of paper and a fountain of fees. Most of the major law firms in Seattle and Tacoma had a piece of the case, and most of them secretly hoped that it would never end.

Slattery threw open the doors to reveal a forest of gray steel, floor-to-ceiling document shelves that filled the entire sixth floor of the building. The rows between each shelf were filled with the nasty blue glow of fluorescent lighting. "Dworshak?" Slattery called out. "You still alive?"

"Over here. In the computer room," Dworshak replied. He was a diminutive, bearded man with thick black-rimmed glasses, a former accountant with extensive computer database experience who had scraped his way through Columbia Law School, only to find that he hated actually practicing law. Reuben Todd had recruited him from a New York law firm, bringing him to Seattle by a devil's bargain: if Dworshak would design and manage the Bremerton environmental suits' evidence database and keep track of its million documents, they would not only pay him a base salary but allow him to charge other law firms fees for access to the database. Dworshak had taken the tedious job and discovered a latent gift for greed; if the case went on for another two years he might never have to work again.

Dworshak handed Slattery a glossy, photo-laden article from *Food & Wine*. "What do you think? The Chilean wine country. You can rent a cottage for $500 U.S. a month. I was thinking I might need a break from Bali, at least during rainy season."

"Take me with you," Slattery replied wearily, "but in the meantime I need your help."

"Sure. Sixty bucks a quarter hour and I'm yours."

"Fuck you, David. This comes out of your salary. One of the witnesses in the Talbot murder case just called me from the old Kitsap offices in Bremerton. She says she just found some documents Talbot was hoarding and that Ellen's trying to throw them away."

Dworshak shook his head. "Not possible. I worked with Mark from January until May to get all of Kitsap's documents located, organized, and logged into the system. Each original was number-stamped, labeled with a bar code, and laser-imaged onto compact disk. In August I walked through every inch of Kitsap's space with him, just to double-check—the old offices on Burwell, the foundry on National Avenue, the new offices up in Silverdale. Everything. I made Mark walk through it personally because he was going to be deposed as Kitsap's records custodian at the end of September before his wife . . . I mean before he died. And I helped Guzzo review all of Talbot's personal files." Dworshak shook his head stubbornly. "No. I got it all."

"Well, there's something out there. At the Burwell Street office. What kind of records are we talking about, anyway?"

"Five main kinds. First, anything related to old insurance policies. Second, anything about KI itself—incorporation documents, bylaws, minutes. Third, employees—payroll and personnel. Fourth, material—what they bought, what they produced, what kinds of chemicals they might have been using, what they sold. Fifth, anything related directly to waste disposal. What kind are you looking for?"

Slattery grinned. "I don't know. Our case is about sex, David, not about gunk."

"Thanks for reminding me," he said mournfully.

Slattery turned to go, thankful she had never had her career swallowed by a megacase. "I'll go check it out," she said. "One more thing, what's the coding sequence look like on the documents?"

"It's a bar code, for the laser-imaging process," Dworshak replied. "But if it's our document, it'll also be hand-stamped *KI*, with a Bates stamp, before the bar code. We did both on every document, two separate reviews. It's the only way to be sure you've got it all."

Slattery got off the Bremerton ferry just at five o'clock. The light was already starting to fade, even in late September, as the sun fell behind the Olympic Mountains, west of the city. She drove along Burwell, parallel to the high fence that blocked off the white bulk of the Puget Sound Naval Shipyard from downtown Bremerton. In the gaps between the buildings she could see the dark gray hulls of navy destroyers awaiting decommissioning. In a half mile she came to the squat three-story building that once housed Kitsap Industries' main office and machine shops. A few lights could be seen on the third floor; otherwise the building was dark and empty.

Slattery tried the front door, found it open, and walked into the worn, concrete-floored entry. To her left was the staircase that led to the third-floor offices; to her right, a passage led to the old time clock and the paymaster's office, with the machine shops beyond.

Slattery paused in the darkened stairwell, searching for a light switch. Suddenly, lights came on at the top of the stairwell. As Mary crossed the first landing she could see Marcia Wiegand coming down the stairs from above.

"Thank you for coming out," Wiegand said sheepishly. "I hope I'm not making an ass out of myself over this."

"Don't worry, people do it all the time," Mary Slattery replied evenly, joining her at the top of the stairs. "Where are these documents you're worried about?"

"Over here," she said, leading the way across the wide room that covered most of the top floor of the converted factory loft. "This used to be the drafting and office areas," Wiegand continued. "Mark and Ellen's old offices were over on the east side of the building, along the wall, where they had a little view of the water. After we shut this building down, all the records were consolidated out here in the open space, and Mark used this little office to sort through things when he came down here at night."

"Were you with him?"

Wiegand colored. "Yes, but not the way you probably think. He needed some extra help in reviewing the records, and he couldn't leave it to a secretary, so he drafted me to work on some of the old leases and things because I know real estate documents."

"Okay. So what brought you down here today?"

"We're donating the building to the city. It's too old to have any commercial use, and Ellen wanted to be rid of it. I came down to make sure that the salvage company had cleared out the rest of the surplus furniture. They hadn't, and I called them and gave them hell. While I was waiting for a call back I decided to just check the office areas one more time, to make sure nothing was left behind. I was checking the file cabinets when I noticed the one that Mark had used was still locked."

"How'd you get it open?"

"He'd taped a key under this desk in case he ever forgot his." Wiegand stepped to the battered green-painted file cabinet, turned the key, and pulled open the bottom drawer.

Mary looked down and saw four thick redweld folders of documents. She shrugged. "Is this everything?"

"I think so. That's all I saw, I mean."

"Let me take a look." Mary sat down in the ancient vinyl padded

Steelcase swivel chair that Mark had used. She slid the first group of documents out and leafed through them. They were mostly Kitsap corporate records, starting with the first articles of incorporation of Renner Tool & Die Works, dated 1959. Mary licked her forefinger and touched the edge of the document; the ink did not smear. Xerox copies. She took the stack and paged through them from the bottom. Each had a photocopy of the *KI* stamp and bar code that David Dworshak's coding shop had applied.

"It's all right," Mary said. "These are just photocopies of documents that have already been coded for the environmental lawsuit. Mark must have made a working set. You said he was working on a corporate restructuring, turning KI into a holding company, right? He might have needed these as reference materials."

"But why did he keep them down here?" Marcia Wiegand demanded, still unconvinced. "And why do they have notes on them, in his handwriting?"

"Because they're a working set. Look, you're right, technically. These should probably be put in the KI lawsuit archives at our office, and I'll review them personally to see if they should have been produced in response to any of the county prosecutor's requests. But I think you can relax."

Wiegand colored again, the flush of embarrassment plain against her pale skin. She sighed. "I'm really sorry to drag you over. It's just that this whole thing—"

"Has gotten fairly well out of hand," Ellen Arcand said archly. She strode into the office, a small but commanding figure in a dove gray Donna Karan business suit. "I thought I'd come down and sort this nonsense out, but I see Ms. Slattery has beaten me to it."

"It's all right, Ellen," Mary Slattery said. "Ms. Wiegand was right to be worried, since any documents associated with Mark could have been subject to a document request."

Ellen's face was impassive. "I know that all the documents have been properly reviewed, Mary. As I told Marcia earlier. I only wish my word were good enough for her . . . in light of her obvious concern that justice is done." Ellen's voice was heavy with sarcasm. She gestured toward Talbot's files. "Mary, why don't you go ahead and send these to the archives, at your office? I do regret your time being wasted when you have more important things to do for my family."

Ellen Arcand turned to Marcia Wiegand. She was by far the smaller woman, but her authority was overwhelming. "Marcia, I did intend to talk with you at the office, but since you did not return this afternoon, this will have to suffice. I've reviewed the office leasing progress at our project, and it is simply not acceptable. I've retained Grayson Smith & Company to handle all the real estate functions for Kitsap Industries, including leasing the office project. That eliminates the need for any internal real estate staff. I've had a check drawn for two months' severance for you and mailed to your home. You'll receive outplacement assistance and our usual benefits. Your personal items in the office will be sent to you. I'm very sorry this whole affair"—Ellen paused, then bit back the word angrily—"this whole situation came about. I've brought a security guard from our offices; he's waiting for you in the lobby downstairs, and will walk you to your car. This is no longer a safe area for a woman when it is near dark."

Marcia Wiegand stood silent, her shoulder slumped, as Ellen Arcand turned to go. "Ms. Arcand," she said quietly, raising her head.

Ellen turned and stared. "Yes."

"I want you to know that what you do to me doesn't matter. All I'm losing is a job. You're going to lose a daughter."

Ellen stepped forward so quickly that Mary could not stop her, her eyes dark with rage. Her hand flashed, and Marcia Wiegand's head snapped back as the slap landed, the solid meaty *chunk* of flesh striking flesh.

And *this,* Mary Slattery thought, in the dense silence that followed, will make one *hell* of a cross-examination.

Chapter Twenty-eight

The only thing wrong with the Washington State ferries, Mary Slattery thought as she sat in the galley of the MV *Sealth* as it made a stately turn around Point White and headed into Rich Passage, is that you can't get a real drink when you need one. She sipped at the paper cup of black coffee that had long since gone cold, and turned again to leaf through the papers Mark Talbot had assembled. Four volumes of dry corporate papers, many with Mark Talbot's careful, precise margin notes tracing each change in the ownership and structure of Renner Tool & Die as it had grown into Kitsap Industries. She sighed and turned to the fourth redweld folder, expecting more of the same. She picked up the first document, a signed photocopy of the 1972 buy-sell agreement that had given Ellen Arcand the majority interest in the company after Curt Renner's death, checked it for marginalia, then flipped it over. The next document caught her attention. It was a sheet of yellow legal pad paper in Talbot's handwriting. It read:

Laura
Donnelly
Gwynn
Wade D.

Sandy D.
Joni B.
S. Goltz
Harry Ryan

Each name on the first list had been checked off, with Talbot's characteristic reverse check marks. A second, shorter list of names had been printed below a hand-drawn line:

Ellen
Ed
Curt
Larry E.

Slattery stared at the paper for a long time. The names meant nothing to her, with the exception of Ed, Ellen, and Curt, presumably Renner, Talbot's biological father. She leafed quickly through the rest of the paper—more dull corporate documents—then turned back to the page of handwritten notes. She was still puzzling over it when the cellular phone inside her purse buzzed.

"Yes," she snapped.

"It's Will. Where are you?"

"On the Bremerton boat, headed back to town. Where are you?"

"Edmonds, heading for I-5. I just got off the ferry. We need to talk. Want to have dinner?"

"Professional, or personal?"

"Professional, unfortunately. What time are you getting in?"

"Seven-forty-five. Sure you couldn't be somebody else and make it personal? I could use some personal about now."

Hatton chuckled. "Not this month."

"Yeah, you're right. Okay, I'm going to do a Hatton on you. I'm tired, I smell, and I'm going home. Which is Belltown Court, twenty-one hundred block on First Avenue. If you show up with Chinese food and beer, I might let you in. Apartment 623. There's a phone at the street door."

"In an hour," Hatton promised.

. . .

That would be like him, to be on time, Mary Slattery thought, hearing the intercom as she shoved the last of two days' worth of dishes into the washer. She left the narrow galley kitchen, went to the intercom in the hallway, verified it was Hatton, and buzzed him in. He knocked on her apartment door a few minutes later, carrying a six-pack of Tsing Dao beer and a white plastic bag that seemed about to burst open. "Come on in," Slattery said, taking the bag by the bottom before the plastic straps could let go. She put the food on the countertop of the bar that separated the kitchen from the remainder of the long, high-ceilinged living room. Hatton had already slid past her, surveying the room.

"It's no more chaotic than the rest of my life," Mary Slattery said defensively.

"I don't think it's chaotic at all," Hatton replied. He parsed the long narrow room. A cream-colored Italian leather sofa flanked by reading lamps filled a window bay at the far end of the room. Tall windows that rose the height of the nine-foot ceilings took in the view to the south, the neon signs of the Pike Place Market in the foreground, the lighted towers of the financial district rising beyond. A thin slice of the harbor could be seen to the right, the colored neon glow of the tourist piers, and the bright orange stalks of the working harbor's cranes along the Duwamish waterway in the distance. A low Japanese table filled the center of the room, with tatami mats surrounding it. A compact stereo on top of a wide wooden chest played a gentle Segovia rendition of Bach on classical guitar. Hatton glimpsed a small study through an open door to his left, fitted with white floor-to-ceiling bookcases along one wall, a Chinese Chippendale desk in red mahogany, and a subdued but good Turkish kilim laid over the industrial gray carpeting on the floor.

"Have you told anybody down at the law firm that you're a real grown-up?" Hatton asked, impressed.

Mary decided not to be insulted. "Hell, no," she said. "Why ruin a perfectly good bad reputation? Let's eat. I'm starved."

"So am I." A half hour later they had demolished most of two orders of egg rolls, Szechuan chicken, and spicy shrimp, and were sipping beer while sitting on the tatami mats around the low table.

"So, what's on your mind?" Mary Slattery asked. "Not that I'm not grateful for the delivery service."

"A couple of things," Hatton replied. "Actually, a lot of things. Remember how Laura said that Mark Talbot had been trying to help her figure out her dreams, why they were so painful?"

"Yeah. That was on the interview tapes. Was he?"

"Quite a bit, I think. In fact, everywhere I've gone in the past five days, Mark Talbot has been there first."

Slattery frowned, puzzled. "I don't understand."

"I've been following up on what we did last weekend, trying to trace what happened to Laura in 1972. I started with a high school friend of Laura's and mine—a woman named Sandy Demerest. They renewed their friendship after Laura moved back here from New York. Sandy told me that Mark had been asking about 1972—focusing on a keg party on the island that Laura was at the night she disappeared. I interviewed John Stansbury, who was Kitsap County sheriff at the time, looked at the news stories from the island paper about Laura's disappearance, then talked to two men who were with her at the party. It turned out that Mark had done all of those things before he was killed."

"*What?*"

"That's how I reacted. But the stories were consistent—Mark was investigating what happened to Laura in 1972. Was there anything in his Day-Timer, or his computer, that indicated what he was doing?"

"Let me check." Slattery ducked into her study and returned with a sagging rectangular black leather litigation bag. She dropped it on the floor and dug into it, extracting a half-inch-thick black three-ring notebook. "This is the case chronology," she said. "It's updated every day. Tony's paralegal staff should have gotten Talbot's Day-Timer, computer calendar, and anything else even remotely relevant from his computer memory loaded into this by now. What months do I check?"

"June, July, August. Maybe early September, but I think Talbot had gone out of town by then."

Mary opened the book, found the right pages. "Tell me what names I'm looking for."

"John Stansbury. He was Kitsap County sheriff in 1972. Danny or Dan Donnelly. He was dating Laura in 1972."

"The old Rams quarterback?"

"The same. I didn't know you liked football. The third name is Seth Gwynn. He was a theater teacher in the Bainbridge Island High School in 1972. Now he's a wealthy retired actor."

Slattery read through the chronology, and then checked the name index. "No. None of them."

"Was Talbot sloppy about keeping his calendar?"

"No. The opposite. Obsessive about it."

"Then Talbot didn't want anyone to know what he was doing," Hatton said.

"Why, for God's sake?"

"Privacy? Embarrassment?"

"Maybe," Slattery said doubtfully. She paused to think. "Wait a minute. I saw those names, Donnelly and Gwynn, just today. They were on a list in Mark Talbot's files." Slattery went into her study, then returned bearing a white cardboard bankers' box. "These were files that Marcia Wiegand, Mark's real estate assistant, found in the old Bremerton office today. She called me over there because Ellen told her to destroy them. I looked at them; they were just Mark's working copies of stuff from a toxic waste dumping lawsuit that Kitsap is involved in. All except for one sheet. Some notes, in Mark's handwriting. Damn, where did I put them?"

"Why was Ellen involved?"

"I don't know . . . I guess Wiegand called Ellen when she found this stuff, before she called me. Ellen told her to throw the files out, and Wiegand got the crazy idea that Ellen was asking her to destroy evidence. Ellen was plenty angry about it. She came down to Bremerton just after I got there and fired Wiegand on the spot. When Wiegand mouthed off to her, Ellen slapped her."

Hatton sighed. "I never went to law school, but even I know that's not exactly a brilliant move."

"That's what I said. Wait, here it is. I moved it to the back."

Mary handed the single page of handwritten notes to Will. He studied it carefully.

"I couldn't say if it's in Mark's handwriting. Is it?" Hatton asked. Slattery nodded. "I think so. I've gotten pretty familiar with it."

"This list of names," Hatton said, thinking aloud. "Donnelly and Gwynn, that makes sense, he talked to them. Some of the others . . . Sandy D., Wade D.—that's got to be the Demerests. They weren't at the party but they were friends of Laura in 1972. Joni B. . . . Berman? She was in my class. Same for Sam Goltz and Harry Ryan, they might have been at that party the night Laura disappeared. What's the other list about?"

"I don't know. Could Talbot have asked Ed and Ellen about Laura's disappearance?"

"That doesn't seem to fit. Larry E. Wait a minute, that's a Bremerton lawyer, dead a long time now. Lawrence Elder. He was the Kitsap County prosecutor in the 1960s. Talbot asked John Stansbury about him, and Stansbury said Elder had been Curt Renner's lawyer."

Slattery looked back down at the list of names. "Why would Mark have put Renner on this list? Ellen said he was drowned in a boating accident later that summer, after they found Laura."

"He was," Hatton replied. "I saw the stories in the paper when I paged through all of the 1972 issues. They declared Renner missing about two weeks after Laura was found."

"A boating accident," Slattery mused. "Will, I was out to Laura and Mark's house on Tuesday. She wanted some toiletries and personal stuff. When I went back in the house there was a light on in Mark's study . . . one I know was turned off when I was there for the search."

"I don't understand."

"Somebody else had been going through Talbot's study. Have you ever seen it?"

"No. As you guessed, he and I weren't the best of friends."

"It's beautiful, in a manly guy sort of way. Oriental rugs, big roll-top desk, thick cherry-wood paneling on the walls."

"So?"

"Cherry-wood paneling with maps thumbtacked to it. Tide and

sailing charts, for Port Orchard Bay up to Whidbey Island. Was Talbot a sailor?"

"No more than I am," Will replied. "I spent two summers on my grandfather's fishing boat as a kid, hauling net in forty-foot swells in the Bering Sea. Scared the shit out of me the whole time. My idea of good water is a calm lagoon in the Caribbean—no more than six feet deep."

"Then why would Talbot decorate his study like the Chart Room Bar?"

"No idea," Will said slowly. "Do you think the cops went through the house again, without a warrant?"

"Maybe," Mary Slattery replied. "But they'd be taking an awful risk."

Hatton paused, thinking. "Somebody is," he said quietly.

Chapter Twenty-nine

Will Hatton stared across the peaceful expanse of Stenslund Lake, a thin morning mist rising near the far shore. The lake, about a hundred yards across, bounded by stately Pacific maples and Douglas firs, had the serene look of a mountain lake, but was governed by the odd quirks of the island's glacial geology. The lake's impermeable clay bottom sealed in the water from a half dozen hidden winter streams and springs. Its outflow was equally mysterious, giving rise to no creek, only a series of springs on the western hillside leading down to the beach at Crystal Springs.

Hatton circled the lake twice and found no trailhead leading down to the western beach. He sighed, regarded his muddy boots, and headed off in a steady autumn rain back to his car. When he returned to his Jeep Cherokee, he drove out to the park road, followed it down to its junction with Island Center Road, and on a whim, turned left toward Fletcher Bay.

Ed Hauser's farm lay three quarters of a mile northwest. Once a proud eighty-acre homestead growing hops, apples, and berries, it had fallen into disrepair by 1969, when Hauser had acquired the house and its twenty remaining acres cheaply in a tax sale. Hatton remembered his mother and Ed working weekends on the white, foursquare Victorian house, painting and repairing its sagging porches, clearing brush from the overgrown yard, preparing for the spring farm wedding that his mother would never see, struck down by breast cancer at the age of thirty-six. After her death, Ed and Will had continued to repair the old farmstead at a manic pace, work being the only substitute that either of them could find for grief.

Will turned into the gate with a quiet smile, his heart buoyed by the sight of the rolling lawns and orchards rising from the road. He pulled into the gravel circle in front of the house and stopped, drawn to a familiar stoop-shouldered figure patiently cutting dead stems from the raspberry racks on the eastern hill.

"Tor!" he called into the rain. The old man dropped a bunch of dead stems from his left hand onto the burn pile beside him and waved, then ambled toward the drive.

"Good to see you, Will," he said, pulling off his work gloves and offering a scarred, leathery hand. "You never come out here enough. This is going to be your place someday. You'll have to take care of it."

Hatton grinned. "I'm not worried about the farm, Tor—you're going to be running it, like always. Do you have any coffee on?"

"In the kitchen, boy. Let's go get some."

Tor Trolland had joined their lives in the year after Will's mother had died. A Norwegian immigrant fisherman who had once crewed on Will's grandfather's boat, Tor had fought and won a fight with another boat captain in Dutch Harbor in the winter of 1971. Unfortunately for Trolland, the captain died from his injuries, and Tor stood trial for the killing. Ed had secured his acquittal with the aid of eyewitnesses, mostly deckhands from Trolland's own boat, who somewhat miraculously placed Tor's skinning knife in the other man's hand at the start of the fight. Tor had come down from Alaska for a year to work on the farm to pay off Ed's fee. He'd stayed ever since, finding farmwork in the island's rainy climate as congenial as he had at home in his native Bergen.

Trolland sat down at the round oak table and poured coffee into the thick stoneware cups that Will had used as a teenager. Outside, the wind rose and rain rattled the kitchen windows. "It's good to see you, Will," he said. "We missed you this summer."

"Stuck in Texas for a lot of it," Will replied. "How've you been?"

"Worried about the old man." Tor showed no sign of irony in calling Ed that, even though Ed was two years younger than he was. "He smokes those cigars, drinks that booze."

"Like you used to. And worse."

"Yeah, that's true. Time he should stop too. How's Laura doing?"

"Badly, I'm afraid."

"I never liked that husband of hers."

"Me neither. But Laura's the only one who could have killed him."

"Yeah. I suppose."

"Something wrong?"

"Just Ed. He needs that heart operation, not another trial. He's getting too old. I stayed here this summer, rather than going back to Norway like I usually do, because I thought he was going in for it. But he didn't. Now he won't, you know, until he gets Laura squared away."

"Ed's pretty tough, Tor," Will replied. "It'd be harder on him to stay out of it than be in it." He hesitated, and then said, "Tor? You remember the night that Talbot was killed?"

"Sure I do. Ed and I were headed to Westport the next day, three days of fishing we had planned."

"What happened?"

Tor looked suddenly fearful. "All I know is what I saw from up here. You know that, right?"

"Of course."

"That's right. I ain't no witness. I've seen one damned courthouse in my time, never want to see another." Trolland sighed. "Anyway, they was having a party that weekend, Ellen and Ed, down at her house," he said. "I was asleep early, like I should be—we was pushing off for the boat at five A.M. Ed comes back in at one, no, one-fifteen in the damned morning—"

"You're sure about the time?"

"Of course I'm sure about the damned time! I had them people from Ed's office asking me about it. And I always look at the clock when some damn fool wakes me in the middle of the night, the way Ed did."

"What did he want?"

"Wanted to know if I had the damn tackle loaded in the truck and the ice ordered, of all the stupid fucking . . . pardon. Of course I had. Like I don't know how to fish."

"What did you do in the morning?"

"I got out of bed at four. Four-thirty, no Ed, so I had to go in and wake him up. He'd slept through his alarm and looked like hell. Hot and sweaty red. Guess he drank too much after dinner, which might account for his stupid questions for me. Anyway, I rolled him out of his rack, and we left about five. No sooner did we get to Westport, start loading the boat, than Ed turns on his damn phone, you know, the cell phone, and it rings and somebody says Laura has killed her husband. Off her head, she must have been." Trolland shook his head. "Poor damn girl. Ed says he's got to get back there, help Ellen."

"Did you see Laura or Mark this summer, Tor?"

"Not too much. They was working on the beach house, I know. I hardly saw Ed. Ellen had been riding him hard all summer about the lawsuits and some real estate deal. She's a lovely woman, but Ed—I tell him he'd be better off, sometimes."

"Without her?"

"Maybe." Trolland looked defensive. "You won't pass this on, now, will you? Man of a certain age . . . gets set in his ways. I tell him . . . There's a place in Bergen, and a couple places in Mazatlán, where we go in spring for the tarpon. I even know a few places like that around here . . . willing ladies, you know, no questions asked, even for an old bastard like me. Okay, maybe a little money, but what's that? And I tell him . . . but he don't listen. No offense to your mother, may she rest peaceful, but that Ellen is it for him. All there ever was, or will be."

Will smiled. "Amen."

"Maybe," Tor Trolland replied doubtfully. "But that Ellen's hard on him. Always has been."

"Love is that way," Will said.

Chapter Thirty

They were twenty minutes early for the two o'clock motion hearing. Ed Hauser and Mary Slattery sat together in the empty courtroom, huddled over the briefs they had filed for the omnibus hearing on this day, Friday, the third of October.

"Why isn't Reuben arguing these motions?" Slattery asked nervously. "He knows the law better than anyone else."

"Reuben also knows that Judge Cairns needs to see us and size us up," Hauser replied. "Relax, you'll do fine. What did you find out about Cairns?"

"Allison Cairns. A newbie, on the bench for just under a year," Slattery replied. "Forty-one, married, two kids. Came out of Reuben's old shop, the Justice Criminal Division in D.C. Eight years there, moved out here in 1991, spent two years working at Wade & Briggs in Tacoma, then hung out her own shingle in Silverdale after she married a builder who lives in Poulsbo. Three years ago she got two of the *E. coli* hamburger cases, settled them for 3 million bucks, kept a million, and started building up a community service record she could run on for judge. Got elected in 1996."

"Republican?"

"Yes, but not Watkins's kind. Belongs to a country club, not Hezbollah."

"Hobbies?"

"Her kids, and horses."

"How does she run her courtroom?"

"Tightly." Slattery grinned. "She will not tolerate your famous histrionics in front of the jury. Nor will she take shit from the press. Which is why they are all standing in the hallway, cussing her out. She'll let them in when it suits her."

Hauser smiled thinly. "*That's* comforting. Here comes Mrs. Watkins, the La Pasionaria of the Christian right, and her henchman, Terrible Tommy."

"Go be nice."

Hauser rose and greeted Judith Watkins and Thomas Tiernan at the bar of the courtroom. "Counsel," he said briefly, "always a pleasure. Have you given any additional thought to our plea offer?"

"No," Judith Watkins said abruptly. She turned away and busied herself in her briefcase at counsel table.

"Ed," Thomas Tiernan said, reaching out and offering his hand. Hauser took it reluctantly. "Any chance of an extension on the trial date? We're ready, of course, but I do have a couple of—"

"No," Hauser cut in. "Let's just have at it, Thomas. The sooner the better."

They were interrupted by the appearance of Judge Cairns's clerk-bailiff, a stout, plain young woman. "Counsel, the judge will be out in just a moment. She's asked me to hold the press out in the hallway so you weren't distracted, but I'm going to let them in now."

The press filed into the courtroom, clearly disgruntled by being held in the hallway. "Hey, Ed," John Cameron, the courthouse reporter for the *Seattle Tribune*, bellowed, "are you gonna rely on the insanity—"

The clerk-bailiff cut him off with her sharp voice. "All *rise*," she commanded, "and knock off the questions until after the judge—"

"Thank you, Margaret," Judge Allison Cairns said, not unkindly, taking the bench. She was tall and graceful, even in her judicial robes, with a long, pleasantly even-featured face and a deep tan, even in early October, from much time spent outdoors. She wore no visible makeup, and her dishwater blonde hair was pulled back tightly into a horsewoman's bun. "Please sit down, everyone. Counsel, before we begin, I need to address members of the press and the public." She composed herself, folding her hands on the bench. "First, I understand that there will be heavy press coverage of this case because the defendant has been very prominent in the arts. I will be the trial judge in this matter. My staff and I will accommodate your presence as best we can, because our state constitution provides for a public trial, and I take that right seriously. That said, *I* control this courtroom. You do not. Shut off those video cameras, now. There will be no television coverage of this trial, period."

The anchor reporter from Court TV groaned audibly.

"Second, I expect decorum from all members of the press and public. Deviate from that rule, and you will be ejected. Promptly.

"Third, I am imposing a restrictive disclosure order on counsel. While no motion has been made for change of venue, this is a small county, and I will not have the jury pool tainted. Counsel, members of the press, please pick up a copy of the order from my bailiff after this hearing. Now that we understand the ground rules, let's begin. Counsel, make your appearances for the record. Madam Prosecutor."

"Judith Watkins and Thomas Tiernan for the state," Judith Watkins intoned.

"Edwin Hauser and Mary Slattery for the defendant, Laura Arcand," Ed Hauser rumbled.

"Thank you. I have two motions from the defense to exclude certain evidence. I also have the state's motion to require the defense to elect between a defense of not guilty and not guilty by reason of insanity. I will take up the defense motions first, then the prosecution's, then we will complete the omnibus checklist. Mr. Hauser?"

"Your Honor, Ms. Slattery will address our evidence motions."

"Very well. Ms. Slattery, are there any additional authorities you wish to bring to my attention beyond those cited in your brief?"

"No, Your Honor. We have briefed the issue, but I would—"

"Very well. I am prepared to rule." Judge Cairns flipped open a notebook and put on a pair of rimless reading glasses, and reviewed her notes.

We're fucked, Mary Slattery thought. A thin trickle of sweat ran uncomfortably between her breasts.

"Counsel, I commend you on your briefs, which enabled me to

reach two very clear conclusions. The first motion from the defense seeks to exclude any argument or suggestion from the prosecution that Ms. Arcand's suicide attempt constitutes an admission of guilt in this matter. I agree. I am not persuaded that the fact of Ms. Arcand's suicide attempt is an admission of guilt by conduct, as argued by the prosecution, and therefore exclude any such argument. I note for the record that even if I were so persuaded, I would still exclude such argument or suggestion as prejudicial, and not subject to correction by a limiting instruction. Therefore, the defense motion is granted.

"I now turn to the second, and much closer, issue, presented by the defense's motion to exclude the statement made by Ms. Arcand in the emergency room when she briefly recovered consciousness. According to the declaration of Sergeant Martinez, who was present in the emergency room with Ms. Arcand, she briefly recovered consciousness and made the statement, quote, 'I killed them! Oh God, *both* of them.' The defense argues that this statement is both hearsay and not an admission, being ambiguous as to meaning. I find that the statement does not constitute hearsay, since it falls under the excited utterance exception to our hearsay rule, evidence rule 803(a)(2). The much closer question is whether the relevance of this statement, which the state seeks to introduce as an admission, is outweighed by its ambiguity and its potentially prejudicial and inflammatory nature.

"I have thought long and hard about this. Counsel have done an able job of researching and citing cases to the court, and my bailiff and I have joined the hunt, searching for *any* case which can shed light on this type of statement. We have found nothing squarely on point. With that in mind, I must do my job, which is to apply my discretion.

"I will admit this evidence. While it may be prejudicial, I do not find, as evidence rule 403 requires, that the statement is *unfairly* prejudicial. The defendant uttered those words. If she chooses to testify, she can say what she meant. If she chooses not to testify—which I caution everyone is the defendant's absolute right, with no inference to be drawn from it—her counsel may argue, and I will instruct the jury, that such a statement is to be given such weight, or *no weight*, as the jury sees fit, dependent upon the testimony, if any, regarding the nature of the defendant's injuries and her state of mind at the time the statement was made. Because of the importance of these decisions, written rulings with detailed citations will be issued following this hearing."

Cairns removed her reading glasses. "Let's begin the checklist. Mrs. Watkins?"

"I'd like Mr. Tiernan to address that, Your Honor."

The judge's eyes narrowed but she said pleasantly, "Of course. Mr. Tiernan?"

"Your Honor, we've found the defense admirably forthcoming, with one exception that swallows everything else," Tiernan began. "They won't tell us whether they're going to try this case based on the insanity defense, or not."

"They gave you notice of the possible application of that defense, did they not, Mr. Tiernan?"

"Oh, they did. After they gulled us into an early trial date, Your Honor. What they haven't said is whether they're going to *rely* on the defense. That's what we have to know."

"Mr. Hauser?"

Ed rose and settled his bulk comfortably at the bar. "Your Honor, the Washington statute regarding assertion of the insanity defense permits the assertion of alternate pleading. All the statute requires is that notice be given to the state that the insanity defense may be asserted. It does not require the defendant to forgo her right to require that the state prove beyond a reasonable doubt that the defendant actually committed the acts accused. Here, there is only very shaky, circumstantial evidence that Laura Arcand had anything to do with Mark Talbot's death. No one saw the shots that killed Mark Talbot being fired. No witness can place the defendant and Mark Talbot together at the time of his death. The state still is required to prove, beyond a reasonable doubt, that Laura Arcand is guilty of that crime. After that—"

"But that's not the question imposed by the omnibus rule, Mr. Hauser. The question is, will the defendant rely upon the insanity defense at trial?"

"Your Honor." Hauser hesitated. "Your Honor, the defendant does not waive her right to require the state to prove her guilt beyond a reasonable doubt. However, she will, *if the evidence shows,* assert the defense of insanity at trial."

Judge Cairns's eyes narrowed and her voice tightened. "Mr. Hauser, your craft at the time of arraignment was, I suppose, admirable. This is not the time for craft. Did your client fire the shots that killed Mark Talbot, and does she assert that she did so while in an insane state of mind?"

Hauser squared his shoulders at the bar. "Your Honor, with all respect, you do not have the right to demand an admission of guilt from the defendant," he said stubbornly. "We stand on what I just told you. The state cannot evade its obligation to prove guilt beyond a reasonable doubt."

Cairns bit her lip and appeared to be swallowing a considerable amount of anger, as Hauser remained at the bar, unmoved. "Very well, Mr. Hauser. The court takes your statement to mean that the defendant will assert a defense of insanity at trial, and rely on it. You will therefore not dispute that Laura Arcand did indeed fire the shots that killed her husband. Have you made your expert witness disclosure to the state?"

"We're prepared to do so now, Your Honor," Mary Slattery said, rising to her feet to defuse the confrontation. "The defense will call Dr. William Hatton, M.D., Ph.D. I tender a complete copy of his vita and his report to the state. They can depose him tomorrow, if they so desire." Mary ostentatiously handed the file of documents to Thomas Tiernan.

"Mr. Tiernan? If you're inclined to claim surprise and prejudice here, I would be willing to entertain a motion regarding the trial date."

Tiernan leafed quickly through the documents regarding Hatton's testimony, a worried expression on his face. He started to rise. Judith Watkins quickly seated him with a brusque motion of her hand, and rose in his stead. She fluffed a bit for the press as she addressed the court.

"I think we will be just fine with the trial date, Your Honor," she said. "Just fine. You see," she said triumphantly, playing again to the press gallery behind her, "we kind of figured this was the way they would have to go. And *our* expert is ready. He doesn't even need to interview the defendant. You see, he's her former treating psychiatrist, Dr. Robert Darrington Treadwell. Treated her right until a week after the murder. And *he* doesn't think Laura Arcand was insane at all."

"Thank you, God," Mary Slattery said under her breath, her voice masked by the excited buzz from the press benches. "Thank you. You made her just as fucking stupid as we thought she was."

Chapter Thirty-one

Will knocked on the door frame of Ed's office, then stepped in. Ed, Mary Slattery, and Ellen Arcand were seated at Ed's conference table with the glassed-in vista of the waterfront from the Duwamish piers to the Space Needle behind them. Ed looked up, surprised.

"Will? We're doing witness prep, son. Can't have you here for that."

"I know. Can you break for half an hour? Mary and I have been trying to get the two of you together for over a week now."

Ed sighed. "Is it important? Ellen and I were hoping to finish up by six, have dinner with Laura, then get back to the island."

"It could be important, Ed. Some questions I can't figure out."

Ed started to demur but Ellen laid a hand on his arm. "Will's right, he's been calling and I've been putting him off. Have your secretary call Grace and tell her to put her feet up and take the night off, and to send Owen back with the car. We can spend the night in town. That's why you bought that overpriced penthouse of yours, anyway."

Ed grinned. "Overruled, as usual. Come on, grab a seat. It's nearly five. I'm going to have a drink. Anybody else?"

Hatton took a beer, Ellen scotch. Mary refused. "I'm working late tonight, so I'd better stick with coffee."

"It's about Mark Talbot," Will began when they had settled back down at the table, "and what he was doing just before his death."

"You mean for the company?" Ellen asked, puzzled. "Everything, I'm afraid. Our restructuring, the environmental suits, our real estate projects . . . It was too much. I know that now," she added sadly.

"Not exactly," Will said. "Did you know he was investigating Laura's background, talking to people about her disappearance in 1972?"

"No," Ed said slowly, taken aback. "Why would he do that?"

"I was hoping you could tell me. He interviewed at least a half dozen witnesses. John Stansbury, the former Kitsap County sheriff; Sandy Demerest and a couple of other students from the high school; and Danny Donnelly and Seth Gwynn, who were at the party with Laura just before she ran away. He got pretty personal with them, accused Donnelly, and then Gwynn, of raping Laura."

Ed drummed his fingers on the tabletop, thinking. Ellen Arcand sat silently. Will watched her carefully. Surprise. No, more than that. Shock.

"I never thought," Ellen said, stunned. "*Mark* was accusing Seth Gwynn? Wasn't he a teacher? Why would Mark think that he . . ."

"Gwynn was the last person to see Laura before she disappeared, Ellen. He took Laura to the beach cabin after the party, stayed with her while she took LSD. Gwynn denies raping her, denies any sexual contact with her. He says he heard a boat scrape up on the beach near the cabin, then ran because he knew he'd lose his job if someone found him with Laura."

Ellen clenched her fists and looked away. "I will *never* forgive myself for that summer," she said bitterly. "Never. The counselor we saw said it was just a phase, give Laura space, let her roam a bit and she'd get through it. I should never have let her stay in that cabin by herself . . . That bastard! Damn. Damn." She closed her eyes and started to shake with long-suppressed tears of guilt and rage.

"Ellen . . ." Ed rose and eased her up from her chair, held her until the angry sobs had subsided. "Look," Hauser said, still holding Ellen tightly in his arms, "maybe Mark started doing this because of all the trouble Laura was having this past summer. I thought Laura said she told him about the dreams."

"She did," Hatton interjected. "But I don't know if she related them to her disappearance. Somehow Mark figured that out on his own."

"Hmph." Ed turned to Mary, on the visible edge of anger. "Why wasn't any of this in the case chronology?" he demanded.

"Mark didn't list any of his appointments with the people he talked to in his daytime log or his computer," Slattery answered. "I'm going to put it into today's chronology update; that's why I'm staying late tonight. But we were hoping that you could shed some light on what Mark was up to. You two were the closest to him, aside from Laura."

"I'm afraid I can't," Ellen said sadly. She slipped out of Ed's arms. "Thank you," she whispered, patting his cheek. She sat back down at the table and composed herself. "I suppose it's good to know that Mark really cared, was trying to help Laura," she added. "It's one small bright thought in this awful tragedy."

"Mark was also asking questions about some people with connections to the company, Ellen," Mary Slattery said. She took a copy of the handwritten notes that had been found in Talbot's files. "Curt Renner and Larry Elder." She handed the paper to Ellen. Ed stopped and moved behind Ellen to read over her shoulder.

"I don't understand this," Ellen said slowly. "What could Curt and Larry Elder have to do with all of these people who were friends of Laura's? They've both been dead for years."

"Probably nothing," Ed boomed, pacing the room with a tumbler of scotch in his hand. "Jesus, Mark was always making lists of things only he could understand."

"What was Elder's connection to Kitsap Industries, Ellen?" Will insisted.

"Ancient," Ed cut in dryly, rubbing the heel of his hand against his cheek as he returned to his chair. "Larry Elder was Curt Renner's lawyer."

"So why would Mark Talbot have been looking for Elder now?"

"It's this restructuring thing," Hauser replied. "Mark insisted that we had to have KI's corporate records in clean shape before we could complete the restructuring to turn KI into a holding company and take it public. To do that we had to have a complete list of every transaction in stock and every insurance policy Renner Tool & Die had ever taken out—and the records were a mess. My fault—I should have cleaned everything up after Elder died. But by then, Ellen had owned all of the company, except for Mark's ten percent, for nearly four years. At the time it didn't seem to matter." Ed turned to Ellen with a rueful smile. "I told you you should have fired me, honey, and gotten yourself a real lawyer."

Ellen smiled thinly. "Larry Elder drafted the stock purchase agreement when I bought into Renner Tool & Die, and then later drafted the buy-sell agreement that I had with Curt Renner," she said, fleshing out what Ed had told them. "When we began to talk about forming a holding company and possibly going public this past spring, Mark insisted that we locate the *original* buy-and-sell agreement, even though we had Xerox copies in the office files, and the stock book showing the transfer of the stock to me after Curt's death, and the insurance payment to his estate. Mark said Wall Street would insist on it. He also said we needed it for all these ridiculous environmental lawsuits, too, but we couldn't find it. The original was filed in court, part of Curt's estate. The court microfilmed all its files, and all the originals were thrown away."

"That would explain why Mark was looking for Elder," Will said slowly. "He was probably trying to locate Elder's old office files." He took a copy of Talbot's notes out of his own briefcase and read it over. "Probably why he had Curt Renner's name written down, too." Hatton reluctantly folded the paper in half and stuck it back in his briefcase. "I guess that covers it. But I wish I knew how Mark had connected Laura's dreams to her disappearance."

Ed was looking at Ellen. "See? I can't even keep my own expert witness in line. You can still get another lawyer. It's not too late."

Ellen smiled back at him. "You do have other talents," she said dryly.

It was Ed's turn to grin. He looked at his watch. "Twenty minutes to six. Let's get rid of these children and go eat."

Ellen smiled briefly at Hauser, then turned to Hatton and Mary Slattery. Anger returned to her face. "I want you to go after Seth

Gwynn," she commanded. "If you can prove what he did to my daughter, I want him prosecuted. Or sued. Ruined."

Mary Slattery detoured to the office kitchen to pick up a spinach salad she'd had delivered for dinner. When she returned to her office she found Hatton sitting in her client chair, leafing through the corporate documents in Mark Talbot's private files.

"Something wrong?"

Hatton looked up. "Why would Talbot be so insistent about having the original of the buy-sell agreement? Isn't something like that a done deal after twenty-five years? Statute of limitations or something?"

"Should be. The six-year statute of limitations for written contracts would apply and you can use the Xerox copies as proof of any agreement, especially if a document is lost or fairly old." She shrugged. "Corporate lawyers get pretty weird about that stuff. That's what Talbot was, really. Maybe he was just obsessive about it."

"Maybe," Hatton said dubiously.

"You're thinking . . . ?"

He shook his head. "Nothing. I just remember something Ed told me once, years ago, when I was clerking in his office. That a document examiner needs an *original* document to determine if a signature has been forged."

Slattery looked at him for a long time, then shook her head. "Don't go there, Will. We've got enough problems to solve. The trial's just over two weeks away."

Chapter Thirty-two

"I don't think I can do this," Laura Arcand said grimly. She rubbed her hands together nervously. "My God, Mary, I thought I wasn't going to have to testify."

"We don't plan on it, Laura, but we have to be ready in case something goes wrong. If you do have to testify, I'll be there with you, helping you through it. Now, on cross-examination, the key is to keep your composure and listen, really listen, to what you're being asked. Most of the questions can be answered just yes or no. If you want to explain something, do it, but keep your answers short." Mary Slattery looked down at the long list of possible cross-examination questions she had prepared. We'll never get through all of this today, she thought. Maybe just a few simple ones for now.

"Okay," Mary said, "let's try this. Pretend that I'm the prosecutor."

"Ms. Arcand," she began, "I'd like to start with the state of your health this past summer. You were being treated by Dr. Treadwell for depression, weren't you?"

"Yes. Well, actually, manic-depression."

"And he prescribed medication for your condition, correct?"

"Yes."

"And you chose to stop taking that medication, didn't you?"

"Yes. Well, not for all of it. I was trying to paint again. You see—"

Slattery shook her head. "Too long. Try to—"

"I am fucking trying!"

Slattery closed her notebook and sighed.

The silence was broken by a persistent buzz from Mary Slattery's cellular phone. "I'm sorry," she said. "Let me see who this is. It won't take long."

Slattery picked up the phone. "Yeah . . . Tony? Uh-huh. Hot damn. Where? Hoquiam? *Hoquiam?* God, no wonder they couldn't find him. I'd never think of looking there. Okay. Tell Will to pick me up at my place. With the traffic, it'll take an hour. No, keep on him. We're going down there tonight."

Mary turned back to Laura, barely able to contain her excitement. "That was my investigator, Tony Guzzo. He's found Steven Terry."

"Who?" Laura looked suddenly drawn and out of focus, as though her depression had slipped back into her through her skin.

"Dr. Terry. He's the psychiatrist you saw when you were fourteen, right after they found you. It's great news, Laura! He can confirm that you were . . . traumatized. It fills the hole in your case that Will has been worried . . ." Slattery stopped abruptly and stared at Laura.

Laura sat rigidly in her chair. She nodded pensively, her lips pressed hard together in a single thin line, gripping the table in front of her, as though to brace herself. Despite Laura's effort to hold her body still, her shoulders and chest began to move, to convulse. "Mary . . . ," she whispered through clenched teeth.

But Slattery had already begun to move, out into the corridor. "You! Nurse!" she shouted. "Get in here! My client's having a seizure."

Two hours later Will returned to the smoking area outside the hospital's main entrance, where Mary had been waiting for him, pacing, smoking, and talking on her telephone until the battery finally ran out.

"How's Laura?" Mary said.

"All right. Sedated. Dr. Richter came back in to examine her."

"Oh God, Will, it's my fault. Laura seemed to be getting better. I knew today was going to be tough, getting her ready to testify if we need her, but most of the times I've talked with her she seems alert, thoughtful. I thought she could handle it. But there's no way we can put Laura on the stand. No way. And I really hoped she was getting better."

Will shook his head, no. "Laura likes you and she's making an effort. But she's not really getting better. Laura is still very depressed, very near the edge. And still very stressed by something she won't admit to. The seizure is similar to the one she had when I interviewed her for the tape. Psychogenic in nature—which is shrink talk for we don't know what really causes it."

"You mean there's no physical reason for it?"

"Not at all. There's plenty of physical—actually, electrical—activity. Think of the brain as a very complex electrical system. Then imagine every fuse or control shorting out. It's like a thunderstorm inside her brain." Hatton looked at his watch. "It's past six. It'll be nine or ten by the time we can get to Hoquiam. You're exhausted. Should we wait?"

Mary Slattery shook her head. "Terry works as a counselor in a crisis clinic down there. He's working tonight and doesn't get off until eleven. I've got an overnight bag in my car with a change of clothes, and some jeans. I don't want to take the chance of missing him. Or losing him. Can I sleep while you drive?"

"Sure. What about your car?"

"Tony and Michael are coming to get it. I put the keys behind a tire and gave them the plate number so they could tell it from all the other Beemers in the doctors' lot."

The crisis clinic was housed in what was once the lobby of an old three-story wood-frame hotel on the wide, nearly empty main street in Hoquiam. Like the other timber towns on the Washington coast, Aberdeen and Forks, Hoquiam had never recovered from the decline in logging that started in the early 1990s, when the last few stands of old-growth timber in the national forests had been set aside by federal court order as protected habitat for the spotted owl. This gray coast, with its burned-over fields of stumps, leaden skies, and lashing rains, had produced the angry working-class rock bands like Nirvana and Soundgarden that gave the world the misnamed Seattle sound.

It was just past ten o'clock when Will Hatton and Mary Slattery walked into the old lobby, now divided into several cubicles by sound-deadening dividers. They waited as a tall bearded man in his early sixties, graceful despite his bulk, shepherded a tearful, grossly overweight woman out of his cubicle, a comforting arm around her shoulders.

"Try not to worry about Tim between now and the hearing," he was saying. "I think the court will order drug rehabilitation instead of jail time. But let me know if he's using again. That could hurt his chances."

The woman nodded and shook the man's hand, then left quickly, her coat pulled over her head against the rain.

Mary Slattery stepped forward. "Steven Terry?" she asked.

The heavy man shook his head. "Sam Deutsch. I'm a family counselor here. Is there—"

Slattery shook her head. "Please don't waste our time. Your real name is Steven Terry, you were a psychiatrist in private practice in Seattle in 1972. We'd like to talk to you informally, but here is a subpoena for your testimony to be taken by deposition, and another for your appearance as a witness at trial." She handed the papers to Terry, who took them without resistance, glancing down at the court caption.

"I see," he finally replied, blinking. "I've got another client in about five minutes. My last of the night. Then we can talk."

An hour later they were seated in a booth in an all-night coffee shop in Aberdeen.

"I don't know where to begin," Steven Terry said. "I suppose the traditional question is, how did you find me?"

"We hired a national skip-tracing firm. They couldn't find you. Then we paid your former wife, Sheila, a large sum of money. She told us."

"That's what I get for being sentimental." Terry finished his ham steak and eggs and pushed the plate aside, signaling for more coffee.

"You're representing Laura Arcand?" he asked, pointing to the court caption on his subpoena.

"Yes," Mary replied. "Do you remember her?"

"Of course. But the one rule I never broke was the privilege. Possibly the only ethical rule I never broke."

Will said, "I have her power of attorney here. You can talk to us." He slid the document across the table.

Terry glanced at it, then nodded. "Mind if I keep it?"

"No."

"Fascinating case. I know who you are, Dr. Hatton. You probably see cases like this . . . but I never had, before Laura."

"Do you know where your practice records are?" Mary Slattery asked.

Terry shook his head. "I left them in my office . . . when I departed. I thought the lawyers would preserve them. I should have turned them over to the state board. Idiotic, in retrospect. Like much else that I've done."

"Any chance they could be recovered?" Slattery persisted.

"I don't think so. Not if you haven't located them already. I'm sorry."

"What can you remember about Laura's case, Doctor?" Will began, his voice soft.

"She came in by referral from her GP, after a runaway episode," Terry replied. "Her medical records showed some fairly substantial injuries, as I recall. Do you have the GP's records?"

Will passed a file containing Laura's records across the table. Terry read them silently as outside the storm lashed rain against the café's plate glass windows. He closed the file. "That helps. It was the head trauma, of course, that most interested me. When I first saw Laura— I'd guess about a week after she'd returned from running away—she was healing physically but not mentally. She had no memory of where she'd gone, or why. She had a very diminished affect . . . her mother called it sullen, but it wasn't a pose. Much more related to fear. Laura was very anxious, very skittish about any kind of physical contact at all."

"What did you think caused the runaway episode?" Will asked.

"My first thought was sexual abuse. But I confronted the mother, who became very angry at the suggestion. The mother was a widow, I think? An attractive young businesswoman, fairly well off. And very insistent that she did not actively date men or allow any man to spend significant time in the household."

"What else did you consider?"

"When I received the police reports from the family's lawyer—I had to insist, as he was most reluctant to turn them over—I guessed that Laura had been raped. Possibly by one of the boys at the party she had been to just before she ran. She told me she was not a virgin, but unfortunately no tests were conducted when she was taken to the hospital from Juvenile Hall. So I was never able to substantiate the basis of my concern."

"How did her treatment progress?" Will asked.

"Slowly. I prescribed imipramine—about all we had at the time for working with depression. The depression seemed to lift somewhat in about six weeks, and Laura became more verbal, although she was suffering from the side effects of the imipramine, especially a heightened anxiety level. Despite her anxiety, Laura was very insistent that she was fine, she was in control again, and didn't want to continue with therapy."

"Did she have any other issues? Her mother, her schooling, anything like that?"

"She was something of a loner as far as social adjustment, as I recall. Just a few friends, mostly other students in her art classes. Not so much from her own desire, but she was clearly an alpha-type person—her artistic ability, her looks—she was really quite a beauty, even as a teenager. She changed schools later that fall, to the boarding division at Seaside, and seemed to prefer that environment. As to her mother, that was an intense relationship. Very close, very competitive. The mother was fully invested in her emotionally. By boarding away at school, I think, Laura gained some necessary distance. She said something to the effect that she loved her mother and had tried to help her, but that she wanted to have time alone."

"Laura tried to help her mother? With what?" Mary Slattery asked.

"I was never sure."

"Did you attempt hypnosis?" Hatton asked.

Terry looked sharply at Hatton, then grinned. "Very good guess.

Hypnotic memory reconstruction. Very much in vogue at the time. I took care not to be suggestive. I still think it's a valid tool. It's a shame the repressed-memory hacks have so abused it."

"And?"

"Completely unsuccessful. Laura was difficult to put into a trance state. But she did go under once. She got close to something, I think."

"In what way?"

"She began to talk about colors while under hypnosis. Good colors, bad colors. A boat. A man. Great fear. But when I tried to get closer to the core memory, I had to terminate the session."

"Why?"

"Laura became hysterical. To the point of a seizure, or seizurelike symptoms. Scared the hell out of me." Terry paused, as though looking inward. "I was never a psychoanalyst, in the full sense of the word. I didn't like my own analysis, from my training—I was more cognitive in approach. I found that extracting some horrors from the unconscious could, and did, hurt some patients. If it did, I stopped. I stopped with Laura."

"Did you ever consider or learn that LSD use might have been part of the experience she suffered?"

"No. In fact, as I remember, she denied any drug use. But that would have explained a lot. At least in terms of the way she approached the memory under hypnosis. Had she been using LSD?"

"Apparently so, on the night she ran."

"Interesting. I wish I could have done more for her. Knowing that might have helped."

"How long did you treat Laura?"

"Just a couple of months. Her mother learned that I had used hypnosis, to poor result. I told her what little I had learned, and at what cost to Laura. Her mother became very angry. She terminated me at that point. I asked to discuss that decision directly with Laura but was told not to. By her mother's attorney, a rather ferocious man, as I recall."

Will paused, frowning. "You mentioned Laura's family dynamics. What did you make of her relationship with her mother?"

Terry hesitated. "Difficult," he said at last. "The mother also seemed very stressed. She was only about thirty, was running quite a large business, if I remember correctly." He shut his eyes to concentrate. "The mother was also very aversive. I had them both together for a couple of sessions. Sometimes they interacted more like siblings."

Will considered the answer, then moved on. "Did you ever reach a conclusion about what happened to Laura?"

"Oh, yes. Even though her mother didn't want to hear it."

"And?"

"I was firmly convinced Laura was raped or sexually abused by someone she knew, or knew of. With violence. And that is why I think she either suppressed her memory or chose to deny it."

"How did Ellen—Laura's mother—respond?"

"That was when she fired me."

Will fell silent. "There's more, I think. But it's nearly one and I am too far gone to think straight. Can we talk tomorrow?"

"Surely. I have Saturdays and Tuesdays off."

"Can I ask a question here?" Mary Slattery asked. "One I'm sure you're not going to like, Dr. Terry."

"Let me guess. You want to know how I got here, so that you can prepare me to be cross-examined, if I testify at trial."

"Exactly."

"The short version is that I was arrogant, Ms. Slattery. Very arrogant. When I finally realized what I had done to my patients, the only way I could survive was to run away. I can give you more details tomorrow. Or you can read about it in Proverbs." Terry stood to go. "Thanks for dinner. No, I don't need a ride, it's only a few blocks away. Here's my telephone number." He scribbled it on a scrap torn from the paper menu. "Call me after ten. Good night." Terry ambled away, whistling tunelessly. He paused at the door to raise the hood on his anorak against the rain, then disappeared into the night.

Will sat silently, the check in one hand, his wallet poised in the other, thinking.

"Proverbs?" Mary Slattery asked quizzically. "What in hell was he talking about? I hope Terry's not crazy, too. I've had enough crazy people for one case."

Will shook his head, no. "Pride goeth before destruction," he said quietly, "and a haughty spirit before a fall."

Chapter Thirty-three

They stood outside the all-night café in awkward silence. The rain had diminished to a thick mist that silvered the light from the streetlamps. It was just past one-thirty in the morning.

"Do we need to talk to Terry tomorrow?" Will asked, yawning. "I'm beat."

"Tomorrow," Mary replied firmly. "He's cooperative now, but that could change in a hurry. That comment from the Bible still gets me, Will. I don't want Terry to flake out on us. We need to open him up on everything we might ask him in court, then get him committed to a declaration, before we tell the rest of the civilized world that Steven Terry is alive, if not well, and living right under their noses."

"You think it's going to be that bad for him?"

"Probably. There're a lot of people looking to get him to pay serious money."

"He hasn't got it anymore. Not from working here."

"They won't know that. At least not right away. They're going to try to make him bleed first." Mary Slattery looked up at the leaden night sky. "Well," she added, "let's stay at the best joint in town. The Motel 6 by the highway, I think."

"If they'll answer the door. I've got another idea. I have a place on the beach about thirty miles north of here. It's not much, but the wine list is better than any place in Hoquiam."

"Sold," Mary Slattery said. She yawned. "You know, I think I'm getting hungry again. Let's go."

Hatton drove carefully up the winding coast road, uncertain how long the quart of coffee he had consumed in the last three hours would keep him awake. Mary Slattery had leaned her seat back and fallen asleep almost immediately, her face gentle in the reflected light from the gauges on the Jeep's dashboard. When they reached the chain that closed off the road to his cabin from the highway, he stopped the car and got out to unhook it. When he got back into the Jeep, Mary smiled sleepily. "We there?" she asked thickly.

"Almost."

She woke fully, rubbing her face, as they bounced down the half mile of rutted sand road, over the dune and through the dense bank of coast pines that shielded the cabin from sight of the highway. As they approached the water, the roar of the breakers could be heard, the rollers nearly thirty feet high, driven by the storm surge until they broke on the flat wide beach. Will rolled down his window to breathe the salt air and let the rain blowing in from the west sting his face. It was, he always thought, as though you could feel the planet breathing, nothing to stop the course of the great currents of water and air between here and Japan.

Will hoisted their bags out of the back of the Jeep and led Slattery to the door of the low shingled beach cabin. "It's not much, and it's too close to the breakers," he said, struggling with the key in the salt-crusted lock. "I'm going to lose it in the next couple of years, if we get a big storm. But I haven't got the heart to tear it down and re-build further back on the dune."

Slattery nodded and followed him into the cabin. Hatton flicked the light switches and found the circuits dead from the storm. He quickly lit a pair of hurricane lamps on the stone mantel, then dropped to his knees and lit the chunks of driftwood already laid in the fireplace. They flared up and cast their light around the cabin. It was bare and simple, with whitewashed wooden plank walls. There was one main room, with a bare fir floor covered with an old threadbare Oriental rug. A great fat pig of a leather sofa, salvaged from some old hotel, faced the fireplace, with a wooden sea chest serving as a table in front. "There's a bedroom and bathroom off to the left," Hatton said. "The kitchen's not much, but there's a woodstove I can heat soup on, and some cheese and flat bread in the freezer." He disappeared into the kitchen and returned with two jelly glasses half full of cognac.

"Thanks," Slattery said quietly, accepting the glass. "I look like hell. Let me scrub off what's left of my makeup and I'll be back."

When she returned she found Hatton on the couch, silent, staring at the fire. "I'm cold," she said, draping an old gray Pendleton blanket over her shoulders. She sat cross-legged, next to the fire, nibbling on the sausage and cheese and flat bread Hatton had laid out on the table. She poked him in the knee to get his attention, but Hatton did not stir.

"Why the brown study?" she asked, her voice bright as the brandy revived her. "We couldn't have expected Terry to remember much more than he did. What he does remember verifies everything we've been trying to find out. Laura *was* raped, *did* develop a blocked memory that caused her PTSD. Your theory was right, Will."

Hatton shook his head, smiled ruefully. "Maybe it's just three o'clock in the morning blues," he finally replied. "I can't shake the worries. Whether we have enough. Terry's story is good, but . . . I hoped there'd be more. There's something wrong with this whole case, Mary. Some piece that we're still missing that would make me see it whole. Terry verified that something horrible happened to Laura, and the PTSD reaction seems to make psychological sense, but why did she bury her pain for all these years? Why didn't she ever get better? People recover from rapes, they recover from childhood sexual abuse. It's not easy, it always means pain, but most of them do. Why not Laura? She's not a coward. Remember those paintings of hers? She was reaching out, trying to confront what happened to her. But every time she tries, the stress nearly kills her. I can't help thinking there must be something else. Something that makes it impossible for her to really confront her past." Hatton's voice grew intense, taking on an almost angry pitch. "And what in *hell* was Mark Talbot up to? What was he looking for? Goddamnit, I've *known* these people, some of them half my life, and even I can't figure them out. Maybe that's the fucking problem." Hatton fell silent, buried in frustration.

Mary Slattery was silent. "You can only do so much, Will," she finally said, her voice gentle. "If you hadn't known Laura, hadn't known about the places she lived, the way she was as a kid, you could never have pieced together as much as you have. And Laura would spend the rest of her life in prison. Now she's got a decent chance of being acquitted."

Hatton took a long pull at his brandy, shaking his head in disagreement. "I shouldn't be in this case, *because* it involves someone I've known for a long time. I'm right up to the line on the ethics of this, probably over it. Those are good rules, Mary. They're there for a reason. To prevent a psychiatrist, a clinician or a forensic, from getting their own feelings involved. From seeing only what they want to see. I'm afraid that's what I'm doing here."

Mary dragged on a cigarette and tossed it into the fire. "Look," she said, "you can't take on that much responsibility for Laura. It's still her life. All we can do is try to keep her out of prison. There're some things Laura has said to me—I know I've probably talked to her too much. But as much as she's depressed, even psychotic, she wants us to understand that she really did love Mark and didn't want to hurt him. The way she sounds, acts, even breathes . . . I believe her. I didn't want to, but I do. Which means that her madness must have been the driving force in her mind when she shot Mark. That's what we go with. That's what we try to make people understand."

"I know," he said. "She's said the same things to me. Over and over again. I believe her too. That's the hell of it, isn't it?"

"So let it go," Mary replied. She rose and joined him on the couch, then slid one leg over both of his and straddled him. She looked into his eyes, saying nothing, her hands on his shoulders, feeling the frustration and tension in him begin to ease away. She wrapped the blanket around both of their shoulders and dropped her face to kiss him. The kiss was long and slow and she felt his hands moving, grasping her hips, then slipping inside the loose shirt that she wore. She reached down and guided his hands to her breasts, sighing as he cupped them. He began to stroke her, touching her nipples with his fingertips as they hardened. She felt a sudden flood of moisture between her legs, something she had not felt in a very long time.

She leaned down to kiss him again. After a long time she lifted her lips away from his and smiled. "Now, please," she whispered, as his lips found the hollow at the base of her throat. Her voice grew urgent. "No more case. No more talk. No more hesitation. Only this."

Part IV

Trial

November 3–December 4, 1997

Chapter Thirty-four

"This is a simple case," Judith Watkins began slowly, standing in front of the jury box on Monday, November 3, her hands resting flat on the rail. "A simple case of murder."

She paused to let the words sink in for the jury, then continued, her voice low. "Mark Talbot was a successful businessman. He was born in Kitsap County, and he was the president of one of our county's largest employers, Kitsap Industries. Three years ago, Mark Talbot married Laura Arcand, the daughter of Ellen Arcand, Kitsap Industries' chairman. Mark Talbot worked hard, managing that business. His life should have been a long one, full of honor and dignity. But Mark Talbot's life was cut short. In the very early morning on September 9, 1997, Mark Talbot died a lonely death on the western beach of Bainbridge Island."

Judith Watkins paused again, letting the jury absorb her words. "Why did Mark Talbot's life end like this? Because Mark Talbot, tired and upset by business problems on a trip to San Francisco, made a mistake. He committed adultery with his assistant, Marcia Wiegand, a dedicated employee. Both of them knew that they had done wrong. Like most good people who have sinned in a way that hurts others, they decided they would not do it again. And they would not tell those whom they had hurt."

Judith Watkins stepped away from the jury box and retreated to the narrow podium in the plainly furnished courtroom. Even her clumsy walk seemed to lend her an odd kind of stumpy dignity. Reaching for her reading glasses, she checked her notes, and continued.

"You on the jury come from several different types of religious backgrounds. Some of you don't profess a religion, and that's your choice, your right as citizens. But when I think of this case, I can think only of something that I learned through my religion: that we must hate the sin and love the sinner. Whatever your personal beliefs are, I think you'd have to agree that is pretty good advice. And a pretty fair way of dealing with the ones we love.

"But Mark Talbot's life is over because his wife, Laura Arcand, *there*"—Watkins paused, and pointed across the courtroom. Laura Arcand raised her head to confront Watkins's glare, as she'd been taught, and then looked away from Judith Watkins to meet the eyes of the jury. Watkins's voice rose when she resumed. "Laura Arcand took it on herself to hate the sinner. And at two-oh-five on the morning of September 9, 1997, in the city of Bainbridge Island, in Kitsap County, Laura Arcand took her husband's life by shooting him, twice, on the beach below her mother's home. We believe the evidence will show you that Laura Arcand shot her husband, then hid the gun with which she killed him. After hiding that gun, Laura Arcand decided that the best way to deflect justice, the best way to hide—"

Edwin Hauser rose silently. "Objection," he said quietly.

Allison Cairns nodded from the bench. "Sustained. Madam Prosecutor, please confine yourself to what state contends the facts will show. Any inferences to be drawn about the defendant's state of mind are the province of the jury."

Judith Watkins colored with anger, but nodded. "Of course, Your Honor." She turned back to the jury box and paced slowly forward until she again grasped the rail. When she spoke again her voice was soft. "The judge is absolutely right. Let's talk about the facts to be found in the evidence we will present to you.

"It is a *fact* that Laura Arcand's marriage to Mark Talbot was a troubled one. It is a fact that you will hear from Laura Arcand's friends, and read in her own journals.

"It is a *fact* that Laura Arcand suspected her husband of adultery. And vowed, in her own private diary, that she would kill him.

"It is a *fact* that Laura Arcand and Mark Talbot joined eight other people at her mother's estate on Bainbridge Island on September sixth, for a weekend meeting to discuss the business of one of Kitsap Industries' real estate developments. You will meet some of those guests during this trial.

"It is a *fact* that at dinner on Monday night, September eighth, Laura Arcand confronted her husband and Marcia Wiegand, Mark Talbot's assistant, in front of those other guests. She accused them of adultery, using a drunken vulgarity I won't dignify by repeating here. She threw a drink in Mark Talbot's face and stormed out of the house, to the beach house on the property where they were staying.

"It is a *fact* that her husband went to comfort Laura Arcand. He later returned to her mother's house, spoke to her mother, Ellen Arcand, and Mr. Edwin Hauser, the defense counsel, who, as the judge has explained to you, has had a long relationship with Ellen and Laura Arcand.

"It is a *fact* that Mark Talbot, who did not himself drink any alcohol that night, returned to the beach house at one o'clock in the morning.

"And it is a *fact* that, at five minutes past two that morning, Laura Arcand shot her husband dead on the beach beside the cabin."

Watkins paused, holding the jurors' attention. I never thought she'd be even this good, Mary Slattery thought. She's actually working them. She stole a glance at Ed Hauser, caught a glimmer of grudging respect in his eyes.

"It is also a *fact,* ladies and gentlemen," Watkins continued, "that no one in Ellen Arcand's house heard the shots that killed Mark Talbot. The bluff there is very high—thirty-two feet, to be exact. We know the time those shots were fired because they were heard across the water of Rich Passage, in Illahee. But no one who heard them could know from where they came. No one knew to call for aid. And that is why Mark Talbot died on that beach.

"It is a *fact* that Laura Arcand, sometime after shooting her husband dead—and we don't know how long after—disposed of the gun with which she shot him."

Hauser rose again. "Objection," he called out.

Judge Cairns looked thoughtful. "Rephrase, Mrs. Watkins. Jurors, please disregard the prosecutor's last statement. As we have discussed, the opening statements of *both* counsel are not evidence."

Watkins bit her lip. "Forensic evidence from the bullets recovered from Mark Talbot's body will show that the murder weapon was a Smith & Wesson .38 caliber Ladysmith revolver. Such a gun was registered to Mark Talbot. And though *all* of the other guns registered to Mr. Talbot have been located, the Ladysmith—a gun designed for use by women—has never been found.

"And finally, it is a *fact* that Laura Arcand, sometime after shooting her husband, attempted to slash her wrists. At roughly four A.M., Jack Stephens, one of the party guests, was out for an early-morning walk on the beach. There was very little light at that hour. But Mr. Stephens, who served with the San Francisco police for seven years before becoming a well-known writer, saw that something was wrong. He found Laura Arcand and Mark Talbot, and raced back to Ellen Arcand's house to call in this medical emergency. It was too late to help Mark Talbot. Laura Arcand was airlifted to Harborview Hospital in Seattle. She was taken to the emergency room. She briefly recovered consciousness.

"And it is a *fact* that in that emergency room, Laura Arcand admitted killing her husband, Mark Talbot.

"And that, ladies and gentlemen, is the people's simple case of murder."

Watkins turned away from the jury to point again to Laura Arcand. "And what is the defendant's answer to this?" she demanded indignantly. "What *is* her answer? That she was unable to tell right from wrong, because her mind was disordered. That her own mind was ill—an illness she failed to follow her doctor's advice on, an illness she failed to allow them to treat. An *illness* which her own physician, the distinguished psychiatrist Dr. Robert Treadwell, will tell you did not prevent Laura Arcand from knowing right from wrong when she shot her husband to death on that cold, lonely beach."

Watkins turned away from the jury after her parting words. With her back to them, she paused long enough to favor Laura Arcand with a long look of pure hatred, then stumped, ungainly, back across the courtroom to take her seat.

"Thank you," Judge Cairns murmured. "Mr. Hauser?"

Edwin Hauser sat still for a long moment. Mary Slattery looked at him, suddenly concerned. They had agreed from the beginning of their trial planning, nearly three weeks ago, that they would reserve opening argument until the prosecution had completed its case. "Better than I thought," Hauser whispered, shaking her off. "We have to get to them now." He rose slowly, without notes.

"Thank you, Your Honor," he rumbled gravely. "With your permission, I will speak for Laura Arcand."

Cairns nodded. Hauser walked slowly to the well of the court, then stood in front of the jury, a bare six feet away. He sighed and raised his hands, his palms open.

"The judge has told you how I've known Laura Arcand for twenty-five years, and Mark Talbot for fifteen years," he said simply. "I won't try to tell you all the things I knew and learned and experienced with those two wonderful people. But I am here to speak for Laura Arcand."

He stopped, seemingly almost tongue-tied in front of the jury. His head dropped to his chest and he stared at the floor. When he raised his head to face the jury, every eye was on him.

"There's so much you need to know," Hauser said, his voice husky with emotion. "For this is *not* a simple case of murder."

Hauser stepped back to the corner of the defense table and rested a hand on Laura Arcand's shoulder. "I want you to know who this woman, Laura Arcand, *is*. Because you hold her life in your hands.

"An art critic will tell you that if she never paints another picture, she will be remembered as one of the greatest American painters of this century.

"Her mother will tell you that she was a special and troubled child, determined to make the most out of the incredible artistic gifts she was given.

"And both of the psychiatrists who will testify in this trial will tell you that those artistic gifts came with a terrible price. For Laura

Arcand has been afflicted with mental illness throughout her life.

"The evidence will show you that there is a well-understood scientific relationship between Laura Arcand's artistic ability and Laura Arcand's underlying mental illness, which is known to medical science as bipolar disorder. Most of us still call it manic-depression. What it means is that in her life—*for all her life*—Laura Arcand has been subject to terrifying, intense heights of feeling and sensation—and the most horrible depths of the black night of the soul. If that were the only illness Laura Arcand suffered from, we would not be here. But it is not.

"The evidence will show you that in the spring and summer of this past year Laura Arcand's bipolar illness deepened and grew more severe. She began to be afflicted with dreams—terrifying dreams of violation, of pain, of fear.

"Those dreams were not imaginary. Those dreams were not made up. Those dreams are not the sweet, restful dreams that you and I know. They were pain, distilled, unique—a pain that, if you took the worst days or nights of your lives, you would not begin to experience.

"These dreams were rooted in reality—in Laura Arcand's past. In the summer of 1972—on the night of August 24, 1972—Laura Arcand was raped and brutalized. She was just fourteen years old. An unknown assailant forced this sensitive girl into oral intercourse. He beat her when she tried to fight him off.

"The evidence, unfortunately, does not tell us—not to a certainty—who committed this terrible crime on the body and developing young mind of this adolescent girl. The evidence *does* tell us that this assault was devastatingly real.

"Here is what happened.

"Laura Arcand went to a party with graduating seniors from Bainbridge Island High School. An innocent kegger to celebrate the departure of the senior class to their new lives. Laura was there, young as she was, because she had skipped two grades and was already in high school. Inexperienced with alcohol and drugs, she left the party with an older man, a teacher. She returned to the beach cabin at her mother's home . . . the same beach house, twenty-five years later, where she stayed with Mark Talbot on the nights before his death.

"During that night she was raped, and fought her rapist, and fled. She ran all the way to Seattle, where she spent three days on the streets. Three days, with no money, no friends, no *memory* of who she was or where she had come from. During those three days, Laura Arcand was beaten again . . . and then beaten *again* inside Seattle's Juvenile Hall. When the police finally identified her, she had been subject to four days of the most base human brutality that most of us will ever likely see."

Hauser stopped, seemingly spent. He shook his head like an aging boxer fighting to focus his eyes. "I'm sorry, ladies and gentlemen, to be so long winded. But there's so much you need to know. When Laura Arcand came home from this traumatic ordeal, she had no *conscious* memory of it. But it was there, buried deep, what the immortal playwright William Shakespeare called 'a rooted sorrow in the mind.' The psychiatrist who treated her after she was found, Steven Terry, tried to extract and understand this wounding experience. But every time he tried, Laura Arcand suffered a seizure. Whatever she recalled from her experience had been simply too much to bear."

Hauser paced now, striding in front of the jury box, demanding their attention.

"The scientific term for this condition, as our expert forensic psychiatrist, Dr. William Hatton, will tell you, is 'posttraumatic stress disorder,' or PTSD. It, too, is a scientifically understood and recognized disease of the mind. And for twenty-five years, Laura Arcand has had this affliction as well. And it, too, is more painful than any condition most of us will ever have to bear.

"Now let us return to the near present, to the summer of 1997. Laura Arcand is in the deepening grip of depression. She is approaching psychosis—the state when the mentally ill lose connection with reality. Her wounded dreams have returned. She does not try to hide them. She shares them with her husband, and her therapist, Dr. Treadwell. Her husband tries to help. He senses, with the intuitive gift of a loved one, that there is something buried in Laura's past which wounds her. He tries to help her—far more than Dr. Treadwell, who ignores these new symptoms in favor of pills, a lecture, and his own several-month vacation in France. Together, Laura and

Mark struggle to find the answer. They can't. It is too deeply buried. Laura struggles on, tries to paint out what happened to her, the form of expression that she knows the best.

"Now it is September eighth. Laura is angry with Mark, angry not because he has had a brief affair—she knows that their life has not been perfect. She understands and would forgive—but the other woman is there, in her mother's house, and the indignity stings. She threw a drink at Mark Talbot . . . *but that is all she did from anger.* Mark goes to her, in the beach house, for more than an hour . . . if jealousy was Laura's motive, why didn't she shoot him then? Because it wasn't. Because it wasn't."

Hauser's voice dropped to a low but not theatrical whisper. "Mark Talbot left Laura for more than two hours and came back to the house to talk business. Why? *Because he wasn't concerned with Laura's anger.* There is no other explanation. For Mark Talbot, the more important issue was the business of the day.

"None of us entirely knows, because none of us were there, what happened when Mark Talbot returned to the beach house. But Dr. Hatton will testify to a scientific certainty, based on Laura Arcand's own videotaped examination, which you will see, that Laura Arcand, alone, late at night, in the same beach house where she was raped and brutalized, lost contact with reality. Laura Arcand believed herself back in 1972, believed she was about to be raped, and did what you or I would do: she defended herself. There was a weapon—a .38 caliber revolver that Mark Talbot, a man who believed in arming himself, tragically brought to the beach house. Laura—and again, none of us can fully know—must have seized that weapon.

"What we do know is this: when the storm of her mental illness lifted, Laura Arcand tried to lay down her life. Her suicide attempt was not a game or a deception, as the prosecution would like you to believe. It was in deadly earnest. For Laura Arcand, with nothing sharp at hand, took her diamond solitaire wedding ring and literally gouged the veins out of her wrists. And bleeding on the cold, wet sand, lay down beside her husband to die.

"Dr. Black, the emergency room doctor who saved Laura Arcand's life, will tell you two things. First, this is one of the most painful and directive suicide attempts he has seen in six years as an emergency room doctor. Second, that when a patient, like Laura Arcand, is in deep shock, they will, if they suddenly recover consciousness, say or do almost anything without actually speaking with a conscious mind, without knowing what they said or did."

Ed Hauser fell silent. Tears ran down his face, dampening the front of his suit.

"Mr. Hauser?" Judge Cairns asked. "Mr. Hauser? Please finish your opening statement or I will conclude it."

Hauser turned back to the jury. "Listen," he implored. "Please listen. Because this is *anything* but a simple case of murder."

"It's past four," Judge Cairns said. "Bailiff, please excuse the jury. Members of the jury, recall what I have said. You are instructed not to read or listen to anything about this case tonight. Court will be in session tomorrow promptly at nine-thirty A.M. We are in recess."

Chapter Thirty-five

Will Hatton and Ellen Arcand left the Northlake Hospital together; it was nine o'clock.

Ellen was smiling. "I'm proud of Laura," she said. "I think she's held up pretty well today."

Hatton failed to answer her.

"Will?" she asked, puzzled.

"Oh, I agree," he replied, still distracted. "She should be fully ramped up on the antidepressants now, which can at least keep her mood reasonably level. Unless . . ."

"Unless?"

"Nothing. I'm worried about her response to the testimony she's going to hear. Neither Dr. Richter nor I can determine the source of her psychogenic seizures. Other than stress."

"I'm sure she's going to be all right," Ellen said stubbornly. She looked at her watch. "If Owen and I are going to make the next ferry, I should be going. Is there something else you wanted to talk to me about?"

"There is," he agreed, still remote. "Can you stay in town long enough to have supper?"

"At this hour? I'm not sure I could eat."

"A drink anyway. How about the bar at the Sorrento? They have a late-night menu if you decide you're hungry."

Ellen smiled. "I could use a drink. I'll meet you there."

Forty minutes later they were seated in the snug walnut-paneled bar of the Sorrento Hotel on First Hill. Ellen took a long sip of her scotch and soda and lit a cigarette. "Why the long face, Will? Something wrong?"

"I want to ask you some questions," he said slowly. "About the night that Laura disappeared, in 1972."

"Why? You know far more than we ever did. I'm very grateful to you for that."

"I'm still troubled. About Seth Gwynn's testimony. I read his deposition again today, and there's a part of it I don't understand."

"Such as?"

"It's the part where he says he ran away."

"Why should that *trouble* you," she asked, suddenly angry. "For God's sake, Will, the man *raped* my daughter."

"I agree he's the best suspect," Will replied. "And if I have to, in court, I'll let the facts point that way. But it bothers me."

"Why?"

"Gwynn's very specific. He says that he heard a boat's engine, then heard the boat land on the beach in the cove. He stayed in the cabin—afraid to show his face, and for good reason. But he goes on to say that he watched the man who landed the boat take the path up the bluff. To your house. And that the lights went on after the man started crossing the meadow."

She looked at him scornfully through the smoke of her cigarette. "Was this," she asked acidly, "before or after he tried to force my fourteen-year-old daughter into oral sex?"

"He's not going to admit that."

Ellen's eyes narrowed. "And so what are you asking me, Will?"

"Was there someone else who came to your house that night, Ellen?"

"For heaven's sake, Will—*no.*" She picked up her glass and swirled the ice. "I suppose you have to ask this. But you should know that in those years I was very shy of gentlemen callers."

"You were thirty, Ellen. You're human. If there was someone you were seeing—"

"I lacked all interest in sex until Ed came along," she snapped, glaring at Hatton. "As a sixteen-year-old who got knocked up and had to face the consequences, you might understand why I was reluctant to get involved with men for a very long time."

"I'm sorry," Hatton said. "But Ellen, if . . . just tell me, all right? You had the right to be human and not on guard for your business and for Laura every second of your life."

"Let me tell you again, Will," she said severely. "For the last time, I hope. I was home that night. Alone. Working on the company books. I knew Laura had gone to a party with her school friends. I checked the cabin at two A.M. When Laura wasn't there I sat up the rest of the night, worrying. And called the police at six o'clock the next morning, frantic with fear for my child."

"I believe that, Ellen. I know how much Laura means to you. But there're other things that don't fit. When you checked the beach house at two A.M., both Laura and Gwynn were gone, correct?"

"Yes. Although now that I think about it, I do remember smelling cigarette smoke. I didn't think much about it at the time. I just assumed that Laura had stolen a pack of cigarettes from the house."

"But what about the blood, Ellen? I have to assume that Laura's fractured memory is partly accurate. She says she shot her attacker in the arm, *in the beach house.* Why didn't you notice the blood spatter, or the smell of blood, when you went into the beach house?"

Ellen looked at him blankly. "Blood?"

"And cordite, the smell of gunpowder. Couldn't you smell that?"

She paused. "I only went as far as the door, Will. I just wanted to see if Laura had come home."

"But you opened the door enough to smell cigarette smoke. Why not cordite? Or even blood?"

"I—"

"And about the gun, Ellen. Just where did the gun Laura shot her attacker with come from? I know you've always kept a handgun in the house, but how did Laura get a gun in the beach house? Did you give her one? At fourteen?"

"Will, I—she must have taken my handgun from the house."

"Which is not something you ever told John Stansbury when he interviewed you after Laura disappeared. I've read his notes of your interview with him, Ellen. I've also read his investigators' notes, the men who went through the beach cabin. They didn't find any blood, or any indication that a gun had been fired. And they searched it within the hour after you called them on the Friday morning after Laura disappeared."

Ellen Arcand closed her eyes for a long moment, then spoke. "I never thought you would turn into my accuser, Will. And as for your questions . . . all I can guess is that Laura chased her attacker onto the beach, shot him there. I wouldn't have heard that from the house, would I? No more than—"

"No more than when Mark was shot," Hatton said harshly. "But which story do I credit, Ellen? Laura's? Because that's what I have to do. Otherwise her entire PTSD case falls apart."

"Why are you doing this?" Ellen Arcand said anxiously. "*Why?* Don't you know I have to go into court this week—"

"And testify," Will agreed. "I'm just warning you, Ellen. *Think.* Look back to the exact events of that night. Because someone on the prosecutor's staff probably has been. And frankly, we haven't."

Hatton watched her gather her jacket and purse from the booth. When she turned, he braced himself. But no storm of anger emerged.

"Please remember who the victim was, Will," Ellen Arcand pleaded softly. "A fourteen-year-old girl. My Laura."

"I know that," he replied.

Chapter Thirty-six

The prosecution opened their case with Jon Sorenson, the Kitsap County coroner. Sorenson efficiently described the procedures he had followed and quickly established the nature, time, and cause of Mark Talbot's death, identifying the murder weapon as a .38 caliber Smith & Wesson revolver.

"Now, Doctor, were you able to identify any specific weapon as the one that fired the shots that killed Mark Talbot?" Tiernan asked.

"No," Sorenson replied. "Test firings were conducted of every .38 caliber weapon found at the Arcand home. There were two, one registered to Mrs. Ellen Arcand, the other to Edwin Hauser."

"The defense counsel?"

"Yes sir."

"And the result?"

"The test bullets did not match those taken from Mr. Talbot's body."

"Who conducted the test firings?"

"The Washington State crime lab, under the supervision of Eugene Welch, the firearms testing supervisor there."

"Did it surprise you that no weapon tested matched the bullets taken from the body of Mark Talbot?"

"No sir."

"Why not?"

"Because no weapon was found at or near the crime scene."

"Was a search made?"

"Of course, but not under my supervision."

"We'll ask Chief Engelhardt about that," Tiernan said, facing the jury. "Let me ask you this: were the bullets taken from Mr. Talbot's body consistent with having been fired from a .38 Smith & Wesson Ladysmith revolver?"

"I specifically requested that information from the crime lab. Their conclusion was they were consistent with having been fired from that specific type of weapon."

"Why did you make that request?"

"Because we found no weapon at the scene. And because Mr. Talbot had such a weapon registered to him."

Edwin Hauser grunted under his breath. Mary Slattery looked at him sharply.

"What?" she whispered.

Hauser waited, then replied, whispering, as Tiernan paused beside the jury box to review his notes. "Nothing. That would have been a priceless answer in any other case, that's all. Neither Sorenson nor the cops ever considered any suspect other than Laura. Hell of an investigation technique. Typical fucking small-town cops."

Tiernan was wrapping up now. "Dr. Sorenson, is there any scientific doubt that Mark Talbot was murdered in the manner that you have described for the jury?"

"No reasonable scientific doubt," Sorenson replied.

"Pass the witness," Tiernan said, making his way back to counsel table.

Slattery rose, glancing back at Hauser. He shook his head a fraction of an inch. "Way too short," he said. "They might be laying in the weeds with something damaging. Be careful."

Slattery nodded, made her way to the lectern in the center of the courtroom.

"Good morning, Dr. Sorenson. It's correct, is it not, that you examined Mark Talbot's body only after he had been completely submerged in seawater for several hours?"

"Two hours and forty minutes, based on the tide tables," Sorenson agreed.

"That had an adverse effect on your ability to conduct a scientific examination of the crime scene, did it not?"

"Of course. A number of things we would normally examine were simply washed away. We were not able to effectively examine Mr. Talbot's body for hair or other substance samples, or to determine if there was any gunshot residue on his skin, or even the pattern of blood spatter."

"So let's make a list for the jury," Slattery said, crossing the courtroom to a trial pad mounted on an easel that faced the jury.

1. NO HAIR/SUBSTANCE SAMPLES FROM BODY, she wrote in heavy black marking pen. "That means you could not determine whether Mr. Talbot had been in physical contact with anyone immediately prior to his death, correct?"

"That's correct, basically. Although . . ."

"Yes?"

"You'll note from the autopsy report that Mr. Talbot had apparently not had sexual relations in the twenty-four hours before his death."

Slattery returned to the defense table and rummaged for the autopsy report. As she did she avoided looking at Laura for confirmation or denial. "Here it is," she said, turning back to Sorenson. " 'No ejaculation twenty-four hours.' Is that the note you were referring to?"

"Yes."

"That doesn't mean Mr. Talbot couldn't have had an erection in that twenty-four-hour period, does it?"

"No."

"It's possible he tried to initiate sexual intercourse with the defendant?"

"I couldn't say. All I can tell you is that if he did, he did not complete the act, Ms. Slattery."

"Thank you." Slattery paused to let the jury ponder the point; it left intact Will's theory that Mark might have attempted sex with Laura, which acted as a trigger for the PTSD response.

"Next," Mary Slattery said, writing in large block capitals on the easel pad: *2. GUNPOWDER RESIDUE.* "You examined Mr. Talbot for such residue?"

"Yes. If any had ever been present, his submersion in the water removed it."

"Please tell the jury why you made that examination."

"If such residue is present on the body of a shooting victim, the location and density of the residue can be used to determine the distance and angle from which the gunshot or shots were fired."

"And you could not do that in this case, correct?"

"Correct."

"Third." Slattery turned and wrote on the pad: *3. BLOOD SPATTER.* "What is blood spatter analysis, Dr. Sorenson?"

"It is a type of analysis based on the fact that blood, when suddenly released from the body because of a wound, is under hydrostatic pressure and spatters into the immediate area of the wound, or even further. If an artery is opened, the blood may fountain several feet from the body of the victim."

"What can be learned from blood spatter analysis?"

"Again, it can tell us about the distance and angle of the gunshot. In many cases, the victim's blood spatters so far that traces of it are found on the person who killed them."

"Was any of Mark Talbot's blood ever found on Laura Arcand, Dr. Sorenson?"

"No. We could not make an effective examination for much the same reason that we did not find spatters on the body of Mark Talbot. Ms. Arcand was found at least partially submerged in the water. Her body was sponged by both the emergency medical technicians and the treating physicians. Any traces of blood would have been removed."

"In fact, you don't know if there was ever any blood on Laura Arcand's body, do you?"

"That's correct," Sorenson agreed.

"While we're on the subject of blood, Dr. Sorenson, did you take any samples of the sand on the beach around either Mr. Talbot or Ms. Arcand?"

"We did. There was some blood present, but it was so heavily degraded by the salt water and other chemicals present in the sand we could not learn anything meaningful."

"Let me make sure I understand. Because Mr. Talbot's body was found in the water, you did not have any evidence from which you could determine whether Mr. Talbot had been in physical contact with anyone immediately prior to his death; you could not determine the distance or the angle from which the shots were fired, and you could not even determine if Ms. Arcand fired the shots, correct?"

"I thought your defense was based on insanity, Ms. Slattery, and that the defense had admitted that Ms. Arcand fired the shots that killed her husband," Sorenson said, irritation entering his voice for the first time.

"Move to strike, Your Honor. Nonresponsive legal testimony from an unqualified witness."

"Granted. Members of the jury, please disregard Dr. Sorenson's last answer. You will take your understanding of the law from the instructions I give you, and nowhere else."

"Dr. Sorenson," Mary Slattery said, "how tall was the person who fired the shots that killed Mark Talbot?"

"Laura Arcand is five feet, nine inches tall."

Slattery wheeled on him sarcastically. "Is that your *scientific opinion,* Dr. Sorenson, based on the ballistics analysis of the bullet wounds left in Mark Talbot's body?"

"No."

"In fact, Dr. Sorenson, what was your *scientific* analysis?"

"It was extremely difficult to make any determination. The presence of salt water affected the skin surfaces of the wounds."

"Dr. Sorenson, is that what you wrote in your initial report?"

Sorenson stared angrily at Slattery. "No."

"In fact, Dr. Sorenson, you wrote that you could not trust any entry wound analysis because it appeared to you that the shooter must have been eight feet tall?"

Sorenson nodded unhappily. "I wrote that," he said. "I assumed that if the entry wound analysis had any validity, the shooter must have been standing above Mr. Talbot on the beach, or at least from some point of greater height. But you're right, Ms. Slattery, the analysis simply couldn't be made with any degree of accuracy."

Slattery paused to think. "I'd like prosecution exhibit 14 placed on the easel," she said to the clerk, who nodded and removed the exhibit, a large photograph mounted on cardboard, from the rack that had been installed on the far side of the courtroom, away from the jury box, and placed it on the easel.

"This is the vertical-view photograph taken during your initial examination of the crime scene, correct?"

"Yes. I identified it earlier today. It was taken from twenty feet in the air, using a pole-mounted camera with a wide-angle lens."

"Quite right. Describe the orientation of Mr. Talbot's body as it appears, in relation to the beach and the water."

"Mr. Talbot was lying on his back, partially submerged in the tide pool, with his feet pointed almost directly toward the waterline at the foot of the beach."

"Can you tell the jury, *scientifically,* that that is the way Mark Talbot fell after the shots were fired?"

"No."

"Why not?"

"Mr. Talbot would have lived between one and four minutes after the shots were fired. He may have crawled, twisted, tried to stagger up, rolled over. Because his body was in the tide pool and presumably floated, at least partially, the movement of water may have shifted him. His wife may have moved him. We cannot know."

"So it is a fact, is it not, that there is no *scientific* evidence to tell us what transpired on the beach that night, other than that Mark Talbot was shot and died from his wounds?"

Sorenson hesitated, then answered cautiously. "There was very little physical evidence, aside from what we were able to learn from examining Mr. Talbot."

"And there is no *scientific,* physical evidence from which you can draw *any* inference about whether Laura Arcand was sane or insane on the night of her husband's death, correct?"

Sorenson chose not to fight any further. "That's correct."

Mary Slattery returned to the defense table. She paused there, standing with a hand on Laura's shoulder, the better to draw to the attention of the jury the silent tears that rolled down Laura Arcand's face.

• • •

The phone rang as Hatton completed his daily search through the computerized Medline database, searching out any new or breaking research in PTSD and related disassociative disorders. He glanced up at the clock mounted above his worktable in the office at the rear of his loft: 3 P.M., too early for his daily call from Michael Spellman, the law clerk on the defense trial team, giving him a quick summary of the trial day.

"Will Hatton."

"This is John Stansbury, Will. How are you?"

"Fine, John. What's up?"

"Two things I thought you should know. First, I've been watching the trial on and off from the bleachers. In fact, I'm still at the courthouse. We just broke five minutes ago."

"And?"

"I was handed a trial subpoena by one of my old deputies as I walked out of the courtroom."

"Did he say why?"

"No, but I can guess. Something about the investigation I ran when Laura disappeared in 1972."

They've spotted it, Will thought blackly. They must have seen the discrepancies between Laura's story and Stansbury's records. "When are they going to interview you?" he asked.

"Tonight. Mike Showalter, my old deputy, said Tiernan wanted to see me at seven o'clock."

Will thought hard, knowing anything he said now could and would be pulled out of Stansbury in the courtroom. "John, all we want is the truth, you know that."

"I know."

"What's the other thing?"

"Your Mr. Talbot asked even more questions than you thought."

"I don't understand."

"Chuck Marshall—he retired as chief of detectives on the Bremerton city police force about ten years ago—was at the courthouse this morning. Chuck's a bit of a wheeler-dealer type, into real estate. We got to talking, and he said he'd seen Talbot before he was killed."

"Did he say what Talbot was doing?"

"Yes. Marshall said Talbot paid him a thousand bucks to go back into the Bremerton police archives and copy the old records for him about Curt Renner's drowning."

"Where can I find Marshall?" Will asked quickly.

"Probably on his boat. He's got a big forty-eight-foot motor sailor at the Illahee Marina. Takes it down to Catalina in the fall, then Ensenada and Cabo."

"I didn't know the city of Bremerton paid such good pensions," Will said dryly.

"They don't," Stansbury replied abruptly. "But Marshall was a smart one. You'd better try him pretty soon. He said he was heading south this week, soon as he gets some investments taken care of. He'll be at his boat tomorrow morning. Slip 24."

Chapter Thirty-seven

By midmorning on Wednesday, November 5, the prosecution had finished with the technical witnesses from the Washington State crime lab. With each witness, Mary Slattery had methodically established the same points she had with Jon Sorenson, that no technical, scientific, or chemical testimony could answer the question at the top of the jurors' minds: what had actually happened when Laura shot her husband to death?

"They'll try to tell it chronologically now," Reuben Todd said as they huddled in the empty jury room of the adjoining courtroom at the morning break. "They'll put on all the party guests to build the tension like a soap opera: the faithless husband, the morose and distant wife during the weekend party, the appearance of the scarlet woman to send the wife over the edge."

"How should the crosses go?" Ed Hauser asked, sipping anxiously at a cup of bitter, cold, courthouse coffee.

"Quickly, I think," Todd replied, turning to Mary Slattery. "Be charming, Mary. 'So Laura smiled at you when you arrived, Mrs. Stephens? She looked pleasant? Even happy?' Just stay with Laura's surface demeanor. None of the guests knew her well. If you catch someone stretching their knowledge too far, just snap them back with that. Then get on to Wiegand."

"Should I take Wiegand, Reuben?" Ed asked. "I know we've planned for Mary to do it, but I think we're going to have to feel our way through her cross."

"No," Todd replied emphatically. "It's got to be Mary. The jury will associate you too much with Laura and Ellen, with their feelings and, they assume, anger about Wiegand's affair with Mark. After the incident with Ellen slapping her, we need to save your credibility with the jury for the police witnesses and Dr. Treadwell."

Ed nodded, frustrated. "All right. And Mary's tack with Wiegand?"

"Psychologically, the jury will want to have someone to blame for what happened, Ed. They won't blame Mark, or at least not enough, because he's dead. We can't let them blame Laura. So—"

"I rip Marcia Wiegand apart," Slattery cut in.

Todd bared his teeth with his thin harsh grin. "Do your damnedest, Mary."

"I am so sorry," Marcia Wiegand said tearfully, concluding the narrative of her weekend affair with Mark Talbot.

"Oh, Christ," Laura muttered, her eyes cast down at the table in front of her. "I need a drink."

"Shut up," Mary Slattery hissed back, her teeth clenched. "Eyes up, damn it, *up*. Look at Wiegand, look at the jury."

Laura nodded grimly and forced her eyes up to look at Marcia Wiegand. I've done what I can, Slattery thought, but no one on the jury is going to miss that anger in her eyes.

Marcia Wiegand caught it too. For a moment her eyes shifted away from Judith Watkins, standing in the well of the court, and locked with Laura's.

"What was Mark Talbot's state of mind when you returned from San Francisco?" Watkins asked.

"Mr. Talbot was still very upset," she continued. "Our meetings with the prospective investors in the Elk Run project had not gone well. He was also extremely worried about his wife. He called home several times that afternoon, both at the airport and then from the telephone on the plane, the Skyphone, but she was not there."

"Why was he worried?" Judith Watkins asked.

"Because Ms. Arcand had been—well, irrational. She'd stopped taking her medications, he said, and she was behaving—"

"Objection," Mary Slattery barked out. "This witness is repeating hearsay at best, offering nonqualified medical testimony at worst."

Judge Cairns looked thoughtful. "Overruled," she said at last. "It's close on the hearsay, Ms. Slattery, but I think it goes to the decedent's state of mind, and I'll allow it under that exception to the hearsay rule."

Judith Watkins nodded. "Go on, Ms. Wiegand."

"Mark told me that Laura had started to disappear. Sometimes she was gone for two days. She'd leave their house, or her mother's house, and go into Seattle. Sometimes she'd be gone for two or three days. When she was home, she was drinking, her moods going up and down. Mark was afraid she'd become violent."

"*Violent?*" Judith Watkins asked, mock surprise in her voice. "Violent against Mr. Talbot?"

Wiegand looked squarely at Laura. "That's what he told me," she said.

"Is that why you decided to keep your affair with him secret?"

"Yes, of course. I had no desire to hurt Mark, or his marriage with Laura. And I had my own relationship with Tom Guenther, and I didn't want to hurt him. It was just . . . we had worked together so closely, we were such friends . . . I'm sorry, Mrs. Watkins. I can't explain it beyond that." Tears flowed again, for the fourth time in Marcia Wiegand's direct testimony.

Judith Watkins was beneficent. "It's all right." She turned, triumphant, to the defense table. "Your witness."

Mary Slattery rose casually. "Ms. Wiegand," she began, "do you see Laura Arcand at the defense table there?"

"Of course."

"How much would you say she weighs?"

Wiegand paused. "Is that a joke, Ms. Slattery?"

"Not at all. How much?"

"I really couldn't say. She's very thin."

"Would it surprise you to know that she weighed a hundred and twenty-four pounds when admitted to the hospital?"

"No."

"Now Mark Talbot. How much did he weigh?"

"I don't know."

"You'd agree he was broad shouldered, deep chested, very strong?"

"I . . . I can't say."

"Well, you *were* in a position to tell us that, weren't you, Ms. Wiegand?"

A quick bright laugh broke out from one of the younger jurors, a bachelor with carefully razor-cut hair and stylish clothes who worked as a highly paid navy yard nuclear engineer. The remainder of the jury got the joke and did their best to hide their laughter behind coughs or cupped hands.

"Objection!" Judith Watkins stormed out of her chair. "This is harassment, pure and simple! I have never—"

"Thank you, Mrs. Watkins," the judge replied. "I'll sustain your objection, but only as to the form of the question. Proceed, Ms. Slattery, with a little less sarcasm."

"I'm sorry, Your Honor. Ms. Wiegand. Would it surprise you to know that Mark Talbot stood six feet, two and a half inches tall, and weighed two hundred and twenty-six pounds at the time of his death?"

"No," Wiegand answered sullenly.

"Mark Talbot owned seven firearms, did he not?"

"I don't know."

"He was an expert shot, was he not?"

"I don't know."

"Weren't you his invited guest at a trapshooting meet on Saturday, July 19, 1997, just two months before his death?"

"Several of us from the office went to watch Mark shoot."

"And he scored ninety-three straight targets?"

"I don't remember."

"Well, surely you recall that he won a medal and the second-place prize of $5,000, having lost by only one shot?"

"Mark won something."

"Five thousand dollars is just 'something'? You have a way with money, Ms. Wiegand."

"Objection," Watkins ventured grimly.

"Strike counsel's comment," Judge Cairns ruled. "Answer the question, Ms. Wiegand."

"I remember it was $5,000," she said reluctantly.

"You also recall that Mark Talbot attended the United States Naval Academy for three years, where he received basic military training, including unarmed combat training?"

"I knew Mark was at the navy academy. I don't know what they do there, okay?" The rhetorical question was flustered. Marcia Wiegand's neck and face began to grow red with anger and frustration.

"Of course, of course," Mary Slattery said lightly. "Would you like to look at his transcript from the academy, Ms. Wiegand? Mark Talbot won special honors in physical combat training."

"I did not know that."

"Assume it now, because it's true. Is it really your testimony, Ms. Wiegand, that six-two, two-hundred-and-twenty-six-pound, crack-shot, combat-trained Mark Talbot was afraid of his wife?"

"She killed him, didn't she?" Wiegand spat out, with a mixture of frustration and triumph.

"And if the prosecution's theory of the case is true," Mary Slattery said quietly, "*you* were the reason. Now," she added, her voice rising in intensity, "answer my question."

"Mark was afraid for them. For Laura too. Afraid that she was going crazy, and that was going to hurt their marriage."

"Just so," Mary Slattery said, looking intently at the jury. "Going crazy. *Thank you,* Ms. Wiegand."

Marcia Wiegand started to leave the witness stand. Slattery forced her back into the chair with a wave of her arm and a sharp reprimand. "Oh no, you're not done, Ms. Wiegand. Not even close. Sit down."

"Now," Slattery added, "this matter of Ellen Arcand slapping you. Because, you said, she was trying to hide documents?"

"Yes."

"You're aware that all of those documents were turned over to the prosecution?"

"I don't know that."

"What?" She turned to the prosecution table, arms spread wide in surprise. "Didn't Mrs. Watkins tell you that?"

"No."

"I'm surprised. And you left out of your testimony what you said to Ellen Arcand before she slapped you, didn't you?"

"I don't remember what I said. The slap was so shocking."

"I do. It was, 'All I'm losing is a job. You're going to lose a daughter.' Correct?"

"I suppose," Wiegand answered reluctantly.

"Don't you think that was a bit of a taunt, Ms. Wiegand?"

"I don't know. I was in shock. I'd just lost my job."

"Oh, yes, your job. It's a fact, is it not, that Ellen Arcand fired you and replaced you with a commercial real estate firm because the leasing on the Elk Run project you were working on was less than half the planned amount?"

"I don't know if it was less than half. About half, I thought."

"And is half good enough? When the owners of the project were losing money every day?"

Wiegand was stubborn. "Mark thought it was good enough."

"Oh, yes. But then, he'd had *other* reasons to be pleased with you, didn't he?"

Silence.

"Never mind. One last set of questions, Ms. Wiegand. Have you ever gone by another name, other than Marcia Wiegand?"

The silence this time was apprehensive, not wounded. "Another name?" Wiegand asked.

"Yes. Specifically, Marcia Louise Decker."

"That was a married name."

"Yes, it was."

"I had a short, unhappy marriage, Ms. Slattery. In San Diego. That was twelve years ago. I took back my maiden name."

"I understand. And I'm sorry to bring this up. But Marcia Louise Decker was the name, was it not, under which you pleaded guilty to two felony counts of making false statements to a federally insured lending institution?"

Wiegand closed her eyes. "I thought I . . . My husband and I were in the real estate business, and we—"

"Were engaged in a fraudulent real estate practice known as 'flipping' to get loans from savings and loan institutions in amounts greater than the properties were actually worth. Correct?"

"I never . . . I mean, Jack was the one who—"

"And you divorced Jack Decker and testified against him, which is why you were sentenced to probation and not jail. By the way, I'm reading from your probation report, Ms. Wiegand. Would you like to review it to see if I am reading accurately?"

"No. No."

"Your Honor, we tender as defense exhibits 43, 44, and 45 Ms. Wiegand's guilty plea, certified record of conviction for violation of the Financial Institutions Reform Act, and the probation report submitted to the United States District Court for the Southern District of California, San Diego division. Ms. Wiegand certified under oath, in open court, to the accuracy of the statements made in the probation report at the time of her sentencing. As set forth in the statute, these are crimes involving fraud and/or the making of false statements under penalty of perjury." Slattery handed copies to Thomas Tiernan, who handled them as if they were radioactive.

Thick silence filled the courtroom. "I hear no objection," Judge Cairns said grimly. "They will be admitted and provided to the jury. Do you have any more questions for this witness, Ms. Slattery?"

Before Slattery could answer, Marcia Wiegand burst out, hissing. "What makes people like you so horrible?"

"Because people like you come to court and lie," Mary Slattery replied distinctly. "No more questions, Your Honor," she added, and returned to the defense table as the hailstorm of objections from Judith Watkins washed over the courtroom.

Will Hatton arrived at the *Bremerton Sun*'s two-story brick offices by 8 A.M. on Thursday as instructed, to use one of the two microfilm reader-printers the paper maintained in its archaic newspaper morgue.

He quickly scanned through the microfilmed roll of newspaper pages from August 1972, until he reached the front page for August 29.

RENNER TOOL & DIE FOUNDER MISSING; FEARED DROWNED, the headline read. The text offered very little else.

BREMERTON, AUGUST 29
By Marion Shively, Sun Reporter

Curt Renner, owner and chief engineer of Renner Tool & Die Works, was reported missing yesterday. The missing persons report was filed on Renner, 54, after he failed to appear at work on Monday, by Ellen Arcand, Renner Tool & Die's office manager, and Carl Schurz, the production foreman. Police authorities say they feared possible drowning because Renner lived on his boat, Steel II, at the Bremerton Yacht Club during the summer months, and the skiff he used to visit friends around south Puget Sound was missing. Renner Tool & Die is a major navy subcontractor that has grown rapidly in the past five years and now employs near 200 area workers. Mr. Schurz reported that all shifts are continuing to work normally, although the employees are very concerned for Mr. Renner's well-being. Bremerton police sources indicate that, although no possibilities are being ruled out, the case is being investigated as a possible boating accident.

Four days later the *Sun* reported Renner's boat had been found.

Bremerton, September 2. Concern deepened today about the fate of Bremerton business leader Curt Renner as the coast guard reported finding Renner's skiff, an open Boston Whaler, foundered in Colvos Pass, off the southwest shore of Whidbey Island. Renner, 54, is the principal owner and chief engineer of Renner Tool & Die Works. He is divorced, with one son, naval academy cadet Mark J. Talbot. Mr. Talbot is on a naval academy training cruise in the South Atlantic and could not be reached for comment. Ellen Arcand, office manager of Renner Tool & Die, has assumed management of the firm with the assistance of Carl Schurz, the production foreman. The firm reports that all of its employees are very concerned about Mr. Renner, who was well liked on the shop floor, but continuing to fulfill their obligations on navy administered contracts.

Over the next two weeks several small stories on the inside pages confirmed that no progress had been made in the search for Renner. Finally, on September 29, the *Sun* reported that the Kitsap coroner had declared Renner dead.

Bremerton, September 29. Kitsap County coroner Miles Brady announced today that his office had officially declared Curt Renner, 54, principal owner of Renner Tool & Die Works, dead by drowning as the result of a boating accident. Renner is believed to have drowned on Sunday night, August 27, in Admiralty Inlet when his skiff foundered in a sudden heavy thunderstorm. The coroner's decision was supported by Lawrence T. Elder, Kitsap County's longtime prosecuting attorney, who said that his office had assisted the coroner and reviewed his decision. "Under Washington law," Elder said, "there is no requirement that a body be recovered, or a certain amount of time pass, before a person may be declared deceased. What matters is the evidence. After careful review with Coroner Brady, for whom I have the utmost respect, we have both concluded that all of the evidence confirms that Mr. Renner's unfortunate death resulted from drowning. There is simply no evidence of any kind of planned disappearance, or of foul play. We hope that our prompt review and decision will help all of Mr. Renner's family, friends, and coworkers begin to accept and heal from this tragic loss."

Ellen Arcand, office manager of Renner Tool & Die, a major Bremerton employer, confirmed that the company will continue business. "Everyone at this company," she said, "will continue to work to fulfill our contracts with the navy and our other customers with the same excellence that Curt Renner showed us every day of his life. We are saddened, but we are far from defeated."

Mrs. Arcand, who is just 30 years old, stated that the company would have an announcement with respect to its ongoing ownership and management in the next several weeks, but that she and Carl Schurz would jointly manage the company's business until that time. Corporate records indicate Mrs. Arcand was Mr. Renner's co-owner in Renner Tool & Die Works, with a 30 percent ownership interest.

Will continued to search the microfilm for another six months' worth of daily papers. He read Curt Renner's reported obituary three days later, which listed Mark Talbot as Renner's son, even though Renner's parental rights had been terminated and Talbot adopted by his stepfather. A small business page story three months later caught his eye.

Bremerton, December 9. Renner Tool & Die Works announced its new ownership, management, and name today. Some four months after the death of its founder, Curt Renner, Renner Tool & Die will become Kitsap Industries, a privately held corporation with the majority of shares held by its new president, Mrs. Ellen Arcand. Court records from the estate of Curt Renner show that Mrs. Arcand acquired the majority of shares through a buy-sell agreement she and Mr. Renner executed just a month before his death. Carl Schurz, former production foreman, will become vice president of fabrication. Frank Johnson, formerly of Boeing Aircraft, will become the firm's new vice president of engineering. Mrs. Arcand will retain her present position of treasurer. When asked about the change of corporate name so soon after Mr. Renner's death, Mrs. Arcand said, "These changes were already in process before our founder's tragic death. Curt Renner personally selected our new name, because it reflects the expansion of our business beyond custom steel fabrication to include the manufacture of marine, aircraft and automobile specialty parts, both cast and machined. Curt Renner gave us our wings. Now it is up to us to fly."

Hatton rolled his eyes. "Bullshit," he muttered as he punched the button for the last print and waited for the copy.

Chapter Thirty-eight

"Good morning," Will Hatton called out to the tanned, fit, white-haired man loading boxes of supplies aboard a handsome motor-sailer, *Rough Justice,* moored at slip 24 at the Illahee Marina. It was not quite noon.

The man turned. His long face screwed itself into a suspicious frown. "Who the hell are you?" he barked.

"My name's Will Hatton. Are you Chuck Marshall?"

"I'm Chuck Marshall but I'm pretty damn busy. Most of this stuff is going into the freezer locker."

"Then let me help. I need to talk to you."

Marshall finally nodded. "Let's get this stuff aboard and I'll talk to you."

Ten minutes later Hatton sat down on a dock piling under a cloudy but dry autumn sky. Marshall emerged from his boat, handed Will a cup of coffee, and said, "So what's this about?"

"John Stansbury told me that Mark Talbot came to see you a couple of months before his death and hired you to obtain some old investigation files about Curt Renner's death."

"Sure did. I've got a private investigator's license, still do some consulting. What's your interest?"

"I've been retained by the defense counsel for Laura Arcand."

"You an investigator? No, wait, I've heard your name before. You're the forensic psychiatrist." Marshall made a face. "I don't like insanity defenses better than any other cop," he added. "Why do you guys do it, anyway?"

"In my case? Four grand a day."

Marshall laughed abruptly. "I don't usually talk about what I do for clients. Why should I now?"

"Talbot's not going to complain, and there's another thousand bucks in it."

Marshall thought it over. "I guess there's no harm, though I can't see that it has anything to do with why his wife killed him. Talbot came to me because I was the Bremerton homicide detective assigned to investigate his father's death, back in 1972."

"Was he after something specific, or just the records?"

"One specific thing: the exact date that Curt Renner disappeared."

"I thought that was in the papers. Sunday night, August 27, 1972."

"That's what we told the papers, all right. Renner wasn't reported missing, officially, until he didn't show up for work on Monday, August twenty-eighth. And it's what we thought, at least at first. When the missing persons report was called in, we checked with the people out at the company and they'd said Renner called in sick on Friday, the twenty-fifth. The office manager out there at Renner Tool & Die said she'd talked to Renner on Sunday, the twenty-seventh, to tell him she wouldn't be at work on Monday because her daughter had run away, and Renner'd said okay. That's how we pegged it to the twenty-seventh."

"Did something change your mind?"

"Not exactly. We just came across a different story. Renner lived on his boat in the summers, a thirty-six-foot cabin cruiser that he kept moored at the Bremerton Yacht Club. He was a wheel in the club, had been their commodore a couple of years running, so he was well known at the marina. When we questioned people out there, we found a woman—a young navy wife whose husband was the exec on a destroyer at Subic Bay—who said she'd seen Renner pulling out in his Boston Whaler on the night of the twenty-fourth."

"Was she certain it was him?"

"She said she talked to him. They'd made plans to do some fishing on Sunday, but Renner never showed."

"Fishing?"

Marshall grinned wolfishly. "Boner fishing, I suspect. Renner cut a pretty wide swath with the grass widows and the lonely navy wives from Bremerton on up to Kingston. Anyway, after we talked to her we checked around the marina some more. No one had seen Renner after Thursday night."

"What did you do?"

"What we could. The Whaler was missing, all right, and the following Friday the coast guard reported it foundered on the south end of Whidbey Island."

"Whidbey's pretty far, isn't it?"

"Not that far by water. Renner used the Whaler to get around the sound, from Tacoma to Anacortes, in good weather."

"What else did Talbot want to know?"

"He wanted to know why the case got closed so quick."

"Meaning?"

"It's pretty damned unusual to close a no-body drowning in a month. The waters around south Whidbey were searched, but we never found Renner's body."

"What did you think?"

"Well—Renner was a pretty heavy drinker. The woman we talked to at the yacht club said he'd been drinking heavily when she talked to him. Whether Renner went on Thursday or Sunday night, if he'd been drinking, it was all too easy for him to fall overboard out of an open boat. And the weather that Sunday night was rough. The weather reports had thunderstorms moving in fast, right through that convergent zone at south Whidbey. So I figured it was a drowning, despite the discrepancy about the time Renner left."

"Did you check out any other explanation?"

"Sure. I toyed with the idea that Renner faked his own death. But when I checked up on him, he was solid financially—money in the bank, healthy stock portfolio, no sudden withdrawals. And his company was doing real good—Renner Tool & Die had three years' backlog of navy contracts. Renner was taking out fifteen grand a month without the company books even starting to break a sweat. That was serious money twenty-five years ago."

"What about the angry husbands of errant wives?"

"Yeah, we checked that out too. There were a couple of guys who were pretty pleased that Renner was dead. But the three we knew of all had solid alibis—and not just from their wives, either."

"You said the case got closed quick. How did that happen?"

"How things used to happen in Kitsap County. Larry Elder, the prosecuting attorney, pulled the case out of my hands three weeks after Renner was reported missing. He met with Miles Brady, the coroner, and the company attorney, Ed Hauser. When they came out of the room, Renner was officially history—accidental death due to drowning, signed, sealed, and ready for the archives."

"I thought Larry Elder was the company's lawyer."

Marshall grinned, sourly. "He usually was. But he couldn't be both prosecuting attorney and company lawyer, now, could he?"

"Are you saying the decision to declare Curt Renner dead from drowning was fixed?"

"Me?" Marshall looked amused. "Hell, no. I was just a dumb cop, Hatton. Hadn't made chief of detectives, didn't get there until 1976. In 1972 I didn't get paid to do any thinking. None at all."

"Is Brady still alive?"

"Nope. Met his maker in '79."

"Did you ever ask Elder why he closed the case on Renner so quickly?"

"Sure. He made it sound pretty good, actually. He said that since all the evidence pointed to a drowning, they couldn't leave the company hanging. Renner Tool & Die had gotten to be a pretty big employer in the county by then. There was insurance involved, and the company needed to get the insurance money and move forward, or else they might lose their existing contracts. I figured Elder was going to get some fat legal fees from the company after that, but what he was doing wasn't so wrong that I was ready to go to the mat. I figured Renner was a successful drunk, but he was still a drunk who liked to putz around in an open boat late at night. The evidence fit a drowning."

"How much of this did you tell Mark Talbot?" Hatton asked.

"All of it. With my records."

"When did you give Talbot the information?"

"End of August, about ten days before Talbot bought it."

"Get me the same records," Hatton said.

"Cash's the stuff that talks, Dr. Hatton. Meet me over at Shilshole Marina, in Seattle, tomorrow at four. I'm sailing for Ensenada tomorrow at noon, but I'll get the file out of my storage locker and drop it to you on the way."

Hatton nodded. "Four o'clock." He paused, then added, "Now I know how you got the boat."

Chapter Thirty-nine

Jack Stephens twisted uncomfortably in the witness chair, struggling to get the tails of his slightly too small suit jacket unstuck from the back of the chair. He was middle aged, close to fifty, with a blunt, almost flat, wide-jawed face, a thick weight lifter's neck that bulged over the starched collar of his shirt, wide shoulders, and an incongruously sleek recent haircut.

Mary Slattery pressed a hand to her cheek to hide her grin. "Looks unhappy on that side of the courtroom, doesn't he?" She smirked.

Hauser gave her a grim look in reply. "Thank God he's a witness," he said. "Otherwise he'd be writing about this case. Ellen would just hate that."

Thomas Tiernan hovered close to the witness box. He gestured to the jury. "Please tell the jurors about your career history, Mr. Stephens," he said.

"Career history? Oh, a summary. Right." Stephens grunted and cleared his throat. "I graduated from the naval academy in 1974," he began. "That's where I met Mark Talbot. Talbot was a second-year man in my unit."

"Summarize your naval experience, please."

"After I was commissioned I was a junior officer on a destroyer for two years. Then they shipped me back to Washington as a public information officer. I couldn't get more sea duty, and I didn't like desk work, so when I finished my four-year hitch I resigned. I bounced around for a while. In 1983 I became a police officer in San Francisco. I was made a detective in 1985, joined the homicide squad in 1987. In 1986 I'd started to sell some freelance writing I'd been doing, mostly hunting and fishing stuff, then some true crime stories. In 1989 I sold my first book, about a murder trial I had a role in, that happened up in the wine country, Sonoma County. It sold pretty well, and I left the SFPD in 1990 to become a full-time writer."

"What kind of writing do you do now?"

"I still do a few magazine pieces, mostly travel, outdoors, adventure. I wrote one novel in 1992. It got published, but I still have most of the copies, stacked under my bed at home. Anyway, after that I went back to writing about crimes and trials, and had some good success with that. Done it ever since."

"You've told us how you met Mark Talbot at the naval academy. Did you keep up that relationship in more recent years?"

"In the past five years, yes. I moved up to Port Angeles from the Bay Area in 1992. After that, I ran into Mark at a couple of shooting competitions—mostly sporting clays and trap. We had a couple beers after those meets; it turned out we weren't living that far apart, him in north Kitsap and me on the peninsula, and so we'd get together every three months or so if we were both in the area. Mark was a good bloke, good shot."

"Did you ever meet the defendant, Laura Arcand?"

"Laura? Sure. Lovely woman, great painter. My wife and I would go out with her and Mark, make a night of it. It's a damn shame . . ."

"Yes, I know," Thomas Tiernan said, cutting him off as smoothly as he could.

Laura turned to Mary. "The longest nights of my life," she whispered sarcastically. "All 'bout huntin' and fishin' and writin' and stuff." Mary patted Laura's hand. "Keep looking devastated, Laura," she whispered. "All those fond memories." Laura nodded and fell silent.

"Please tell the jury how it was that you were a guest at Ellen Arcand's home on the weekend of September seventh," Tiernan continued.

"Well, that's a bit of a story. A couple of years ago Mark and I got to talking about investments. He was planning to develop the Elk Run project—that's our office complex—in the north part of Kitsap County, north of Silverdale. His theory was that Silverdale got too junked up, too ugly, and that a properly planned, attractive office development in north Kitsap aimed at the high-tech market could stimulate a lot of high-quality residential development in the same area. So it was a two-part deal, two partnerships. One to put up the office project, the other to buy up the inexpensive property around it, then just wait out the natural course of things." Stephens cleared his throat again, realized he'd gone on longer than Tiernan or the jury wanted. "Sorry. Is all this—"

"Oh no, it's fine. But perhaps you could tell the jury how much you invested."

"Sure, $250,000 in each deal. Anyway—"

"Mr. Stephens," Judge Cairns cut in gently, "perhaps you might wait for Mr. Tiernan's questions before you go on."

"What? Oh, sure." He grinned ruefully. "Sorry, Judge. I've been in a lot of courtrooms researching my books, but I've got to say it looks a little different from this chair."

Judge Cairns gave way to momentary laughter, joined by the jury. "It usually does. Mr. Tiernan? A question?"

"Of course. Why did you come to Ellen Arcand's house on September sixth?"

"We were going to have some meetings about the projects. The investors, I mean. Ms. Arcand wanted it to be gracious, so she invited us all down to her house for the weekend. Great house, by the way."

"Were the meetings acrimonious?"

Stephens looked amused. "I don't think I've ever written 'acrimonious' in a story," he said. "Too big a word for most of my readers. But not angry, no. Mark was pretty upset because the office park wasn't leasing up very fast, and he took responsibility for that. But I think it was a good concept, still do. We all felt the same way. Besides, I was just the little guy in the deal, kind of a favor from Mark. Everybody else had a lot more dough in it."

"After the meetings, there was a dinner?"

"Yeah, Monday night. Labor Day."

"Did you see Laura Arcand at the dinner?"

"Sure. She sat across from me."

"What did you observe?"

"Well, she looked unhappy. And she was working through the wine pretty fast. Ms. Arcand had the dinner catered, so there were people serving—I just noticed that Laura was raising a finger to the wine server pretty quickly."

"What happened then?"

"Not much. A lot of people were putting questions to Laura. You know, about her painting. She was so famous for a while, then nothing—I'd always admired that, a J. D. Salinger kind of thing, demanding her privacy, letting her previous work speak for her."

"Did you observe Laura after dinner?"

"Sure did. You mean when Mark was tending bar?"

"Yes, exactly."

"I saw her go out for a smoke after dinner. She took a wineglass with her. When she came back, Mark was pouring a brandy for Marcia Wiegand, his property manager. Laura came into the room—we'd moved from the dining room to the big living room by then, kind of all standing around the fireplace. She came up to the bar. She had a kind of shiny look about her—like the alcohol had hit her. And she was pissed. I could see that in her eyes, just royally pissed." Stephens stopped and gazed at Laura for a moment. "Then she lit into Mark," he added.

"How?"

"Oh, she just talked to him. Hissed, actually."

"What did she say?"

"Well, she kind of gestured at Marcia with her wineglass. 'So how is she?' Laura said. 'At giving head.'"

"Were you the only person who heard Laura Arcand say that?"

"No. The whole room must have. Laura kind of whispered it, but you could hear it fine. Like a stage whisper. What do they call it? Sotto voce?"

"What did the others at the party do?"

"They all kind of froze. One of those nasty husband-wife moments you get at parties sometimes. Then Laura threw the wine in her glass in Mark's face. And stormed out."

"What did Mark Talbot do?"

"He shrugged it off, at first. He got a little high color, mopped his face with a handkerchief, embarrassed. Finally he just smiled and took off out of the house, headed for the beach cabin, I suppose. That's where he and Laura were staying."

"What happened then?"

"At the party? Not much after that. We really didn't know each other that well—just investors in the same project. Laura and Mark's fight made things pretty quiet. So my wife and I went upstairs to our room."

"Any particular reason?"

Stephens grinned. "Just that we've got kids that are two and four, and they were home with the baby-sitter for the night, Mr. Tiernan. This was the first night my wife and I'd had to ourselves in a long while."

This time even Tiernan joined in the laughter. "I won't ask you about the next hour or so," he said, still smiling. When the laughter died down, Tiernan reassembled his somber demeanor. "Did you see Mark and Laura again?"

"Yes sir, I did. I went out for a walk along the beach, around three-thirty that next morning."

"Why so early?"

"I've got insomnia, and it gets worse if I drink. I'd had a drop or two that night."

"So you decided to walk it off?"

"Sure."

"Tell the jury where you went."

"Well, Ms. Arcand's place is set back, on the bluff," Stephens replied. "There are two paths down to the beach. I took the north path, out to the north edge of the property, where it switchbacks down to the beach. Then I walked south, along the beach. I was maybe twenty yards from the beach house, inside the little cove there, when I saw them. Laura and Mark."

"What did you see?"

"Mark was lying on the sand at the edge of the tide pool that sits below the beach house. He was almost half in the water. Laura was—well, kind of wrapped around him. I started to turn away."

"Why?"

"I thought they'd been making love. It was a fine, warm night, Mark was naked, and Laura just had on a T-shirt, and I thought— well, like I said."

"Did you look back?"

"Yes, I did. I called out something—I think it was, 'Oops, sorry about this, you guys'—and I didn't hear anything back. They didn't move. So I went closer."

"What did you see?"

"They both looked very pale, even in the light from the moon. Then I saw one of Laura's wrists. It was—gouged. A big bloody mess of hamburger. So I went up to them, saw that Mark wasn't breathing, and that Laura was barely breathing. I pulled her away from him and saw the wounds in Mark's chest."

"What happened then?"

"Laura was breathing, shallow but regular. Mark was gone. So I figured that I could either give Laura CPR and try to dress her wounds, or call in the medics. It looked like the wounds on her wrists had clotted up, so I headed up the hill, hell-bent for the phones in the house. I called 911, asked for a medevac, but they gave me to the local police. I got a patrol sergeant, who said he'd call. I told him how to get down to the beach, then I grabbed a couple of towels from the downstairs bathroom to make bandages. When I got back there, Laura was still breathing, thank God. She felt cold, so I took off my sweatshirt—I'm a big guy, so there was enough fabric to wrap around her. And I bandaged her wrists and tried to keep her warm until the cops came."

"When did Sergeant Martinez arrive?"

"Couldn't have been more than five minutes later. Good copper. Anyway, he said he'd called the medevac, but forgot the flares. So I ran back up to his car, got his flares out of the trunk, and lit up a landing zone on the beach, as he'd instructed. The chopper dropped in about four minutes later."

"You did very well, sir," Tiernan observed warmly. "One last question. When you were helping Laura Arcand, did you see a gun?"

"A gun? No. I wasn't really looking, but I did look around a little when I saw the wounds in Mark's chest."

"And you saw nothing?"

"That's right."

Tiernan nodded. "Your witness," he said, striding back to the prosecution table.

"One question," Mary Slattery said, rising. "Why did you think that Laura and Mark were making love, Mr. Stephens?"

"Well . . ." He paused, coloring a bit. "Laura's a beautiful woman, Counsel. Mark was always—well, you go out with a couple, you see things. The little touches, the contact. They had that. And the light— there was a half-moon shining across the beach, and there were Mark and Laura, on the sand beside these three little stone towers, or piles. It looked romantic—like they'd been playing on the beach, piling up rocks, talking—hell, I guess my imagination took over. It was a pretty romantic scene."

"Just so," Mary Slattery said. "Thank you, Mr. Stephens. And thank you for your quick action. You may have saved Laura Arcand's life."

Slattery returned to the defense table, satisfied. The jury would re- member Stephens's touching description of Laura and Mark's ap- pearance on the beach, she curled around him as though they had just made love. As she reached the table she looked directly at Laura to flash her a confident smile.

Laura was rocking in her chair, face down almost to the table, then back in her chair until her head and neck arched until she was looking at the ceiling. Slattery looked closer. Beads of sweat had popped out on Laura's forehead. The sweat had matted her hair at the temples. When Laura's head dropped again, she saw nothing but the white of her eyes as they rolled back in their sockets.

"Ed!" she hissed. "Get the nurse!" She whirled around to face the bench. "Your Honor!" she called out urgently. "We request a recess. Our client is having a seizure."

Chapter Forty

Will towered over Dr. Susan Richter as they stood in the corridor of Northlake Hospital's psych wing. Richter stood scarcely five feet tall but, even in her fatigue, filled the space around her with the projective force of her personality. Concern was etched tightly on her plain features.

"It was a bad one, Will," she said, sighing. "Nearly eleven minutes by the nurse's count, but it could have been longer. Ed says he was distracted by his preparation for the next witness, wasn't keeping a close eye on Laura. And the seizure was well in progress by the time Mary finished the cross-examination and noticed what Laura was experiencing."

"Any idea what the trigger was?"

Richter frowned. "Possibly the testimony, describing Laura as she appeared with her veins opened on the beach, huddled around Mark. She has such strong feelings for him—she's still in the grieving process, you know, which makes our task of prying her out of the depression even harder."

"I know. You're doing a wonderful job, Susan."

Susan Richter shrugged, disclaiming credit. "If she's alive and well in a year, then you can congratulate me." She paused, then added ruefully, "And if she's not in some god-awful penitentiary, Will, then I will congratulate you."

"Is it all right for me to talk to Laura?" Hatton asked.

"I think so, yes. She's sketching. Some kind of energy burst, a short second wind. Don't stay too long."

"I won't." Hatton offered a brief hug, which Richter accepted before departing for her Kirkland home.

Hatton strode down the psych wing corridor, worried. They had to expect the tension of sitting through the trial, watching and listening to the details of Mark Talbot's death, would shock and further depress Laura. But the severity of today's seizure unnerved him. What, he thought, was the specific trigger?

He stepped into Laura's room and found her seated by the window, a sketch pad in her hands. "Hey, there," he said, with an effort to keep his greeting casual.

"Hell," Laura Arcand replied, letting the oversize pad fall to the table, "I should pass out in court every day. I get visitors, maybe even cigarettes."

Will handed her the box of Marlboros he carried for her, then retreated to the bathroom with an empty cup for water to create a makeshift ashtray. "Still in thrall to demon nicotine?" he asked lightly as he handed her the cup.

"Still," she replied. "Susan sneaks them to me, and Mary too."

"We're part of a new group, doctors and lawyers for vice. What happened today?"

"I decided to show the jury what a crazy person looks like."

"No, I'm serious. What was the last thing you thought of before you had the seizure?" He sat down in the other chair at her table as she lit a cigarette and blew a plume of smoke toward the open window. He caught her eye and she stared at him, blue-gray eyes wide with fear, he thought. And something else. "What?" he repeated.

"Rocks," she finally replied.

"Be serious."

"I am!" she said indignantly. "I got through the worst of it, Will, I really did. The forensic stuff, the autopsy, all those god-awful pictures of Mark lying dead on the sand. I did that. Then . . ."

"Who was the witness?"

"Jack Stephens. He was talking about how he found us. Mark and me. On the beach, wrapped around each other like we were making love . . . and he mentioned the rocks."

"What rocks?" Will asked, exasperated.

"Three little stone cairns. They showed up in a picture the police took after . . . after Mark was dead. I remember now. I built them . . . at the top of the tide pool. At the high tide that afternoon, before Mark . . . before I had to go up to that awful dinner."

"What did the rocks mean to you?"

"Nothing at first. Just a flash of memory, one for that afternoon, one I hadn't had before."

"Why did you build these—what did you call them—cairns? What are they?"

"Just little piles of rocks. You know me, I'm always fiddling with whatever is around me, trying to make things, things that look different. Cairns are rock piles, used in a lot of different cultures. They mark things . . . trails, graves, food caches, underground springs for water . . . the Plains Indians used them for that."

"Were you trying to mark something?"

"Not that I remember; just fooling around, I think. That tide pool by the beach shack always meant a lot to me. It used to be higher up, on the beach, but the pool has shifted. I liked to float in it, years ago, because it was so warm, compared to the water of the sound."

Hatton thought hard, remembered a day when Laura had been painting at the old beach shack on a hot July afternoon. She had taken him outside after the high tide, late in the afternoon, and they'd stripped to their underwear and T-shirts and soaked in the pool. He tried hard to shrug away the memory. "What happened after that?" he finally asked.

"I had a second flash. A memory flash."

"And?"

"It was night. I was standing on the deck of the beach shack—the new shack, Will, on the deck we built, not the old one." The words tumbled from her in an excited rush. Her eyes widened again—with fear or understanding, Hatton could not tell. "And I saw."

"What?"

"Mark. Standing on the beach, on the far side of the tide pool. Naked, like he'd just come out after a swim."

Hatton closed his eyes, bracing himself for the worst. "What are you doing?"

"Watching. Just watching."

"Anything else?"

"I don't have a gun, Will. I'm not holding a gun."

"What were you feeling?" Hatton asked quickly. "Anger, fear, what?"

"Some anger. Mark's made me unhappy, made my mother unhappy. But it's not burning anger. It's anger . . . with a kind of understanding. Acceptance. I want Mark to be with me despite the anger."

Hatton took a deep breath. "What do you think it means, Laura?"

Laura looked at him steadily. It was late, nearly ten o'clock. Weariness filled her eyes.

"Oh, Will," she said desperately, "I hope it means I did not kill Mark."

Hatton saw a crease of light above him as he rode the ancient freight elevator up to his loft on the top floor of the old Christiansen Fisheries building. He tensed at the sight of the light, knowing damn well he had not left the lights on when he left that morning to meet Chuck Marshall at the Illahee Marina.

Hatton slid the elevator gate open cautiously. He paused in the vestibule, peering cautiously around the solid sixteen-inch Douglas fir post into the living room of the loft.

Ed Hauser sat in Hatton's fat leather reading chair, glancing pensively at an open deposition transcript, a glass of brandy in hand and one of Hatton's carefully hidden Cuban cigars smoldering in an ashtray on the side table beside the chair.

"Ed?" Hatton asked, surprised. "What the hell are you doing here? It's after eleven. You've got to be in court in Port Orchard tomorrow morning."

"I know that," Hauser growled. "But we need to talk."

"About what?"

"About whatever the hell you think it is you're doing in this case, damn it."

Hatton's eyebrows went up in surprise but he said nothing. He went to the refrigerator in the kitchen, got a bottle of mineral water, and returned to the living room. "By the way, how'd you get in here?" he asked casually.

"The emergency key you keep in my office safe."

"This is an emergency?"

"Goddamn right it is," Hauser roared, tossing the deposition on the floor. "What in hell do you think you were doing the other night, taking Ellen out after she'd been to see Laura and putting her through the third degree? Don't you understand the kind of stress that woman is under, seeing her daughter on trial for murder?"

"Of course I do," Hatton said mildly. "As I see it in you, which is why you're not being shoved into the elevator for the street right now. I've long since grown up, Ed, and I no longer take guidance in my professional life from you."

"Maybe you fucking should. What was all this crap about the condition of the beach house after Laura disappeared? You scared Ellen half out of her wits."

"Good. She needs it."

"What in hell are you talking about?"

Hatton slid into the chair facing Hauser and leaned forward. "Think, Ed. I know you're on trial, but think. I was going back through Laura's taped interview, charting each detail. We depend on that tape, Ed. At least, I sure as hell do. And Laura not only described the old beach house, she described the shooting in it. Which means blood, Ed, lots of it. On the floor, maybe on the walls, sprayed who knows where. When I asked Ellen about it, just to be sure, she didn't have an answer for me."

Hauser looked suddenly sober, and cautious. He reached for the cigar, found it dead, knocked the ash off it, and relit it. "Ellen was barely in that beach shack after Laura disappeared," he said. "She couldn't stand it."

"Couldn't *you?* You were an FBI agent for six years before getting your law degree, you've seen lots of crime scenes."

"Sure, I looked. If there was blood, it was maybe outside the door. Laura's memory may not be exact as to where she fired the shots."

"She was pretty specific. So how do I credit part of what she said on that tape, and not the rest?"

"You won't have to. Nobody else was there."

"Sure there was. John Stansbury, the Kitsap County sheriff in 1972, has been attending the trial. He got served with a trial subpoena yesterday. They're going to call him in rebuttal to me, Ed. Because he doesn't remember seeing any blood in the beach cabin. None at all. That's why he thought Laura got snatched on the road after she left the party out at Stenslund Lake. That's why he ordered an all-island search, not just a search of Ellen's place and the surrounding area."

Hauser drew carefully on his cigar. "This is making something out of nothing," he said scornfully. "You think if I'd found blood in that beach cabin I would have just passively searched the island? Fuck, no. I'd have known what it meant. All I'm telling you is that Laura must have been mistaken in this one detail. That maybe she shot at whoever tried to rape her as he was going out the door, or shot him on the beach, just the same as Mark. It doesn't take away from your PTSD analysis."

Hatton was skeptical. He took a mouthful of water straight from the bottle. "Maybe so. I'd like to think so. But there're two other problems."

"What?"

"The gun, Ed, the gun. Same as now. Ellen told me that Laura had taken the gun that she shot at her rapist with in 1972 from Ellen's house. But something must have happened to the gun, Ed. It wasn't found at the beach cabin, and Laura didn't have it when they found her in Seattle."

Hauser sat in stubborn silence, thinking.

"There's more, Ed."

"What?"

"Seth Gwynn. His testimony bothers me."

"Why?"

"It's when he ran, Ed. He admits being at the cabin, but he says he ran when he saw a boat land on Ellen's beach, and a man go up the path to the main house."

"Sure," Hauser scoffed. "If I was a rapist I'd say that too."

"Maybe. But if Gwynn raped Laura, where the hell's his gunshot wound? Laura was too specific, Ed. It can't be Gwynn, he wasn't shot. And who was the man in the boat who went up to the house, Ed? Gwynn has no reason to lie about that. Does Ellen?"

Hauser tried to change the subject. "Laura could be as wrong about hitting Gwynn as she was about shooting someone inside the beach house. You know how people react when they see a gun and hear gunshots, or hear the bullet passing them. They dodge, they duck, they act like they've been shot. Laura was stoned out of her head on alcohol and LSD, Will. She's hardly an accurate witness for details. So she never hit Gwynn. It doesn't mean that he's not her rapist."

"Maybe not. But who was the man in the boat, Ed?"

"There wasn't one."

"Oh yes, there was. I think it was Curt Renner."

"Curt Renner?"

"Renner was supposed to have disappeared four days after Laura was raped, Ed. But there was one witness who said he left Bremerton in his boat on Thursday night, August twenty-fourth."

Hauser was incredulous. "You've got this witness?"

"No. In 1972 she was a navy wife whose husband was at sea, living on a boat at the Bremerton Yacht Club. She said Renner took off on the night of the twenty-fourth, promising to take her fishing on Sunday. Renner never showed up for their date."

Hauser grunted disgustedly. "Renner was probably fucking her. Who'd you get this from?"

"Chuck Marshall."

"Oh, for chrissakes, Marshall," Hauser said heavily. "There's a dirty cop, in spades. Will, I *know* Renner was alive the following Sunday. I heard Ellen on the phone talking to him, telling him she wouldn't be in to work because Laura was missing."

Hatton considered the answer in silence.

"One last question," he finally said. "Why did you get Larry Elder and Miles Brady to declare Curt Renner dead so fast? Four weeks must be some kind of record for a no-body death."

Hauser stared at him coldly.

"Well, you have done your homework," he said at last. "Should have expected it. And if your question is, did I dance with the devil to keep KI alive, protect Ellen, then the answer is, you bet your ass I did. Ellen and the company paid Larry Elder a hundred grand in retainers over the next five years, the corrupt bastard."

"To fix it?"

"Hell, no! To save the company. We knew Renner was dead, but we had to have a death certificate. Otherwise the buy-sell wouldn't work, the insurance wouldn't get paid, the company would have been caught up in a probate, contracts would have gotten canceled. Even a few months' delay would have killed us. All of the work that Ellen had put into the company would have been wasted. And a couple of hundred people Ellen cared deeply about would have lost their jobs."

"I get the point," Hatton said. "You did what you had to do."

"Damn right I did." Hauser shrugged his big shoulders, trying to release some tension. There were deep rings under his eyes; his cheeks had slumped into gray pouches. "And I'm still doing it," he said, rising to go.

Hatton nodded. "But Ed—what if Laura didn't kill Mark Talbot?"

Hauser shook his head. "I'd like to believe that," he said. "But I can't. And if you back off from your testimony, Laura's as good as dead."

Hatton watched as Ed Hauser entered the elevator and descended to the street. When he heard the elevator stop, he closed the gate on his floor and turned away, his thoughts dark with worry. For the first time in his life he was not sure he could trust Edwin Hauser.

Chapter Forty-one

On the following Monday the prosecution picked up the thread of its story with Sergeant Martinez of the Bainbridge Island police, who had responded to Jack Stephens's urgent 911 call and called in the emergency medical evacuation helicopter that had taken Laura Arcand to Seattle. Martinez was stiff and superficially unemotional on the witness stand, but could not keep the undercurrent of excitement from his voice as he recounted how Laura had burst out of her coma and into confession on the emergency room table.

Edwin Hauser listened for the note of pride in Martinez's voice, heard it, and decided to change his planned cross-examination on the spot.

"Good morning, Sergeant," he said warmly, buttoning his suit coat as he rose from behind the defense table. "Sergeant, before we begin I just want to thank you. If it hadn't been for your quick and sure response to this tragedy, Laura Arcand would not be alive today."

Martinez nodded, gravely accepting the accolade he believed due him. Ed paused to give the stocky sergeant another minute to bask in the warm regard of the jury, then began, softly. "Sergeant, I just have a few questions about the timing of events," he said. "Remind us, you received Mr. Stephens's 911 call exactly when?"

"Four-oh-six A.M., sir."

"Where were you?"

"I had just passed Lynnwood Center, part of my usual night patrol pattern. I received the call, turned on my lights, and proceeded due west on Baker Hill Road."

"What time did you arrive at Ellen Arcand's home?"

"Four-ten A.M., by my watch."

"Remarkable. It's hard to find, isn't it?"

"Sir, I've memorized the island's roads and address systems. If you don't do that, they can be confusing. I knew exactly where the house was."

"And what time did you reach Mr. Talbot and Ms. Arcand?"

"Within four minutes. Four-fourteen on my watch."

"Excellent. What did you do then?"

"I checked both Mr. Talbot and Ms. Arcand, saw that Ms. Arcand was still breathing, and put through a radio dispatch call to summon the emergency medical helicopter."

"Which we know was dispatched at four-twenty-two A.M., from the EMT records." Hauser smiled again. "While waiting for the EMT chopper, you and Mr. Stephens administered first aid to Ms. Arcand?"

"Mr. Stephens had pulled her out of the water. We replaced the towels Mr. Stephens had used to bandage Ms. Arcand's wrists. At one point Ms. Arcand stopped breathing on her own, and I gave her mouth-to-mouth resuscitation. I sent Mr. Stephens back to my patrol unit for flares to create a landing square for the chopper on the beach. The tide had dropped and I wanted to get Ms. Arcand off the beach as soon as possible, rather than have to carry her up the hill."

"That decision probably saved Laura's life, Sergeant. Well done." Ed's voice was even warmer, more deferential than ever. "What time did the chopper arrive?"

"Four-thirty-one. Flight time is nine minutes from Harborview."

"And during those nine minutes you were busy saving Laura's life."

"Yes sir."

"So, there was just no time to create a crime scene control perimeter on the beach?"

"No sir."

"When did you call for backup?"

"Well . . ." Martinez hesitated. "There just wasn't time, sir. I spent seventeen minutes, total, on that beach."

"Of course, of course. When and how did backup get called?"

"I did call for more units. When I got to Harborview."

"That call was recorded in at five-eighteen, was it not?"

"That's right."

"That was after Ms. Arcand was brought into the emergency room?"

"Yes sir."

"And after she came out of the coma long enough to shout something at Dr. Roy Black?"

"Yes sir."

"That whole situation was fairly unnerving, wasn't it, Sergeant?"

"I don't understand the question, Mr. Hauser."

"This was a woman that you had just given mouth-to-mouth resuscitation to, and who was very nearly dead not thirty-five minutes before, correct?"

"Yes."

"Didn't it startle you when she came out of the coma and started shouting?"

"Well . . . yes. But not so much that I didn't hear what Ms. Arcand said."

"Of course. I didn't mean to suggest that. What I meant was, did the fact that Ms. Arcand screamed, 'Oh God I killed them . . . both of them,' make you concerned that there might have been a second person injured on the Arcand property?"

"Yes sir."

"And that's what reminded you to call for backup units to be sent, correct?"

"Yes."

"And to your knowledge, the first thing those units did was to search the property for a second victim, correct?"

"That's right."

"And of course, there was no one else on the property who had been injured, correct?"

"That's correct."

"You thought that was puzzling, I'm sure."

"I still do." Ed paused to let the answer settle on the courtroom air. Any hint of puzzlement or uncertainty by the police officer who heard Laura's words would do far more to persuade the jury they could not be relied on than anything else the defense could do. "So, because of the immediate need to locate and help any other person who might be injured, no search was mounted for the gun that had fired the bullets that killed Mark Talbot until well after the search for a second possible victim ended?"

"It's in the reports, Mr. Hauser. We started the search for a weapon at nine-thirteen A.M. that morning."

"That's four and a half hours after you left the beach with Laura Arcand, wasn't it?"

"Yes." Martinez began to look around the courtroom, concerned.

"And what time did the Bainbridge police set up a control perimeter around Mark Talbot's body?"

"Not until Chief Engelhardt got there at eight A.M."

"Just over three hours?"

"Yes sir."

"Thank you, Sergeant. You really did save Laura Arcand's life, and we're all in your debt. I mean that, son."

Martinez allowed himself to grin at last, both from pride and relief. "Thank you, sir," he said.

Hauser returned to the defense table with a grave, firm walk. He winked at Mary Slattery when his back was turned to the jury.

Not bad for an old man, she had to admit to herself. Not bad at all.

The best cross-examinations, she knew, were those where the witness remained on the stand, smiling, long after his or her throat had been cut.

Chapter Forty-two

Bainbridge Island police chief Wayne Engelhardt dressed like a model small-town plainclothes cop: wrinkle-free polyester blue blazer, gray slacks, white short-sleeved shirt, gray-and-red striped tie, dark socks, black leather walking shoes with rubber soles. When the jacket gapped you could see a pocket protector stuffed with pens. Only the .38 police special in a side holster distinguished Engelhardt from the manager of the local utility office or the vice principal at a local middle school.

"I agree, Mr. Tiernan, that it took us a long time to set up a crime scene perimeter and begin searching for the gun," Engelhardt said. In his mid-forties, Engelhardt had a round face atop a rapidly thickening body, receding salt-and-pepper hair, and a gray toothbrush mustache that just barely touched the corners of his mouth. "But for the need to search for a possible second victim, based on Laura Arcand's statement, we would have started much sooner."

"But your search was thorough, wasn't it?" Tiernan asked. He was engaged in a mock cross-examination of his own witness, trying to shore up the Bainbridge Police Department's shaky performance in the eyes of the jury by appearing to be tough on them.

"Very thorough," Engelhardt continued. "We divided the Arcand property into sections, each section fifty feet by fifty feet, and searched each one with a combination of my force, off-duty county personnel, and Explorer law enforcement volunteers from Kitsap, Clallam, and Jefferson Counties. The search took nearly two days."

"And you found nothing?"

"Nothing. That gun was hidden, and hidden well, by Laura Arcand. There is no other explanation."

Slattery looked over at Hauser, expecting him to explode into an objection. He sat with his eyes narrowed, distaste for the bumptious little police chief plain on his features. He shook his head, no. "I think they're almost done," he whispered. "And I'm going to feed him that statement."

Hauser was correct; Tiernan finished with Engelhardt a few questions later, and tendered him to Hauser for cross.

Hauser rose to his feet briskly. "Mr. Engelhardt—"

"It's 'Chief,'" Engelhardt cut in.

"I beg your pardon?"

"I'm called 'Chief Engelhardt,' Mr. Hauser."

"Really?" Ed Hauser drawled as he approached the witness box, his bulk looming over the smaller man. "I believe you testified that your first name was 'Wayne.' Am I wrong?" The jury broke out in open laughter. Thomas Tiernan rose to object but Judge Cairns waved him down before he could open his mouth.

"Mr. Engelhardt," Hauser said acidly, "you testified, did you not, that because your search was thorough, Laura Arcand must have 'hidden the gun, and hidden it well.' Correct?"

"That's right."

"Did you see Laura Arcand hide the gun, Mr. Engelhardt?"

"No, of course not."

"Did anyone on your force see Laura Arcand hide the gun?"

"No."

"Did any witness, to your knowledge, see Laura Arcand hide the gun that was used to shoot Mark Talbot?"

"Not to my knowledge, no. At least none has come forward."

"I see. And so your conclusion that Ms. Arcand hid the gun is entirely based on a search that did not begin until seven hours and eight minutes after Mark Talbot was shot, correct?"

"It was a thorough search."

"Oh, I agree," Ed said sarcastically. "Thorough, but late."

"Well, we had to—"

"Yes, you've already said that. Now, sir . . ." Ed paused, went to the rack of blown-up exhibits, and removed a large aerial photograph of Ellen Arcand's estate. "Prosecution exhibit 4, Your Honor." Hauser placed the photograph on an easel so that the jury could see it. "This is an accurate aerial photograph of Ellen Arcand's property, isn't it?"

"Correct."

"What is shown at the north end of the property?"

"Well, it's a fairly thick stand of trees, mostly fir, some alders, and vine maples."

"It's very thick and brushy, isn't it?"

"Yes, we had to hack through it some, with machetes, to search it."

"Thick enough so that someone standing, or even walking in it, wouldn't be easy to see?"

Engelhardt began to see the direction Hauser was going, and didn't like it. "We had dozens of people out on the property. It would have been very difficult for anyone to remain unobserved."

"After you got there," Hauser cut in.

"I . . . yes."

Hauser pointed to another section of the photograph, a thick swath of trees moving up the bluff, east of the beach cabin. "What's in this area, Mr. Engelhardt?"

"It's a creek bed. The water comes from a spring someplace up the hill, and empties into the tide pool."

"Is it wooded?"

Engelhardt hesitated. "Yes, very. Mostly alders and some firs, what you'd expect around a creek bed on the island."

"Did you search it?"

"We did."

"Did you use your machetes?"

"Yes. Parts of it were a little cleaner—it looked to me like there was an old trail through there at one time, running up along the creek. But the ravine had apparently slid some since anyone used the trail, and so parts of it were blocked and grown over."

"Where does the ravine go?"

"Right up to Crystal Springs Drive. The stream runs under the road there, in a four-foot-diameter culvert."

"It would be hard to see someone up in that ravine, wouldn't it, Mr. Engelhardt?"

"Even when we were searching?"

"Yes."

Engelhardt thought. "I suppose, yes. Harder in there than in the woods on the north side of the property. There's more brush, bigger trees in the creek bed."

Hauser turned toward the jury, pointing at the thick cover over the creek bed in the photograph. "In fact, Mr. Engelhardt, it's quite possible, isn't it, that someone could have entered the Arcand property through this creek bed trail, removed the gun, and left the same way? Especially before you had your search organized?"

Engelhardt's expression turned bland. "I guess so, in the sense that anything's possible. But why would someone want to do that?"

"Why, indeed? That's a good question, Mr. Engelhardt. Let's work on that. But first, let's establish one other possibility. During the search, it would have been possible for someone who found the weapon to remove it to the creek bed, and then take it out later without being seen, correct?"

Engelhardt thought for a long time. "As long as you say 'possible,' I'd have to agree. But it would have been harder. The searchers worked in adjoining fifty-foot squares, and they were mostly visible to each other."

Hauser smiled. "That's fine. So it would have been possible for one of the searchers to find the gun, secrete it, and carry it away later without being seen?"

"I really doubt it. I mean, why on earth would one of us hide the gun? We were trying to find it."

Hauser's smile thinned. "Again, why indeed? Now, you're aware, aren't you, that the prosecution in this case has argued that since Laura Arcand ostensibly hid the gun that was used to shoot Mark Talbot, she cannot be insane. Correct?"

"I guess so. I wasn't here for the opening arguments."

"No, you weren't. But you've talked with Mr. Tiernan about the case, haven't you?"

"Yes."

"And specifically about the search portion of your testimony, correct?"

"Yes."

"In fact, Mr. Tiernan told you on the Tuesday morning that Mark Talbot died that it was very important that the gun be found or, absent that, a very intensive search be made?"

"He said something like that."

"So you knew from the outset that if the gun was not found, it could be argued that Ms. Arcand had hidden it and was not insane?"

"I don't think I had anything figured that far out, Mr. Hauser."

Hauser turned to the court. "Your Honor, with your permission, my law clerk, Mr. Spellman, will set up a tape recorder to play a portion of the radioed conversation between Sergeant Martinez and Mr. Engelhardt. The tape was made by the Kitsap County Communications Center in their ordinary course of business, and was produced to us pursuant to subpoena. I tender a copy of the transcript to the court and to opposing counsel. The tape counters and other authenticating information appear on the transcript."

"Why wasn't this listed as an exhibit?" Thomas Tiernan demanded.

"It is impeachment. We could not know that it would be necessary to use this evidence until just five minutes ago."

Judge Cairns ran through the transcript quickly. Her eyes widened. "I'll allow this. Proceed, Mr. Hauser."

Michael Spellman set up the tape recorder in front of the jury, then played the tape. It was full of the buzz and hiss of recorded radio conversations, but reasonably audible.

Martinez: Chief, I just left the operating room here. The Arcand woman woke up and said she killed her husband.

Engelhardt: Good, that makes our job easier. There's going to be a lot of heat on this one, Bill. He was president of Kitsap Industries. She's supposed to be some famous artist. We'll have the media on our ass for sure. How'd the woman look when you got her off the beach?

Martinez: Bad.

Engelhardt: I heard she's supposed to be crazy. I suppose we'll get an insanity defense for sure.

Martinez: She sure looked crazy when she came out of that coma, Chief. Like a ghost.

Engelhardt: You find the gun?

Martinez: No. It wasn't in her hand or anything. I didn't see it.

Engelhardt: You look?

Martinez: No. No time. I looked right around her, as the EMTs got her loaded in the chopper. I didn't see it. I don't think Stephens saw it either. Think she hid it?

Engelhardt: She must have. Be kind of sweet if she did. It would sure as shit mean she wasn't crazy.

Martinez: Yeah.

Engelhardt: I'll get the warrant to Seattle to hold her at Harborview. You bust butt back here, okay?

Martinez: Okay. [There was a long static-filled pause, then Martinez added,] "Wait, Chief! The Arcand woman said something about killing 'both of them.' There could be another victim!"

Engelhardt: Christ, we gotta search. Get back here.

Hauser turned a withering stare on Wayne Engelhardt. "You had it figured out, didn't you"—he paused maliciously—"Chief."

Engelhardt stared at him, breathing hard. "Mr. Hauser, I swear to you, I never told anyone to get rid of that gun. And there's no witness that saw any of my people do anything like that."

"Just," Ed Hauser replied distinctly, "as there's no witness that saw Laura Arcand hide the gun that killed her husband." He turned away from Wayne Engelhardt. "Your Honor, I'm done with this witness," he concluded, disgust in his voice.

Chapter Forty-three

Hatton paged through the photocopied police reports, then the official coroner's report on the death of Curt Renner. They didn't add much until he reached the final item: an incident report from the Kitsap County sheriff's office, a phone complaint of a possible prowler who'd landed by boat on the west shore of Bainbridge Island, called in by a man who lived across the narrow stretch of water on the mainland. Marshall had attached a note to the top of it. It read:

"We picked this up because it was a boat reference on the night of the 24th. I interviewed the guy who turned it in, an old man known in the neighborhood as kind of a nosy Parker. Nobody reported seeing Renner on the island that night, so we disregarded it. But I gave it to Talbot, so I thought you should have it. That was the deal."

Will arrived at Northlake just after dinner. Laura seemed relaxed, even upbeat. "Ed had a wonderful time today," she reported, "sort of batting the cops around the courtroom like they were tennis balls. It's fascinating, in a horrifying sort of way."

"More like chess, or fencing," Will agreed. "Strategy, skill, invention, preparation."

"Don't worry, Will, I'm not thinking of taking up a new career. But I am feeling better. Really."

Hatton hid his worry behind what he hoped was a reassuring smile; bedside patient manner had never been his best skill. "Any other memory flashes?" he asked, keeping his voice as casual as he could.

"No. Just the one . . . I keep playing it back in my mind, seeing Mark on the sand, alive. But then I think it through rationally and ask myself who else could have killed him, if not me? Ellen? Ed? Some weekend guest? Because they were unhappy about a real estate deal? It's absurd." Laura raised the cigarette in her hand to her mouth and drew on it, her hand shaking. "I know that. But I like to keep it . . . like a little piece of daylight."

"There's no reason you shouldn't do that," Will replied, "as long as you don't raise your own expectations too high. It may be a sign of healing—that you are coming to grips with your loss of Mark, and the fact that you were not morally responsible for what happened, because you were insane."

"I'm trying. But I sit in the courtroom every day, with the eyes of the jurors on me, and Mark's parents sitting there. Oh, I know they've refused to testify for the prosecution—so far. Ed talked them out of it, promised them in return that he wouldn't try to make Mark look bad because of his silly business-trip fuck with that awful Wiegand woman. But they're judging me, too. I can feel it. They're waiting to hear what the doctors will say, what you will say."

"I'll say pretty much what I've told you, Laura. But there's—"

"I know. More questions."

Laura got a small bottle of apple juice from the refrigerator she'd had installed in her room. Laura hated summoning nurses for such things, preferring, like many patients coming out of a deep depressive episode, to exert as much control as she could over her immediate surroundings.

"Okay, Doc," she said, swigging directly from the bottle. "Ask."

"Can you take yourself back to the party at Stenslund Lake the night before you disappeared?"

She nodded. "Danny brought me, I remember that much. He was interested in some other girl, so I drifted over to the keg."

"Do you remember Seth Gwynn?"

"Vaguely. But not the things he described to you, not my taking him down the path to the beach shack."

"Can you see him in the beach shack?"

"No. My paintings—I never got further than that. All I could see was the blackened shape of a man, like a silhouette. Will," she added with sudden urgency, "what happened to those paintings I did over the hardware store? I don't want them out—some ghoul of a collector would probably want them. Not as paintings. The final work of crazy Laura Arcand. I couldn't bear that."

"It won't happen. They're in court custody. When the trial is finally over, all appeals done, if there are any, they'll be released to you. You can destroy them."

"Good. I've never let bad work out of my studio, not if I could help it."

"They won't get out. Have you given any thought to who else could have been in the beach shack, Laura? Someone other than Gwynn."

"I don't even know that it was Gwynn, Will."

"Could it have possibly been Curt Renner?"

She froze, cigarette halfway to her mouth. "Mark's biological father? My mother's old boss?"

"Yes."

"Good God, no. Why?"

"Because he may have disappeared the same night you were raped."

Laura paused, her face twisted in a quizzical frown. "I thought it was later."

"That's what your mother says."

She shook her head, puzzled. Hatton pressed on.

"What was Renner's relationship like with your mother?"

"Ordinary, I think. He took her out sometimes, company dinners, industry meetings, entertaining navy brass or some other important customer. I don't think Ellen ever slept with him, if that's what you're getting at. Getting knocked up at sixteen gave Ellen a rather dim view of sex. At least that's what she tried to drill into me. Obviously, the lesson never took."

"Until Ed came along. For your mother, I mean."

Laura's laugh was bawdy. "And wasn't that the conquest of the century? Good God, she must have been the hardest case Edwin Hauser ever had to crack. I'd love to have been a fly on the wall that night."

"Was Renner in your house a lot?"

"What are you getting at, Will?"

"I'm not sure, Laura. It's just—"

"What, Will?"

"Things don't fit," he finally admitted. "They're close. I can make this case for you, Laura. It's what I do, what any forensic psychiatrist does. Fit together all of the pieces of information about people's lives that conflict, then reconcile them. But there's something—"

"I can't help you, Will. Not yet. It seems the person I know least about is myself." She yawned. "I'm sorry. I get up so early, it's two hours to the courthouse from here. I'd better take my pills now. But don't worry. You will do what you can for me, I know. God knows why."

Hatton left soon after. He dropped his keys to his Cherokee in the dark hospital parking lot, had to inch his way under the car to retrieve them, cursing. When he finally retrieved them he opened the door and slid into the driver's seat. He pounded the steering wheel in frustration.

You've finally hit bottom, Hatton, he thought. Now you're taking comfort from a crazy woman.

Chapter Forty-four

"We're willing, Your Honor," Edwin Hauser called out acidly, "to stipulate that Dr. Treadwell meets the *minimum* requirements to qualify as an expert in this court."

Thomas Tiernan shot Hauser a look that should have stuck four inches out of his back. "And the jury is entitled to hear those qualifications," he replied waspishly.

Mary Slattery rolled her eyes. This has the makings of a very long day, she thought. But Ed had better be careful. Treadwell had the look of a classic courtroom expert witness: handsome, confident, smiling just enough, making good eye contact with the jury. She could already see the jury warming to him, their body language relaxing as they listened, jotting a note or two on their pads.

"I've testified as an expert in court on fourteen occasions," Treadwell continued, finishing the recitation of his credentials. "And perhaps forty more times by deposition, in cases that were resolved prior to trial."

"On what subject matters have you given testimony in court?"

"Nine times as a clinician, a treating physician, in cases involving claims of malpractice," Treadwell replied. "Five times in a forensic capacity, in criminal matters."

"For the prosecution, or the defense?"

"For the defense. This is the first time I have been retained as an expert by the state."

"Dr. Treadwell, you're also here today because you treated Laura Arcand, served as her psychiatrist for five years. Please tell us how your relationship with Laura Arcand started."

"By referral from John Adler, Laura Arcand's internist."

"Did Laura Arcand seek that referral?"

"Yes, she did. She was experiencing recurrent depression, as she had earlier in her life, in New York City, during 1984 and 1985. Dr. Adler suggested she contact me because I have had considerable experience in treating other artists—I have treated several prominent painters, persons in the ballet and opera, a number of writers. Dr. Adler thought I might have some insight into Laura Arcand's problems because of that experience."

"How did you begin her treatment?"

"With a complete medical history, of course. I obtained her medical records from her treating psychiatrist in New York, Dr. Herbert Milstein. I oversaw a complete physical examination. I met with Ms. Arcand several times, to assess her as a person, and administered several psychological tests."

"What type of tests?"

"Projection tests, a thematic apperception test, and an MCMI Two."

"What is an MCMI Two?"

"It is the Millon Clinical Multiaxial Inventory, version two."

"What is it designed to do?"

"It is designed to provide information about the makeup of a patient's personality, a list of characteristics."

"Is it a diagnostic test?"

"It can be. I do not use the MCMI for that purpose, which is why I keep it in a separate file from my treatment chart notes. I use the MCMI to gauge for myself what kind of person the patient is, and how I might most effectively treat them."

"We'll return to the MCMI in a moment, Doctor. First, what diagnosis did you make of Laura Arcand?"

"That she suffered, and still suffers, from bipolar depressive disorder, with some intermittently mixed disassociative tendencies."

"What is bipolar depressive disorder?"

"It is a form of mental illness characterized by cycling between depressed mood and an excessively elated mood. Its mechanism is not yet perfectly understood, but it is related to the level of a chemical substance in the brain known as serotonin, as well as several other brain enzymes. In overly simple terms, there is a chemical malfunction of the brain, often characterized by inadequate levels of serotonin."

"Is that sometimes known as manic-depression?"

"It has been called that, but 'bipolar disorder' is the more precise medical term."

"Then we'll use that term. What causes bipolar disorder?"

"It can be several things. In most cases it is the interaction of genetic heritage—the disease shows a pronounced tendency to appear in family groups—and environment. Depression can be set off by grief, by workplace stress, emotional upset—a variety of influences. But it always has an organic—that is a physical, body—component."

"Let's turn back to Ms. Arcand. What was the basis of your diagnosis that she suffered from bipolar disorder?"

"Several, really. First, Dr. Milstein had reached the same conclusion, eight years before. Bipolar disorder is a chronic condition; it can, and usually does, recur several times in a person's life. Second, Ms. Arcand's own description of her symptoms and feelings. She had returned to Seattle from living in New York City after a series of personal and professional reverses. Her painting, which I believe very beautiful, no longer met with the kind of critical acclaim and success she was used to. She had feelings of worthlessness, fatigue, inability to concentrate, and was unable to enjoy food or her social life. The generally low mood level had been punctuated by several episodes of manic behavior—weeklong shopping sprees; work sessions in her studio that lasted several days, prolonged with stimulants, followed by collapse; sexual encounters with strangers."

"Was Ms. Arcand using drugs?"

"Yes, primarily alcohol and stimulants. She was not an alcoholic in the classic sense; she was using alcohol and stimulants, occasionally cocaine, more often amphetamines, in an effort to self-medicate away the pain of the depressive episodes and prolong the manic phases."

"Were those episodes painful for Laura Arcand?"

"Very." Treadwell turned to the jury, his face a proper mask of grave professional concern. "Depression is among the most painful psychiatric disorders. In Laura Arcand's case, the pain was manifested in her general low mood, but also in a series of painful nightmares that involved feelings of pursuit and fragments of vivid, pulsating color. Laura Arcand's pain was, I can assure you, very real."

"And how did you proceed to treat her?"

"Very carefully. That is where the results of her MCMI come in."

Tiernan busied himself with the overhead projector in the well of the court and flashed the summary page of the MCMI scales on the screen. "These scales represent the relative degree to which certain personality traits are present in the patient. The results of the MCMI for Ms. Arcand were disturbing, to say the least. She has very high levels of diffuse anger, deceptiveness, and a willingness to engage in antisocial behavior."

"Can antisocial behavior and anger indicate a propensity to engage in violent conduct?"

"Yes, it can. Very much so."

"And how did that affect your treatment plan?"

"Quite simply, I had to be careful in evaluating the information I received from Ms. Arcand because of her willingness and capacity to deceive others, including me, for what she perceived to be her own selfish interests. Given the possibility of antisocial, angry behavior, I had to presume that she could pose a risk to herself or others. That suggested an immediate need to stabilize her condition."

"What did you do?"

"We began with imipramine, a broad-based first-generation antidepressant. It can have some unpleasant side effects, but it is broad based—it has a positive effect on most types of depression. When Ms. Arcand was stabilized, I placed her on a course of lithium, which tends to control the bipolar tendency."

"In addition to these drugs, did you analyze Ms. Arcand?"

Treadwell chuckled gently. "No." He turned to the jury. "Psychoanalysis is a form of mental health treatment pioneered over a hundred years ago, by Sigmund Freud. You may have seen this depicted in old movies, particularly from the 1950s. In analysis, the patient meets with the therapist three or four times a week and engages in a

process called transference, whereby the patient projects, or trans-
fers, various characteristics onto the therapist, in an effort to resolve
conflicts that Dr. Freud believed were inherent in the human unconscious. The theory was that when the conflicts were confronted and
resolved, the patient would be healed." Treadwell smiled at the jury.
"Yes, it's confusing, isn't it? And not very scientific. It's not the way
we treat depression today, except in a very small number of cases."

"Does that mean you can just hand pills to a patient like Laura
Arcand, and she'll get well?"

"Heavens, no. I talked to Laura Arcand endlessly, about her work,
her family dynamic, her life goals. That's a very necessary part of
treatment. One must always listen to the patient and adjust the medication accordingly, as I did with Laura Arcand."

"How did her treatment progress?"

"Well, at first. She was motivated to treat because she wanted to
continue her work as a painter, and the physical deterioration caused
by her self-medication—the alcohol, the cigarettes, the amphetamines—were threatening her skills. Later, she met her husband, Mr.
Talbot, and continued to progress well."

"Did something later change?"

"Yes. In 1995, Ms. Arcand was very dissatisfied with the progress
of her painting. She had changed styles away from the abstract work
that had originally made her famous; she confided in me that she felt
she had nothing new to say. She experimented with representational
art, with Asian and primitive artistic influences, but nothing seemed
to please her. She said"—Treadwell fixed the half glasses on his nose,
then thumbed through his chart notes—"Ah. 'I feel like I'm painting
dead things. And my painting is dead.'"

"What happened?"

"Ms. Arcand deceived me, frankly. She said that she was continuing to take her prescribed lithium dosage and avoid alcohol, but in
fact she had stopped taking her medication and had resumed her old
lifestyle, including long, exhausting painting sessions of several days'
duration. Her husband, Mr. Talbot, was very concerned, and finally
contacted me."

"How was Ms. Arcand's condition?"

"She had relapsed into a generally severe depressed state. At my recommendation she was hospitalized for sixty days while we reestablished her equilibrium."

"What else did you do?"

"I counseled her to consider a sabbatical from painting, focus on her own physical health and her relationship with her husband, who seemed both patient and supportive. She did that, to the best of my knowledge, right through the spring of this year."

"Did that help?"

"It seemed to. She was excited earlier this year about rebuilding a beach cabin on her mother's estate. She and her husband were going to work on it together. She took up exercise, reduced her smoking, drank very little. She and her husband attempted to conceive a child, as well. The failure to conceive was a disappointment to both of them. I counseled her about the other options, such as adoption, but she seemed disinterested. In early summer I sensed a darkening of Laura's mood. She reported some of her characteristic dreams had recurred, especially in the wake of her medical inability to conceive a child. Since I was going to be gone for much of July and August, I urged Laura to contact Dr. Winterbauer, on my staff, to continue to bring any problems to his attention for evaluation. She promised she would. She obviously did not."

"Dr. Treadwell, at any time prior to the death of Mark Talbot, did you observe any mental disease or defect in Ms. Arcand that would preclude her from knowing right from wrong?"

"No, I did not. And frankly, I think it's almost absurd to suggest it. At no time in the five years in which I treated Laura Arcand did I ever observe any mental disease or condition that caused her to enter psychosis, that is, the state in which she would not have contact with reality. Laura Arcand is not and never has been schizophrenic, has never been delusional, has never lost the ability to discern right from wrong."

"Dr. Treadwell, you continued to treat Laura Arcand after she killed her husband, did you not?"

"Yes, I did."

"From what point in time?"

"From three days after her attempted suicide. Ms. Arcand's legal counsel obtained her transfer from Harborview Hospital, where she was initially treated, to Northlake Hospital, where I am an attending physician. When Ms. Arcand emerged from the coma she was difficult, evasive. She would not work with me. I made a number of efforts. Finally, I had to give up, transfer her to the care of Dr. Susan Richter. I could not seem to reestablish a good relationship, and when that happens, the caring therapist must step away."

"But did you have an opportunity to observe her condition?"

"Oh, yes. I oversaw a physical examination, including a PET scan and a CAT scan, to determine if there was any kind of organic brain abnormality that could somehow account for Ms. Arcand's actions."

"Did you find any?"

"None. There was a very slight lesion near the hippocampus portion of the brain, and what appeared to be a fully healed hairline fracture that she suffered as a child. Nothing that, in my medical opinion, could have caused psychosis."

"How did she appear to you?"

"Depressed, angry, evasive, hostile. But she seemed in every way capable of understanding her circumstances, and fully in touch with reality."

"Is that what you would expect to find in someone who was recently in a psychotic state, who had so lost contact with reality that they could not determine right from wrong?"

"No sir. It is not."

"Your Honor," Thomas Tiernan said. "It is nearly three, and I understand the court has a legal matter to tend to in another case. At this time we would ask to defer the forensic portion of Dr. Treadwell's testimony to the rebuttal stage of the case, as he will be, to some extent, reviewing Dr. Hatton's testimony and the testimony we understand will be presented in the defense case as part of his expert analysis. We ask that the court declare a recess at this time."

"Do the people have other witnesses?"

"Not at this time, Your Honor. However, I would like to complete Dr. Treadwell's fact testimony prior to making a decision to rest."

"Mr. Hauser? Any objection?"

"None at all, Your Honor," Hauser said mildly, rising to his feet. "None at all."

"Very well. We're in recess until nine A.M."

Chapter Forty-five

"Dr. Treadwell." Edwin Hauser stood squarely in the well of the court, facing the witness stand. The jury was attentive, fresh from their morning coffee. At the defense table, Ellen Arcand had joined her daughter and was holding her hand tightly.

"Yes sir." Treadwell was attentive, polite, but wary.

"In all of your chart notes, there is no mention of the fact that as a fourteen-year-old girl, Laura Arcand was sexually traumatized by oral rape, suffered an amnesiac episode, and disappeared for four days, during which she was further brutalized on the streets of Seattle."

"Some of that is supposition by Dr. Hatton."

"Please answer the question, Doctor. There is no mention in your chart notes of any of those events, correct?"

"Assuming that they occurred and are not supposition, that is correct, sir."

"Assume, for purposes of my questions, that they occurred, Doctor. Would it be important to you, as a practicing psychiatrist, to obtain such information from your patient as part of your initial workup of the case?"

"For what patient, sir?"

"Please don't fence with me, Doctor. For a patient who presented in the same manner as Laura Arcand."

"Possibly."

"Would any of the events I described be unimportant to you?"

Treadwell hesitated. "They are things any reasonably skilled practicing psychiatrist would want to know about a patient, yes."

"And you never learned them?"

"I don't accept that some of them happened."

Hauser turned to the court reporter. "Please read the question back to Dr. Treadwell, ma'am." She did.

Treadwell colored slightly. "I did not learn of them."

"Thank you. Now, Doctor—"

"I asked Ms. Arcand questions about her childhood and upbringing, Counsel. She did not volunteer information about these events."

Hauser smiled silkily, savoring the outburst. "You just did not ask the right questions, did you, Doctor?" he said.

Treadwell paused. "I asked the questions I considered appropriate."

"Which did not include the correct questions." Hauser turned to the clerk. "Defense exhibit 28, please. Now, Doctor, you've seen defense exhibit 28 before, haven't you?"

"Yes."

"What is it?"

"It appears to be a compilation of medical records. From a general practitioner."

"That's Dr. Ted Wilson, who practiced on Bainbridge Island?"

"It appears to be."

"When did you first see these records, Doctor?"

"I don't recall, precisely."

"It was after you were retained by the Kitsap prosecuting attorney's office to serve as their expert witness in this case, wasn't it?"

"Yes."

"So you never obtained these records as part of your medical history of Laura Arcand?"

"No."

"Had you done so, as part of your original patient intake of Laura Arcand, you would have learned that at age fourteen, Laura had disappeared, suffered an amnesiac episode, and had a head injury that Dr. Wilson believed had caused a hairline skull fracture?"

Treadwell looked at the records. "If I had them, yes. Ms. Arcand never mentioned any of this, never referred to this episode in any way."

"Really? But I thought you told us Laura Arcand was secretive, Dr. Treadwell? Based on the MCMI inventory you administered to her."

"I believe the word I used was 'deceptive.'"

"And a patient with tendencies to be deceptive might be secretive about her own past, Doctor?"

Treadwell seemed to struggle for a moment, then conceded the point. "I suppose."

"Which would give you reason to probe deeper into such a patient's past, would it not, Doctor?"

"Not necessarily."

"Ah. Not necessarily. So you wouldn't make use of the information from the MCMI for the purpose of better understanding how to treat the patient? Was there some other purpose?"

"I would use the MCMI information for determining how best to treat the patient and manage the therapeutic relationship. And I had no other purpose."

"I want to be certain of this, Doctor. It is your *sworn* testimony that your sole purpose in administering the MCMI to Laura Arcand was to determine how best to treat her and to properly manage the therapeutic relationship?"

"Yes, that is my sworn testimony."

Hauser turned to the court reporter. "Ma'am, would you please place a clip on the testimony at that point? I may wish to have you read it back later."

The reporter, a stocky woman in her fifties with graying hair, nodded without removing her hands from the keys of her stenotype machine. Treadwell seemed puzzled.

"Thank you. Doctor, you testified on Friday that one of the reasons you concluded that Laura Arcand was suffering from bipolar disorder was that she had been similarly diagnosed by Dr. Herbert Milstein, of New York City, in 1985. Do I have that right?"

"That was a reason, yes."

"Do you know of Dr. Milstein's reputation, Doctor?"

"Not in detail. When I spoke to him he seemed qualified."

"He is board certified in psychiatry, is he not?"

"I believe so."

"Did you have any reason to doubt his competence?"

"No."

Hauser looked at his watch. "Perhaps this might be a good time for our morning recess, Your Honor."

"We are in recess."

Hauser returned to the bench for a huddled conference with Mary Slattery and Reuben Todd. "Is the jury listening?" he demanded in a hoarse whisper.

"Yes," Todd replied. "All but two. The rest are wondering how Treadwell could have missed so much of this."

"They'll wonder more. Get Michael ready. I may want the equipment in here before lunch. I'll try to time it so that we offer the tape just before the jurors go to lunch, but I'm not sure I can get everything in."

"Don't try to time it, Ed," Mary suggested. "Just get through the points. They're following."

He nodded. "Negligent bastard," he said under his breath.

"**Dr. Treadwell,** just before we took our morning recess, you told me that you had no reason to doubt Dr. Milstein's competence, correct?"

"That's right."

"And when he sent you his chart notes and patient file for Laura Arcand, you reviewed them in detail?"

"Of course."

"Of course. Dr. Treadwell, one of the painful aspects of Laura's depression was the intrusive nightmares she had, was it not?"

"Yes."

"Did you consider them medically significant in your workup of her case?"

"I considered them, yes. I don't do dream interpretation, Mr. Hauser. Nor do I read palms."

The joke fell flat on the jury, who remained silent. Treadwell glanced their way, with a hint of anxiety, Slattery thought. "Hit him, Ed," she said under her breath.

Hauser did. He turned to Treadwell and took two steps toward the witness stand, his bearish frame seeming to fill the well of the court. "Doctor," he said softly, his voice contrasting with his angry body language, "is this a joke to you, sir?"

"Objection," Thomas Tiernan called out. "Argumentative."

"No, Mr. Tiernan. Answer, Doctor."

"No, of course not. And I apologize. What I meant was—"

"Please answer the prior question, Doctor. Did you consider these painful intrusive dreams medically significant in the case of Laura Arcand?"

Treadwell nodded. "Anything that causes pain to the patient is medically significant, Mr. Hauser."

"Thank you, Doctor. Thus, having determined that these dreams were medically significant, you reviewed Dr. Milstein's chart notes on the subject with care, did you not?"

"I'm sure I did," Treadwell said. "May I review—?"

"Yes, of course. Madam Clerk? Defense 32, please."

Hauser took the exhibit from the clerk and handed it to Treadwell. "Page fourteen, I believe, Doctor."

"Yes." Treadwell reviewed the chart notes. His eyes seemed to widen.

"Please read to the jury Dr. Milstein's chart notes for October 3, 1985."

"Read them?"

"Aloud, please."

"'Ten/three/eighty-five. PT Laura Arcand returned after two-week absence, visit home to mother in Washington State. PT continues on ten-milligram imipramine. PT seems reasonably in balance but reports recurrence of intrusive dreams since visit home. Describes dreams as pulsating and broken lights similar to broken glass, accompanied by feelings of fear, anxiety. When questioned PT stated that dreams had been experienced since runaway episode as child, four days on streets with considerable injury but no memory by PT of events. Have suggested PT keep dream diary to record frequency of dreams as PT relates to stress. Helpful to identify stressors? PT depressive mood complicated by anxiety. May be related to repressed and/or amnesiac response to flight from home? Why recur now?'"

When he had finished reading, Treadwell looked up, wary.

"In fact, Doctor, had you *carefully* read Dr. Milstein's notes, as you testified, you would have had ample reason to inquire into both Laura Arcand's medically significant, painfully intrusive dreams and her disappearance when she was fourteen years old, would you not?"

Treadwell decided to tough it out. "All I can tell you, Mr. Hauser, is that while I considered Laura's dreams, they didn't appear to be of sufficient medical significance to inquire into an episode that was eighteen years in the past at the time."

"That's because you never investigated, did you, Dr. Treadwell?"

"I did what I believed medically sufficient."

Hauser looked at Treadwell coldly. "Is it really the best clinical practice, Doctor," he said softly but distinctly, "to *not* investigate medically significant information?"

"Objection! Argumentative!"

Hauser eyed Treadwell skeptically. "I withdraw the question, Doctor. There are others who can testify on that issue."

Slattery watched juror 3, the young nuclear technician, carefully. His expression as he looked at Treadwell verged on distaste. She jotted a note for Reuben Todd: "We may have No. 3. Watch him."

"Doctor," Hauser continued, "you testified that Laura Arcand's condition was worsening in the spring of this year, correct?"

"I would say deteriorating, yes. I modified her medication dosage and tried to schedule Ms. Arcand for weekly visits. She resisted that, so we stayed on a twice-a-month plan."

"Through June, yes?"

"I don't understand."

"Doctor, you spent the days from July ninth through August thirty-first in Provence, in France, did you not?"

Treadwell looked sour. "Yes."

"What were you doing there, Doctor?"

"Vacation," Treadwell replied abruptly.

"What kind of vacation, precisely?"

Treadwell looked pained. "Classes in wine tasting and cooking, Mr. Hauser."

Juror 3 rolled his eyes. The rest were stone faced. "Good," Slattery muttered.

"Doctor, to whom did you assign Laura Arcand's patient care while you were improving your palate in the south of France?"

"Objection."

Judge Cairns looked bemused. "On what ground, Mr. Tiernan?"

"It's—well, it's—"

"Accurate," Hauser said dryly.

Cairns nodded. "Overruled. Answer, Doctor."

"Dr. Winterbauer, of my office. As I believe I testified."

"Did you prepare a transfer-of-patient memorandum for him?"

"I don't see one in my file," Treadwell admitted. "I must assume that we talked about the case. And he had my chart notes."

"Yes, the chart notes. How long are your chart notes on Laura Arcand for the month of June, Doctor?"

"How long? I don't understand."

"Please answer the question. Prosecution 24, Clerk."

Treadwell reviewed his notes and colored slightly. "Seven lines, total."

"Please read them."

"'Six/fourteen/ninety-seven. PT L.A. Office visit. Reports continuing upset over work, fear for relation with husband, failure to conceive. Modify dosage up five milligrams.'"

"And for 6/28/97?"

"'PT L.A. Office visit. Anger over rebuilding house. Reports sudden reappearance of intrusive dreams, associated pain. Denies alcohol use increase. Counseled adherence to medication.'"

"That was the last note you made before you departed for Provence?"

"Yes."

"This verbal conversation you had with Dr. Winterbauer. Please tell the jury, as exactly as you can, word for word, what you said and what he said."

Treadwell colored. "I'm sorry. I have a rather poor memory for—"

"Which is why it is your normal practice to prepare a memorandum, correct?"

Treadwell said nothing. Judge Cairns said, "Please answer, Doctor."

"I suppose that's correct. But I am sure we discussed her case in detail."

"There's just no chart note and no memorandum to show that any such conversation took place, correct, Doctor?"

"There is no memorandum or note," Treadwell conceded.

"Fine. Let's move on. Shortly before you resigned as Laura Arcand's treating physician you had a meeting with Dr. Hatton, correct?"

"We had a conversation, yes."

"You taped that conversation, did you not, Doctor?"

"I did. As an aid to note taking. I later transcribed the tape to notes, and reused the tape. That's my customary practice for consultations with other physicians."

"I see. So it is fair to say that you considered the taping of that conversation acceptable to you?"

"I don't understand. I taped it, so of course it was done with my consent, if that's what you're getting at."

"It is, thank you, Doctor. Could you read the note you made from the meeting? It's the last item in your chart notes, before you recorded your resignation."

"Certainly. 'Nine/twelve/ninety-seven. Met Wm. G. Hatton, M.D. Forensic evaluation of L.A. for defense counsel by Dr. Hatton. Told him regretted L.A.'s sudden refusal to cooperate in my treatment, my decision to resign, my observation that L.A. bipolar, no psychosis, no impairment of ability to tell right from wrong.'"

"That note doesn't record everything that was said in that conversation, correct, Doctor?"

"It's a summary."

"But it is not a complete summary, is it, Doctor?"

"It records the parts I thought pertinent."

Hauser returned to the center of the court, directly in front of the witness stand. "It's a fact, isn't it, Dr. Treadwell, that Dr. Hatton accused you of neglecting Laura Arcand's case?"

Treadwell reddened. "He made a suggestion along those lines. I told him that was nonsense, for the reasons I've told you—I assured continuity of care through Dr. Winterbauer."

"Continuity, Doctor? Isn't it a fact that Laura Arcand went to one half-hour appointment with Dr. Winterbauer, then never returned, because he did not seem to know anything about her case?"

"That would be her reconstruction of events, not mine."

"It's a fact, isn't it, Dr. Treadwell, that no other appointment was ever scheduled for Laura Arcand before the death of Mark Talbot?"

"I can't keep patients from skipping appointments, Mr. Hauser."

"No, you just charge them anyway. But you didn't listen to my question, Doctor. Listen, please. I said, it is a fact that no other appointments with Laura Arcand were scheduled by you, Dr. Winterbauer, or anyone else from your office, prior to Mark Talbot's death. Is that correct?"

Treadwell checked his chart notes. "That's correct," he said reluctantly.

"I see. You've been sued for malpractice four times, correct, Dr. Treadwell?"

"Every treating psychiatrist is."

"I agree. You've been found liable on two of those occasions, have you not?"

"Not quite. Both cases were appealed and settled by the insurance company during the appeal process."

"And both those cases involved continuity-of-care problems, did they not?"

"There were many issues. It is so easy to second-guess when treatment is not successful—"

"That means yes," Hauser said, heavily.

"Yes."

"You don't like malpractice cases, do you, Doctor?"

"No one does. I'm sure it's the same for lawyers too."

"It is. So, you were angry when Dr. Hatton suggested that you might have committed a third instance of continuity-of-care malpractice?"

"I would say that I thought Dr. Hatton's suggestion was very wrong."

"Very wrong. And is that why you told Dr. Hatton that if you were accused of malpractice, that you would come into Laura Arcand's trial for the murder of her husband, and using the MCMI scores which you created, depict her as a deceptive, hostile, angry woman, 'who could easily kill her husband'?"

"I said no such thing."

"I'm quoting from a tape recording, Dr. Treadwell."

The courtroom was stunned silent. Slattery looked at the clock: 11:53 A.M. Right on time.

"We will recess for lunch, now, members of the jury," Judge Cairns said. "The bailiff will escort you out into downtown Port Orchard for a lunch at McHenry's Restaurant. I'll expect you back at two. There are some legal matters I need to discuss with counsel."

Chapter Forty-six

The argument raged through the lunch hour in the judge's chambers. No one thought about food.

"This is outrageous, Your Honor," Tiernan spat, his choleric face deep red in anger. "This is more than just unethical secret taping, it's a violation of the Washington criminal statutes, which require that all parties consent to the tape recording of a conversation. Dr. Hatton is guilty of a criminal gross misdemeanor."

"Nonsense," Edwin Hauser said serenely. "Treadwell consented to taping, because he was taping the conversation himself." He passed three declarations to the judge across her desk, handed copies to Tiernan. "This is Dr. Hatton's declaration as to the circumstances of the taping. The second is the declaration of Joseph Atwell, an expert recording engineer. He has examined the original tape, which we tender into evidence for impeachment purposes. He found the tape unaltered. The third is that of the transcriptionist, court reporter Joan Eddington, who certifies as to the accuracy of the transcript."

"Let me read," Judge Cairns said. When she reached the critical part of the transcript, her eyes widened. "This is serious. Very serious." She paused. "Mr. Tiernan? I'm inclined to agree with Mr. Hauser that the taping did not violate the statute and the tape is not inadmissible on that ground. Any other reason I shouldn't let it in?"

"It's a blatant violation of the discovery rules, Your Honor. We specifically asked for all of Dr. Hatton's notes and work papers. If this was just note taking, as Dr. Hatton's declaration says, then Mr. Hauser violated the criminal rules by failing to produce this document. It's trial by ambush, Your Honor, pure and simple. The only fair remedy is to exclude it."

"Mr. Hauser?"

"Your Honor, this is a copy of the state's discovery request," he said, passing it over. "Please read number six. It states, quote, 'All notes and work papers reflecting the source or basis of Dr. Hatton's expert opinion.' This tape is neither a source nor a basis of Dr. Hatton's opinion, nor does it reflect the basis or source of his opinion. His opinion does not rely in any way on Dr. Treadwell's statements on the tape, his opinion, or his testimony. Dr. Hatton's opinion is based on those things referenced in his report, and every document that went into the making of that report has been produced. This is no more within the scope of the discovery request than was the prosecutor's opening statement, or this morning's *Seattle Tribune* story about this case. It's about the subject matter of this case, yes. But it is not a document within the fair reading of the request, as drafted by the prosecution."

Judge Cairns looked troubled. "I've warned you before, Mr. Hauser, that my courtroom was not the place for lawyer's tricks."

"This was not a trick, Your Honor. We did not ask Dr. Treadwell to perjure himself. We were simply prepared to expose it if it came. And bias is a fair attack on any witness. Particularly when a woman's life is at stake."

Cairns sighed. "I'm forced to agree. The tape comes into evidence."

The jury listened intently. The voice of Robert Darrington Treadwell was muffled, but clear enough to be heard and recognized.

"But mark this, my friend," Treadwell's disembodied voice said as the tape concluded. "You and I both know this is going to end with a trial in which Laura's sanity is put in issue. And if you and her

lawyers think I am going to sit still and allow my professional conduct to be attacked, you will be very wrong. I *will* make the jury understand that Laura is a lying, jealous, violent woman who could
easily kill her husband—and is legally sane. I've sweet-talked a hundred juries, and they will believe me. Do you understand?"

"I've heard you," Hatton answered.

"Do remember what you've learned here today, Doctor, about the
defensive practice of medicine."

"I think we all will," Hatton had replied. The tape ended.

The courtroom remained silent.

"Are those your words?" Hauser growled.

Treadwell, pale and anguished, nodded. "They are."

"For chrissakes," muttered juror 3.

"**Your Honor,**" Thomas Tiernan said, rising to address the court after a brief, sharp disagreement with Judith Watkins at the end of that
very long Thursday, the thirteenth of November, "could you ask the
bailiff to excuse the jury? We have a legal matter that we would like
to address to the court."

Judge Cairns frowned, but nodded. "It's three-thirty. Members of
the jury, thank you for your attention today. You are excused until
nine A.M. Monday morning. Please bear in mind the court's instructions as to your conduct." There was a pause while the jury filed out,
following the bailiff and the Kitsap County deputy assigned as a
courtroom guard. When the door was closed and the guards had returned to their positions at the jury and courtroom door, Tiernan
rose again.

"Your Honor," he said, "the state would at this time request a mistrial."

"On what basis?" Judge Cairns demanded.

"We ask for this very reluctantly, Your Honor. But the conduct of
Dr. Treadwell, which was never disclosed to the prosecution, com-
pels us to request this. Dr. Treadwell never told us of his possible
conflict of interest in facing a malpractice suit from the defendant as
a result of his treatment of her. He never told us that his conduct was

in question at all. Given the outrageous statements Dr. Treadwell made on the tape, the state does not believe that it can receive a fair trial."

"I gave you the opportunity to obtain a trial delay for purposes of retaining other experts in rebuttal to Dr. Hatton, Counsel. Mrs. Watkins rather vehemently rejected the offer."

"I know, Your Honor, and obviously we erred. But Dr. Treadwell's failure to disclose—"

"Was a matter for you to deal with. Mr. Hauser? What do you say?"

Edwin Hauser rose, shaking his head. Mary Slattery grabbed his arm and pulled him to her. "Take it, Ed. Take it now," she hissed. "They'll deal, they have to. We own them."

"Wait," Laura cut in, whispering. "What's happening? Will they—"

"Your Honor," Hauser began. "A moment to confer, please."

"Very well."

Ed turned to Mary. "What the hell is wrong with you? We're winning, damn it."

"Think, Ed. Even if there's a retrial, you can pull Treadwell in as a fact witness and blow him up all over again. He'll taint any expert."

"I demand to know what it means," Laura whispered.

"It means that this trial will be over," Mary said. "They'd have to try you again. But we've damaged them so much, they might not, or agree to let you spend a minimal sentence in the hospital at Western State, where you'd continue your treatment. I know it's a hard choice, but—"

"I understand. Ed, do what Mary says."

"But—"

"Please, Ed. I can live with more treatment. I think I need it."

Hauser rose again, reluctantly. "Your Honor, the defense will not object," he said.

Judge Cairns stared at him, shocked. She mulled it over.

"Mr. Tiernan. Will the state seek a retrial?"

Judith Watkins nodded vehemently. "Yes, Your Honor," Tiernan replied.

She frowned. "I'm going to take five minutes," she said. "Then I'll rule. We're in recess."

They waited anxiously. Reuben Todd joined them at the defense table. "I'll admit I'm surprised," he said. "But I'm inclined to think they'll deal now, Ed. I concur."

"We'll see if the judge does," Hauser said sourly.

The answer came a precise five minutes later, as Judge Cairns had promised.

"The motion for a mistrial is denied," she said, on returning to the bench. "While the defense does not object, the decision to declare a mistrial is solely within the power of the court. This has been an expensive and time-consuming trial. Both parties are entitled to a conclusion. I do not believe the conduct of Dr. Treadwell, while the jury may make of it what it will, justifies the waste of judicial resources. The state has had an opportunity to obtain different or other witnesses. It chose not to. It must live with that choice."

Cairns looked up from her notes and removed her reading glasses. "Does the state have any further witnesses at this time?" she demanded.

"Your Honor," Judith Watkins said desperately, "we would like a continuance to retain a new psychiatric expert. You said how much we had been prejudiced by Mr. Hauser's trick pleading tactics. We must have an opportunity—"

"No, Madam Prosecutor. The state has been given those opportunities. It has squandered them. You must live with your decisions. Do you have any additional witnesses to put on at this time?"

"We do not," Judith Watkins said bitterly.

"Then on Monday you will rest your case. We're in recess."

Edwin Hauser remained seated at counsel table long after the courtroom had emptied, slumped in exhaustion. Mary Slattery waited until Ellen and Laura departed for Northlake Hospital, each pausing to kiss Hauser good-bye, before she spoke.

"That was fucking brilliant, old man," she said simply.

Hauser shook his head. "Never celebrate until it is over," he said quietly. "Never." When he rose to go she was startled to see tears in the corners of his eyes.

"Ed? What's wrong?" she asked, suddenly concerned.

"Nothing," he said, his voice quavering. "Just tired, that's all. Tell Ellen I'm not going to the hospital with them tonight. I need to rest for a while."

"Of course. I'll be ready for Monday morning."

He nodded. "All right," he said, his voice again strangely hollow. He left the courtroom quietly, his firm stride reduced to an old man's shuffle.

It was only later that night that Mary Slattery remembered Ed's strange demeanor as a premonition. But by then, seven hours later, Laura Arcand had once again tried to kill herself.

Chapter Forty-seven

"How?" Will Hatton snapped, at ten minutes past midnight.

"With a metal bottle cap," Susan Richter responded grimly, her mouth twisted from frustration and grief. "Laura must have picked it up in the courthouse somewhere and hidden it. She palmed her meds tonight—we found them on the floor under the bed. If the duty nurse hadn't come back in . . ." She shook her head and paced restlessly in the antiseptic hospital corridor.

"Goddamnit, Will, why can't Laura get better? Why? She isn't a coward. You know that. But *this* attempt . . ." Richter shuddered. "Not the wrists this time, the neck. Straight for the carotid artery. The pain must have been incredible."

Susan Richter closed her eyes and wept, weary bitter tears. Hatton put his arms around her and held her until her sobs subsided. His own mind was churning with a mess of conflicting emotions, fear and anger and frustration and grief.

Richter stepped out of Will's embrace and dried her eyes with her hands. "I'm sorry, Will. I'm so sorry. I've let you down, and worst of all I've let Laura down. But I am at my wit's end. She *was* progressing in her therapy. I simply can't explain this. It's as if there is some internal conflict that she cannot resolve, and it overcomes her. I can see it, but I can't reach it."

"Stop blaming yourself, Susan," Hatton replied. "If Laura wants only to die, there is nothing you can do to give her the will to live. But why does she want to die so badly? The trial is going well. She's probably going to be acquitted. What was it about today that brought back the suicidal impulse?"

"The only thing I can think of is that the judge ruled that the trial was going to go forward," Richter replied. "It's as though she cannot face the end of it."

"Or face it going on," Hatton said, thinking aloud. "But why? The prosecution case is over, and there's only a few defense witnesses—Roy Black, the ER surgeon, Steven Terry, me, you, a couple of her friends, and her mother. There's no one who's going to be accusing her—"

"Only Laura herself," Susan Richter replied. "And maybe it is facing herself that Laura finds to be the hardest thing of all."

"Perhaps," Hatton replied. "Are you monitoring her?"

"Of course. She's back on suicide protocol. We put her on IV Valium to sleep after Dr. Briggs sutured the wounds."

"Are Ed and Ellen still outside her room?"

"Still. But there's nothing they can do tonight."

"I'll send them home. Can I stay with her?"

"I don't think she'll wake."

"I know, but I'd feel better being here in case she did."

Susan Richter smiled ruefully. "And this way I'll go home, right?"

"Right. I'll see you tomorrow morning, around six."

Laura lay quietly on her back in her hospital bed, her neck swathed in bandages, her chest rising evenly, her breath soft and regular in her drug-induced sleep. Hatton selected a reclining chair across the room, dimmed the lights, and stared at Laura until sleep claimed him as well.

He woke just past four, from the clatter of a water bottle that Laura had knocked to the floor.

"Will?" she whispered painfully.

"I'm here, Laura."

"Water, please."

"Of course." Will found the water bottle on the floor, rinsed it, filled it with fresh water, and gave it to Laura. She drank thirstily through the straw. When she had finished she began to drift again into sleep.

"Laura," Will said insistently, placing a hand against her cheek. "Laura."

"Hmm?" she asked, still groggy from the drug.

"Why, Laura? Why did you try to kill yourself again?"

"No way," she muttered. "No other way."

"Why, Laura? Why is there no other way?"

"No way out," she whispered. "But I want you to know, Will."

"Know what, Laura?"

Her eyes widened and stared sightlessly at the ceiling as she fought to hold on to the edge of consciousness. Her words were forced through drug-numbed lips. *"I did not kill Mark."*

Before he could press her further, Laura slipped back into sleep.

Hatton poured himself a fourth cup of coffee, black. It was just past seven-thirty on Saturday morning. Hatton had slept just six hours in the last forty, and fatigue had seeped into every bone and muscle.

Gray steel light from a morning of November rain filled Mary Slattery's living room. Mary Slattery sat quietly on the leather sofa by her rain-streaked bay window, watching Hatton pace the length of the room.

"You can't rely on what Laura said, Will," Slattery told him. "She probably wasn't even conscious, and she was pumped full of Valium. It's no more believable than what she said in the emergency room after her first suicide attempt, when she said she *had* killed Mark."

"I can't testify to what I don't believe, Mary. And I don't believe that Laura killed Mark Talbot. Not any longer."

"Will," Mary said, her voice soft but insistent. "Are you willing to put Laura's life at risk? Because if you change your testimony we could lose this trial. As it stands now, the jury's so mad at the prosecution and at Treadwell, they're ready to acquit. All you have to do is give them a reason."

"You might think that now. But if the prosecution gets Ellen on the stand about what happened on the night Laura disappeared in 1972, and she's contradicted by John Stansbury, they're going to be able to blow some pretty big holes in my testimony."

"Why? Just because no one found a gun in the beach house that night?"

"That, and more. Curt Renner had to have been the man in the boat that Gwynn says he saw. It doesn't make sense any other way. And Mark Talbot knew that."

"Talbot's study," Mary said slowly.

"What?"

"His study, Will. Remember? When I went to the house for the second time, I went into his study again. He had marine charts tacked to the walls of his study. Like he was trying to figure out the currents around Bainbridge Island."

"What is the direction of the current in the pass off of Ellen's place?" Will asked her.

"South," Mary Slattery replied, remembering what Jon Sorenson had told her on the morning after Talbot was killed.

Hatton shook his head. "Renner's boat was found off Whidbey Island, ten or fifteen miles north. He didn't drift there by accident, Mary. Somebody took his boat north to make it look like he was lost in a storm. Talbot had figured it out. He must have gone to Ellen, confronted her with that."

"But Talbot didn't have any proof that Ellen killed Curt Renner and stole the company from him," Mary said stubbornly. "Ellen could've just told him to stick it. He wouldn't have confronted her unless he had some kind of proof, some kind of evidence that she killed Renner, or had him killed."

"Maybe it was proof that she stole the company," Hatton replied. "Maybe Talbot found an original version of the buy-sell agreement, proved that his father's signature was forged. And that's why Ellen was so spooked when Marcia Wiegand called you from KI's old offices in Bremerton, thinking that Wiegand had found something."

"But if he did have a document, we'd have found it, Will. We've checked everything—the house, his office, his computers. And we didn't find anything like that."

Hatton shook his head, no. "Talbot was a smart guy," he insisted. "He hid it somewhere."

"But where? We even checked his lockers at his gun club and the gym he worked out at. Every place he had access to has been searched."

"Maybe," Hatton said slowly, "he hid it in plain sight."

"How?"

"You can't find a needle in a haystack, right?"

Slattery shook her head, frustrated. "I don't follow."

"You can't find a needle in a haystack because it looks like every other piece of hay. So if you're clever, you'd hide a piece of paper in a stack of paper. And who's got the biggest stack of paper about Kitsap Industries in the entire world?"

"Oh, shit," Mary Slattery said suddenly. "*We* do."

Chapter Forty-eight

The light in the mag card reader on the sixth floor of the Northwestern Bank Tower switched from red to green.

Mary Slattery removed her security card from the reader and switched on the lights. Rows of metal floor-to-ceiling document shelves, each filled with numbered redweld folders containing the documents generated by the Kitsap Industries environmental lawsuits, marched away from them, two hundred feet in each of three directions, under a harsh blue fluorescent glare.

"Can you access the database from the computer in your office?" Will asked.

"No. It's on the office LAN—local area network—but it's security guarded. I never had reason to load the access codes onto my computer."

"How can we search it then?" Will asked, frustrated.

"David Dworshak—the record custodian—has the database on the hard drive of his PC, so he can update the data every day. He puts the updated database back on the network after the rest of us have gone home, so it doesn't tie up the LAN when we're using it."

They entered Dworshak's office on the southwest corner of the floor and switched on the desk light. Mary turned on Dworshak's PC and booted it up.

"Who coded all the documents?" Hatton asked.

"Small batches are coded by the staff here. But most of them were coded offshore."

"Offshore?"

"Yeah. The documents are actually coded by university students in China and the Philippines that are reasonably proficient in English. They work for four bucks an hour."

"But how can they understand what they're reading? Hell, I can't understand the insurance policy on my building."

"They don't have to. At the start of a big case, they get a week of training, telling them how to sort documents by type, title, data, author, recipients, who produced it, where it was found, that sort of thing. Objective data. Each coder has to enter three initials that identify them, so their work can be reviewed. The lawyers here read them after they're coded, and add a special field that contains the lawyer's subjective assessment of the relevance of the document and its evidentiary value."

The PC opened to the Windows screen and Mary scrolled through the Explorer utility until she found the Bremerton Litigation Database directory. When she tried to open it, the first screen came up, demanding a password.

"Shit," she said. "I don't . . . wait. Dworshak showed me his password once. What was it?" She frowned, deep in thought, looking around Dworshak's office. Her eyes lit on a shelf of travel books Dworshak kept there. She grinned.

BALI, she typed.

Will laughed over her shoulder. "Bali?"

"Dworshak's a little bit arrested," she said. "You'd probably like him. Or want to analyze him, one of the two. Here we go." The system opened to a new screen with icon-based commands.

"How do we search?"

"We can search the objective codes by field. We can also go into the scanned text database and do a keyword search for particular kinds of subject matters."

Hatton scanned the list of fields and thought. "Is someone who signs a document an author of the document?"

"Yes, at least a coauthor. Even if it's a draft."

"Try Curt Renner."

She did. "Twenty-one hundred and sixty-two documents accessed. You still think Mark found the original copy of the buy-sell agreement between Curt Renner and Ellen Arcand?"

"I think it has to be. Or some form of it. An original that either could be proved to be a forgery or would somehow show that the official signed version of the agreement in the company files had Renner's signature forged on it."

Slattery clicked on the "type" field, got a subdirectory, and clicked on "contract."

"Down to four hundred and thirty-three documents. Making progress."

"Title field?"

Slattery nodded, accessed the title field, entered PURCHASE W/25 SALE.

"A hundred and twenty-six documents," Hatton said, reading over her shoulder. "Shit. Mark must have had some way to get to it fast, identify the one document from all the others that looked like it. Maybe some phony date or other information he knew wasn't correct, that he somehow coded?"

"I think we'd better look at all of them, Will. We still don't even know what we're looking for. No, wait. I wonder . . . I think Talbot was trained on this system, Will. Let me . . ."

She clicked on the coder ID field and entered the initials MJT.

One document, the system read. "That's it," Hatton said.

Mary Slattery saw it too. "Oh my God," she said. "Let's take a look."

"Where is it stored?" Hatton asked.

"Every document gets bar-coded and laser-imaged after the initial hand-coding. Dworshak's people have a system for coding and imaging documents found after the initial bulk document productions are done. I think they've been doing about a hundred docs a day for months now. Talbot probably just slipped it in the production queue for bar-coding and imaging." She clicked on the 'Image/Print' icon.

The screen filled with the laser-stored image of the first page of a document, the agreement for purchase and sale of stock in Renner Tool & Die Works. The top of the page had been written on in a precise engineer's hand, the capital letters bold and clear.

LARRY: I WON'T SELL THE COMPANY TO THAT BITCH. NOT AFTER TODAY. IF I'M DEAD, THE COMPANY DIES TOO. TEAR THIS FUCKING THING UP. CURT.

"It's hand-dated," Hatton said slowly. "August 24, 1972. That's the day Curt Renner died."

"But I thought the signed buy-sell agreement was dated August third."

"Of course. When Talbot found this, he knew Ellen Arcand wasn't supposed to own Kitsap Industries. Ellen and Ed forged Renner's signature, then brought in Larry Elder, who had been acting as Renner's lawyer, to notarize the forgery. Look." Hatton produced his own photocopy of the buy-and-sell agreement bearing Curt Renner's forged signature. "Elder's notary seal is right through Renner's signature. He must have been in on it."

"How could Ellen have missed this other document after Renner's death?"

"Renner never sent it to Larry Elder. Ellen never knew it was there. It probably got shoveled up with the contents of his office after he was declared dead, and stuck in a file somewhere in the old Burwell Street machine shop in Bremerton."

"Then Ellen's never seen this."

Hatton shook his head grimly. "No, I'll bet she has. A photocopy, at least. On the night Mark Talbot was murdered."

By eight o'clock Sunday morning Will Hatton was standing next to the beach cabin on Ellen Arcand's estate, staring up at the bluff. The searchers had cleared enough of the brush out of the canyon rising from Ellen Arcand's unnamed cove that the remnants of the old trail could be glimpsed between the now-bare branches of the alder trees and blackberry canes that still flanked the streambed. Hatton started up the canyon, walking up the creek bed where the trail had been washed out, placing each step carefully on the slippery smooth stones. The stream ran thick over its cleared stony course, swollen from the fall rains. At the road Hatton had to scramble up a steep gravel bank to the asphalt paving. On the far side of the road the stream disappeared into a green tangled wall of blackberry, salal, Oregon grape, and young Douglas firs. Hatton, steaming inside the rain suit from exertion, swigged from his water bottle, dropped it back into his fanny pack, and hacked his way forward with the machete, following the sound of flowing water.

The brush thinned as the tree canopy over the creek emerged. Hatton made good time up the slope of the island's long western ridge, again wading into the creek where the trail had washed out, the numbingly cold water flowing over his boots. In fifteen minutes he found himself standing beside a natural stone cistern, water springing into a pool between two layers of the harder, upthrust rock that formed the southern part of the island. Hatton had never been more than an amateur geologist, but he guessed that the fracture in the rock layers released water from deep in the ground beneath the hillside, flowing even during the dry summers.

"Laura's spring," he said, wondering why she had never brought him here, even in the summer that they had been close, so long ago.

Hatton pressed on. In another ten minutes he crested the top of the ridge and found himself in a grove of hundred-foot Douglas firs. To the south he heard a loon's cry, then the sound of drumming wings as a flight of Canadian geese passed overhead.

Stenslund Lake, he said to himself, still puffing from the climb.

He looked around. The remnant of the old path curved north, slippery with rain, narrow and overgrown, but with the trace of broken branches, several months old, pointing the way. A second path crossed it and ran southeast, back toward Stenslund Lake. Hatton stayed on the main path, sure now of where he was. The path stopped suddenly, cut off by a barbed-wire fence.

He did not need to cut the fence. Beyond it he saw a familiar hillside planted with old breeds of Northwest apple trees—Gravensteins, Kingstons, Jamaica blacks. He had planted some of those trees himself, twenty-five years before. In Edwin Hauser's orchard.

Hatton jogged back down the trail toward Crystal Springs Drive. Tor Trolland's words, spoken six weeks ago, echoed in his head. "He'd slept through his alarm and looked like hell, hot and sweaty red. Guess he drank too much. . . ."

No, Hatton thought. It wasn't drink, Tor. The old man, weakened heart and all, had been running, crashing his way up the old trail.

When he reached his car he took out a state of Washington map and gauged the distance. It was just after 9 A.M. It would take about three hours, but he could make it down and back today.

Within minutes he was off the island, over the Agate Pass bridge to the mainland of Kitsap County, headed for the Pacific coast.

The Westport marine pier was empty at quarter to one, the looming black clouds over the boiling Pacific promising one hell of a storm in the next twenty-four hours. Will quickly found his way to slip 9, the moorage for Ed's boat, the *Ellen IV*. At nearly fifty feet, the *Ellen IV* could handle anything up to and including the Bering Sea, though Will, mindful of his two terror-stricken fishing seasons on his grandfather's boat, had never taken up Ed's offers of a fishing trip up to Dutch Harbor, Alaska. The boat had been an open ocean salmon trawler Ed had cannily bought from the Fisheries Administration disposal program at ten cents on the dollar of construction cost. He'd refitted it for comfort, lining the cabin below with teak, fitting out the galley with a full kitchen and a warming propane stove, stocking the deckhouse with the latest in radar and global-positioning gear. Will paused on the deck, waved at the dockmaster, and then headed below.

An hour's search of the cabin yielded nothing. Frustrated, Will returned to the aft deck, fitted out for trawl lines and with deep-sea-fishing chairs, for Ed had taken the boat as far south as Mazatlán for the winter tarpon season. Hatton thought, trying to remember Tor's words. The ice. Something about ice. Will's eyes turned to the sides of the boat.

"The bait wells," he muttered.

There were six on each side. Hatton plunged his arms into the wells, to the shoulder, the brine frigid on his skin.

It was in the third well, on the port side, sealed in a gallon-size thick plastic freezer bag, bound with rubber bands. Hatton opened the bag, careful not to touch the .38 caliber Smith & Wesson revolver inside. The word LADYSMITH had been etched into the blue steel frame, just below the barrel.

Chapter Forty-nine

Allison Cairns took the bench, as was her habit, precisely at 9 A.M. on Monday morning. She momentarily lost her composure and stared at Laura Arcand, sitting in a wheelchair beside the defense table, her eyes vacant, her neck swathed in a white bandage.

"Ms. Arcand," Cairns said, "are you prepared to continue? If your medical condition will prevent you from attending this trial, I will postpone it."

Laura shook her head painfully. "No, Your Honor," she whispered. "I would rather go on with this."

"Are you certain? Is your treating physician here?"

"Yes, Your Honor," Susan Richter replied, rising from the first row of benches behind Laura. "I am here, and will monitor Ms. Arcand's condition. She is not well—but I believe she is capable of understanding the proceedings and working with her counsel as necessary."

"Very well. Mr. Hauser?"

Hauser rose. "Yes, Your Honor?"

"I have read the medical reports you faxed me about Ms. Arcand's condition on Sunday. I want to proceed as normally as possible, but you are to have Dr. Richter notify me at the *first* sign that Ms. Arcand's condition may be troubling her."

Hauser nodded. "I understand, Your Honor, but my client's condition is—"

"Something I want Dr. Richter to monitor, sir," Cairns responded, cutting him off. "Now to the matters pending. The prosecution's motion for a mistrial was denied on Thursday afternoon," she continued. "An emergency motion for reconsideration was filed by the prosecution on Saturday morning. I have reconsidered the matter, and affirm my original decision. A written opinion will be issued later today. Does the state have any other witnesses?"

"Not at this time, Your Honor," Judith Watkins said sullenly. "The state rests, subject to calling additional witnesses in rebuttal."

"Very well. Is the defense prepared to proceed?"

Mary Slattery rose. "We are. And we call William Girard Hatton, M.D."

"Dr. Hatton, is Laura Arcand mentally ill?"

Hatton looked out over the courtroom, the better to draw the jury's eye to Laura's silent ghostly presence. "She suffers from severe mental illness, yes."

"What is your diagnosis?"

"Laura Arcand suffers from a long-established condition known as bipolar disorder, which we used to call manic-depression. Her condition is severely complicated by posttraumatic stress disorder, with attendant problems of organic and hysteric amnesia, and disassociation."

"Have you made that diagnosis to a medical certainty, Dr. Hatton?"

"Yes, my diagnosis is medically certain."

"How has Laura Arcand's mental illness manifested itself, Dr. Hatton?"

"Her symptoms are varied and complex. She suffered, and still suffers, from extreme variations in mood, from deep depression to heights of manic behavior. When she was younger, she was able to use those mood swings to produce some of her finest artistic work, painted at the height of her manic phases. But for nearly fifteen years, she has not been able to control or deal with those mood swings. She has been hospitalized three times for her bipolar illness, each time because the highs and, particularly, the depths of depression became too painful to bear. She also suffers from repeated and intrusive dreams and fragmentary memories that cause her great pain and fear. These symptoms occur most often during the depressive phase of her bipolar disorder."

"You also said that Laura Arcand's illness was severely complicated by posttraumatic stress disorder. What is that disorder?"

"It is a recognized form of mental illness that arises from a severe traumatizing episode, one that is terrifying or painful beyond the range of normal experience."

"What are the symptoms of that disorder?"

"Persistent, recurring, and intrusive recollections of the stressful event, both consciously and in dreams; avoidance of things or places associated with the traumatizing event; psychogenic amnesia; feelings of estrangement from others; hypervigilance and physiologic reactivity."

"Can you explain those symptoms to the jury, Dr. Hatton? What would a person having those symptoms be like?"

Hatton turned to the jury. "A person experiencing those symptoms would be a great deal like Laura Arcand. Such a person would often be difficult or irritable to deal with, and would sometimes appear evasive or deceptive, because they would want to avoid any feelings or thoughts that could trigger a memory about their trauma. Like Laura Arcand, a person suffering from PTSD would be afraid of places and things that reminded them of the trauma suffered. As with Laura Arcand, the memory of that trauma might be repressed, or even consciously forgotten, but would leak out in other ways—as through frightening dreams. Like Laura Arcand, a person suffering from PTSD would be very quick to react to any threatening information, and would exhibit visible physical signs of stress, ranging from sweating and tremors to full seizures of the type Ms. Arcand has had, including one that happened in this courtroom."

Slattery watched the jurors carefully through Hatton's long answer. They seemed to listen intently and showed no signs of tension or dislike, only a kind of somber acceptance of what they were hearing. *He's got them,* she thought to herself. *If only I knew what he was going to do.*

"Dr. Hatton," she continued, "you testified that PTSD is caused by a severe trauma. Have you identified the trauma which caused this condition in Laura Arcand?"

"Yes, I have. It was an attempted, or partially successful, rape. The rape took place in 1972, in the original beach cabin that was located on her mother's property on Bainbridge Island, when Laura Arcand was just fourteen years old."

"What happened?"

"Laura Arcand returned from a party with her high school friends, late at night, and went to the beach cabin with a man named Seth Gwynn, a teacher at her high school. With Mr. Gwynn's assistance, she took LSD. While she was under the influence of LSD, she was attacked."

"By Mr. Gwynn?"

"No. I do not believe it was Mr. Gwynn."

There was a sharp gasp from the courtroom benches behind the defense table. Ellen Arcand leaned forward, face flushed, and tried to reach Edwin Hauser. Hauser shook her off and kept his eyes focused on Hatton, dark worry etched on his face. Hatton turned slightly to look at Laura; her eyes were glazed with fear.

"No," Laura whispered. "Don't, Will."

Slattery paused. "If not Mr. Gwynn, who took her to the beach cabin so she could take LSD, then who was it?"

"I believe that Laura was attacked by a man named Curtis Renner, her mother's business partner. Mr. Gwynn's testimony in his deposition was very specific: he heard a boat land on the beach near the cabin, saw a man emerge and walk up the trail that led from the beach to Laura's mother's house, up the bluff. Mr. Gwynn says that he fled shortly after that, not wanting to be found with a teenage student under the influence of an illegal drug. While Mr. Gwynn's conduct was absolutely reprehensible, I believed him."

"Why, Dr. Hatton? Gwynn had the opportunity. He has a history of—"

"I know. But the persistence of Ms. Arcand's trauma, the fact that she never really was able to recover from it, only suppress it, leads me to believe that the man who traumatized her had a much closer relationship to Laura and her mother."

"Tell the jury about the persistence of Laura's trauma, sir."

"It has persisted, that is perhaps the most unique thing about it. For twenty-five years, Ms. Arcand has had repeated, intrusive memories of a man who attacked her—yet it was a man that she could not name. That suggests to me that there was a family relationship involved."

Mary Slattery stopped. It's too late, she told herself; I have to let him go on. "How did Ms. Arcand deal with these memories?"

"She could not. That is why they became the cause of her PTSD disorder. After she was attacked, she believed that she shot her attacker; and then she fled the beach house. She was beaten in the attack, which caused a hairline fracture of the skull and a substantial concussion. Laura was on the streets in Seattle in that condition, and was beaten again while on the street and in juvenile custody. She never recovered a complete conscious memory of what happened to her that night. Laura did have severe, repeated, painful dreams of that attack, which caused her to relive the rape, over and over. She tried to capture those memories, control them, by painting about them. But she was never able to make them stop. She relived those memories on the night her husband, Mark Talbot, died."

"You said Laura Arcand believed she shot Curtis Renner after he attacked her. Did she?"

"She believes that, yes. I do not know whether Laura actually fired a gun at Curtis Renner. The county sheriff, John Stansbury, and his officers searched the beach cabin the morning after Laura Arcand disappeared, and they found no weapon, and no evidence—blood, bullet holes, spent shells—that a gun had been fired in that beach house in August 1972."

"How do you account for this discrepancy?"

"I can't. Laura is very firm in her belief that she fired a gun that night, and shot and wounded her attacker. The only other explanation is that someone cleaned up any evidence prior to the arrival of the police."

Mary Slattery took a deep breath.

"Dr. Hatton, you said that Laura Arcand relived this memory on the night she shot her husband, Mark Talbot. Can you testify, to a medical certainty, whether in your opinion Laura Marie Arcand was unable, by reason of mental disease, to know right from wrong when she shot her husband, Mark Talbot?"

Hatton paused and locked eyes with Mary Slattery.

"I did not say that, Ms. Slattery. And I cannot answer your question. Because I no longer believe that Laura Arcand shot her husband, Mark Talbot."

Allison Cairns broke the stunned courtroom silence.

"Bailiff," she said quietly. "Lead the jurors out. We have some legal matters to attend to."

She waited while the jury, still bewildered by Hatton's testimony, filed out. When the door to the jury room had been locked, Cairns turned in sudden fury on Edwin Hauser.

"Stand *up*, Mr. Hauser. Stand!"

Hauser slowly rose to his feet, his face grave.

"I warned you, Mr. Hauser. Repeatedly. I told you that I would not tolerate chicanery in this trial. And what trick is this?"

Hauser remained mute. He looked away from the judge and stared at Hatton, then spoke a single tortured word.

"Why?" he asked.

Will returned Hauser's wounded stare with fierce anger. "Because Laura Arcand has the right to know the truth about her past," he said hotly. "Because she has the right to heal—and she cannot heal without knowing the truth." Hatton reached to his feet and opened his briefcase and brought out the .38 caliber Ladysmith revolver and handed it up to the judge. Cairns took the gun, still wrapped in a plastic bag and musty from immersion in seawater, and placed it on the bench in front of her.

"Is this—," she began, her voice filled with confusion.

Hatton nodded. "I believe this is the gun that was used to murder Mark Talbot," he said. "I found it yesterday afternoon. In a bait well on Edwin Hauser's boat. I believe Mr. Hauser took the gun there and hid it on the morning after Mark Talbot was murdered."

Allison Cairns reddened with fury. "Explain yourself, Mr. Hauser. Now."

Hauser, still standing, shook his head. "No," he whispered.

"What?"

"No," Hauser repeated, his voice cracking. "I will not."

Cairns turned to Hatton, stunned by Hauser's refusal to speak. "What are you suggesting, Dr. Hatton? Did Mr. Hauser murder Mark Talbot?"

"Edwin Hauser is not a murderer, Your Honor. But I believe that he covered up two murders. The murder of Curt Renner, twenty-five years ago. And the murder of Renner's son, Mark Talbot. I think he hid this gun so that if Laura Arcand was convicted, he could plausibly claim that he killed Mark Talbot and free her." Hatton's voice broke, and his eyes filled with tears, but he continued. "At least I hope that is why he did this."

"I don't understand," Cairns said, dubiously. "Why was Mark Talbot murdered?"

"For two reasons, Your Honor. First, because he discovered that Ellen Arcand murdered his estranged father, Curt Renner, in 1972. Ellen Arcand was Curt Renner's partner in Kitsap Industries. Renner died on the same night he attacked Laura Arcand, August 24, 1972. After Renner was murdered, his body was sunk in Puget Sound, and his boat taken north, to waters off the south end of Whidbey Island, and his boat scuttled there to make it look as though Renner had died in an accidental drowning. After Renner was killed, Ellen Arcand and Edwin Hauser forged Renner's signature on a shareholder agreement, a buy-sell agreement that gave Ellen Arcand most of the stock in Kitsap Industries.

"When Laura Arcand began reexperiencing her violent memories of being raped this past summer, Mr. Talbot tried to find out what had happened to her. He contacted the same witnesses I did, trying to reconstruct what had happened to his wife. He found out the same things I did, including the fact that his father's death and Laura Arcand's disappearance were linked. He also found a document in Kitsap Industries' old files that proved that Curt Renner's signature on that buy-sell agreement was forged. Here it is." Hatton passed the copy of the agreement with Renner's handwritten instructions on it to the judge.

"I believe that Mark Talbot confronted Ellen Arcand with what he had learned on the night of his death," Hatton continued. "He accused her of stealing Kitsap Industries from him, and killing his father. And that Ellen Arcand killed him later that night, on the beach, with her daughter's gun." Hatton stopped abruptly, suddenly worn down by the weight of days of tension without sleep.

The dense courtroom silence was broken by a low keening wail. Laura Arcand rose unsteadily to her feet, her face a mask of rage.

"You!" she hissed bitterly, turning to her mother. "You told me I had killed Curt Renner! You said you were *protecting* me! How could you?" Her voice took on a childlike cadence. "Oh, Mother, how could you?" Laura collapsed to the floor, as though beginning a seizure. Susan Richter rushed to her and dropped to her knees to hold Laura, shoving the wheelchair away so that Laura would not crash into it if she convulsed.

"Order!" Allison Cairns commanded. Hatton rose from the witness stand and turned to face her.

"No, Your Honor," he said. "Please, let Laura speak. Let me help her."

Cairns leaned back from the bench and thought, then nodded. "Go ahead, Dr. Hatton. Madam Reporter, take this down. All of it. We're still on the record."

Hatton stepped down and crossed the well of the courtroom to where Laura remained in Susan Richter's embrace, half sitting, half collapsed, stunned into silence.

"Laura," Will said, as evenly as he could. "There is another way, Laura. *Listen to me*. The memory that you have of killing Curtis Renner is false. And you know—*you know*—that you did not kill Mark. Stop protecting her, Laura. Stop protecting Ellen. You do not owe her your life. You do not have to throw away your life to protect her any longer. Please, Laura." Hatton paused, his heart pounding, waiting for some sign of agreement from Laura. When she finally nodded, he helped her to her feet.

Laura Arcand stood and faced the courtroom. "I did not kill my husband," she whispered painfully. She coughed, and when she spoke again her voice was firm. "*I did not kill my husband.*"

Laura shook loose of Will's arm and went to Ellen Arcand.

Ellen Arcand sat rigidly in the first row of courtroom benches, her jaw clenched. When Laura reached out to her, she pushed her daughter's searching hands away.

Chapter Fifty

The videotaped examination began, as before, with Laura Arcand seated pensively at a table in the physicians' library at Northlake Hospital.

"It's ten A.M. on December 4, 1997," Hatton said softly. "Laura, are you feeling well enough to talk about your past today?"

She nodded nervously. "Where do you want to begin?"

"In 1972, Laura. Tell us what happened when you came back to the beach cabin with Seth Gwynn."

"We heard the boat," she began simply. Laura's voice was tense, but her words were adult, in control. "The acid I took was a bust, or at least it hadn't started to work. I was pretending to be stoned because I didn't want to have sex with Seth Gwynn. He had his hands all over me until I went limp." She shivered.

"The boat," Will prompted her gently.

"The boat. We went to the cabin window and looked. When the man got out I knew right away who it was. Curt Renner." Laura's face twisted in disgust. "You know about Ellen and Renner, don't you?"

"No," Will replied. "I can guess, though. Ellen traded sex with Renner for the chance to buy into the company."

Laura shook her head, no, her expression sad and bitter. "Traded," she snorted angrily. "Try forced. When my mother first went to work for him he courted her, all kind words and flowers. And she had a relationship with him, for a while. But when she understood him, saw what a bastard he was and tried to end it, Renner wouldn't let go. Oh, she could leave him, all right. So long as she lost her job and went packing without the money she'd invested in the company." She paused, then spoke again, quiet vehemence in her voice. "When I was little, Will, and we still lived in Bremerton, in the D Street house, Renner used to come around the house late at night, drunk. He'd pound on the door, demanding that she let him in. My mother and I used to sit huddled in the kitchen, Ellen holding me. And then, very slowly, she would put me away in bed, in the little bedroom she'd made for me on the walled-in back porch. And I would wait for her, Will. Sometimes it was quick. Sometimes it wasn't. Finally, when he was gone and she had stripped the bed and put on clean sheets, and had the blankets back in place, she would come for me and we would sit in her bed, sing songs, and read books, until I finally fell asleep." She paused, a gathering anger in her face. "Then sometimes he'd come around sober. Like they were going on a date. My mother fussing with her hair, giving instructions to the baby-sitter. And he'd *stroke* me, touch my hair, telling me how smart and pretty I was. And I'd have to be *nice* to him." Laura shook with disgust. "When I was older . . . past twelve, my breasts popping out, my hips spreading . . . he'd touch me. When my mother wasn't looking. I let him. I thought it would help mother. And I never said a word." Laura looked up at him, her eyes dark with remembered hatred. "My mother bought our life by having sex with Renner. And I swore to myself, one of those deep angry childhood vows. When I was old enough I would kill Curt Renner for her."

Hatton prompted Laura further. "Tell me what happened at the beach cabin," he said again.

"My mother had a huge fight with Renner that day. She told him that it was over, to leave her alone, threatened him with a lawsuit if he didn't. She'd been working with Ed by then, and Ed told her she could take Renner for her share of the company if he didn't leave her alone. That night, after the party at Stenslund Lake—when we heard Renner's boat—Seth ran out to see where Renner was going. He followed him up the beach path, saw that he was headed for the house. I tried to explain, but when Seth figured out that Renner was going to see my mother he took off, panicked. I stayed in the beach shack. I wanted to go and help my mother, but I was afraid . . . afraid of going to the house, where Renner was, afraid of staying where I was, alone, in case he came back. I was so terrified I couldn't move . . . and then the LSD started to hit me. The room started to quiver. Colors began flashing into bright squares, then each pane of color shattered, like glass." Laura looked up, her face twisted with self-loathing. "Do you have any idea of how I hated myself for that?" she asked. "*Any* idea? I was old enough, strong enough . . . and I let him go to my mother. *Again.*"

"I know, Laura. No, that's not right. I can't know. I can understand, though."

Laura nodded. "Then Renner came back," she added.

"What did he do?"

"He was drunk. He tried to rape me. He hit me." Laura clasped her hands together to stop their trembling. "I've seen the earlier tape we made, Will. Susan thought it would help. It did, I guess. Because it was like I said on the tape . . . when I thought I was talking about Mark. The beating. The . . . rape." She shuddered.

"How much can you remember after that, Laura?"

"Not much. The LSD was really on me—the world was exploding. Stars flared into color, then shattered. Until Ed and Ellen came down the path from the house, calling my name. Then, just for a moment, I could see clearly again, really sharp, really clear."

"Where were you?"

"Outside the beach house." Laura's voice was shaking now. Sweat beaded on her forehead and upper lip and dampened the hair at her temples. She swung her head from side to side, as though trying to control a sudden bout of nausea. "Curt Renner was sprawled face-down on the beach. I thought I'd killed him. And that was when I ran away."

"Why couldn't you remember this before, Laura?"

Laura shook her head, as if to clear it. "I was afraid to, Will. Because when I got home again my mother told me that I had killed Curt Renner. And that I must never tell anyone, to protect us. I believed her. I really did. And so I tried very hard to forget what happened. After a while I couldn't remember anymore. But I could never escape the dreams."

"I want to go forward now, Laura. To the day that Mark died. What happened when Mark came back to the beach cabin that afternoon, before you went up to the house for dinner?"

Laura shuddered with remembered pain, her eyes closed.

"He was so *angry*, Will. So angry . . . my mother had humiliated him in front of all those people, made him look like an idiot . . . He told me how she'd stolen the company away from his father, away from *him*. How he thought she had killed his father. I told him he could have the damn company, that I would help him get it back, if that was what he wanted. I pleaded with him to forgive her. I stripped off my clothes, told him to take *me*, hit *me*, fuck *me*, take his anger out on *me* and leave it there. I was his wife, for God's sake . . . when he was in pain I wanted to help him bear it. But Mark wouldn't. He just looked down at me . . . cold. I'd never seen such cold anger. He turned his back and left me there."

"And that night, when Mark finally came back to you?"

Laura was sobbing openly now, deep gasps of fresh pain. "I don't *know*, Will. I still don't. Not for certain. When Mark came back to the cabin that night . . . it wasn't Mark. It was as I said . . . all I could see was Curt Renner, *there*, and I was going to be raped again.

"Then Mark was gone. I heard voices outside the beach cabin. I went to the deck and saw Mark standing naked on the beach, by the tide pool, near the little rock cairns I'd made earlier that day."

"How long was Mark standing there, Laura?"

"Not long. A minute, at most. Then I heard voices again. Mark called out to someone standing up the beach, near the foot of the bluff. I couldn't see who it was. But the voice that answered him was my mother's voice."

"And then?"

"Two shots. Like flashes of blue lightning."

"What did you do?"

"I wanted to run away. But I loved Mark. I knew that the things I'd told him about my dreams, about what happened at the beach house—that had led him to confront my mother, had gotten him killed. But I still had to protect my mother, the way she had protected me. And the only place I could go was to be with him." Her voice dropped to a broken whisper. "To be dead with Mark."

"When did you know all this, Laura? When did you know that you hadn't killed Mark?"

"On the night I tried to kill myself for the second time. Not until then."

Laura slumped wearily in her chair, eyes closed. Hatton's voice spoke on the tape. "It's twelve-forty-two P.M. I'm concluding this session."

Douglas Wilcox, the Washington special assistant attorney general in charge of the state's criminal division, turned to Will Hatton. They were seated, along with Mary Slattery, in a dull green institutional conference room in Olympia, the state capital.

"So what was your final diagnosis?" he asked.

"PTSD," Hatton replied, "with severe disassociation effects and amnesia, driven by the false memory Laura developed of having killed Curt Renner."

"How's that different from a repressed-memory case?" Wilcox asked, probing.

"True repressed memory is quite rare. Most of the therapists who claimed to find it during its heyday in the late eighties and early nineties were actually 'discovering' memories that they themselves suggested. Most of the studies debunking repressed-memory theories did so by showing how easy it was to implant a *false* memory, a false belief. And that's what Laura's mother did—implanted a false memory in Laura's mind that she had murdered Curt Renner, as a way of ensuring that Laura would never tell anyone about what had really happened to Renner." Hatton shook his head. "And I missed it. Mary was right—I was still emotionally involved with Laura. I wanted to save her if I could. And so I bought into the idea that she was reliving an accurate memory and killed Mark in a PTSD-induced flashback, rather than looking at the evidence. If I had, I'd have seen that Laura's false memory didn't fit the facts. Some of the facts, yes. But not all of them."

"I can't comment on that," Wilcox said. "But personally, I think you were working with what you had. If you'd known the truth about Renner's relationship with Ellen Arcand, you'd have pieced it together sooner."

"Maybe," Hatton said doubtfully. "Maybe."

"Did Hauser cover up both murders?" Wilcox asked.

Hatton nodded. "I think so. He was working with Ellen by the time she killed Curtis Renner, and we know he was there the night Renner died. After Ellen shot Renner they took his body and sank it in Elliot Bay. Ed knew about Renner's habit of taking his boat around the sound late at night, and scuttled his boat off Whidbey Island to make it look like a drowning."

"Why didn't Hauser just dump Laura's gun after Ellen had shot Talbot with it?" Wilcox asked.

"Because he needed it in order to take the blame in case Laura was convicted," Mary Slattery said, breaking into conversation.

"Maybe so," Wilcox said. "It could have worked the other way, too—maybe he thought by keeping the murder weapon he'd be able to protect himself from Ellen Arcand. She'd committed two murders to steal that company of hers and hang on to it. When you've killed twice, killing a third time is mostly just a matter of opportunity." He shrugged. "But with Hauser standing mute, we'll never know."

"I can't believe that," Hatton said. "Not the last part. Ed was trying to protect both Ellen and Laura. He knew Laura's medical history and thought that by trying the case with an insanity defense, he stood a reasonable chance of getting Laura acquitted. If she was found not guilty by reason of insanity, no one could ever accuse Ellen because Laura would have already admitted firing the shots that killed Mark. And he thought that even if I discovered the truth, I'd still go along with it. That's why he wanted me to stay in the case."

The cold December rain drummed on the windows of the conference room.

"Will you charge them?" Mary Slattery asked.

Wilcox's expression was flat. He nodded. "Hauser, for obstruction of justice in hiding the gun. That's all we've got."

Mary Slattery reddened. "Come on, Doug, show some balls here. You've got motive, opportunity—"

"And a shooting where the only witness was certifiably insane at the time of the murder. That's not enough, Mary, and you know it. The AG pulled this case from Kitsap County precisely so Watkins couldn't make a hash of it again. And we aren't going to make the same kind of stupid mistakes that you and Hauser exploited." Wilcox shrugged. "We'll do our best to turn Hauser after we indict him. But he's a tough old bastard. I don't think he'll ever talk."

"He won't," Will Hatton said. "He did what he did for love. He won't turn on Ellen now."

"So Ellen Arcand walks away from this?" Mary Slattery asked, still disappointed.

"Not quite. You looking for work?"

Slattery nodded. "Hauser and Todd is dissolving. Reuben Todd offered to take me in, but I didn't think it was right."

Wilcox smiled. "Open your own shop. I've got a client for you. He's got a good case, I think. Fraud, and wrongful death. He's rich, and he's pissed. If you win it'd make your reputation."

"Who?" Slattery asked.

"Admiral Luther Talbot. He's the executor of Mark Talbot's estate. And he wants to sue Ellen Arcand—"

"For about a hundred million dollars," Mary Slattery said happily.

Part V

Daylight

May 29, 1998

Chapter Fifty-one

She stood with her back to him, right hand on her firm, cocked hip, surveying the canvas that lay on the painting table in front of her. With the left hand she held a brush in the air, undecided, then flicked it at the canvas, as if much depended on that single stroke. The late-afternoon heat in the top floor loft was oppressive, rare in intensity for May. Grinding street noise, punctuated with the impatient blare of horns, drifted up through the open windows from the crowded quitting-time traffic on Burwell Street below.

When she heard his step on the last creaking stair she turned and stared at him, her features first tense, then slowly warming into a smile.

"Will," she said simply.

"Laura." Hatton smiled in return. She looked, he decided, much as she had years ago, in their brief time together in New York. Her tan skin was flushed and sweating from hours of hard work in the hot studio, her dark hair a loose wild mane, tied back with a cheap blue bandanna. Her tight faded jeans were smeared with paint, her piercing gray-blue eyes bright in the slanting sunlight pouring through the windows and skylights above.

She looked so much now as she had then that the memory tore at his heart. He let the pain stay with him for a moment, and then put it carefully away, in the place he had kept it locked away for the past dozen years. And that is where it will stay, he thought to himself. For good this time.

"Want a beer?" she asked. A dark curved line of sweat between her breasts stained the thin white cotton shirt she wore.

Hatton nodded, silent. Laura reached two long-necked bottles of Corona out of a steel washtub half filled with watery ice, cracked the caps with a church key, and passed one over to him. "Hot summer days," she said, clinking her bottle to his, then taking a long pull at the cold bitter beer.

"Say something, Will," she added. "You know it makes me crazy when you don't talk. I feel like I'm on the couch again."

He looked her over again, and then nodded. "You well?"

"Susan Richter seems to think so. I feel well."

"Good." Hatton gestured toward the painting on the table. "Mind if I look?"

"Go ahead."

Hatton walked around her to the painting table, looking down at the painting. It was a riot of hot yellows and burnt oranges and reds, underlaid with a structure of girded black lines. After a moment he realized that beneath the abstraction the masses of paint marched away in perfect perspective, putting him in mind of a series of low buildings climbing into the distance on a rising street.

"Architecture," he commented.

"It's just a sketch, in oil. Practice. What a street in San Miguel de Allende felt like. To me, anyway. I was down there for a couple of weeks."

Hatton ignored the explanation, still focused on the painting. "It's good," he concluded.

"They teach art appreciation in medical school these days?" Laura Arcand teased, not too harshly.

"Probably should," Hatton agreed. "God knows there's enough crazy artists in the world."

"No shit," she agreed. The thick, corded scars on her wrists showed white against her skin when she took the brush up again. "I'm going to stay here," Laura Arcand said briefly.

"Here? Bremerton?"

"Why not? I was born here. I bought this building. I'm going to keep this floor as a studio, build it out so I can live here. I'll divide up the floors below, turn them into live-work spaces for other artists. Half the artists in Seattle have been forced out by all the new development, and rents they can't afford. A lot of them are coming over here. I can build a space for them, help them the way I got help when I was starting out in New York."

Hatton considered the idea, and then nodded. "I think that's good. Not that you need my approval. Just as long as it's what you want."

"It's time," she said. "Time I gave something back. If I can't paint again . . . well, that's something I'll find out. But even if I can't, I can help others get their chance."

She paused to light a cigarette, scraping a kitchen match in a long arc along the top of the painting table. "So what's troubling you, Will? Why are you here?"

"Ed's gone," he said simply. "Heart failure. I thought you should know."

"Did he—"

"No. He's never said a word."

She closed her eyes and was silent for a long moment. When she opened them again she said, "I'm sorry, Will. I mean that."

"I know you do."

"He had to choose, Will. And he chose to protect the woman he loved. I can understand that. It's not so different from what you did for me."

Hatton nodded. "We didn't leave you with very much," he said quietly.

Laura stepped away from her painting table and looked at him intently. "Don't ever believe that, Will. Not for a moment. Because tonight I will sleep without dreams. In the morning there will be daylight. And for me, that's enough."

Author's Note

This book was written during some of the darker times in my own life. My thanks go to the friends who stuck with me against what would surely have been their better judgment; to my editors, Michael Korda and Charles Adams; and, above all others, my patient and caring literary agent, Clyde Taylor, who passed away on January 5, 2001.

There are no words of thanks enough for my wife, Dr. Colleen Huebner. This book is forever hers, as I am.

F.D.H.